Jesse.

The bridge of time snapped, butting her past up against her present.

The serving tray she carried slipped from her grasp and clattered to the floor. Flynn smelled peanut oil, lemon, and her own deep-seated fear. Instantly, she squatted and started scooping up catfish.

To her horror, Jesse crouched beside her.

"Don't . . . I can . . . please." Studiously she wrangled hushpuppies, tomato relish, mashed potatoes, anything to keep from looking him in the eyes.

His hand reached out to lightly touch hers. Damn if her heart wasn't beating so hard she feared it was going to explode. She didn't know what to think, had no idea what to do with these feelings shifting around inside her. He kept his hand on hers until she finally had no choice but to look at him.

"How you doin', Dimples?" Jesse said in his sexy Southern drawl that still curled her toes. "Long time no see."

By Lori Wilde

THE SWEETHEARTS' KNITTING CLUB

Forthcoming
THE TRUE LOVE QUILTING CLUB

THE *Sweethearts'* KNITTING CLUB

LORI WILDE

AVON

An Imprint of HarperCollins*Publishers*

AVON BOOKS
An Imprint of HarperCollins*Publishers*
10 East 53rd Street
New York, New York 10022-5299

To Lucia Macro—
Thank you for taking a chance on Twilight.
Your wisdom and insight have been invaluable.

THE
Sweethearts'
KNITTING
CLUB

CHAPTER ONE

Jesse Calloway voted boy
most likely to end up in prison
—Twilight High, 1999

"You got anybody special waiting for you on the outside?"

Jesse Calloway froze with the only surviving remnant from his good-for-nothing father, his battered old Timex, half-strapped onto his wrist.

Immediately the image of Flynn MacGregor, looking the way she'd looked the last time he'd seen her, peppered his mind. Wearing that pink dress that made her shine like a springtime tulip. Her soft, dark brown hair curling to her feisty shoulders, hands clutched into tight fists, bottom lip caught up between her teeth, her hazel eyes wide in stunned disbelief as Sheriff Clinton Trainer had handcuffed him and stuffed him into the backseat of his patrol car.

Slowly, he stabbed the strap of the Timex through

the loop, completing the cinch, the weight of it unexpectedly heavy against his wrist after all these years. The watch had stopped. Ironic when you thought about it. Stopped watch, stopped life. He wound the stem, and then looked up to meet Warden Neusbaum's eyes.

"No," he said. "There's no one."

The warden nodded as if the answer did not surprise him and passed Jesse the new, but cheaply made suit and lace-up dress shoes supplied by the state of Texas. In the pen they stripped you not only of lace-ups, but of your entire identity. For ten years he'd been nothing but a number. Now he was supposed to go out into society and became Jesse Calloway again. How was he going to do that? He'd spent his entire adult life behind bars. Framed and incarcerated for a crime he hadn't committed.

Resentment tasted as brackish as burnt coffee beans on the back of his tongue, but he shook off the emotion. No sense getting pissed off. What was done was done. After all, revenge was a dish best served cold, and he'd been in a deep freeze for a very long time.

"For what it's worth . . ." Warden Neusbaum paused and shifted his bulk, clearly uncomfortable with what he was about to say next. "I'm gonna miss you. You've been an exemplary inmate, and what you did for that boy . . ."

Jesse took a deep breath, inhaled the institutionalized smell of fear, testosterone, blood, body odor, Lysol, and badly prepared meals. The haunting smell was routine now, but he could still remember the way it had hit him the first time those cell doors had clanked closed behind him. The same way it must have hit Josh Green. In prison, empathy was a stupid thing, and it had almost gotten him killed.

He shrugged. "Yeah, well, you know."

"Don't shrug it off. You put your own life in grave peril to save that boy and you stopped a prison riot."

"Don't go makin' a hero out of me, Warden. I was just bucking for an early release." Jesse flashed the grin that had once worked so well at charming the panties off young women.

"Well, you did something right for once. The kid's alive and you got two years shaved off your sentence. Now for the standard speech. Good luck out there and don't ever let me catch your ass back in here again."

Jesse clenched his jaw. "That it?"

"Since you've got no folks coming to fetch you, a guard will put you on a bus and give you instructions about contacting your parole officer." Neusbaum nodded toward the bathroom adjacent to his office. "You've earned the right to some privacy. Go get dressed."

Jesse picked up the suit and shoes and headed toward the bathroom, not sure what he was feeling. He supposed he should have been excited. Today he would walk away from Huntsville prison a free man. But his emotions were complex.

Hollowness carved out a hole in his brain. Regret slithered along his spine. Anxiety swirled through his every breath. Resolve crouched on his shoulders. Revenge burned his gut.

But in his heart . . . in his *damnable* heart . . . he felt hope. And that's where trouble boiled.

As much as he wanted revenge to matter more, it didn't. Sure he wanted to get even with Beau Trainer. Certainly he ached to mete out real justice. Yes, he itched to expose the new sheriff of Twilight, Texas, for the fraud he was. But underneath it all, he wanted Flynn more.

According to Jesse's Aunt Patsy, Beau had asked Flynn to marry him four times, but she turned him down even as she kept dating him. Jesse ground his teeth. Why? Could it be that some small part of her still harbored feelings for him?

Even after ten years? Even after he'd been to prison? Fat chance of that.

Yet the hope flickered.

Hope. What a stupid, dangerous thing.

Jesse shook off the rough cotton prison jumpsuit, letting it drop to the cement floor, and stepped into the ill-fitting Wal-Mart suit. Not much of an improvement, but at least he looked like a human being again. Good-bye prisoner number 87757310.

Once dressed, he kicked off the slip-ons, sat down on a bench, and jammed his feet into the new shoes. It had been ten years since he'd done up laces, and he wondered if he'd forgotten how to tie his own shoes.

He raised his right leg up to the bench. The laces felt thick and clumsy in his fingers. Freedom was within his grasp. The flavor of it was on his tongue, and it tasted like Flynn. Sweet, with just the right amount of underlying tartness; juicy, warm, and welcoming.

There was that hope again.

Jesse tried to crush it. Reminded himself that she'd been sleeping with his mortal enemy, but he couldn't manage to summon up any anger toward her. He reserved that for Trainer. All he really wanted was to see Flynn again.

What if she doesn't want to see you?

She probably didn't. If he was smart, he would forget all about her. But if he was smart, he wouldn't have landed in here in the first place. He looped the laces, pulled them tight, his fingers regaining their memory.

Flynn.

The woman he'd dreamed about every night. The image of her smiling face had saved his sanity inside these prison walls.

Flynn.

He tugged the knot, making sure it held secure. He was breathing heavily now. Hope fluttered around in his heart like some damn butterfly. Christ, he was acting like a schoolgirl.

Flynn.

Had he completely fabricated the feelings they'd had for each other? Had it all been in his head, lopsided and pathetic? Doubt smashed the butterflies. Fear kicked hope in the teeth. Who was he kidding? He wasn't good enough for her. He'd known it then and nothing had changed.

Yet she hadn't married Trainer. Why not?

"Calloway," Neusbaum called to him.

Jesse stood up and looked down at his perfectly bound shoelaces. New beginning. New start. He opened the door and stepped back into the warden's office.

"Guard's here to escort you to the bus."

The guard waited for him in the hallway. Neusbaum clasped Jesse's hand, told him good-bye.

Unshackled for the first time in ten years, Jesse followed the guard out into the light.

"Where you headed?" the guard asked. "Home?"

"I've got no home," Jesse said. "Never have, never will."

"I gotta know where you're going. For the bus ticket."

"I'm headed for Twilight."

"Twilight?" The guard looked confused.

"Twilight," he confirmed. "It's a town, outside Fort Worth."

"What's in Twilight? A job? A woman?"

"A wrong that needs righting."

"Hey," the guard said, "don't do anything to send your ass back here. That'd be stupid."

Stupid it might be, but Jesse didn't care. His plan had been ten long years in the making. He was going back to the town where it all began. Back to even the score with the man who'd ruined his life. Back to collect the justice he'd been denied.

Back to claim the woman who should have been his.

Flynn MacGregor pulled her clunky old Ford Ranger out of the parking lot of Froggy's Marina Bar and Grill. The café hunkered on the banks of the Brazos River at the juncture where it flowed into Lake Twilight. She'd grown up on this river and she was as much a part of it as the sand cranes and snapping turtles. The smell of the water was in her blood; this place anchored her heart. The early evening mist cloaked the valley in a moisture shroud, causing Flynn's hair to frizz like a 1970s Afro.

Yeah, okay, she loved the river; the humidity, not so much.

She raised a hand in a vain attempt at taming her unruly locks, forgetting all about buckling up her seat belt. Dammit, she'd spent an hour last night ironing it straight. Naturally curly hair and river life didn't mix. She had half a mind to say, "Screw it," and stop the ironing, but Beau preferred her hair sleek and tamed. Honestly, so did she, but battling nature was hard work.

So was getting ready for the Friday night all-you-can-eat-catfish dinner crowd at Froggy's. Especially since her father had yet to show up for his shift and she was due to host the Sweethearts' Knitting Club at their house in half an hour. Flynn tried not to assume the worst, but she immediately started worrying. Had Floyd fallen off the wagon again?

He's been clean and sober for a year. Take a deep breath. He's probably got a very good reason for being late.

Still, that didn't stop her from making a beeline for home—which lay just half a mile north of Froggy's. She had to get there before the ladies from the knitting club started arriving and found Floyd half into a bottle of Wild Turkey, doing his best imitation of Tom Cruise in *Risky Business*, sliding across the hardwood floor to the tune of some Elvis ditty. Last time it had been "Burning Love." Flynn cringed at the memory of her father in his underwear, crooning into a hairbrush, as dotty octogenarian Dotty Mae Densmore applauded and asked if he was available for bachelorette parties, while the rest of the knitting club had looked on in stunned shock.

And then she heard the *whoop-whoop* blast of a squad car siren, saw red and blue lights twirling behind her pickup truck.

Oh crap, now what? Feeling just a bit cheesed off, she pulled to the side of the road. The cruiser snugged in behind her.

The trooper swung out of his vehicle, cocked his Stetson back on his forehead, sank his hands onto his hips, and sauntered up to her window. He looked like a cross between Dudley Do-Right and The Terminator—precision military haircut, large firm jaw, shoulders you could iron a linen shirt on, service weapon strapped to him more securely than a body part. The twinkling star on his chest confirmed his identity—sheriff of Hood County, Texas.

"Ma'am," he said, leaning in to rest his forearms on her windowsill.

He was playing a familiar little sex game, but honestly, she wasn't in the mood. "Listen Beau, I gotta go. Floyd didn't show up for work and I've got the knitting club on the way and—"

"Flynnie," he interrupted. She wished he wouldn't call her that, but he seemed to enjoy it so much that she'd never worked up the courage to tell him she didn't care for the moniker. "Take a deep breath and be in the moment. You're letting your mind run away with you again."

She hated how well he knew her. It was almost as irritating as it was comforting.

"Deep breath," he insisted.

Rolling her eyes, she took a deep breath.

"Good girl. Now how come you didn't have your seat belt on?"

"Is that what this is about?"

He pulled his ticket book from his back pocket.

"You're not serious."

"Click or ticket, ma'am," he said with a deadpan face.

He was still playing the game. Or at least she hoped he was. Beau was such a straight arrow it was often difficult to tell when he was teasing or when he was toeing the line beyond all reasonable human expectations.

Flynn batted her eyelashes at him, playing along just to get this over with so she could go home and make sure Floyd was not blitzed on the Jägermeister she suddenly remembered her sister, Carrie, kept hidden behind the paint thinner underneath the kitchen sink.

"Oh, Officer, is there anything I can do to get out of this ticket?" Flynn asked.

"Are you attempting to bribe an officer of the law?"

"Um . . . no . . . not at all. Unless it'll work."

"Ma'am, I'm going to have to ask you to step out of your vehicle and follow me to my patrol car."

She sighed, resigned to playing out the scenario. She opened the door, followed him to his patrol car, and got into the passenger seat.

"Your hair's frizzing," Beau said, back to being himself as he got in beside her.

Flynn reached up to tuck a wild strand behind her ear. "I know. I'm sorry."

"Hey, you don't have to apologize. You can't control the weather. It's just that it makes you look wild."

Maybe I wanna be wild for once.

"Um, could we please get the show on the road? I've got a lot to do and—"

"Flynnie," he interrupted, "We've got something really important to discuss."

"I know, I know, I should have worn my seat belt."

"That's not what I'm talking about, but yeah, you should have." He shook a chiding finger.

"Can't it wait?" She waved a hand in the direction of her house. Flynn could see it from here— down-home farm-style, painted buttercup yellow, wraparound veranda. Rocking chairs on the front porch. Bucket of colorful yarn parked beside the rocking chairs to keep up the appearance that she actually knew how to knit. "Floyd, the Sweethearts, Froggy's . . ."

"I know you're stretched thin, but I need for you to focus. Take another deep breath."

She complied.

"Good girl," he said again, and she halfway expected him to pat her on the head and give her a liver treat. Then he took something out of his pocket that made her heart vault up into her throat.

A black velvet ring box.

"Beau . . ." She was shaking her head before he ever cracked the box open.

He raised a finger. "Before you say anything I want you to just hear me out. Can you do that?"

She nodded mutely, overwhelmed by the tightness in her chest. She did have a tendency to shoot her mouth off without knowing all the details.

Beau opened the box. This time the ring was a three-carat marquise cut surrounded by a flotilla of baguettes. It must have cost him at least six months' salary. It was twice as big as the last one. She had to bite down on her tongue to keep her promise of hearing him out.

He reached for her left hand. Flynn was startled to realize she was shaking. What was she feeling? Resistance? Fear? She rolled both those words around in her head. No, no. That wasn't it.

She and Beau had known each other their entire lives. High school sweethearts, dating on and off for ten years. He was a rock-solid guy. The salt of the earth. Yes, he was a little rigid in his outlook and he could be a bit judgmental, but that went with the territory. He was squeaky clean. A real Goody Two-shoes. Once she'd even made him a musical playlist that included the Adam Ant "Goody Two Shoes" song.

He doesn't drink, he doesn't smoke. What does he do?

That was the thing. The guy was a comic book superhero, and no one could live up to Beau's expectations. How the hell had Lois Lane managed it?

Was that the reason she'd put him off every time he'd asked her to marry him? Of course, she had other reasons. External reasons. Good reasons. Or was her real reason something else entirely? Or perhaps she should say *someone* else entirely.

And then—*boom*—there he was nibbling at the back of her conscience as he'd done off and on for the past ten years.

Jesse.

The wild side that she'd never gotten to explore. Her one serious regret. Just the thought of him took her breath in a way Beau never had. Immediately she felt disloyal and bit down on her bottom lip.

"Flynnie, look at me."

She forced herself to meet Beau's chocolate brown eyes underneath straight, black brows. Good ol' reliable Beau. Everyone in town loved him. He was a war hero, having earned a Bronze Star in Iraq. He was a pillar of the community. A man that people looked up to and admired.

Goody, Goody Two-shoes.

God, what was wrong with her? She was secretly pining for a convicted criminal incarcerated in Huntsville prison while this decent and law-abiding man, who'd never been anything but kind to Flynn and her family, was sitting here asking her to marry him. She was lower than river sludge. Why couldn't she just pull the trigger and say yes?

"Before you turn me down again there's something very important I have to say," Beau said.

"I—"

"Ah, ah." Beau pressed his index finger to her lips. "Shh, shh."

She pantomimed zipping her lip, and his smile crinkled up the corners of his eyes. She really did love the big lug. Just not in the way she should. Not the way her mother had loved her father. Not the way the members of her knitting club all loved their high school sweethearts.

Her heart twisted. Honestly, what in the hell was wrong with her? Why couldn't she give him her all?

The thing of it was, she had always expected to

marry Beau eventually. Her mother had certainly wanted it for her. As she lay in the final throes of dying, Lynn Dupress MacGregor had made her eldest daughter promise two things.

One, that Flynn would open a yarn store so the knitters of Twilight didn't have to make the forty-mile trek into Fort Worth whenever they felt a yen for something more sophisticated than the basic Wal-Mart skein. And two, that Flynn would one day accept Beau's proposal of marriage.

Flynn had pointed out that with the proliferation of the Internet it was now feasible for the citizens of Twilight to meet their knitting needs online, but her mother insisted it wasn't the same. All her life Lynn had dreamed of owning a yarn store where she could host knitting circles and give lessons to pass on her love of the craft. Flynn had agreed to both promises, fully expecting to keep them.

One day.

First on her list, find the right property—and the financing—to start Lynn's Yarn Barn.

But now here was Beau, pushing for the second item.

"You remember the first time I asked?" Beau crooned, giving her hand a gentle squeeze.

"It was your high school graduation," Flynn said.

The day after the night Jesse had made out with her for the first and last time. Made out with her on the old Twilight Bridge, gave Flynn her first orgasm right through the fabric of her panties and rocked her teenage world.

It was also the same day Beau's father had arrested Jesse on cocaine trafficking charges and possession of an illegal firearm. He was supposed to have graduated that day as well.

"You looked so gorgeous. You were wearing a pink sundress." His voice softened.

Little did Beau know she'd worn that dress because Jesse had told her she looked pretty in pink. Flynn's cheeks warmed at the memory. She'd thought . . .

You were sixteen. You had no clue about who Jesse really was. You barely knew him. Let it go. She wished it was that easy. She felt guilty somehow—like she'd betrayed Jesse—and she didn't know why. If anything, she'd betrayed Beau.

Okay, here came the full-on guilt.

"It was thoughtless of me to ask you then," Beau was saying. "I understood that you were too young. I just wanted you to know how I felt. I wanted to know that you were mine before I headed off to college."

Flynn forced a smile. Beau's hand was warm and moist around hers, his grip just a tiny bit too tight. Panic fluttered against her chest wall the way it always did when he asked her for a solid commitment.

"My timing has always been off when it comes to us. What with your family problems, my stint in Iraq, then my extensive rehab after being wounded, my father's stroke. We've been through a lot and yet we're still together. You've always given me hope that one day you'd be ready to wear my ring."

"Beau, you're a wonderful person." This time she squeezed his hand.

"I love you, Flynnie. I've loved you for years. You're my oldest and dearest friend. I think it's important to be friends with the person you marry."

They *were* good friends and they knew each other so well.

"But as much as I love you, as much as I want you to be my wife, I can't keep waiting." Beau cleared his throat. "I know you have a problem with commitment and I get why. You had to assume the role as head of the household when your mother got sick and your dad went off the deep end. You were only thirteen years old and you were cooking dinner and changing diapers and making sure the bills got paid and taking care of your mother . . ." He shook his head. "I admire you so much, Flynnie MacGregor. You're my hero."

Aw shit, she was gonna cry. She ducked her head, stared down at her sneakers stained with grease from Froggy's. "Beau . . ."

"Shh, listen, listen to me good." He hooked two fingers underneath her chin, raised her face up to meet his gaze. "I'll be thirty next year and Hondo Crouch is running against me in the upcoming sheriff's race. I need a wife by my side to help me win. Not to mention that I'm ready to start a family."

"I know."

"No, this is different." He paused. "I realize you haven't had a chance to sow your wild oats. That you've been so busy taking care of everyone that you've never taken care of Flynn, and I've tried to be considerate of that. I didn't take offense when you turned me down the last four times."

No, no he hadn't.

"I understood and I waited."

Yes, yes he had.

"So I have to have an answer. One way or the other. Will you marry me?"

The squad car suddenly seemed to close in around her. She tried to draw in a deep breath but her lungs wouldn't expand properly. "I . . . I need time to think."

"You've had ten years to think, Flynn; if you don't know the answer by now—" He broke off, shook his head.

"Are you—" She stopped, gulped. "Giving me an ultimatum?"

"I am. Either agree to wear my engagement ring or I'll find someone who will." He couldn't have shocked her more if he'd reached out and slapped her across the face. "You've taken me for granted and I've allowed it to happen because I've wanted this so much. But you aren't the only woman in Twilight. I've had lots of offers."

A sour taste spilled into her mouth. It tasted like guilt. She *had* taken him for granted. Assumed Beau would always be there. Waiting for her. She saw now how unfairly she'd treated him, keeping him dangling on a string. He was right. She should say yes or let him go.

"All your excuses are gone," he continued. "Cassie grew out of her wild phase and turned her life around. Froggy's is finally in the black. Your twin brothers graduate from high school next May. Your father is on the wagon. There's nothing you have to do for anyone else, Flynnie. You deserve to pursue your own happiness."

And of course he thought pursuing her happiness meant marrying him, becoming the sheriff's wife. In all honesty, Flynn had no idea what constituted her own happiness. She'd never had an opportunity to give it much thought.

He took the ring from the box and held it out to her. "This is it, Flynn MacGregor, your last chance. I won't ask again. I've got to have a definitive answer once and for all. Will you marry me or not?"

Flynn opened her mouth to speak but no words came out.

"Yes or no?" Beau demanded.

"I . . . I . . ."

"Yes or no, Flynn, it's a simple question."

Emotions crowded in on her. Anger with him for springing this on her, irritation with herself for dragging her feet, desperation at his challenge, fear that she was never going to figure out who she really was outside of being everyone's go-to girl.

And beneath it all lay a bone-deep sadness. *If you say yes, you forever close the door on Jesse.*

Jesse, that vulnerable boy who'd come to live with his Aunt Patsy his junior year. He'd swaggered into Twilight High all tough bravado and oozing tortured-loner cool. Leather jacket, skull tattoo on his upper arm, pierced tongue, chip on his shoulder twice the size of Texas, laser-sharp stare that sent chills of excitement chasing up a girl's spine.

But Flynn had immediately seen past the façade. The minute she looked into his intelligent gray-blue eyes, she'd known they were the same. Pretending to be something they weren't in order to keep their chaotic worlds in balance. He was faking being a bad boy; she had donned the role of responsible good girl. He'd touched her heart in a way no one ever had and she'd fallen in love with him.

And then to her ultimate dismay she discovered she'd been wrong about Jesse. That he truly was a bad boy involved with drugs and guns. But still, some small part of her refused to believe it. Some part of her still *yearned*.

What in the hell was she thinking? The door had closed on Jesse years ago. That was just a foolish girlhood longing. She'd grown up. She'd stopped believing in soul mates and kismet and sexual chemistry so urgent it scared the hell out of her. Marrying the steady, reliable man who'd stood by you through thick and thin was good enough. It wasn't settling. It was sensible. Right?

"Flynn," Beau prompted.

She looked down at the diamond sparkler and everything it represented—home, hearth, husband, family. She should want this, but the truth was she was up to her ears in home, hearth, and family. The only new addition would be husband.

His gaze burned her cheeks. She forced herself to meet his eyes. Caring and concern for her shone there, and for the briefest moment, she spied a flicker of panic. He rubbed his thumb over her ring finger. "Flynnie?"

"Why today, Beau?"

"What do you mean?"

"Why not yesterday? Why not tomorrow?"

He shrugged. "I guess I just made up my mind that I can't keep hanging in limbo. I gotta know once and for all, will you be my wife?"

"Could you give me twenty-four hours?"

His lips pressed together to form a hard line. "You've had ten years. Will twenty-four hours make that much difference?"

No, of course not, but she needed time alone from him to think this through. "I wasn't expecting an ultimatum and the knitting club will be arriving any minute and my father is AWOL and—"

Beau heaved a long-suffering sigh. "It's always about your family." Flynn bristled, but then he lightly touched the tip of her nose with his index finger. "Good thing your devotion to those you love is one of the things I adore most about you. Yes, okay, twenty-four hours. But that doesn't mean I'm not serious about this. My ultimatum still stands."

"Okay. You're right. You deserve an answer." She moved to get out of the car.

"Flynnie?"

"Yes?" She turned back to look at him, and that's when Beau gathered her up in his arms for a kiss.

As kisses went it was one of his best. Firm, warm, moist but not wet—full of passion, yet properly controlled. He tasted of mouthwash and toothpaste. She realized he'd recently brushed his teeth. Rehearsed this.

She found that fact both endearing and bothersome, and she couldn't really say why. She knew Beau was a man who did nothing without forethought and preparation. Eagle Scout all the way.

He pulled his lips from hers. "Keep that in mind as you do your thinking."

She nodded mutely, got out of his patrol car, stumbled in the ditch on her way back to her Ranger. As she climbed onto the running board, Beau poked his head out of the window. "And don't forget to buckle up," he hollered.

Flynn waved a hand, but had the strangest impulse to raise a finger. God, he was such a stickler for rules.

And what's wrong with that, river sludge? He only wants to make sure you're safe.

She got in and buckled her seat belt, looked back, and saw Beau making a U-turn, then spied a car on the overhead bridge that she recognized. Patsy Cross's ruby red Crown Victoria packed with carpooling members of the knitting club.

Crap!

At best she had only a two-minute head start. Flynn gunned the engine and zoomed to the end of the road. She slammed the Ranger into park, tumbled out, sprinted up the back steps, and banged in through the screen door.

CHAPTER TWO

*Beau Trainer voted boy most likely
to be brought home for Thanksgiving dinner*
—Twilight High, 1999

For as long as he could remember, Beau Trainer had struggled to overcome the image of his larger-than-life father. Clinton Trainer was a throwback to the lawless days of the Wild West when men were men—drinking, whoring, gambling, smoking, fighting, shooting off guns for sport—and the women put up with it because they were scared not to. His father called every boy Bubba and every girl Sissy-babe. He had a picture of a hula dancer with oversized bosoms tattooed on his forearm, and until his stroke he'd always kept a whiskey flask tucked into the top of his cowboy boot.

The Trainers hailed from a long line of lawmen, dating back to some of the first Texas Rangers. And when Clinton married Kathryn Loving and her family's cattle money and used her wealth and his boldness to get elected sheriff of Hood County, his place in Twilight history was cinched. No one dared cross Clinton Trainer except Kathryn, and that was only because she held the purse strings.

When Beau was eight years old his father took him behind the woodshed, pulled a cigar from his pocket, bit off the end, and spit it into the field. "Let's see how tough you are, little man," Clinton had grunted. "Smoke this."

He remembered being simultaneously repulsed and seduced. He'd brought the cigar to his lips. Clinton fired a match with his hoary thumbnail. "Now suck," he commanded.

Beau sucked. Acrid smoke filled his lungs. It tasted like wet, moldy leaves set on fire. He'd coughed and tried to hand the cigar back to Clinton. "I don't like it."

"Keep smoking," Clinton growled with that don't-give-me-no-shit look on his face.

Knees trembling, tears burning at the backs of his eyes, Beau took another hit. The second time was worse than the first. "I can't do it," he'd whimpered.

"Again."

"Daddy, don't make me."

"You want me to take off this belt?" Clinton settled his thumbs on his belt buckle. " 'Cause I will."

He couldn't hold the tears back any longer as he took another horrible drag off the vile cigar and promptly vomited in the sand.

"Pussy." Clinton curled his nose in disgust and walked away.

When he was ten, Clinton took him deer hunting. When it came down to pulling the trigger and annihilating the defenseless animal, Beau had shot wide, missing on purpose.

"Pussy." Clinton reached out and slapped him across the face.

When he was twelve, Clinton took him to the Horny Toad Tavern and told Earl Pringle to serve Beau a whiskey.

"I can't do that, Sheriff," Earl had said, looking nervously at Clinton's badge, no doubt wondering if it was a test.

"Then give me a whiskey."

Earl served him and Clinton pushed the glass to Beau. "Knock it back in one swallow, kid."

Beau tried, he really did. Honestly, all he wanted was to please his father, but it turned out like the cigar. Vomit on the floor.

"Pussy." Clinton grunted and finished off the whiskey Beau hadn't been able to down.

Then when he was fourteen . . . Beau closed his eyes against the memory of the whorehouse and the naked woman who'd touched him. All he heard ringing in his ears were his father's parting words as he slammed the door behind him. "Pussy for a pussy."

It was at that moment Beau realized that no matter what he did he could never impress or please his father. He also realized something else. His father was morally bankrupt and he wasn't a man worth emulating. And Beau recognized that from then on, he was going to have to father himself. Find his own blueprint for the way a man was supposed to be. He was going to make his own guidelines, develop his own moral code, police himself so there'd be no need for anyone else to police him. He'd adhere to the letter of the law and he'd live up to his image of what a real man should be. From that moment on, Beau made it his life mission to be better than Clinton in every way. He'd be everything his father was not—ethical, fair, honest, and self-disciplined.

And then at sixteen he'd fallen in love for the first time. Madly, deeply, blindly in love, the way that only a teenager could fall. Jodi was beautiful, impulsive, and exciting. Beau was drawn to her, moth to a flame. She strung him along, then broke his heart by leaving town with a thug so much like Clinton it crushed his soul. When he heard a few weeks later that she'd been killed in an accident on the back of the guy's motorcycle, he took it personally. If she'd just stayed with him, she would still be alive and safe. After that, he'd drawn up his image of the perfect woman. She would be a good person, hardworking, responsible, generous, and practical. She wouldn't let her head be turned by some swaggering bad boy.

And then he met Flynn. She fit his mental blueprint perfectly, and he set about falling in love with her in a calm, rational manner.

They were getting along good, she was his perfect mate. Even though they were still in high school, he was already picturing their children. Then Patsy Cross brought her nephew to Twilight and ruined everything.

Beau blew out his breath, parked his cruiser in front of the sheriff's office, and got out, the black velvet ring box weighing heavily in his pocket. He'd put up with a lot from Flynn because he knew she was right for him and he was right for her. They'd been through so much together. For the most part, he was willing to give her the time and space she needed. He had been happy with their current relationship.

That was until Warden Neusbaum called him to tell him Jesse Calloway was getting out of prison on early release and Beau knew he had to get his ring on Flynn's finger before that bastard came roaring back into town. Because he knew Flynn didn't take commitments lightly. Once she committed to something, she was in for the duration.

And he was going to make sure that he was the one she committed to. He'd be damned if he let her end up like Jodi. Once and for all, he was saving her from that low-life scumbag, if it was the last thing he ever did.

Her sister, Carrie, stood in the kitchen tying a green and white Froggy's apron around her waist. Flynn screeched to a halt and said breathlessly, "Red alert. Knitting club is right behind me, where's the afghan?"

"Don't panic. The living room is set up for the meeting. Afghan is by your chair. Your dark secret is still safe. Cookies, sandwiches, and tea . . ." She motioned to the sideboard. "All laid out."

Flynn stared. Her sister had come through for her and in a big way.

Carrie wrinkled her nose. "Why are you looking at me like I'm Jezebel singing in the church choir?"

All those years of bailing her sister out of trouble—shoplifting charges, underage drinking and pot smoking, annulling her ill-conceived marriage. Carrie was going to be okay.

"You're not supposed to work tonight," Flynn said. "I thought you had a date with Logan."

"I'm taking Dad's shift." Carrie pinned her name tag to her chest.

"Where is he?"

"AA meeting."

Relief that her father hadn't fallen off the wagon was as strong as the dual twist of concern. "What happened?"

Carrie shook her head. "Today would have been their twenty-eighth wedding anniversary, Flynn."

May 28. How could she have forgotten? Flynn smacked her forehead with her palm. "I'm such a dumbass. It completely slipped my mind."

"You can't be expected to remember everything." Carrie turned for the door, uncharacteristically cutting her some slack. "You're giving me that look again."

"Who are you and what have you done with my sister, you evil pod person?"

"How come *you're* late?"

"Beau gave me an ultimatum."

"Oh?" Carrie paused, one leg in the kitchen, the other on the porch. "What kind?"

"Marry him or he's going to find someone else."

"He's bluffing."

Flynn shook her head. "I don't think so. Not this time."

"I guess he's getting the urge for babies."

Flynn covered her ears with her palms. "Don't say that. I'm not ready to hear that. I'm not ready for babies."

"Remember twins run in our family." Carrie scooped up her purse.

"You're evil, you know that?"

"I thought you just said I was a pod person."

"Okay, my mistake. You're still the same old Carrie. You just lured me in there for a minute with these lovely little sandwiches with the crusts cut off."

"Honestly, Flynn, you're finally going to say yes, right? I mean you guys are meant for each other. Mr. and Mrs. I Walk the Line. Of course, I pity the kids. They'll have no choice but to rebel, but look at the bright side; they'll have Auntie Carrie showing them the ropes." Carrie headed across the veranda.

Flynn followed her. "You think I should say yes?"

"Beau's crazy about you."

"I know."

"So why the hesitation? You guys fit like peanut butter and jelly. Although there is the issue that you've never dated anyone else. That's gotta be weird, having only been with one guy."

Except Jesse. Sort of.

But Carrie didn't know about that. Nobody knew about her and Jesse except Jesse's Aunt Patsy.

"We all can't have your colorful past with the opposite sex."

Carrie hummed a line from an oldies song, "Going to the Chapel."

"Who's going to get married?" Patsy Cross asked as she and three other members of the knitting club—Dotty Mae Densmore, Terri Longoria, and Marva Bullock—walked up on the porch.

Patsy owned the Teal Peacock, a curio/souvenir

shop situated on Ruby Street catty-corner from the Twilight Playhouse on the town square, where in the summers, touring companies performed Broadway musicals. It drew visitors from the Dallas/Fort Worth Metroplex, infused extra money into the town. This month *Mamma Mia!* was on the playbill. Patsy also served on the town council, and people sought her advice because of her sound, logical outlook on life. She possessed round cheeks, a rounder waistline, and a precise, measured way of taking stock of people and situations. She wore her hair short and dyed blond and she reminded Flynn a bit of Debbie Reynolds, just not as perky. She'd never had any kids. Last year, her husband had been diagnosed with early-onset Alzheimer's and she'd been forced to put him in a home. Flynn's mother had once told her to be extra kind to Patsy, because she'd had a very hard life, but she'd given her no details.

"Beau and Flynn," Carrie supplied in answer to Patsy's question.

"Finally?" Dotty Mae Densmore squealed with excitement and clapped her hands. "It's about damn time."

Dotty Mae was a former Miss Twilight, 1942. She had the outer appearance of a typical great-grandmother—blue hair, floral print housedress, a rash of liver spots on the backs of her hands, thick glasses perched on the end of her nose. But it was all a guise. Dotty Mae cussed like a Green Beret, played the Lotto every Saturday, and never missed the biannual Twilight senior citizens' bus trip to the Indian Casino in Choctaw, Oklahoma. Her passion for the Dallas Cowboys rivaled that of any Joe Six-Pack. She smoked clove cigarettes and had a certain fondness for peppermint schnapps. Flynn had discovered that last tidbit when Carrie had come home staggering drunk at age twelve, reeking of cloves and peppermint. Dotty Mae had called her up to bawl her out for letting Carrie go around stealing old people's hooch.

"That's wonderful," cooed everyone except Patsy. They converged on her in a group hug.

Carrie winked and abandoned her to the smother of well-meaning bosoms. If she hadn't been so proud of her sister for stepping up to the plate and taking care of things, she might have been irritated. Then Flynn's gaze met Patsy's gray-blue eyes, which were the exact same color as Jesse's. She stood back from the group. Something flickered on Patsy's face. An accusation? A challenge? Disapproval? Whatever it was, it quickly disappeared.

The others pelted Flynn with questions as she escorted them inside through the kitchen and into the living room.

"When's the date?"

"Are you getting married at his church or yours?"

"Have you picked your colors yet?"

"Um . . ." Flynn said. "I'm afraid Carrie was putting the cart before the horse. I haven't exactly accepted Beau's proposal yet."

"But you're going to this time," Terri said firmly.

At thirty-seven, Terri was the youngest member of the knitting club besides Flynn. Her husband was chief of staff at Twilight General, and Terri owned Hot Legs Gym. She loved salsa dancing and bowling, and she held the title of best female slalom skier in Twilight. Her biggest claim to fame was an appearance on a reality show called *Fear Nothing* where she'd systemically gulped down a bucket of earthworms and won ten thousand dollars for the disgusting honor. However, her most prized accomplishment was her plump little four-year-old, Gerald. No one had the courage to tell her the kid was a complete brat, and Flynn breathed a sigh of relief that she hadn't brought him with her tonight. Gerald had a sordid history with knitting needles.

"I'm surprised someone hasn't stolen Beau away from you already," Marva said. "Half the single girls in town are in love with him."

"And a few of the married ones too," Dotty added.

"It's such a shame that your mother won't be here for the wedding," Patsy said quietly and that caused everyone to pause and look toward the photograph of Flynn's mother on the wall over the fireplace mantel.

The photograph had been taken thirteen years earlier, just before her mother had received the devastating news she had amyotrophic lateral sclerosis—a progressive and incurable neuromuscular disease made infamous by baseball great Lou Gehrig. In the picture she was only thirty-five, with a smile so bright that it made Flynn's heart ache. Her soft blond hair, which Carrie had inherited, curled down her shoulders, and her blue eyes danced mischievously. She was a far cry from the way she'd been at the end; her body weak and helpless, but her mind fully aware of what was happening to her.

"Lynn would approve," Marva murmured. "She was crazy about Beau, and she wanted nothing more than to see you happily married to your childhood sweetheart."

Marva and her mother had been best friends since high school. Marva was as dark as Lynn had been fair. With her cocoa-colored skin, ebony hair plaited in neat cornrows, and lean body, Marva looked years younger than forty-nine. She had a son, Ashton, who was Flynn's age, and a daughter, Kiley, a year younger. They'd both moved away from Twilight to better job opportunities in Dallas. Marva's husband, G.C., worked as an electrician, and she was the principal of Twilight High. At first glance it was impossible to see what her mother and Marva had in common other than their kids, but they'd both shared an almost rabid love of knitting.

That love led them to start the Sweethearts' Knitting Club the very same year her mother posed for the photograph. The genesis for the club came from the fact that as part of a romantic Twilight tradition, both Marva and Lynn had married—and stayed wedded to—their high school sweethearts. They formed a knitting club among other women who could claim the same thing.

Twilight was founded on the Brazos River in 1875 and today it functioned mainly as a regional tourist destination. To keep a steady influx of cash pouring into a town that claimed a permanent population of just under six thousand, a cottage industry had sprung up around a local legend whose authenticity was the topic of heated debate.

The prevailing legend, among the romantics, involved two teenage sweethearts separated during the Civil War. Jon Grant had been a soldier for the North; Rebekka Nash, a sweet Southern belle. Circumstances tore them asunder, but they never stopped loving each other. Fifteen years later, they met again at twilight on the banks of the Brazos in the same spot where the town now stood.

In the early 1900s a statue in the lovers' honor had been erected in the park near the town square. Rumor had it that if you threw pennies into the park's fountain, you'd be reunited with your high school sweetheart. Whether it was true or not, the legend worked. Twilight was officially nicknamed Sweetheart Town in the *Fort Worth Star-Telegram* in 1910, and there'd been a steady influx of romance-related tourism ever since. Many reunited high school lovers came to Twilight to get married under the Sweetheart Tree, and in fact Belinda Murphey, one of the other ladies of the knitting club, ran a thriving matchmaking business focusing on helping people reconnect with long-lost loves.

"Once you and Beau are hitched, you'll be an official member of the club," Terri said. "Having qualified by marrying the only man you've ever really loved."

Thoughts of Jesse circled Flynn's head again. Why was he on her mind so much today? She hadn't thought about him in ages . . . well, except in an occasional lusty dream. She slid a stealthy glance over at Patsy, who sank down in her designated rocking chair near the television set. She was startled to find the older woman glaring at her.

Unnerved, Flynn snatched her gaze away.

"Wow, you've made a lot of progress since last week," Terri said, plucking up the afghan Carrie had knitted for Flynn and studying the needlework. "How do you find the time? Running Froggy's, looking after your dad and Carrie and the twins, keeping house, dating Beau . . ."

"Idle hands," Flynn said, and reached for the afghan. She clutched it to her chest. She didn't want anyone looking too closely. "With the twins away at basketball camp in Iowa for the entire summer, I've got some extra time on my hands." That was true enough.

"You're getting really good." Terri nodded in approval. "I love this pattern. When did you learn to do that stitch?"

"Oh, you know," Flynn shrugged. She hated lying, but she'd been pretending for so long, how did you just suddenly come out and confess that you were a fraud?

"Your mother would be so proud."

Guilt stabbed her. This was her secret shame.

The lie had started innocently enough not long after her mother received the crippling blow that she would be slowly wasting away until she died, losing her abilities to do all the things she enjoyed most. Combing her daughters' hair, cooking her husband's dinner, rocking her twin sons, knitting crafts for family and friends.

Her mother had been hands-down the best knitter in the county. Some said even the whole of Texas. She'd won the state fair competition three years running.

Flynn had been thirteen at the time and her mother had been trying for almost a year to teach her how to knit. Flynn couldn't seem to wrap her head around it. Knitting was tedious, not relaxing as her mother claimed, and when it came to yarn, all ten of Flynn's digits turned into clumsy thumbs. But more than anything else in the world, she'd wanted to please her mother, so she kept trying.

One day, while Flynn was in the bedroom she'd shared with Carrie, knitting needles clutched in her hands like handle bars, yarn in her lap, cussing up a blue streak because she couldn't make it work, Carrie got up off the floor where she was coloring and walked over. She took the knitting needles and yarn from Flynn's hands, sank down on the bed beside her, and just went to town.

Flynn's mouth had dropped open. "How . . . how'd you learn to do that?"

Carrie had given her an it's-no-big-deal shrug. "I watched Mama showing you how to do it."

"You . . . you're a natural."

"It's easy."

Flynn had wanted to slap her. "Does Mama know you can do this?"

"Naw, if I told her she'd pester me to do it all the time like she does with you."

"I'll pay you to knit something for me."

Carrie looked surprised and pleased. "Ten bucks."

"Done."

Carrie had knitted her a scarf. Flynn had presented it to their mother as her own work. Lynn had been overjoyed that she'd finally gotten through to her oldest daughter. She called all her friends and bragged up a storm. Carrie bought a bagful of candy with her money and a copy of *Teen Beat*.

And so Flynn's big fat lie began.

When it came to the Sweethearts' Knitting Club,

she was a fraud in every sense of the word. She didn't know how to knit, and while she'd dated Beau in high school, he hadn't been the one she'd first given her heart to. If these women knew her secrets, they'd boot her right out of the knitting club that her own mother had started.

The doorbell rang, signaling the arrival of more Sweethearts. Flynn got up to answer the door. Raylene Pringle waltzed over the threshold. Raylene had been a Dallas Cowboys cheerleader back in the Tom Landry/Roger Staubach days and she still dressed the part even though she was rapidly approaching sixty. White knee-high boots, blond hair teased big, false eyelashes, short skirt, an expertly hand-knitted Dallas Cowboys sweater vest, and lots of flashy attitude. She and her husband, Earl, ran the Horny Toad Tavern down off Highway 377.

"Hey y'all," she called.

"Belinda's not with you?" Flynn asked, checking the front porch to see if Belinda had lingered to smell the honeysuckle. Usually Belinda and Raylene carpooled together because they both lived in Rio Vista Estates on the other side of the dam.

"One of her kids is sick."

"Which one?" Patsy asked.

Raylene waved a hand. "How should I know? She's got too many to keep track of."

"Is it Kimmie, Kameron, Karmie, Kyle, or Kevin?"

"Kameron maybe."

"What's wrong with the kid?"

"She's throwing up."

"Then it's not Kameron. Kameron's a boy."

"Whatever."

"Was it Kimmie?"

"Why do you care?"

"How can I send the child a get well card if I don't know which one it is?" Flynn asked.

"She's a kid, she'll be well tomorrow, and if you sent her a card she'd probably just eat it and throw up all over again. Save your money."

"Or just send her a funny e-mail," Terri suggested.

"How can I do that when I don't know the kid's name?"

"It was Karmie," Raylene said.

"You're sure?"

"Positive."

"Now was that so hard?" Flynn asked.

"Guess what?" Dotty Mae said as Raylene set down her knitting bag near her rocker.

"Dotty, we're too old for guessing games. You got something to say just spit it out."

"Flynn's engaged to Beau."

Raylene's eyebrows shot up. "No, really?"

"She hasn't said yes yet," Marva said.

"Oh, so nothing's changed." Raylene plunked down, crossed her legs at the knee.

"It's different this time," Terri added. "He gave her an ultimatum."

"No shit? Whatcha gonna do, Flynn?"

"I'm going to go get the tea," Flynn said.

"But you will say yes." Marva nodded, getting up to follow Flynn. Once she was in the kitchen, she hoisted the tray of finger sandwiches to help serve. "Beau adores you."

"What in the heck *is* holding you back, honey?"

Raylene called from the living room. "That man is delicious. If you don't want him, I'll take him."

"What would Earl have to say about that?" Patsy asked.

"Oh, you know Earl." Raylene waved a hand. "I could shave my head bald and walk through the house stark naked and he wouldn't blink twice."

"Don't forget you'd have to have Kathryn Trainer for a mother-in-law," Terri pointed out.

"Ugh," Raylene said to Terri. "Maybe that's why Flynn's said no all these years." Then to Flynn she said, "You got a beer, honey? I'm not in the mood for tea. Earl and I had a knock-down-drag-out and I need to let off some steam."

Flynn rolled her eyes at Raylene's dramatics and bit down on her bottom lip to keep from saying something snarky. "We don't keep alcohol in the house."

"Oh yeah, since your daddy got dried out. I forgot."

"Earl?" Patsy raised an eyebrow. "A knock-down-drag-out?"

"Okay, it was more like I pitched a hissy fit and he ignored me, but you get my drift. He refused to buy me a mink stole for my birthday. Cheapskate. Like he's not sitting on a big pile of his grand-daddy's oil money. I gotta go around with the last name of Pringle, least he could do is make sure I had a stole to keep me warm."

"Good grief, Raylene, what do you need a mink stole for? It's Texas," Patsy said.

"You sound just like Earl."

"And it's the twenty-first century," Terri added. "It's not politically correct to wear fur."

"*Phttt.*" Raylene gave a one-fingered salute. "That's what I think of political correctness."

"More tea, anyone?" Flynn interrupted before a knock-down-drag-out occurred in her living room. Terri's temper could escalate as quickly as Raylene's.

Raylene held out her cup. "Dotty Mae, you got any of that peppermint schnapps in your purse? That oughta fix this tea right up."

The women ate and chattered and then got down to serious knitting and even more serious gossiping about what was going on in Twilight. As she did at every meeting, Flynn stayed on her feet making sure everyone had enough to eat and drink, then she bustled around cleaning things up. She sat a time or two and pretended to knit, but luckily her role as hostess gave her an excuse to flit.

"So Flynn, how are plans coming for the Yarn Barn?" Marva asked toward the end of the evening as everyone was packing up her knitting supplies.

"I haven't found the property that both meets our needs and is something I can afford," she answered, stacking teacups on the serving platter now littered with sandwich crumbs.

"Oh"—Terri waved a hand—"you won't have time for that once you're married to Beau. He'll have you popping out babies lickety-split."

"I'm not a toaster," Flynn said. "I don't pop."

"Your biological clock *is* ticking, dear," Dotty Mae threw in.

"Whose side are you on?" Usually Dotty Mae was all for women waiting until they got their careers established before having babies. She'd had her two sons when she was in her late thirties after she'd become the first female department head of Montgomery Ward.

"Well dear, waiting tables at Froggy's isn't exactly a career and you are so good at taking care of people. I'm sure Terri just assumed you'd be eager to start your family once the nuptials were over." Dotty Mae tried to smooth things over.

"I'm starting the Yarn Barn. That's going to be my career."

"Oh," Dotty Mae said. "Well then, never mind."

Raylene rubbed her hands gleefully. "We're taking sides? I'm in. Popping out babies?" She mimed a chopping motion. "Way overrated."

"You only say that because Earl Junior turned out to be such a turd," Patsy said. "I still can't believe that boy didn't even call you on Christmas."

"Well at least he didn't end up in prison like someone's surrogate son," Raylene sniped.

The entire room inhaled sharply. And everyone looked anywhere but at Patsy. No one ever mentioned Jesse in front of her.

"For the sake of our friendship I'm going to pretend you didn't say that." Patsy straightened her shoulders. "My nephew was wrongly accused. He's innocent."

"Yeah, just like he was innocent of blowing a hole in the Twilight Bridge with that M80."

Jesse *had* been guilty of blowing a hole in the old wooden suspension bridge. Flynn had been there when he'd done it. She still remembered the illicit thrill she'd felt when he'd grabbed her hand and they'd jumped off the bridge together just as the potent firecracker had erupted behind them in a shower of sparks.

"You know what?" Flynn said. "It's getting really late." She faked a yawn, stretched.

Everyone got the hint and headed for the door.

"Tell Beau yes," Terri said on her way out.

"But tell him he has to wait to set a date until you get the Yarn Barn going," Dotty Mae said, clearly trying to make amends. "He can't tie you up until you've tied that up."

Precisely her thoughts. Tired of being subtle, Flynn made shooing motions. "Night all."

"G'night."

"Take care."

"Tell your father we asked after him."

Yes, yes, go, go. "Will do." She pasted a smile on her face.

"Honey," Marva whispered, leaning in close. "Seriously, don't make the mistake of letting Beau get away. You could be living in the biggest house in Twilight."

"Yes, because hey, it's all about the size of the house, right?"

Marva gave her a strange look, and Flynn smiled wider to prove she was only kidding.

The minute they were all out, Flynn locked the door and sank against it, both physically and mentally drained. Some days it just didn't pay to get out of bed. Why the hell had Beau picked today to issue his ultimatum? Why couldn't he have waited until . . .

When? When would be a good time for your boyfriend of ten years to demand you make a permanent commitment to him or walk away forever?

What was the matter with her? Beau was perfect.

Every woman's dream. He was rich, good-looking, patient, and . . .

Okay, all right, the problem was all her. She was a commitment-phobe and she was damn lucky Beau had put up with her this long. But finally he'd had enough and he'd given her twenty-four hours to make up her mind.

The grandfather clock by the door chimed nine. *Bong, bong, bong.* Only twenty-one hours left to make the biggest decision of her life.

CHAPTER THREE

*Patsy Calloway voted
most likely to end up governor of Texas*
—Twilight High, 1969

After dropping off her passengers at their respective homes, Patsy Calloway Cross drove through the silent town square feeling lonelier than she had the day she'd been forced to admit her husband, Jimmy, to Twilight Hills Alzheimer's Care Facility. First she'd lost one of her closest friends in Lynn MacGregor, and then two days later Jimmy had had a complete meltdown, stripping off his clothes, running down the street, screaming bloody murder when anyone tried to touch him.

It wasn't fair, losing so much at once, but Patsy had learned a long time ago that was simply the way the world worked. One tragedy after another, and if you were really, really lucky, you found a shiny spot of happiness for a second or two. It had been a really long time since she'd been lucky.

She turned down Ruby Street and drove past the Teal Peacock. She wondered if she would sleep tonight. Probably not. After tonight's discussion at the Sweethearts' Club, Jesse crowded her brain along with the inevitable sorrow and regret that followed such thoughts.

Poor kid. Poor unlucky boy.

She wished for the millionth time that she'd never gone searching for him, never found him, never brought him to Twilight for his final year of high school. By giving him a home, she'd sealed his fate. She'd thought she was doing a good thing; instead, it had ended up being the biggest mistake of her life in a life filled with gargantuan mistakes.

Patsy bit her lip, remembering the day she'd discovered her hippie, dopehead younger sister, Phoebe, had died in Phoenix, leaving behind a child that she'd never told anyone about. It had taken Patsy more than eight years to track the boy down. Those had been rough times—for her, for her marriage, for Jesse.

You'd think it'd get easier with time. It didn't. She needed to make a trip down to Huntsville. What with running the Teal Peacock and her town council duties and going to see Jimmy in the nursing home every day, more than six months had slipped by since her last visit. She hadn't even called Jesse.

Who are you kidding with those excuses? You haven't gone because every time you do, it's getting harder and harder to look him in the eyes.

And now she was going to have to tell him that this time, she suspected Flynn would accept Beau's marriage proposal. A girl could ignore reality for only so long. Patsy knew that well enough. Inevitably, thoughts of Jesse led her back here. To her own youthful mistakes.

To Hondo.

That's when she realized she hadn't taken her normal route home, but had instead turned down Eton Street, past the fire-ambulance station.

This is stupid. What are you doing?

The ambulance bay door was rolled up. A large square of yellow light fell onto the darkened street. Sphinx moths winged above the gleaming clean emergency vehicle parked in the driveway.

Her pulse quickened. Patsy clenched the steering wheel tighter, held her breath. *Stupid, stupid, stupid.*

There he was, polishing the chrome mirror on the passenger side.

Patsy's heart scaled her throat and for one razor-sharp moment, stopped beating.

Hondo Crouch.

Her first love. The man she'd never been able to forget, not even after almost forty years of marriage to Jimmy Cross.

Hondo had done things. Unforgivable things. But she still loved him. Even after all these years.

He was fifty-nine, but you wouldn't know it by looking at him. He wore his hair clipped short now. Not long and tied back with a leather strap the way he had after he'd come back from Vietnam and gone to Washington, D.C., to protest the war he'd been part of. His hair was mostly gray now, but he still held on to a few jet black stands. Gone too was the bushy mustache she'd once found so sexy, and he wore a crisp white and blue paramedic uniform.

But his shoulders were just as broad as they'd ever been. His arms just as muscular, his waist as lean, his hips as narrow. He walked with a John Wayne swagger, all manly and arrogant. Lines of time etched his face, but nothing could fade the intensity in those deep blue eyes.

He looked up from polishing the chrome.

Patsy scooted down in her seat, stared straight ahead, pretending that she wasn't doing precisely what she was doing. Driving by to see if she could catch a glimpse of him.

What is wrong with you? You're not seventeen. This isn't 1969. You're on the town council, for crying out loud. Don't look, don't look, don't you dare look.

At the last second, she couldn't stand it and peeked over.

He drilled her hard with those eyes, his polishing rag thrown over his shoulder, his features expressionless. You could have wrung more emotion from a chunk of granite.

Then he did something that completely took her breath.

He raised his hand in greeting.

While Patsy was driving past Hondo's ambulance, Flynn was climbing the stairs to bed.

Her father had come home from his AA meeting right after the members of the knitting club had departed. She'd made him a turkey sandwich and they'd sat at the kitchen table talking about her mother. She told him how proud she was that he'd managed to conquer his addiction and he told her how lucky he was to have such an understanding daughter. It had been a rare father-daughter moment for them. Usually Flynn acted as the parent, Floyd the child. Then she told him about Beau's ultimatum.

"Marry him, sugar. Beau will take good care of you."

"I know, Dad. It's just that . . ."

"Why are you hesitating? Don't you love him?"

She shrugged, toyed with a paper napkin. *Just not in the way I think I should.* "I do, but it's just not that simple. I'm so used to being the one taking care of people, I don't know if I can let someone take care of me. It just feels . . . off."

Her father got to his feet, kissed the top of her head. "You deserve to be taken care of, princess. I know I let you down after your mother got sick and it all fell on your shoulders. I can't tell you how sorry I am for that. I'm trying my best to make amends."

"I know you are, Dad. Staying sober is the best gift you could ever give us."

"I'm doing my best, baby girl." He'd gone off to bed and she'd washed the dishes, and then turned for the stairs. Before she reached the top, she heard a knock at the back door. Had Carrie misplaced her key? But no, it wasn't even ten yet. Carrie would still be closing up Froggy's. Had one of the Sweethearts forgotten something?

She bumped back down the stairs and opened the door to find Beau standing there.

"Hi."

"Hi," she said. "What are you doing here?"

"Can I come in?" He wore starched jeans with a sharp crease, a short-sleeved, button-down shirt, spit-polished cowboy boots, and an excited smile. He was without his Stetson for once and his hair was freshly washed and combed. He smelled of Old Spice.

"Dad's trying to get to sleep, he's had a rough day," she said.

"This will only take a minute."

"Yeah, okay, sure. Let's sit on the porch swing."

He stepped back and she walked out onto the veranda, pulling the door closed behind her. He took her hand and led her over to the porch swing. They sat, and he kept her palm clutched in his.

The loamy smell of the river, along with the richly sweet scent of her mother's honeysuckle twining along the white picket fence, drifted over to them. Crickets and cicadas chirped a noisy racket, accompanied by the occasional bullfrog bass. Overhead the stars were scattered like loose diamonds over black velvet. There was no moon in the sky. Beau gently rocked the swing, sending the weathered chains creaking softly. A slight breeze blew in off the water, ruffled her hair.

This was life as she'd always known it. Slow, gentle, conventional. There'd been only a short window of time when her world had seemed full of other possibilities—fast, wild, unpredictable.

Jesse.

"What's up?" she ventured when Beau didn't speak.

"I've been thinking and I realize it was wrong not to give you any wiggle room."

Thank heavens. Flynn exhaled fully. He was retracting his ultimatum. "Okay, good, fine, thanks."

"You were feeling backed into a corner."

"Sort of," she admitted.

"I don't want you to feel that way. Marriage shouldn't be a straitjacket." He sounded thoughtful, pensive.

"No indeed."

Silence stretched between them, comfortable as a pair of worn-out jeans.

"I heard some intriguing news this evening that might interest you." He interlaced their fingers.

"Oh?"

"Pete Grissom's getting married."

"Really? To whom?"

"Belinda Murphey helped him find his high school sweetheart and they just hit it off like thirty years never passed. He's moving to Colorado to be with her and he's looking to sell the picture show cheap just to get rid of it."

The old Twilight Theatre on the courthouse square had been vacant for years, ever since they'd built a fourteen-screen cineplex on Highway 377 leading into Fort Worth. It had originally been constructed as a saloon back in 1878. The downstairs area had housed the bar and the piano. The broad, ornately carved staircase had led upstairs to a gaming parlor that had been highly illegal, but operated without interference from the local sheriff of the day. Over the years, the building had gone through many incarnations. Barbershop, milliner's, candy store. In the 1950s Pete Grissom's father had turned the building into a movie theater, with the upper floor serving as a storeroom/office combo.

"It's a great building, even if it did used to be a whorehouse," she teased.

"Flynn! It was no such thing."

"Come on, saloon, gambling hall, you telling me there wasn't a little sumpin' sumpin' going on in there?"

"We're talking about our founding fathers here."

"And they were all saints? Boys will be boys after all."

"I'm saying there's no recorded history that the saloon was ever used as a brothel."

"Just because no one wrote it down doesn't mean it didn't happen. Besides, Twilightites tend to whitewash their history. Romance rules over reality."

"You like the lurid stuff, don't you?"

"It's fun to talk about." She ran her free hand along the chain of the porch swing.

"Let's just talk about the building. What do you think?"

"It *would* be the perfect place for Lynn's Yarn Barn."

Beau smiled, his straight teeth a flash of white in the darkness. "I was hoping you'd think that."

"I've been thinking that for years, but Pete's always wanted too much money for the property."

"Well, he's in love now and money is no longer his top concern. Time is of the essence." Beau then quoted a price that was well within her range. "I've taken the liberty of speaking to him on your behalf, and he says if you can commit to the deal and arrange financing by Tuesday afternoon, the place is yours. I called Moe, and he said if I cosigned your loan it's a done deal."

Moe Schebly was not only head VP at Twilight National Bank, he was also the town's mayor. But since the reward of the mayoral position was one more of honor than money, he stayed working for the bank. Although being mayor did have its perks, like free downtown parking, free dry cleaning, and a leased car.

Two concurrent emotions took hold of Flynn. Gratitude that Beau had ferreted out this bargain and irritation that he'd done it all without her consent. She wanted this, but his methods left a sour taste in her mouth.

He squeezed her fingers. "Are you happy, baby?"

She bit her tongue to keep from saying something utterly ungrateful. "You didn't have to go to all this trouble on my account. I could have handled it."

"I know." He brushed a strand of hair from her forehead. "You're an independent little cuss. It's one of the things I love about you. No shrinking violet, my Flynnie."

Why was she feeling so bitchy? She forced herself to say, "Thank you, Beau."

"So here's my proposition," he said, and then he took that black ring box out of his pocket again. "If you'll say yes to marrying me, right now, tonight, we'll hold off on setting a date for the wedding until after you get the Yarn Barn up and running and turning a profit."

"That's the wiggle room you're giving me?" A moth in a cocoon had more wiggle room.

He nodded. "If it takes a year, it takes a year. If it takes two, it takes two. Just make our engagement official, Flynnie. Will you do that for me?"

"Beau . . ."

His smile was so eager, so full of hope. She

thought of what everyone had said at the knitting club meeting. They were right. Beau was a good man. She was foolish for keeping him dangling on a string and damn lucky he was a one-woman man or he would have lost patience with her a long time ago. "I know you're scared, but I'm brave enough for the both of us."

Her heart thumped. "We don't have to set the date until after the Yarn Barn is fully operational and turning a profit?"

"Nope."

She took a deep breath.

"There's just one other thing."

She met his gaze. "What's that?"

"I think we should have one of those celibacy pacts."

"A what?"

"You know. Let's do this the right way. Commit ourselves to celibacy until our wedding night."

"Seriously?"

"It would make the wedding night really special."

"No sex until after the wedding?"

"That's right."

"You're sure?"

"It just feels right, you know?"

The request was classic Beau. Mr. Do the Right Thing. "Are you thinking it might make me hurry up and get the Yarn Barn going faster if I'm not gettin' any?"

Beau laughed. "I'm not going to quibble with that."

The man had a great laugh and he smelled so good. And he had enough money to take care of her and her family. He was honorable. He was good-looking. He possessed a strong moral code. He was going to give her time to fulfill her mother's dying wish. What more could a woman ask for?

He slipped the ring from the box. "May I put this on your finger?"

She nodded. Her hand was trembling.

Beau slid off the porch swing and onto one knee. "Flynn Denise MacGregor. For the fifth and final time, will you marry me and make me the happiest man on earth?"

His eyes shone in the porch lamplight. He'd been so good to her, so good *for* her. He'd been kind and patient and understanding. And now he was giving her Lynn's Yarn Barn. She had no reason to refuse other than a silly crush she'd had on a boy back in high school. A boy who'd turned out to be a pistol-toting drug dealer. A boy, she'd discovered belatedly, that she knew absolutely nothing about. A boy she hadn't seen in ten years and probably wouldn't recognize if she did. It was time to let go of those old fantasies that had stopped her from moving on and embracing the future.

"Yes," she whispered, "I'll marry you, Beauregard Reginald Trainer."

"Oh, Flynnie," he said, and his sigh of relief was so heartfelt that all her doubts fled. "You've made me the happiest man on earth." He slipped the ring on her finger.

She held it up to the light, trying to adjust to the unaccustomed weight. It turned easily on her finger. "It's a bit big."

"We'll have it sized on Tuesday when we go apply for the loan to buy the theater."

So many emotions crowded into her throat—

anxiousness, excitement, fear, loss, acceptance—
that she couldn't speak. She didn't even know what
to say.

Beau stood, took her hand. "Come on. Let's go
tell your dad. Tomorrow night we'll tell my parents, and make it official at Mom's annual Memorial Day party."

While Flynn was getting engaged to Sheriff Beau
Trainer, Hondo Crouch stood staring after the tail-
lights of Patsy's Crown Victoria long after they'd
disappeared into the darkness. The past rolled over
him, warm and sticky as the night air, leaving him
with cravings he thought he'd vanquished long ago.
Had she been feeling it too? Was that why she'd
driven by?

Honda swallowed, shook his head. Too late for
thoughts like that. Forty years too late.

Still, he couldn't stop himself from having
thoughts. He wondered what she'd do if he just
went over to her prim house on Market Street,
punched a hole right through her front door with
his fist, and marched inside. What would she do
if he grabbed her in his arms and kissed her the
way he'd been aching to kiss her? Kiss her, hell. He
wanted to fuck her prim, stuck-up majesty within
an inch of her life. He wanted to make her beg. He
wanted to hear her call out his name in ecstasy one
last time before he died.

His cell phone rang. He pulled it from his
pocket; saw that the number scrolling across his
caller ID belonged to one of the men he sponsored.
One-handedly, he flipped the phone open. "How
you doin', Floyd?"

"Not so good, Hondo."

"Get yourself to a meeting, Floyd."

"I just came from one."

"That bad, huh?"

"I gotta drivin' urge to head down to the Horny Toad Tavern."

"But you're not going to do that."

"I . . ."

"You're not going to do it," Honda commanded, full-steel marine.

"You don't understand. It is . . . was . . . my wedding anniversary." Floyd choked up. "I miss Lynn so bad I can't breathe."

He knew the feeling. "Straighten up, man. Do it for your kids. Do it in memory of Lynn. Honor her with your sobriety."

Floyd swallowed audibly. "Does it ever get any easier?"

No. Hondo thought of how it had taken him several tries in detox with trained professionals to finally kick the heroin twenty years ago. And how to this day he still felt those old cravings at the most unexpected times. But he wasn't about to tell that to a man on the verge of taking a drink after being eleven months sober. "You just learn how to man up and deal with it. You realize you want to stop hurting those you love more than you want to take a drink. Do you want to put Flynn and Carrie and your boys through any more shit than you've already put them through?"

"No."

"Damn straight."

"How . . . how do I deal with this?"

"You got a punching bag?"

"No."

"Weights?"

"An old barbell out in the garage and I think Flynn's got a jump rope."

"Good. Go out in the garage and lift weights and jump that rope until your lungs are screaming and your muscles are cramping and your physical pain is worse than the mental pain."

"And that really works?"

"It does." *At least for a little while.* "Now go on and do it. Call me if you get into more trouble."

"Okay, thanks," Floyd said.

Hondo hung up, pocketed the cell phone. He didn't know if Floyd MacGregor was strong enough to conquer his addictions. The man had always been one of those breeze-through-life kind of guys.

Yeah, like you've fully conquered yours? Hypocrite.

No value in judging people. He'd learned that lesson the hard way. It always came back to bite you in the ass.

Hondo started to pull the ambulance into the bay when he heard the familiar sound of a Harley engine. It had been years since he'd ridden one, but suddenly he was *Easy Rider* all over again. Those damn addictions. He stopped, turned. The chopper pulled up beside the ambulance. The rider cut the engine, peeled off his helmet.

Hondo did a double take, blinked. It couldn't be, but it was. *Jesse Calloway.* Out of prison two years earlier than expected.

"Hondo," he said.

"Jesse." Hondo nodded.

"I'm here to call in that favor."

Aw shit, the chickens were coming home to roost. "Now?"

"No time like the present."

Hondo exhaled. "Park your bike around the side and come on in the station house."

He fought back the knot gathering in his gut as he waited for Jesse to park the Harley and follow him inside. This time of night most of the crew were sleeping or watching television. Hondo led Jesse into the empty kitchen area. "You want something to drink? Water, soda, juice?"

"Water's good."

Hondo pulled two bottles of water from the refrigerator, took one for himself, tossed one to Jesse. The kid looked thinner in a black T-shirt and denim jeans than he did in his prison jumpsuit. A couple of days' growth of beard stubble ringed his jaw and accentuated the rebel-without-a-cause thing he had going on. Hondo took a chair at the table, nodded at the one across from him. "When'd you get sprung?"

"A week ago." Jesse twisted open the bottle of water, took a sip.

"Why didn't you call? I would have come to pick you up."

"I had some things I needed to do."

"Like getting the Harley out of storage?"

"Yeah."

They sat there looking at each other. Neither one spoke for a long moment.

"I want to thank you," Jesse said. "For coming to see me when I was inside. It helped."

"I know. You're welcome."

Another awkward silence. In the background they could hear the television from the next room. It sounded like a *Baywatch* rerun.

"How'd you manage to get out early?" Hondo finally ventured.

"Long story, we'll save it for another time."

Hondo inhaled. "So what can I do for you?"

Jesse toyed with the plastic ring from the lid of the water bottle. "You still willing to loan me the money to open my motorcycle shop?"

Hondo remembered what it was like to be young and in trouble with no opportunities, no one to stand by you, no one to care. He recalled the desperate, gritty feelings that made a man do things he shouldn't. He didn't want Jesse to have to go through that. It was the reason he'd taken an interest, gone to see him in prison. That and the fact he was Patsy's nephew. Stupid, he knew, still giving a damn after all these years. But there it was. "Where are you thinking about opening up the business?"

"Right here in Twilight."

An uneasy feeling skittered over Hondo's skin. "You think that's wise, considering Clinton Trainer's progeny is now sheriff of Hood County?"

Jesse slouched back in his chair and lowered his eyelids halfway, dropped his hands into his lap. "I'm not scared of Beau Trainer."

"You should be. One wrong move and he could send you straight back to prison." Hondo shook his head. "He'll be gunning for you, make no mistake about that."

"I welcome the challenge. Besides, I heard you were running against him in the upcoming election. Maybe you'll win."

Hondo had to smile. "I might at that."

"What prompted your sudden political aspirations?"

"Trainer's too young to be sheriff. He only got the position because his old man had a stroke and Beau went off to Iraq and got himself shot. He's not qualified and he's too damn much a stickler for the rules. Sees things in strictly black and white, and we both know how dangerous that kind of thinking can be. But it'd be dumb for you to come back to Twilight if you've got an axe to grind with Trainer. You won't win."

"I'll let you do my axe grinding for me, Hondo."

"It's Flynn, isn't it? That's *really* why you're back."

Jesse was cool, but not so cool that he could completely hide the surprise in his eyes. "Why would you say that?"

"I'm not blind, boy. I saw the way you used to look at that little gal. You had a thing for her. Which ultimately is what landed you in the slammer."

"Nothing gets by you."

"Not much," Hondo admitted. "Not anymore."

"So you know of any places for sale in the area that might meet my needs?" Jesse took his hands out of his lap, stretched them out on the table in front of him.

For the first time Hondo saw the watch on Jesse's wrist up close. He blinked, did a double take. Uneasiness snaked through his body. The hairs on the back of his neck lifted. "Where'd you get that watch?"

"This piece of crap." Jesse scoffed, flicked his

fingers over the watch face. "It's the only thing my old man ever left me."

Hondo moistened his dry lips. He couldn't seem to tear his gaze off the timepiece. He hadn't seen the watch in a very long time. There was nothing particularly special about it. Inexpensive, mass-produced. Rather, it was the band that identified it. Two-tone braided leather. Handcrafted by Navahos selling jewelry at a roadside stand in Arizona, and the telltale notch at the side where it had once caught on a nail. "I . . . I thought you never knew your father."

Jesse shrugged. "I didn't, but my mom gave it to me a couple of days before she died. I hated the son of a bitch, but it's the only thing I have that belonged to him. Stupid, huh?"

"You sure it really belonged to him?" Hondo asked, bouncing his knee up and down. "Maybe your mother just told you that."

"Maybe," Jesse said. "I just know if I ever find the original owner of this watch, I'm gonna cold-cock the bastard first and ask questions later."

CHAPTER FOUR

*Flynn MacGregor voted the person you'd most like
to be stranded with on a deserted island*
—Twilight High, 2000

"Oh my gracious," Belinda Murphey exclaimed.
"Will you get a load of that ring? Harvey, honey,
look at Flynn's ring."

Belinda poked her husband, who was busy
wiping something sticky off their three-year-old's
face. Their four older children were giggling in
time to the lively country music piped in through
the sound system and running unfettered around
Froggy's, zigzagging past waitresses carrying heap-
ing platters of fried catfish, fried chicken, chicken
fried steak, fried frog legs, fried shrimp, and pot
roast.

Froggy's streamlined menu was straight-to-
the-arteries comfort food. You picked from the
six main entries, and it was served at your table
family-style. Each dish came with a huge platter of

mashed potatoes, cream gravy, green tomato relish, coleslaw, hush puppies and/or homemade biscuits, and the vegetable of the day. Today it was Roma green beans fresh from Beau's mother's backyard garden.

When her father first bought Froggy's back when he and her mother were newlyweds, it was nothing more than a boat gas station on the marina with a place inside to buy sandwiches, cigarettes, boating supplies, and beer. Over the years her father had slowly added the outdoor patio deck, expanded the main dining room, and put in the bar at the back. One gas pump remained at the end of the pier, but for the most part, people came there for the food.

After Mom had gotten sick and Floyd had seriously tucked into his drinking, business dwindled as food quality nosedived, and the staff made like sinking-ship rats. Floyd had almost lost the place until Flynn took over managing it after she graduated high school. But since her father quit the hooch, he'd been slowly gathering the reins again. He'd taken over the bookkeeping, the ordering of supplies, and the hiring and firing. Flynn still made out the employees' schedules and filled the gaps in the waitstaff schedule.

Like this Saturday. One of the waitresses was on her honeymoon and Flynn hadn't been able to con anyone else into taking her weekend shift. She wore a Froggy's apron knotted around her waist and a name tag lanyard. Working the floor today put her in a bit of a bind, seeing as how she'd have to rush home to change after her shift was over. Beau was picking her up at seven for his mother's party.

"Harvey, seriously, look at the rock Beau put on Flynn's finger. It's huge. What is that? Two carats?"

"Three actually."

Belinda whistled, and all five of her kids made a beeline for the table. She shook her head. "False alarm, Mommy wasn't whistling for you. Go back to what you were doing."

The gaggle of young Murpheys dispersed.

Harvey looked up, blinked. Somehow the gunk that had been on the three-year-old's face had ended up on his own chin. "Beau and Flynn finally got engaged?"

"That's what I'm trying to tell you." Belinda shifted her gaze from her husband to Flynn. "The ring *does* belong to Beau, right?"

"Who else's ring would it be?" Harvey asked. "He's the only guy she's ever dated."

Flynn rolled her eyes. The joys of small-town life. Everyone knew all your business.

"Honey, hold still, you got some . . ." Belinda moistened her thumb and rubbed the smudge off Harvey's chin.

"See what you get to look forward to," Harvey said. "The ugly side of intimacy."

"And you love every minute of it." Belinda kissed his cheek. "So Flynn, sit, sit." Belinda patted the seat next to her, which was littered with the crumbs of her offspring. "I want to know all the details. How did he pop the question? Have you set a date? Where's the ceremony gonna be at? What about the honeymoon? You know I've got connections. I could get you a great discount on a Padre Island condo."

From the kitchen, a bell dinged twice signaling that a catfish platter was up for delivery. "That bell's for me." Flynn pointed a thumb over her shoulder. "Gotta go."

"Aw shoot, can't someone else get it? I'm so sorry I had to miss the knitting group last night. Karmie had a stomach bug but you couldn't tell it by looking at her today."

Belinda nodded in the direction of her six-year-old, who was doing the chicken dance with a group of servers, her siblings, and various other children. In between the country music Froggy's looped in, they played a few group participation songs like the "Hokey-Pokey" and "Chicken Dance" to heighten the festive atmosphere. One thing was a given, Flynn was *not* playing the "Chicken Dance" at her wedding reception. No "Y.M.C.A." No "Electric Slide."

"We'll chat later." Flynn zoomed away, happy for the excuse of schlepping a platter of steaming hot catfish across the packed dining room. People had been bombarding her with questions all day about the ring and she was tired of talking about it.

The sun was sliding westward as she turned from the kitchen, the serving tray balanced on her upturned palm. No one had yet thought to draw the shades, and the harsh afternoon glare cut straight through the big picture window fronting the water, bathing the main entrance in a band of sultry light.

The front door swung open and a man, cast in silhouette, stepped across the threshold. He was cloaked in shadows, but something about the way he stood seemed very familiar—deceptively casual and self-possessed, but don't-tread-on-me dangerous.

Flynn squinted, blinked. Her gut tightened and her heart slowed to a sluggish beat. The hairs on the nape of her neck lifted and all the air fled her lungs. Her head spun and her knees wobbled. She'd never fainted in her life, but for one precarious second she thought she might hit the floor, catfish platter and all.

Jesse.

Was he real? Was it a trick of the light? It had to be. Jesse had two years left to serve on his prison sentence. He simply could not be standing in Froggy's doorway looking like a gunslinger come for a showdown.

A hostess met him, menu in hand.

It could *not* be Jesse. She was imagining things. This engagement business was muddling her mind. The cold sweat rolling down her back had to be wrong. But he was undeniably masculine, his saunter pure cocky, self-assured male.

The hostess turned, escorting him toward her.

No, no, no.

The "Chicken Dance" was over, the kids dispersed. Silverware clattered against plates. Voices hummed. Shania Twain was singing "You're Still the One."

Closer and closer, he stalked.

Her whole body was trembling now. Willow-tree-in-a-hurricane trembling.

His face was leaner, stripped of the round-cheeked innocence of youth; his jaw harder and ringed with a scruffy five-o'clock shadow darker than his muddy blond hair. He wore scuffed cowboy boots, faded Levi's with a hole in the knee, and a snug-fitting white T-shirt that stretched tight across his bulked-up biceps. A battered old Timex was strapped to his left wrist, and a red bandana peeked from the front pocket of his jeans. Gone was the boy she once knew. Here stood a man, through and through.

Jesse.

The bridge of time snapped, butting her past up against her present, the future weighing heavily on her ring finger.

The serving tray she carried slipped from her grasp and clattered to the floor. Flynn smelled peanut oil, lemon, and her own deep-seated fear. Instantly she squatted and started scooping up catfish.

To her horror, Jesse crouched beside her.

"Don't . . . I can . . . please." Studiously she wrangled hush puppies, tomato relish, mashed potatoes, anything to keep from looking him in the eyes.

His hand reached out to lightly touch hers. Damn if her heart wasn't beating so hard she feared it was going to explode. She didn't know what to think, had no idea what to do with these feelings shifting around inside her. He kept his hand on hers until she finally had no choice but to look at him.

"How you doin', Dimples?" Jesse said in his sexy Southern drawl that still curled her toes. "Long time no see."

She couldn't breathe, couldn't think, she was as brainless as if she'd just been struck on the head by lightning. He was the only person on earth who'd ever called her Dimples.

Say something, but be cool, don't let him see what he's doing to you.

"You're out of prison," she said brightly, plastering a stupid smile on her face, knowing full well she was revealing the dimples he enjoyed teasing her about. Oh God, why had she said that? And in such a chipper tone, like, "You've lost weight."

"Here I am." He spread his arms.

"So you are. How'd you get out early?"

"Time off for good behavior."

"You?" She snorted.

"Yeah, imagine that."

They stared at each other. He reached a hand to her face. Startled, she drew back.

"Easy there, Dimples, just going for that speck of gravy." He rubbed her cheek with his thumb.

Her skin burned where he'd touched. "You that hungry?" she quipped.

"Oh yeah," he said, his tone low and sexy and filled with sizzling hot innuendo. His eyes darkened. "You have no idea."

Flynn gulped and got lost in his gaze. Apparently some things never changed. "Was there really gravy on my cheek?"

"Let's just let that stay a mystery."

The busboy, Carlos, hustled over with a mop and broom. "I clean mess up for you, boss."

"Thank you," she said, happy to have a reason to look away from Jesse.

He stood and held a hand out to help her up, but she ignored it and got to her feet under her own steam. No way was she touching him.

"Well, then," she said, wiping her palms on her apron. "If you're hungry, let's get you a seat."

"Had enough of those in prison. Not very tasty even with salt."

She wasn't going to laugh at his joke. She wasn't about to encourage him. How did he manage to joke after ten years in the slammer? She immediately had ugly thoughts of metal bars, cement floors, stark lighting, and burly men named Bubba with fierce tattoos on their faces. Jesse had been to such a place, and now here he was grinning and joking as if he'd just come back from a prolonged vacation. It wasn't what she expected.

What had she expected?

For one thing, she'd never expected him to come back to Twilight. Not after the way the town had treated him. Why had he come back?

"What'll you have?" she asked.

"I've been dreaming of Froggy's chicken fried steak."

"One chicken fried steak dinner, coming up." She turned to go, but he snaked out a hand and grabbed her wrist. Instantly her womb tightened. "What?" she whispered.

"You want me to just stand here?"

"Oh, yeah, um, you wanna sit outside on the patio?"

"Outside sounds like an excellent idea."

"This way." She crooked a finger and led him to a vacant table near the railing overlooking the river. A sand crane flew by, skimming low to the water, looking for a meal.

Jesse sat, tipped back his chair, propped his feet on the railing, and closed his eyes. He looked . . . peaceful.

"You want a beer or something while you wait?"

"Don't drink," he said without opening his eyes. "Never have, never will. Not joining in on that little family tradition, if you know what I mean."

No, maybe not, but you carried a .357 and sold cocaine.

"Well, me neither. Nothing more than a sip of champagne at celebrations. Not with my father's problem. Alcoholism takes all the luster out of being drunk."

"Yep."

"I'll bring you a glass of water."

He nodded, eyes still closed, sun on his face. Flynn raked her gaze over him, unable to believe he was really there. Maybe this was a dream. That was it. After accepting Beau's proposal, she'd gone to bed and was just naturally dreaming of Jesse to get him out of her system once and for all.

Pinch yourself and see.

She pinched the web of skin between her thumb and index finger. *Ouch. Okay, not a dream.*

He opened one eye. "You still here?"

"Just going."

"Hurry back."

She turned, walked halfway to the door, stopped, turned back, opened her mouth, shut it, then zoomed off to the kitchen. But she didn't get far; Belinda and her brood were headed out the door.

"Yoo-hoo, Flynn," Belinda called and waved at her. She pretended not to hear, but Belinda wasn't the type to believe anyone would intentionally ignore her. "Honey, wait up."

Flynn stopped, sighed, and waited for Belinda

to catch up after she sent Harvey and the five little Murpheys on out to the car.

"Who's the guy?"

"Guy?"

"The hunk." Belinda waved toward the patio. Although she'd been born in Twilight, her family had moved away for several years. She hadn't lived there when Jesse was in high school with Flynn. "He's gorgeous and he's got that bad-boy aura women just love. I have a couple of clients who'd go gaga over him."

Jealousy swept through her, California-wildfire hot. Flynn moved between Belinda and the patio. "I thought your matchmaking business concentrated on hooking people up with long-lost loves."

"Everyone isn't as fortunate as you and me to wind up with our high school sweethearts. Some poor women don't even *have* long-lost loves. There are only so many Beaus and Harveys in the world." Belinda peered around her shoulder trying to get another peek at Jesse. "Do you think that guy is single?"

"Listen, Belinda, it's not a good idea." Why was she warning Belinda off recruiting him for her matchmaking business? Jesse deserved some happiness. If Belinda could conjure him a match, why not encourage her?

"What do you mean?" Belinda lowered her voice, leaned in closer.

"The bad-boy thing?'

"Yes?"

"No act. He's been in prison."

"Really?" Her eyes widened.

"That's why you haven't seen him in here before. He just got out."

"What he'd do?"

"Drugs, guns."

"Do you think he learned his lesson? People can change."

"Belinda! You're not seriously thinking of hooking one of your clients up with an ex-con."

"No, no." She waved a hand, but kept looking at the patio. "Of course not. But if he's learned his lesson and he's really remorseful . . . I mean come on, look at him . . ."

"It's Jesse Calloway, okay."

Belinda looked flustered. "Patsy's Jesse?"

"Patsy's Jesse," Flynn confirmed.

"Why didn't she tell us he was getting out?"

Why hadn't she? "You know Patsy doesn't like to talk about Jesse."

"Still." Belinda sniffed, her feelings clearly hurt. "You'd think she'd say something to her closest friends."

"Wife," Harvey hollered from the doorway. "It's broiling out here in the Suburban and the twins are fighting, shake a leg."

Flynn shook her head. "I'll let you go, Harvey looks like he's about to have a stroke."

"Oh dear, his face is red. Harvey, did you forget to take your blood pressure medication?" Belinda scurried off to her husband.

Flynn placed the order for Jesse's chicken fried steak and tried not to look out the patio doors every time she walked past. When she brought his meal he was still cocked back in the chair, face turned up, enjoying the sunlight.

She settled the platter in front of him. "Grub's up."

He opened his eyes, dropped his legs, settled his chair firmly on the floor, and then he kicked out the chair beside him. "Sit down."

"I gotta . . ." She jerked a thumb over her shoulder.

"You aren't going to make me eat by myself, are you? It's been a long time since I had a meal with a pretty woman."

Flynn felt her cheeks heat.

"Come on," he wheedled. "Five minutes for an old friend?"

Don't do it. Leave, go.

She sat. He'd always been able to coax her into anything.

He tucked into the chicken fried steak with gusto, eating hunched over with his elbows sticking out as if fending off predators.

"That good, huh?"

Jesse seemed to realize what he was doing and where he was. He settled his elbows to his sides, sat up straight, took a deep breath. "Sorry, I picked up a few bad habits in the can."

"I can imagine."

"No," he said, his tone as sharp as the steak knife he held in his right hand. "No, you cannot."

A chill chased through her at the dark look in his eyes. "You're right. That was a very dumb thing to say."

The moment was incredibly awkward. On the river below, a pontoon boat filled with laughing and joking partygoers motored past. Over the outdoor speakers, Shania was singing "Forever and for Always." Who the hell had put on that sound-track?

"Froggy's has changed," Jesse said after a long moment. "No longer just the place you gas up your johnboat, grab a six-pack and a hot dog."

"A lot of things have changed." She wondered how to tell him about her engagement to Beau. *You don't owe him anything. He returned your letters unopened. Never called. Never offered an explanation for what he'd done. It's none of his business that you're getting married.*

"I can see that." His gaze lingered on her bosom. "A lot of things got bigger."

She crossed her arms over her chest, fought back the thrill his perusal brought. *Stop this nonsense.*

"You changed your hair."

She put a hand to her sleek straight locks. "I straighten it now."

"Why?"

"It looks more polished."

"Ah, I see."

"See what?"

"You want to look like furniture."

"What?" She knew he was making a joke but she was suddenly struck by insecurity. She lifted a hand to her hair. "You don't like it?"

He shrugged, " 'S all right."

"You disapprove."

"I liked it wild and curly."

"You were the only one."

"Meaning?"

"I like it straight."

"Just you?"

"And my family."

"Just them?"

"And Beau," she said, reluctantly speaking his name in front of Jesse. Tension spun out between them, taut as wire, thick as tapioca.

"Ah, the Golden Boy, I was wondering when we were going to get to the root of the problem. He's the one who likes straight hair. Not you, not your family."

"Listen, you gave up your right to weigh in on my hair when you decided to sell drugs."

"I didn't—" He stopped, clenched his jaw, fisted his hands against his thighs. "I just don't see any reason why you have to be something you're not. Be natural, be yourself."

"You're saying I'm not polished?"

"I'm saying you shouldn't fight who you are."

"Thanks. I appreciate the sage advice." She scooted back her chair and tried to ignore her rapidly pumping heart. "Seeing as how following your natural outlaw tendencies worked so well for you."

"Hey, now." He rested his hand on her forearm. A jagged scar zigzagged across four of his knuckles. A scar that hadn't been there ten years ago. "I didn't mean to make you mad."

She sucked in a breath filled with concern, sadness, longing, sarcasm, and fear. She twisted her arm out from under his hand. "I did just fine without your advice for ten years."

"You did." He nodded.

"Now you're just placating me."

"I don't want you to go."

"Why are you here, Jesse? Why did you come back to Twilight?"

He leaned forward, placed his arms on the table, pushed his tea glass back and forth between his hands. A nervous gesture? The ice in the glass tinkled; his watch band made a rough noise against the smooth table. For a split second, she prayed he would say, *You.* But he didn't. He just shrugged. "Gotta be somewhere."

"What are you planning on doing here?"

"Opening up a place to sell and repair motorcycles."

"You were always good with your hands," she said, recalling the way his calloused palms had felt running over her soft skin.

"It comes to me naturally," he said. "But I also took courses in prison on small engine repair."

"You can take courses in prison?"

"Sure. Rehabilitation and all that."

"So you're really set on staying."

"I am."

She didn't know how she felt about that. It was unsettling, thinking of Jesse being in town again for good. "We'll be seeing each other around."

"We will."

They stared at each other. Desire flamed in his eyes. He fisted his hands, clenched his jaw. She watched him fight back what he was feeling, but it was a struggle. Did *her* face reveal her own battle?

Fear clobbered the other emotions swirling inside her, pulling ahead like an odds-on favorite at the Kentucky Derby. She jerked her gaze from him, stared down at her hands, and that's when she saw that her ring finger was bare.

"Omigod," she exclaimed. Flynn felt her skin

blanch white, and she bit down so hard on her bottom lip she was amazed she didn't taste blood.

Instantly Jesse was on his feet, on alert, fists knotted, eyes sharp, muscles tensed. "What is it? What's wrong?"

"My ring. I lost my ring. I've got to find it."

"It's all right, calm down. I'll help you find it."

"You don't understand . . . it's really valuable. Oh, oh, I knew something like this was going to happen." She jumped back, eyes to the ground, searching. Beau was going to have a fit. She hadn't had the damn thing twenty-four hours and she'd already lost it. And in less than four hours she was supposed to be at his mama's annual Memorial Day weekend bash, flashing it around for all her uppity friends to ooh and aah over. Proving in his mother's eyes, once and for all, that she wasn't good enough for the likes of her son.

"Let's retrace your steps. When was the last time you remembered having it on?"

"Just before you came into the restaurant."

"You dropped the tray."

Flynn groaned. "I lost it in the food. Or on the floor. Someone probably already found it, kept it."

"Don't freak." Jesse laid a hand on her shoulder to calm her.

That same old electricity shot through her. She tensed beneath his touch and he immediately dropped his hand. Shania was back to "You're Still the One." *Would someone please put a new play-list on?* Several diners at nearby tables peered over at them.

"This is terrible," she moaned, meaning more than just the loss of Beau's engagement ring.

"Worst thing since Vietnam." Jesse nodded solemnly, but his eyes danced with mischief.

Flynn's heart clutched. Part of her wanted to smile, another part of her wanted to throw up. Once upon a time, whenever she was overreacting to some turn of events, Jesse would tease her with the crack about Vietnam, letting her know she was making a mountain out of a molehill. But the message had double meaning. The very last thing he'd said to her as Sheriff Clinton Trainer had stuffed him handcuffed into his squad car was: "Cheer up, Dimples, it's not the worst thing since Vietnam."

But it had been. Jesse's arrest and subsequent conviction had been her teenage version of a devastating war with far-reaching consequences. Not wanting him to know how much their past still affected her—after all, she'd gone on to live a normal life, while he'd endured things she could not begin to imagine—she bantered back, "Horrible, the world will never be the same."

"Scorched earth."

"Devastation."

"Widespread famine."

"Orphans with rickets."

"There'll be monsoons."

"Tidal waves."

"Earthquakes."

"Apocalypse, Mad Max style."

"Sand and rusted tanks."

"And really bad clothing options."

"Damn," he said. "The fate of the entire world hangs in the balance. We have to find that ring."

A giddy warmth filled her and she couldn't stop

herself from smiling, which she was sure had been Jesse's intent.

"There you go," he said. "Showing me those dimples."

The giddiness disappeared, replace by embarrassment and confusion. What was the matter with her? Beau's engagement ring had gone missing and she was flirting with Jesse.

I'm not flirting with him, I'm . . . I'm. . . . What was she doing? *Having a good time.*

Inappropriate. These thoughts were totally inappropriate.

They retraced her steps, searching along the way, and ended up on the loading dock, squatting on the cement ramp, going through the trash. After half an hour, she rocked back on her heels. Despair sagged her shoulders. "I give up. It's gone."

Jesse kept shifting through the guck like he was panning for gold. His head was down, his hair falling over his forehead.

Her stomached tightened. She still couldn't believe it. Jesse was back and she was engaged to Beau.

Jesse grunted.

"What is it?" She rocked forward again.

"I think I found it."

Relief and hope pulsed through her. "Really?"

Between his fingers, he held something covered in mashed potatoes. He wiped it off on newspaper they'd spread on the cement floor. Suddenly the triumphant smile vanished, replaced with a steely expression.

"An engagement ring?" he said. "You didn't tell me we were looking for an engagement ring."

Her heart stuttered. "Didn't I?"

He shook his head, stared at her coolly. "Beau?"

"Yes."

"Right. Who else but good ol' Beau." Something dark and unsettling flickered in his eyes. "When did you guys make if official?"

"We haven't," she admitted. "He asked me last night, I said yes. We're announcing it officially tonight at his mother's annual Memorial Day weekend party." *Now why had she gone and told him that?* "May I please have it back?" Flynn held out her hand for the ring, but instead of putting it in her palm, he slipped it on her ring finger, mashed potatoes and all.

"Congratulations on the upcoming nuptials, Dimples. I hope you and Dudley Do-Right will be very happy together."

Before she could say or do anything, he dipped his muddy blond head and closed his mouth over hers in a hard, unremitting kiss.

The kiss was spontaneous and bold, but it was not a kiss of passion. Rather, it was an instrument of his anger. Rude. Demanding. Orchestrated to shame.

Flynn's body reacted instantly, softening, dampening, hungering. And in that second her mouth seemed to have a mind of its own, kissing him back, gobbling up the taste of him like a starving woman. She felt her lips slip apart, felt his tongue slide sweetly into the space she'd made for him. She was bombarded by sensation. Some old, some new, all of them mind-blowing.

And along with the sensations tumbled a million emotions. She felt speechless, overwhelmed, lusty, bewildered, ravenous, spellbound, ecstatic, ashamed, exhilarated, sheepish, aroused, annoyed.

Too much, it was all too much. It was wrong and it was way more than she could handle. Terrified, Flynn jerked her mouth away and slapped him hard across the face.

Jesse reached up, ran his hand along his jaw imprinted bright red from the impact of her palm. He didn't say a word, just got to his feet and sauntered away.

Leaving Flynn crouched on the loading dock surrounded by garbage, hand stinging, heart thumping, a lump of sorrow and regret lodged solidly in her throat.

Jesse sped away from Froggy's on his Harley determined not to feel a damn thing. But it was a hopeless endeavor. Flynn had always possessed the power to twist him inside out. Tangle him up. The scent of her lingered—spice, honeysuckle, sass.

And her taste!

His tongue tingled with her womanly flavor. His stinging cheek told him he shouldn't have kissed her, but when he'd seen that ring, his cool had slipped away, leaving him with nothing but a desperate, primal need to brand her and claim her as his own.

He'd acted like a caveman.

Why had he kissed her like that? So savagely, so unrelentingly? Had he subconsciously wanted to punish her? He hated to think that was the case, but he couldn't deny she brought out complicated feelings in him.

When he'd seen her again, standing in the artificial light of Froggy's, wearing that apron and her I'm-in-charge expression, he'd been overtaken with longing. Dreaming about her in prison was one thing, seeing her in person was a whole other story. All his best intentions faded away in the face of reality. He was putty in her hands.

She'd grown even prettier since he'd seen her. More self-confident in her movements, more polished in her personal style. Her hazel eyes were the same. Feisty and smart. And those dimples. God, how he loved those dimples. The sight of them beat an antidepressant any day of the week. She was a little thinner than she'd been before, but she filled out her T-shirt quite nicely. Remembering, he felt himself getting aroused.

How he wanted her!

But he'd blown it. Kissing her the way he had. Out of anger and hurt. It was stupid and it was pathetic. He'd seen that ring and he'd lost his cool.

It bothered Jesse that Flynn saw him as a criminal. He wanted to tell her the truth about Trainer, but pride held him back. If she'd really trusted him, if she really had known him as she claimed, she wouldn't for one second have believed that he was selling cocaine. After watching his mother destroy her life with the stuff, he wanted nothing to do with drugs. Flynn should have known that.

But the gun was yours.

Yes, right, the gun. The thing that had tacked extra years to his sentence. He'd gotten it to scare off Trainer. God, he'd been such a dumbass kid with no clue.

And if Flynn couldn't see Trainer for who he was

deep down inside, well then, he was wasting his time trying to recapture their once budding love.

What was he doing here? Why had he come back?

For one thing there were his feelings. He hadn't expected such an odd mix of hope, longing, regret, shame, revenge, and need.

That was starkest of all.

This hungry, insatiable need for her. He hadn't expected this level of burning, yearning when he saw her again. It muddled his head, fogged up his brain.

He needed sex. That was the cure. But he couldn't make himself just go pick up some random woman, no matter how strong his physical urges. Flynn was the one his body craved. Flynn was the one who boiled his blood, hardened his cock. Anything else, anyone else would just be a pathetic stopgap measure.

So what now? What was he going to do? He wanted her, but only if he could have her as his own, totally, completely, forever. But she was engaged to Beau Trainer.

A smart man would walk away. Go to a new town, meet a new girl, start a new life. But when it came to Flynn, when had he ever been smart?

Jesse grunted, hardened his jaw, tightened his fists on the handlebars. So Flynn had gone and gotten herself engaged to that bozo Trainer. He shouldn't be surprised. It didn't matter. It didn't affect his plans one whit. They weren't married yet.

In fact this was better. When he stole Trainer's fiancée from him, one half of his plan for revenge would be complete. He tried smiling, but it didn't fit on his lips.

Flynn wasn't a pawn and he didn't want her getting caught in the crossfire between him and the sheriff.

Sheriff.

Jesse snorted. What a joke. If only the town knew the real Beau Trainer and what he was capable of, they'd be shocked to the core. If they knew what he'd done, they'd impeach him. And that was precisely what Jesse was counting on. Beau Trainer was gonna pay for stealing Jesse's woman and his life, and he was gonna pay big.

CHAPTER FIVE

Patsy, you'll always be the love of my life.
—Hondo Crouch, yearbook entry, 1969

Patsy sat knitting on the top floor balcony of her old Victorian house on Market Street, gently swaying in the rocking chair passed down from her maternal grandmother. It occurred to her—not for the first time—that she had no daughter to pass it down to. From this vantage point, she could see the lake and the sandy beach where families flocked on the weekends.

Colorful sailboats glided past the swimming area. In the distance, jet boats pulled skiers, paddleboats and canoes rocking in their wake. Kids with fishing poles sat on the docks, kicking their bare toes in the water, completely carefree. A red-tailed hawk flew over the tops of the pecan trees in her front yard calling *kreeee, kreee, kree, kreeeeeeee.*

Overhead, the ceiling fan rotated lazily. Mozart spilled from the mp3 player. A glass of iced chamomile tea with fresh honey and a flickering aromatherapy candle called Serenity, which smelled of fresh linen, lilacs, and sea salt, rested beside her on the small wrought-iron table with a mosaic tile top.

From the outside, her life looked quite peaceful. From the inside, it was a different story. Hence the calming aids of beautiful view, inspirational candles, uplifting music, and busy hands.

She knitted continental style, holding both the yarn and the needle in her left hand, picking the stitches through with each loop. Everyone else in the knitting club knitted English, but her French grandmother—the same one who'd given her the rocking chair—had taught her this method and she'd seen no reason to change, even though her friends claimed their method was easier. The trick to continental style was in the way you kept the yarn slightly taut. This required winding the thread over her left pinkie finger and her left forefinger. She liked the tradition of continental style. It made her feel connected to the past. And in a life where she'd lost so much, it was a feeling she treasured.

The music, the water, the tea, the candle, the rocking chair, and her knitting slowly unraveled the nerves she'd jangled last night by driving past the fire station. After seeing Hondo, she hadn't slept a wink. Finally, at dawn, she'd gotten up and driven over to the Alzheimer's Care Facility to check on Jimmy.

It hadn't been one of his better mornings. The minute she'd walked in the door with a basket of fresh-baked cranberry muffins, Jimmy had started screaming, "Help! Help! Police! Police! She's trying to poison me!"

She tried everything she knew to soothe her addled husband but his agitation escalated to the point where the nurse had finally asked her to leave. She'd come back home and taken a fitful nap. Around noon she'd gone down to the Teal Peacock to check on the new girl she'd hired for the weekends. Business was steady. A few locals dropped by to visit, several of them buzzing about Kathryn Trainer's annual Memorial Day party. Patsy hadn't been invited. Ever since Clinton had arrested Jesse, Patsy and Kathryn's relationship had gone from politely cordial to iceberg cold.

Tourist traffic motored along Market Street, headed for Marina Beach. A silent ambulance was in the convoy, more than likely on the way back from transporting a patient to Fort Worth. Was Hondo behind the wheel? Patsy's fingers quickened at her knitting.

Once upon a time this whole area had been affluent residential homes. Houses on one side of the road; the lake, piers, beach, and marina on the other. Now it was zoned as a commercial area, with only a few houses like hers left. Most of the Victorians had been converted into businesses. A bed-and-breakfast next door to the right. A law office beside that. On the other side was an exercise studio, and behind it, the Carriage House (which had once been an actual carriage house), an elegant four-star restaurant, open only in the evenings Thursday through Sunday. Across the street, a set of new townhouses had been erected on the waterfront, blocking part of her view of the lake.

The ambulance was hung up at the red light at the intersection of Graffon and Market. She narrowed her eyes to see if she could make out who was behind the wheel, but her vision just wasn't what it used to be and the windows were tinted. It could be Hondo.

Her needles clacked as she remembered the way he'd waved at her last night. How long had it been since they'd acknowledged each other's presence? Old history weaved its way through her brain along with the smell of Texas Joe's Barbecue from down at the end of the block.

In a blink, she was seventeen again, sitting on her canopied bed in this very house, listening to the new Rolling Stones album, *Let it Bleed*, and crying her heart out because her period was three weeks late. Between the music and her sobbing, it had taken a few minutes for her to hear the pebbles smacking against her window. She'd dragged herself off the bed, swiped at her eyes, smearing mascara tracks over the backs of her hands, and stumbled to the French doors leading out on to the balcony.

The minute she saw Hondo standing on the side lawn in his Jefferson Airplane T-shirt and cut-off blue jeans, fresh tears sprang to her eyes. How was she going to tell him that she might be pregnant?

"Patsy?" he said, alarm in his voice. "Are you okay?"

She'd shaken her head. "No."

"I'm coming up." He'd grabbed for the trellis.

"Shh, my folks are in the living room watching *Hawaii Five-O*. Remember what happened last time?"

The last time her seven-year-old sister Phoebe had caught them kissing on Patsy's bed. She'd threatened to tattle, but Patsy bribed her with promises of a new Barbie. Her parents disapproved of Hondo because he lived with his trash collector father in a trailer park by the river, and they'd forbidden her to see him. The upper-crust Calloways judged people not on who they were, but on where they came from and what they did for a living. Patsy wasn't so narrow-minded. She knew people couldn't help the family they were born into. She wondered how her folks would react when they found out she was carrying Hondo's baby.

You don't know for sure yet.

Hondo scaled the railing onto the balcony like Romeo coming after Juliet. He held his arms out to her and she sank into them. He squeezed her tight. "What's wrong?"

She broke the news. He didn't get angry. Instead he swung her up in his arms and twirled her around. "Why are you crying, silly? This is wonderful, wonderful."

"But I wanted to go to college," she'd sobbed.

"You wanted to go to college."

"We can still go," he said. "We can do this. I'll go to school during the day, work at night."

"Doing what?"

"Whatever I can get."

"How will we pay for an apartment? A baby? College tuition?"

"We'll get grants, loans," he'd said optimistically.

"We need help, Hondo." They both knew help would not be forthcoming from his father. "We have to tell my parents."

"Let's wait," he said, "until you know for sure."

She nodded; he kissed her and told her not to

worry, that he loved her and everything would work out fine. Then he'd slipped off into the darkness, the sound of his happy whistling floating back to her on the night breeze. She and Hondo were having a baby. For the first time she smiled. Imagined a miniature Hondo calling her Mama and giving her sticky-faced kisses.

If only she'd known then what she knew now. Patsy closed her eyes. Mozart played on as a tear slid wetly down her cheek.

A week later, the family doctor who had delivered her confirmed that she was pregnant. She hesitated calling Hondo. She was still trying to figure out how they were going to break the news to her parents. She was in line at the school cafeteria, an egg salad sandwich, bottle of Yoo-hoo, and a package of Cheetos on her lunch tray.

"Patsy," he whispered, "can we talk?" The look in his eyes was one of pure fear. Nothing had ever scared her so badly.

"What is it? What's wrong?"

He'd taken the tray from her hand, set it down, pulled her from the line. Putting his hand to her back, he guided her into a quiet corner. Her heart was thumping, panic spread through her like a wildfire. Instinctively she'd curled her hand around her belly. The baby was the size of a pea, but already she was trying to protect him.

"What's happened?"

He tugged an envelope from his pocket and handed it to her. She opened up the letter, saw the word "drafted," and the next thing she knew she was in the principal's office with the school nurse waving a vial of ammonia underneath her nose.

She convinced Hondo they should elope; surely they wouldn't send him to Vietnam if he had a new wife and a baby on the way. He told her he wasn't a coward. That he didn't run away from his responsibilities.

"What about me and the baby? Aren't we your responsibilities too?"

Finally, he'd agreed to an elopement. He took all the money he'd been saving for college out of his bank account and bought plane tickets to Vegas and made plans to leave in the middle of the night. Patsy was climbing down the trellis when her father caught them. He'd come out on the porch with his shotgun in his hand. Threatened to shoot Hondo for defiling his daughter. The ensuing row had been frightful and angst-ridden.

In the end, they'd lost. Hondo went off to boot camp and then on to Vietnam. Her parents had pushed for her to go down to Mexico and see "a special kind of doctor." Patsy was aghast that they would suggest such an abortion, and she refused their south-of-the-border solution. She was having Hondo's baby whether they liked it or not. It was only years later that she found out from Jimmy Cross that her family doctor had violated patient confidentiality by telling her parents she was pregnant. The very next day, her father had paid a visit to a crony of his on the draft board, with Hondo's name on a piece of paper in his pocket.

When she was six months along, news came that Hondo was MIA, presumed dead since the rest of his battalion had been wiped out. She'd mourned him with the tortured grief of a brokenhearted teen. The only thing that kept her sane was the thought that at least she had a part of Hondo growing inside her. Then Jimmy Cross had come courting. His family had some money, although not as much as the Calloways, and he was pre-law at Texas Christian University. When he asked her to marry him, Patsy said yes. She needed someone to help her care for the baby, and she was desperate to get out of her parents' house. Jimmy was a good man, if somewhat bland, and he didn't seem to mind that she was having a dead man's baby. They married on her eighteenth birthday.

On New Year's Eve 1970, Patsy went into labor. Twenty-seven hours later, a stillborn son was delivered with severe complications. In order to save her life, the doctor had been forced to perform a hysterectomy.

Three years after that, Hondo was discovered in a POW camp, starving, fever-ridden, and strung out on heroin.

Patsy swallowed, looked over at the trellis still twined with ivy, and her heart ached for the girl she'd been, for Hondo, for their sweet lost child.

The crunching sound of tires on gravel brought her fully back to the present. The ambulance had pulled into her driveway. Her heart fluttered, equally apprehensive and hopeful.

The ambulance door slammed closed and Hondo walked around to the side lawn just as he used to do all those many years ago. He sank his hands on his hips, pushed his sunglasses up on his head, tilted his chin up at her. "Afternoon, Patsy."

"Hondo," she said. They'd barely spoken a dozen words to each other in as many years. They stood there staring at each other. The litter of their past was an ocean between them.

"There's something I think you should know," he said.

She walked to the balcony railing, told her stupid heart to stop pounding so rapidly. "What's that?"

"Jesse's come back to town. He's staying with me and I've loaned him the money to buy the Twilight Theatre."

Clinton and Kathryn Trainer owned the largest house in town. Every time Flynn visited, she felt like she was being granted an audience with the King and Queen of Twilight. The mansion, built in 1910 by Beau's great-great-grandfather, sat high on a hill above the lake. From this lofty perch, five generations of his family had sat on their back porch looking down on the town.

Going to the mansion always set Flynn on edge—she was terrified of making some unforgivable faux pas, like using the wrong fork with the wrong course, or grabbing her dinner companion's water glass by mistake—but this evening was especially nerve-wracking. Beau escorted her up the wide flagstone walkway, possessively tucking her arm through his. They arrived thirty minutes ahead of the appointed party start time of eight P.M. in order to break the news of their engagement to his parents before officially announcing it at the party.

Flynn wore the same emerald green, sleeveless

taffeta dress she'd worn last year and hoped Kathryn wouldn't remember. She hadn't had the time or the money to buy something new.

A housekeeper greeted them at the door. "Take a chair in the sitting room," she invited. "I'll let Mrs. Trainer know you're here."

"Thanks, Carmen." Beau smiled and guided Flynn to the sitting room crammed with expensive antiques and elaborate paintings of dead Trainer relatives.

The grandfather clock ticked loudly in the silent room as Beau helped himself to bourbon and branch water from the wet bar in the corner. He wasn't much of a drinker under normal circumstances, but he'd often hit the hard stuff whenever he visited his folks. Even as leery as Flynn was of alcohol, she couldn't blame him. Clinton and Kathryn were a bit hard to swallow without some kind of mellowing agent.

"You want a club soda?" he asked. It was what she usually drank when being entertained at Chez Trainer. "Or maybe, just for tonight . . ." He held up the bottle of bourbon.

"Tempting . . . but I'm good." Flynn eased down on the hard-backed settee, pressed her knees together, and tucked the fingers of both hands underneath her thighs.

"Darling, you're early," Kathryn Trainer said, sweeping into the room in an expensive designer frock perfectly tailored to fit a figure just a shade above anorexic, and made a beeline for her son. She bussed both his cheeks. "Make me one of those, will you?"

"Sure thing."

Kathryn turned to her. "Nice to see you again, Flynn."

"Mrs. Trainer." Flynn nodded.

"Why, don't you look nice in green. That dress is just as pretty on you this year as it was last."

Zing! Kathryn had noticed.

You're marrying into this family, play nice. Flynn bit down on the inside of her cheek.

"How is your father?" Kathryn took the tumbler Beau handed her and sat down in the Queen Anne chair across from where Flynn sat. Beau eased down beside her.

"Fine, great."

"Beau told me your brothers are at basketball camp for the summer."

"They are," she said proudly. "They have a good chance of winning college scholarships based on their basketball skills."

"And that quaint little restaurant with that adorably kitschy name . . ."

"Froggy's." As if the place hadn't been in business for twenty years.

"How are things there?"

"Things are just as kitschy as ever. If things get any kitschier we'll have to break out the gig to keep it from leaping off the lily pad."

Kathryn looked at Beau, clearly confused by Flynn's joke. Beau took Flynn's left hand and squeezed it, reminding her that not everyone was a sarcasm aficionado.

"Did you know Tony Romo ate at Froggy's when he and his girlfriend spent a weekend in Twilight?" Beau asked.

"Tony Romo?"

"Quarterback for the Dallas Cowboys," Flynn supplied.

"Oh, tell that to Clinton, it'll impress *him*."

"Where is Dad?" Beau asked. "There's something Flynn and I would like to tell you both."

"Augustina is bringing him down."

"Who's Augustina?" Flynn asked.

"His nurse."

"I thought her name was Amelia."

Kathryn frowned, or at least she would have if she hadn't been so shot up with Botox. "Is it?" She shrugged, took a sip of her drink. "I could have sworn she said Augustina."

"She's been working for you since Dad had his stroke last year and you still don't know her name?" Beau asked.

"I can't learn the name of everyone in our employ, Beauregard."

Flynn forced herself not to roll her eyes. Later, she would giggle with Carrie over this, but right now she was feeling a wee bit like someone who'd been buried alive.

"Look, here he is." Kathryn got to her feet as the nurse wheeled Clinton Trainer into the sitting room. The former sheriff wore a white Western shirt with a bolo tie, gray suit pants, and a matching gray Stetson. He looked not unlike J.R. from the old television show *Dallas*. He was of that same wealthy, Big Daddy ilk.

Before his stroke, Clinton was known for his booming voice, exuberant glad-handing, and larger-than-life persona. But the stroke had compromised his speaking abilities, reducing him to grunts and monosyllables. Beau said it was the first

time in his life he was able to get a word in edge-
wise. But the old man's mind was still sharp. It was
impossible to miss the frustration and anger burning in the depths of his whiskey-colored eyes.

"Hi, Amelia," Flynn said to the nurse.

"You remembered my name." Amelia looked
both puzzled and pleased.

"Yes, yes." Kathryn waved her away. "You may
go now."

Once the nurse had left the room, Beau took
Flynn's hand. "Mother, Father . . ." He nodded.
"Flynn and I have something to tell you."

Kathryn smoothed down her skirt, set her drink
on the coffee table. "Yes."

He held out Flynn's hand so his parents could
see the ring. "We're officially engaged."

"Finally!" The uptight matriarch dissolved into
a smile just like most any other mother would. "Did
you hear that, Clinton? Oh, this is good news."

Flynn softened toward her. Kathryn wasn't an
awful person. Just different from the way Flynn's
own warm, welcoming, accepting mother had been.
She'd often wondered if part of what Beau liked
most about her was her family. Lynn had treated
him as if he was one of her kids. Floyd joked with
him. Noah and Joel played basketball with him.
Even Carrie liked him, and she was a hard nut to
crack.

"Should I give you a hug?" Kathryn stood.
"Would it be all right if I hugged you?"

"Sure," Flynn said and met her halfway.

The hug was stiff and uncertain, but by golly it
was a hug, and it was the first time ever that Kathryn had made such a gesture toward her. Her body

felt so thin in Flynn's arms, she didn't really know to hug her back. Hugging Kathryn was a bit like hugging a sack full of rosebush clippings, bony and sharp. She ended up just sort of patting her jutting shoulder blades.

Sheesh, you could slice bread with those things.

"Son." Kathryn turned to Beau. "You've made me so happy."

"As Flynn made me when she finally said yes." Beau beamed at her.

Okay, stop with the "finally," people, we get it. I've been dragging my feet.

"So when's the wedding?"

Beau glanced at Flynn. "We're waiting until Flynn has the Yarn Barn going before we set a date."

"Oh?" One of her perfectly arched eyebrows rose up on her forehead as far as the Botox would let it, and her voice took a frosty north turn. "What's that?"

"The Yarn Barn was her mother's dying wish," Beau said. "More than anything in the world, Flynn wants to honor her mother's memory with this endeavor. She fears . . . we fear . . ." he corrected. "If we get married before she gets the business started her dream will get lost in the shuffle of wedding plans, setting up housekeeping, and then having a family."

"So this wedding might not come off for two or three years?"

"That's a possibility, yes." Beau exchanged a look with his mother.

"Could you fellas give us a few minutes alone?" Kathryn asked. "Maybe you could take your father onto the patio for a cigar. I'd like to speak to my new daughter-in-law-to-be in private."

Oops, what was this? Flynn darted a please-don't-leave-me-alone-with-your-mother look at him, but Beau was bending down undoing the locks on his father's wheelchair and didn't catch her eye.

"Sit," Kathryn invited as she returned to her chair. Beau wheeled Clinton out the French doors to the patio beyond the sitting room.

Flynn perched on the edge of the settee. *Ulp.* What was this little private chat all about?

"Now then." Kathryn smiled when the French doors shut after the men.

"Now then," Flynn echoed, not knowing what else to say. *Just don't make some smart-ass quip. Now is not the time.*

"Beau has waited over a decade for you."

"Uh-huh."

"He could have any woman he wanted."

"He's quite the catch."

"Yes he is." There was that north wind again, chilling as it rolled over Kathryn's scrawny shoulder blades and blasted Arctic ice Flynn's way.

"However, my son never wanted any other woman but you . . ." Kathryn paused. "Well . . . there was that awful Jodi Christopher."

"Jodi Christopher?" Who was that?

"Beau never mentioned her to you?"

"No."

Kathryn slid a glance toward the patio, and Flynn had the strongest sense she was being manipulated. "Jodi was Beau's first love."

"Huh?" *She* was Beau's first love.

Kathryn's smile was smug. "You thought you were the only one, didn't you."

Well, yeah. "When'd he meet her? How come I didn't know about this? I mean Twilight is a small town."

"Beau is three years older than you, darling, and it was the summer before he turned seventeen."

That was the same summer her mother had been diagnosed with ALS. Flynn had known Beau then, of course, but she was too young for dating and her life had tumbled in on her at her mother's diagnosis. That summer was a blur of doctors' visits and balancing the twins on her hips as she cooked dinner and cleaned the house and generally took over all her mother's duties. No wonder she didn't remember that Beau had dated this Jodi person.

"That summer Jodi was out of control and her parents sent her to live with her grandmother here in Twilight, hoping it would straighten her out." Kathryn pursed her lips. "She was wild as a March hare and Beau was drawn to her like a magnet. You know how he is. That boy simply can't resist a damsel in distress."

Meaning *she* was a damsel in distress? *Don't be snarky, don't crack wise.*

"Of course Jodi broke his heart. Shattered it right to pieces."

"What happened to her?"

Kathryn shrugged. "She ran off with some low-life and ending up getting killed on the back of his motorcycle."

"How awful."

"You reap what you sow."

Flynn sat there absorbing the information. This

news cast Beau in a whole new light, and she didn't know what to make of it. On the one hand, she sort of liked the notion that he'd had a bit of a past, a smudge on his knightly armor. On the other hand, it bothered her that he'd never mentioned Jodi, not once in the ten years they'd been dating on and off.

Hypocrite. You never mentioned Jesse to him.

No, but she had the feeling he always knew. This Jodi thing came completely out of left field.

"And then Beau started dating you and the light came back into his eyes. I have to admit you weren't my top choice for him, but he loves you. And unlike Jodi Christopher, you're hardworking and trustworthy and I know you have a good heart, Flynn. You won't hurt my boy." The last sentence was a command. Kathryn's eyes were flint. "Because if you do, so help me God, I will—"

The front doorbell rang, breaking off Kathryn's heartfelt threat.

"Well, now," her future mother-in-law said, plastering a smile on her face and going from menacing to jovial faster than a Maserati could shoot from zero to sixty. Immediately Flynn thought of ol' Two-Face Harvey Dent from the Batman movie her brothers had dragged her to see. "I think my party is the perfect place to officially announce your engagement to all of Twilight."

By nine P.M. the outdoor party was in full swing. The five-piece band played "Cotton-Eyed Joe" while the town's upper crust two-stepped across the pavilion strung with Japanese lanterns. The smell of barbecue filled the air—pork ribs, chicken halves, beef brisket, the whole nine yards. Two tables, covered in linen tablecloths, overflowed with platters of corn on the cob, yeast rolls, cornbread, potato and macaroni salad, and cowboy beans served buffet-style on bone china.

Another table held the desserts—banana pudding, chocolate cake, pineapple upside-down cake, apple fritters, peach pie, and cream cheese popovers. To one side, a half-dozen machines labored over various flavors of homemade ice cream.

A full bar was set up on the pathway leading down to the lake dock. Several people had already drifted toward the water, enjoying the breeze as the sun slipped below the horizon. When the song finished, Kathryn stepped to the microphone at the gazebo where the band was set up. "May I have everyone's attention please?"

That was all it took. Heads turned and necks craned.

Kathryn motioned to Beau, who put his hand around Flynn's waist and guided her up the gazebo steps. "You all know my son, Beau—"

Applause broke out.

"—and his girlfriend, Flynn."

The applause ratcheted up a notch; someone whistled. Flynn's cheeks heated. She felt self-conscious. She wasn't a limelight kind of woman.

"They've just given me some news that has made me the proudest mother on this side of the Brazos." Kathryn stepped back from the microphone. "Beau, I'll let you do the honors."

Beau's hand shifted to Flynn's shoulder and he drew her against his side. "Friends, neighbors." He turned to look at her, love shining in his eyes. A lump clotted her throat. "Flynn has consented to be my bride."

A chorus of cheers erupted and several people hollered, "Finally!"

"The waiters are passing out champagne," Beau said. "We want you all to share a toast with us."

He kept talking, telling everyone how happy he was, how special Flynn was to him, giving a little speech she could tell he'd rehearsed in front of the mirror, until all the champagne had been distributed. Someone handed Flynn a champagne flute, and she curled her fingers around the stem.

"To my bride-to-be." Beau raised his glass.

Flynn blushed again. She *really* didn't like this overblown center-of-attention thing. She smiled.

"To Flynn!" the crowd called out, and then it was a simultaneous down-the-hatch.

Flynn took a small sip.

"My turn," Kathryn said, maneuvering her way back to the microphone. "To the happy couple."

Everyone was happy to take another drink.

"Anyone else like to offer a toast?" Beau asked, his words slurring slightly.

That's when Flynn realized he was tipsy and looking at her like she was supposed to say something. How could he expect her to say something? He knew she hated public speaking and she wasn't like him. It hadn't even occurred to her that she'd need to prepare a speech.

"Anybody?" Beau shifted his gaze to the crowd.

"I do," said a deep masculine voice from the bottom of the gazebo steps.

The second she heard it, Flynn's gut clenched. It couldn't be. Not here, not at the Trainer enclave. Cringing, she dared to turn her head.

Yep, greatest fear confirmed. It was Jesse. Decked out all in black. Black jeans, black cowboy boots, black T-shirt, with the skull tattoo on his arm peeking out from under the sleeve.

Every gaze in the place was welded on him as he sauntered up the steps. Flynn felt Beau tense beside her, but she didn't dare look at him.

You coward.

A murmur ran through the crowd.

Jesse sauntered straight over to Beau and audaciously plucked the glass of champagne from his hand.

The crowd gasped.

Flynn stopped breathing and darted a fearful glance at Beau. He looked stunned and . . . *scared*?

Of Jesse?

Beau was a good five inches taller and fifty pounds heavier than Jesse. But Jesse was fast and wiry and he'd been to prison. A fistfight between them was bound to be bloody and protracted.

What should she do?

Kathryn was moving off the dais, obviously going after security.

And here Flynn was, standing there like a ninny as Jesse raised the glass of champagne and locked eyes with Beau. "To Beau and Flynn. I wish you the very best."

Then he shifted his gaze to Flynn.

Her heart flipped.

"Why fight genetics, right, Dimples?" He winked and tippled back a long swallow of champagne.

Jesse, no!

She almost reached out to slap the alcohol from his hands. But she didn't dare say or do anything to stop him from drinking the champagne, not here with everyone watching. She couldn't give the slightest indication that she cared about him at all. She was engaged to the richest, most influential man in town; a man who had the power to send Jesse right back to prison.

Didn't Jesse get that? By coming here tonight, pulling this stunt, he was putting his freedom in jeopardy.

At that moment, the band started playing "I Got Friends in Low Places," and Flynn suspected from the devilish gleam in Jesse's eyes he'd paid the band for their choice of tune and impeccable timing.

The crowd cheered and broke into wild applause.

At that moment, two off-duty sheriff's deputies hustled up onto the gazebo. Kathryn scowled at the band and made cutting motions across her neck.

The Garth Brooks song was quickly replaced by another go-round of "Cotton-Eyed Joe."

"Guess it's time to clear out the riffraff, eh, Trainer," Jesse said.

The deputies reached for Jesse, but he shook off their arms and sent them an expression that had them stepping back a pace.

A chill ran down Flynn's spine.

Jesse cocked a smile at her. "Don't worry, Dimples, I won't embarrass you further in front of your fancy friends. I'm leavin'."

CHAPTER SIX

*Beau Trainer and Flynn MacGregor voted
couple most likely to end up married*
—Twilight High, 1999

Beau and Flynn did not speak of what happened at
the party on Saturday night. She kept waiting for
him to say something, but he never did, and she
wasn't stupid enough to kick a hornet's nest. So
the incident just lay there between them. The eight-
hundred-pound gorilla no one wanted to poke.

On Tuesday morning after the Memorial Day
weekend, Beau showed up on her front porch in his
uniform and bearing a grande Mocha Frappuccino
from Starbucks. "Thought you might need the kick
start."

"You know me too well." She smiled. She preferred cold beverages to hot, even in the winter,
and she'd never sprung for the pricey coffeehouse
stuff herself, but she did love Mocha Frappuccino.

"My little night owl," he said fondly and kissed

the tip of her nose. "It's gonna be tough on you adjusting to my meadowlark schedule."

"You think I'm changing my schedule?" she asked as they walked to his SUV.

He looked puzzled. "I get up at five A.M."

Flynn groaned. "Ungodly hour."

"Mother demands that her cook have breakfast on the table at six."

"Well, that's your mother. Relax, I'm not that regimented. You can eat a bowl of cereal on the couch in your underwear any time of the morning."

Beau frowned. "I suppose that's something we'll have to negotiate with Mother when we move in."

"Whoa, back the train up here. Move in with your parents? Are you nuts?"

Beau tilted his Stetson back on his forehead. "I can see I shouldn't have sprung the idea on you like this."

"If anything, we can move in here." She waved at her house as they drove by. "Or even your apartment."

"That's too small for the two of us."

"Then let's buy a house of our own."

Beau cleared his throat. "That house has been in our family for five generations, Flynn."

"I'm not saying we can never live there, Beau." She spun the oversized engagement ring on her finger. "Just not as long as your parents are alive."

"My mother needs help with the place and with my father. It's all too much for her."

"Okay, how about we buy them a small house near the hospital?"

"Are you suggesting we kick them out of their own home?"

"I can't live in the same house with your parents, Beau."

He splayed a palm against the back of his neck. "We're getting ahead of ourselves here. We won't even be setting a date until you have the Yarn Barn firmly established. My dad's in bad health. Who knows what the next couple of years will hold? Let's take this one step at a time."

It was only then that Flynn realized she'd been holding her breath. Slowly, she let it out. "Yeah, okay, I can do that. I can take a wait-and-see attitude if you can."

"That's my girl." Beau smiled and reached over to chuck her lightly under the chin.

Five minutes later they arrived at the bank. Immediately, Moe's secretary ushered them in to see the mayor.

"Morning Beau, morning Flynn," Moe greeted them. He wore a lime green polo shirt over his ample belly and matching green plaid golf pants. He shook their hands and instructed his secretary to bring in coffee. "Congratulations on the engagement."

"Thanks." Beau beamed.

"That was some shindig on Saturday." Moe patted his belly. "Enjoyed that barbecue. What was the weird deal with that guy who interrupted your toast?"

Flynn held her breath and waited to see if Beau was going to mention Jesse, but he just shrugged and said, "Some drunk. You know how it is."

Moe nodded and went through the necessary pleasantries while Flynn nervously worried the corners of the business plan she'd printed up on her computer.

"May I have a look at that, young lady?" Moe reached for the papers, and she turned them over to him. He put on reading glasses and glanced over the documents for a couple of minutes. Flynn tried not to fidget.

"Everything looks in order." Moe pushed the glasses down to the end of his nose with one pudgy finger and peered at Beau over the top of them. "You are cosigning for her loan?"

Beau nodded. "I am."

"Well, let me just get Pete Grissom on the horn here and find out all the details about the property." He pressed the intercom button and asked his secretary to make the call and patch it through to him when Pete was on the line.

Moe sat back in his chair and beamed. "I'm so glad you kids are finally making it official. You two are perfect together, just perfect."

Beau slung his arm around Flynn's shoulder, pulled her close. "We like to think so."

"Mayor, Pete Grissom is on line one," came the secretary's voice over the intercom.

Moe held up an index finger of one hand and picked up the receiver with the other. "Pete, how you doin'?"

Beau ran his palm up the back of Flynn's neck, splayed his fingers through her hair.

"I've got Sheriff Trainer and his fiancée, Flynn MacGregor, here with me. Beau tells me he's talked to you about selling him the theater." Moe paused, listening to whatever Pete was saying.

Flynn tapped her foot, annoyed that this was turning into the Beau and Moe show. She was the one buying the Yarn Barn.

"Hmm, you don't say." Moe leaned forward. "Well, that's a bit irregular."

What? What was irregular? Uneasiness replaced annoyance. All day yesterday she'd kept having this feeling that things were coming together too easy. Nothing had ever just fallen into Flynn's lap. She'd had to work hard for everything she'd achieved. Why would the Yarn Barn be any different?

"I'm sorry to hear that from my end of things, but I suppose it was a good deal for you. Yeah, yeah, I'll break the bad news to them."

Flynn's stomach slumped to her feet.

Moe hung up the phone, turned baleful eyes their way. "Got some bad news for you kids."

"What is it?" Beau asked.

"Pete's gone and sold the theater out from under you."

"But . . . but . . ." Beau sputtered. "He can't do that. We had a deal. We shook on it."

Moe spread his hands. "Apparently someone showed up over the weekend and wrote Pete a check for two grand over his asking price. Sorry, there's nothing more I can do."

Disappointment sagged Flynn's shoulders as she and Beau drove off. Until now, when it all started slipping away, she hadn't realized how much she'd wanted this. True, the Yarn Barn had started out as her mother's dream. True, she couldn't knit to save her life. True, she often felt like she was living someone else's life. But the Sweethearts meant something important to her. They'd been the glue that held her together after her mother's death. They might squabble and get on one another's nerves, but when it came down to it, they cared deeply for one another, and Flynn longed to give them all the gift of a place of their own where they could gather to share their lives, purchase quality yarn, and knit their love into scarves and sweaters, socks and blankets.

Suddenly Beau trod the brakes, whipped the steering wheel around, and goosed the accelerator.

Flynn stared at him owl-eyed. Normally he was a very cautious driver, and he'd just cut haphazardly across two lanes of traffic. "What are you doing?"

"I'm going to find out what son of a gun bought that building out from under me. It's not as if there are a lot of contenders. How many people in Twilight have the money or the inclination to buy the theater?" He shook his head. "This was a put-up job."

"What are you talking about?"

His jaw was set in a hard line, and he glared intently through the windshield. "What are the odds that someone just happened along on the same weekend Pete promised the property to me, offering him two grand over his asking price? Someone is messing with me."

"Aren't you taking this a little personally?" Flynn asked, grabbing hold of the strap on the ceiling as he rounded the corner onto Sapphire Lane five miles too fast. The tires squealed.

"That's the way they meant it," he insisted.

"They who?"

"Whoever it was that bought the theater."

"You're sounding a bit paranoid."

"Doesn't mean I'm not right."

Actually, she had to agree with him. The timing was suspicious. But most everyone in town liked Beau. He was a much kinder and more diplomatic sheriff than his father had been.

"It is a prime piece of property," Flynn pointed out, playing devil's advocate. "And at Pete's new lower asking price . . ."

"Pete didn't advertise it."

"If he told you, he told other people."

"Whose side are you on?"

"I'm just saying—"

"We'll find out soon enough," he interrupted.

She looked over at him again. Flynn had known Beau for most of her life, had dated him for ten years—breaks notwithstanding—and yet she'd never known that he'd been in love with someone before her. What else didn't she know about him? She'd never thought of Beau as the least bit mysterious before, but now suddenly he felt like a stranger.

"How come you never told me about Jodi Christopher?"

Dammit! Why had she asked that? She'd promised herself she wouldn't ask that, because that question opened the door for Beau to ask her about Jesse.

"Huh?" Beau yanked his head around to stare at her.

"Your mother told me all about Jodi Christopher. She said Jodi was your first love. She's your real high school sweetheart."

He snorted like this Jodi person meant nothing, but his face reddened. "My mother talks too much."

Beau was blushing? Her Beau? She'd never seen him blush. It made her feel . . . What did it make her feel? Surprised. She felt surprised. And curious. Surprised and curious and . . . Nothing else. Shouldn't she feel jealous?

"So technically," she said, "I can't even be an official member of the Sweethearts' Knitting Club when we get married. You're not my high school sweetheart. The point of the Sweethearts' Knitting Club is that it's a group of knitters who married their high school sweethearts. If I can't be a member, then what's the point of me starting the Yarn Barn?"

Well, if you're getting technical about it, you shouldn't be a member because you can't knit!

"The scope of the group is too narrow," Beau said. "And I *am* your high school sweetheart and we *are* getting married. You qualify. Unless you really don't want to do this Yarn Barn thing."

"No, no," she backpedaled. "I want to do it."

"Fine, then we're getting to the bottom of what happened here. That theater is the perfect place for your business and one way or the other, I'm going to make sure you get it," he declared, pulling to a stop at the parking meter on the square."

The theater had been boarded up for several years. The town beatification committee—which consisted mainly of members from the Sweethearts' Knitting Club—had painted a garden-inspired mural over the plywood and planted geraniums and begonias in planter boxes where the ticket booth used to be, in an attempt to camouflage the barrenness. For the most part, it worked.

The minute they got out of the car, they heard

the revved engine of a chain saw buzzing from the back of the theater.

"Didn't waste any time getting started," Beau muttered.

"Look, if someone bought this place, they had a reason, especially if they've already started construction on the renovations. There's no reason to confront them. I'll just have to find a new location for the Yarn Barn."

"This location is perfect," he said truculently. "Come on."

It was the perfect location, she couldn't deny that. But what did he hope to accomplish by calling out the new owner? Reluctantly, she followed Beau around the side of the building; the high-heeled shoes she'd put on to convince Mayor Moe Schebly she was loan-worthy kept hanging on the cracks in the uneven cement, slowing her progress.

Beau didn't wait for her as he normally would have. Usually he was all Mr. Gentleman. Instead he power walked ahead of her, intent on discovering who'd bought the theater out from under him. He turned the corner ahead of her.

The chain saw stopped.

"What are you doing here?" she heard Beau growl.

Flynn rounded the side of the building to see a construction worker in a hard hat, chain saw in hand.

But it wasn't just any construction worker.

The man in the hard hat ignored Beau, cocked a wry grin her way, and said, "Mornin', Dimples."

"Didn't I catch you on an episode of *Cops*?" Jesse asked his nemesis.

"Who hired you?" Trainer demanded.

"Yeah, yeah, I'm sure I did. You were eating doughnuts, writing tickets, and, oh yeah, planting evidence—"

"Shut the fuck up, convict."

"Tsk, tsk. Is that any way for an officer of the law to talk, especially when there's a lady present?" Jesse was walking a thin line. One wrong move and he could end up right back in prison. He knew exactly what the exalted Sheriff Trainer was capable of, even if no one else in Twilight did.

Trainer settled his hand on the butt of his gun.

Oh, so that's the way he was playing it. Jesse hefted the chain saw on his shoulder, showing the blade's jagged oily teeth.

"Who hired you?" Trainer repeated, and took a menacing step forward. "Who bought this property?"

Bluff, bluster. Dudley Do-Right wasn't about to shoot him. Not in front of Flynn. She walked up behind Trainer, placed a restraining arm on his elbow, calling off her pit bull. Jesse couldn't stop his gaze from straying to her.

"Why, Marshal Dillon," he drawled, easily shouldering the weight of the chain saw. "I'm working for myself. Thanks for asking."

Trainer looked stunned, which was precisely the reaction Jesse was shooting for. "You? You bought the property?"

"Got a feather handy, Dimples?" He winked in Flynn's direction. "I think you could knock your fiancé over with it."

Jesse did his best to look casual, cool, and in control. Calm, but assertive, just as he'd learned from reading those mind guru books in the prison library. He was in the driver's seat. Everything was happening just as he'd planned.

Trainer, on the other hand, looked anything but in command of his emotions. The vein at his temple pulsed. His jaw was granite, his eyes daggers. "You . . . you . . ." he sputtered.

"Got something to say? Don't be afraid. Spit it out."

Trainer fisted his hands, took another step toward him. "You bought this place out from under me."

"Don't know what you're talking 'bout, Hoss." Jesse dragged the back of his hand across his sweaty forehead and drilled Flynn with his eyes.

She was standing there looking like she'd love to be anywhere else on earth than in this back alley. He widened his grin. She had her hair pulled back in a ponytail, all perky girl-next-door.

Jesse tracked his gaze down Flynn's profile to her long, swanlike neck. Once upon a time, he'd planted a hickey there, branding her as his. His eyes roved right on over the slope of her shoulders, then braked abruptly at the swell of her breasts in that flamingo pink short-sleeved top. God, she was gorgeous in pink. The strength of the sun in late spring sweltered even at ten in the morning. He felt the old pull, strong as a siren's call.

"Pete Grissom earmarked this place for me," Trainer said.

"I didn't see your name written anywhere on it. Neither did Pete when I handed him a check for more than his full asking price."

"Where'd you get the money?"

"Well now, that's a rude question, Sheriff. Didn't your mama ever teach you it was crass to ask people personal questions about their finances?"

"You're a convict. You went to prison when you were just a kid. You were an orphan. There's no legal way you could have herded together enough money to buy this place. You're up to something nefarious, Calloway, and I'm not going to let you get away with it."

"That sounds an awful lot like a threat," Jesse said. The chain saw was getting heavy, but he wasn't about to set it down. Not in front of Trainer. "You threatenin' me?"

"It's not a threat," he mouthed through clenched teeth. "It's a promise."

"Beau, stop getting so worked up," Flynn interjected and shot Jesse a look that said, *Lay off.* "He bought the place fair and square. Just let it go, forget about it. I'll find somewhere else."

"No," Beau said. "I promised you *this* place."

The cell phone clipped to Beau's belt went off. He swore, jerked it from his hip, flipped it open.

"Yeah?" he barked. "Hang on, I can't hear." Glaring at Jesse, Beau took several steps backward and plugged up his free ear with his finger. "Can you hear me now?"

Flynn's gaze met Jesse's and he felt it in his chest. That snap. That crackle. That pop of familiar chemistry.

They stood staring at each other only a few feet apart, both breathing heavily, the air hazy with the scent of sawdust. The fact they were under Trainer's watchful eye only served to escalate the tension. And heighten Jesse's arousal. He desperately wanted to ask her if she remembered that long ago night on the old Twilight Bridge, but he was too afraid of her answer to ask. If she said no, that would slam-dunk his ego, and if she said yes, well, hell, that would hurt even more. To think that maybe she still cared. Even just a little bit.

"He was buying the place for you?" Jesse asked, freaked out by the way his heart reeled. He lowered the chain saw, shrugged his shoulder to work out the kinks.

"It doesn't matter," she said, looking wide-eyed and sounding breathy, like she'd been caught off balance. Good. It was precisely how he wanted her to feel.

"It does." That fact complicated everything. "Why did he want to buy you the theater?"

"He wasn't buying it for me," she bristled. Damn, but she was beautiful when she had her back up. "He was going to cosign so I could qualify for the loan."

"And you were going to do what?"

"Start a specialty yarn store. The theater was an ideal location on the square and the upstairs has that huge room perfect for a knitting circle but . . ." She shrugged, a hapless gesture. "I'll find another location."

"You?" Jesse hooted.

Flynn glowered. "What's so funny?"

"You. Starting a yarn store." He shook his head. "That's hysterical."

She sank her hands on her hips. Glowered in that cute little way that only Flynn MacGregor could. "Why is that?"

"You can't even knit."

"How do you know?" Her voice went up an octave. "It's been ten years since you've seen me. Maybe I've become a world-class knitter in the interim."

"Dimples, there's a lot of things about you that are world-class." He dropped his gaze past the hem of her skirt to take in the fine curve of her calves. "You can bring home the bacon and fry it up in the pan, but knitting is not one of your talents. When it comes to crafts, you're all thumbs, and even ten years of constant practice isn't going to make you Mozart of the Skein. Don't fret it, we all have our talents; knitting just doesn't happen to be yours."

"Shh," she hissed, and pressed her index finger to her lips. "Beau might hear you."

Jesse's grin widened. "Seriously? Trainer doesn't know? Oh, he's gonna be surprised when you can't knit booties for his babies."

Flynn's face flushed. "He's not going to find out."

He clicked his tongue. "Perpetuating lies with your intended? What would the marriage counselors say?"

"It's none of your business." She huffed.

"It is if I'm keeping your dirty little secret."

"Please Jesse, you can't say anything. No one knows but you and Carrie."

"Ah, young Carrie. Your partner in crime." He chuckled. "A codependent relationship if I ever saw one."

"Hush it."

She looked honestly distressed, and Jesse relented. "Why do you want to start a knitting store when you can't knit?"

"It's complicated."

"I get it." He nodded. "Still trying to please Mommy, even from the grave."

Flynn gasped, glared. "You bastard, I can't believe you said that."

"What? You can't believe that I spoke the truth? When have I ever lied to you?"

"If you say a word to Beau about this—"

"Don't worry, Dimples, your secret shame is safe with me." He supposed he should be feeling guilty for upsetting her, but the truth was her staid little life needed some serious shaking up.

Flynn narrowed her eyes at him. "How *did* you get the money to buy the theater, by the way?"

"I'm afraid I'm not at liberty to say."

"Was it"—she dropped her voice—"drug money?"

If she hadn't sounded so laughable, he would have gotten mad. "Yeah, big drug money."

She hissed in her breath and her eyes widened.

"I became a millionaire behind bars. My book comes out in next spring. *How to Make a Hot Million While You're Sitting in the Cooler.*"

The surprise on her face quickly turned to irritation. "You're yanking my chain."

"You think?"

"Okay, that was a stupid thing to ask. I suppose this is where you're putting your motorcycle shop."

She looked genuinely interested. Jesse swallowed, caught off guard by this turn of events. When Hondo told him Pete Grissom was selling the theater, it had seemed ideal for his shop, and then when he'd learned from Grissom that Trainer was interested, snagging it had gone from ideal to idyllic. "It is."

"Oh." She blinked. "So you really are back in Twilight for good."

"That's the general idea."

She tilted her head, studied him for a moment. "Did you really get drunk on Saturday night after you left the party?"

"What do you care?"

"Jesse, I don't want anything bad to happen to you."

"Horse has already gotten out of the barn on that score, Miss MacGregor."

She cringed, and he felt guilty for baiting her. What was wrong with him? She wasn't his target, Trainer was.

Trainer strode back over to them. "That was Madge," Beau said to Flynn. "I gotta go. Someone stole a riding lawn mower from the outdoor display at Ivey's hardware. Come on, I'll give you a ride home."

"That's okay," Flynn said. "You go do what you need to do. I can find my own way home."

Trainer looked like she'd reached out and slapped him hard across the face. "Wh—wh—?"

"I need to drop by the gym and see Terri. She has a pattern for a sweater I want to borrow."

Trainer's gaze shifted to Jesse. Damn if he didn't look downright scared. Jesse widened his smile. *You better be scared, you son of a bitch. I'm gonna expose you for the fraud you are.*

The sheriff folded his arms over his chest in his best badass lawman stance, but Jesse could see he was fighting hard to hold on to his self-control. "I'm not leaving you here alone with him."

Flynn's eyes flared with defiance, but she said

nothing. She just stood there between the two of them, caught in a dilemma. Did she knuckle under to the good boy, or rebel and side with the bad boy?

Who are you kidding that she'd pick you? She's already hitched her wagon to Trainer's tin star.

Still, a small part of him didn't want to give up on her, and not simply because seducing her was part of his plan to make Trainer pay for stealing ten years of his life. The truth was, he'd never been able to get Flynn out of his head. But he couldn't risk letting her know that she held such power over him.

"Don't worry 'bout me, Hoss," Jesse drawled. "Stop fretting. I ain't interested in your little girl-friend. I got work to do. Now if you'll excuse me." He slipped his goggles back down over his eyes and pull-started the chain saw.

Then, with a pounding heart, Jesse turned his back on them and attacked the wall with renewed vigor. Even so, he could feel the heat of Flynn's gaze on him, and it was all he could do to keep from spinning around, throwing down the chain saw, and gathering her up in his arms, the sheriff be damned.

But he had to be careful, play this cool. If he kept his head while Trainer lost his, everything Jesse had ever wanted was well within his grasp.

CHAPTER SEVEN

Calloway, what comes around goes around,
watch your back.
—Beau Trainer, yearbook entry, 1999

Anger spurted through Beau. It was all he could do to keep himself from attacking Calloway on the spot. He knew the bastard was angling to goad him into doing something he shouldn't do, and after the stunt he pulled at their engagement party on Saturday night, this backstabbing subterfuge of stealing the theater right out from under him was just topping on the shit cake.

The worst of it had been the way Flynn looked at the convict. Like a moony-eyed teenager. It was almost more than Beau could bear. You'd think after ten years she would have let go of those stupid bad-boy fantasies. What was it with women anyway?

Buck up. Be strong. You're sheriff. He's nothing. You have all the control. Give him enough rope and he'll hang himself. As long you stay calm, everything will be okay.

Good advice if only he could heed it. As it was, he couldn't help wondering what Calloway and Flynn had been whispering while he was on the phone with Madge.

The whole time old man Ivey was blabbing about the stolen riding lawn mower, Beau stood on the sidewalk, notepad in hand, gaze trained on the theater. He didn't hear a word the man said until he made sure Flynn had rounded the corner and gone into the Hot Legs Gym. He let out a long-held breath. She'd been telling him the truth. Not that Flynn wasn't honest. It was just that he never quite trusted others to do what they said they would do.

"I'll get on it, Joe," he said to Mr. Ivey. "I'm sure it's just kids."

"I want to press charges."

"Okay."

Mr. Ivey went inside his store and Beau shifted his gaze back toward the theater.

Bile burned his belly. The old familiar anger churning. Dammit, he shouldn't let external circumstances get him so worked up. *Okay. Deep breath. Not angry. I'm not angry. I'm in complete control of my emotions.* He clenched his jaw, did what he always did, stuffed down the rage, denied it. Because if he ever let it out of its box . . .

He didn't want to think about that. About the ugliness he was capable of when pushed to the wall. The battlefields of Iraq flashed in his mind, and he closed his eyes against the onslaught.

"Sheriff?"

Beau blinked and opened his eyes to see the local veterinarian, Dr. Sam Cheek, standing there.

Behind his back everyone called him Steady Sam because he was the most even-tempered man in town. Beau had never seen Sam lose his cool. Not even on that Boy Scout camping trip they'd gone on together to Big Ben National Park way back during their junior year. Tenderhearted Sam had come upon a wounded mountain lion and tried to help it. The animal had swiped a paw at him, leaving Sam with gashes across the top of his head. Beau had panicked, while Sam sat down in the dirt and calmly told him to go for help. Then when Beau came back with the scoutmaster and game warden, Sam had lain across the mountain lion, all the while bleeding profusely, and without raising his voice or showing any emotion told the game warden he was going to have to put a bullet through him first if he planned on killing the animal. Of all the citizens in Twilight, Beau admired Sam most.

Sam was not a loquacious man. He didn't say anything else, just waited with an are-you-okay expression on his face, the edges of the silvery scar visible through the sheaf of thick dark hair covering his forehead. The dusting of dog hair on his shirt nagged at Beau. He had an urge to whip out a lint roller and whisk him off.

"I'm fine." Beau nodded, packing down that anger even deeper. "I'm fine, Sam, thanks."

"You sure?"

"Yeah."

"Office door's always open."

Sam was a good listener, but Beau didn't feel like talking. "I appreciate it."

Beau hitched up his belt and headed toward his office. He was the sheriff of this town and he was going to behave like one. He had to set an example. He had to be perfect. And that meant toeing the line and waiting for Calloway to screw up.

Because he would screw up. The bad guys always did.

For the rest of the week Flynn tried not to think about Jesse, and for the most part, during the day at least, her busy life held her on track. She worked at Froggy's, kept tabs on Floyd, called to check on her brothers at basketball camp, continued searching the real estate ads for another location for the Yarn Barn, while also researching yarn wholesale suppliers on the Internet. By the time Friday rolled around, she was looking forward to the camaraderie of her weekly knitting club.

But it was the nights, oh, those long treacherous nights, that did her in.

She would lie in bed beneath the ceiling fan with the windows open, listening to the bullfrogs' medley, smelling the river, feeling the muggy humidity steam up her thoughts. She kept thinking about the kiss Jesse had given her on the loading dock at Froggy's. She could still smell the mashed potatoes, still taste him on her tongue. All alone in the darkness, her mind ran nimbly back to the past and she was sixteen again.

The minute Jesse hit Twilight High with his bad-boy attitude, skull tattoo, charming good looks, and wicked grin, the gossip started swirling. He'd been arrested in Arizona, said the whispers. Car theft. Joyriding. And there was a shoplifting charge.

Potted meat from the A&P. He'd never known his father, so the stories went, and his mother had died of a drug overdose. Shocking stuff for Twilight. That rumor immediately raised Flynn's sympathy. She had an ailing mother and a father who liked his alcohol a bit too much.

Jesse sassed teachers, broke rules, and challenged Sheriff Clinton Trainer in a public forum over curfew for teens. People were agog at his audacity. The town had no idea what had hit them. He stole the affections of teenage girls and struck terror into the hearts of parents.

He went for football and outshone Beau, eventually replacing him as first-string quarterback, and their rivalry began in earnest. Beau glowered under a black-cloud mood for a month. In the hallways at school, Jesse would saunter past Flynn, arm thrown over one girl or another (sometimes two), sending her sexy looks with his troublemaking gray-blue eyes. She'd square her shoulders, tip up her chin, and look down her nose at him. Not because she thought she was better than he was, but simply to stop her wobbly knees from collapsing.

How come she was always feeling like she was coming down with a fever, all hot and achy and restless, whenever she was around him?

Then on Valentine's Day she came home late from school because she'd stopped off at the florist's to barter her sweeping services for a small bouquet of red carnations to give to Mama. She arrived home to find her father sprawled across the living room couch reeking of sour mash whiskey and sobbing drunkenly. Her mother had been rushed to the hospital, feverish with pneumonia. Carrie had taken the news hard and run off.

Patsy had gone with her mother to the hospital. Marva had come by to pick up the twins. They'd both known Floyd wouldn't be able to handle the crisis, so they'd stepped in. Flynn helped her father to bed and then went in search of her sister.

Flynn took the family canoe and headed for Carrie's favorite spot on the river—a tributary that flowed into a wide swimming hole that camouflaged a series of underground caves where Jesse James supposedly hid out while being chased by a posse.

The spot could be accessed by land, but it required crossing the old suspension bridge and trespassing on the Fairfield ranch. She and Carrie used to go there once in a while, in the summers, before Mama got sick and everything changed. But traveling by water was swifter and negated the need for dodging cow patties and the Fairfields' prize-winning (but excessively ornery) Brahman bull, Ferdinand.

Before she turned that last bend in the river that led to the pool, she heard voices. And smelled cigarette smoke. Someone was already there. Good, she could ask them if they'd seen Carrie. She dipped her oar in the water, ready to push the canoe on around the corner when she recognized the voices.

Carrie.

And Jesse!

The bad boy of Twilight High was alone in a secluded spot with her baby sister, and from the smell of it they were smoking. Anger rushed her, and—even if she didn't want to admit it—so did a twinge of jealousy. She was torn between charging around the corner and reading them the riot act, or sitting there and eavesdropping on their conversation.

"You shouldn't smoke," Jesse said.

"You sound just like Flynn," Carrie had replied petulantly.

"You should listen to her."

"Blah, blah, blah, she thinks she's my mother. She's not my mother."

"She's raising you as if she is."

"Well, I didn't ask her to do it. I don't want her to do it. I want my mama to get well, I want my sister back, I want my family back the way it used to be, I want . . ." The sound of Carrie's sudden sobs wrenched something deep inside Flynn. She sat frozen in the canoe, listening to Jesse murmur soothing words, experiencing a mixed bag of unpleasant feelings.

"Come on," he said after a few minutes. "I'll walk you home."

"No, that's okay." Carrie sniffled.

"Don't want to be seen with me, huh?"

"It's not that. It's just that I told all my friends you were my secret boyfriend and if anyone sees you walking me home, they'll know that's a lie."

Jesse's laughter bounced through the treetops. "Maybe they'll think I'm your real boyfriend."

"Oh no, that would ruin everything."

"Ah, I get it. You want the bad-girl rep without having to actually be bad."

"I knew you'd understand! Thanks, Jesse. You really made me feel better."

"Before you go, put out that cigarette."

A couple of minutes passed. Flynn took a deep breath, stuck her oar in the water, and paddled around the corner.

Jesse lay stretched out on the bluff above the swimming hole, staring up at the clouds, hands cupped behind his head. "How much of that did you hear, Dimples?"

"You knew I was listening?" Flynn paddled closer. He'd called her Dimples. Her stomach gave a crazy little swoon. He'd given her a nickname.

Jesse sat up. "I could see the canoe from up here. It's Day-Glo orange, Flynn."

She cringed. "Cross covert spy off my list of career possibilities. Did Carrie see me?"

He shook his head. "Don't think so. She was too upset about your mom to pay much attention."

"Thank you." She pulled the canoe up on shore a few yards from the bluff.

Jesse had gotten to his feet and was staring down at her. She shaded her eyes against the late afternoon sun. He looked at once terribly solitary and fiercely independent—that lone wolf isolated from his pack and pretending not to care. "You coming up?"

She hesitated. She shouldn't, she should just go on back home, retrieve the twins from Marva, start making dinner. But there was Jesse at the river's edge, holding out his hand, ready to help her on shore.

Heaven help her, she'd taken his hand and he'd pulled her up beside him. They climbed the bluff together, sat overlooking the river, saying nothing for the longest time. He sat close, but not touching her.

"You know what I'd like to see?"

She shouldn't have played along. It was asking for trouble, but she'd done it anyway. "What?"

"You on the back of my motorcycle. Your hair blowing wild and free."

"Ain't never gonna happen."

"Never say never."

She wrapped her arms around her, planted her elbows in her palms. Closing herself off. Holding him at bay. "You don't even own a motorcycle."

"I'm saving up for one."

"Pipe dreamer."

"You know what else I'd like?"

"I don't care," she lied.

"You in a pink Harley jacket while you're holding on to me as we ride on my motorcycle."

"You're so full of it. There's no such thing as a pink Harley jacket."

"There is if you have one custom made."

"I tell you what, custom make me a pink Harley jacket and I'll ride on your bike with you."

"Really?"

"Oh yeah, 'cause that plays so well into my good-little-girl act."

"You've got a mean tongue," he said. "I like it."

"Thank you."

They lapsed into silence. Finally, he took a deep breath. "You want to talk about it?"

She shrugged. "What's to say? My mama's dying and my daddy's a drunk."

He nodded. "Life sucks."

"You said it. I've got nothing that's all my own. I share a room with my sister. I get hand-me-down clothes from my cousins. Even my name isn't my own. Half Floyd, half Lynn. Flynn. It's my parents' names morphed together. Who does that? If my dad's name had been Clifton and my mother's name Deloris, would they have called me Clitoris?"

Jesse had snorted a laugh. "Hey, look at it this way. At least you didn't get named after an outlaw. Jesse James. Talk about setting someone up for a prison record. Who names their kid Jesse James?"

"You've got a point."

"Feeling any better?"

"I'm getting there. You're a good listener."

"You're a good talker. Here, maybe this will help." He reached into the front pocket of his shirt and withdrew something wrapped in red foil. It was a milk chocolate candy heart. "You can have my heart."

Their eyes met, their fingers touched over the chocolate. He must have realized how that sounded, because he quickly rushed on to make a joke of it. "Now you can't say I never gave you anything."

"I'll share," she said, unwrapping the chocolate and breaking it into two pieces right down the middle. "It's the least I can do."

Simultaneously, they popped the chocolate into their mouths. The candy melted warm against her tongue. Jesse's eyes lit up. They stared into each other. It felt strangely like communion.

"If you ever need to talk," he said, "I come here a lot after school."

After that day, whenever Flynn could sneak away, she'd meet Jesse at the underground caves. Sometimes they'd arrive—she by water, he by land—to find fishermen had usurped their spot or other teenagers bent on swimming or making out, and they'd be forced to give up their rendezvous.

On the days they were alone, they talked for as long as Flynn dared stay away from home. Thirty minutes most of the time, an hour if they were lucky. Quickly she came to see past Jesse's cocky, bad-boy façade to the wounded soul beneath. She was drawn to his intense nature and his enigmatic gray-blue eyes. They had something in common. Jesse had lost his mother to a drug overdose when he was eight, and Flynn was slowly losing her mother to ALS. Jesse had never known his father. Flynn's father had disappeared inside a whiskey bottle. Circumstances had forced them both to abdicate their childhoods far too soon.

Jesse understood her in a way no one else did. He didn't judge her for her snarky, smart-ass comments, and he shared her wicked sense of humor. She felt as if she could tell him anything. He gave her tips on how to deal with Carrie's rebellion. She gave him pointers on fitting in at Twilight High.

They were just friends, she told herself. She was going steady with Beau, and Jesse hadn't tried to kiss her. But she could see the fire in his eyes when he stared at her lips, and she felt a corresponding heat burning in her chest. She wanted him to kiss her, but wanting it made her feel ashamed.

And then came that night on the bridge . . .

"Flynn?"

Someone was calling her name.

"Flynn? Hello, anybody home?"

"Huh?" Blinking, Flynn looked around at the Sweethearts assembled in her living room. She'd been daydreaming of Jesse again, and right smack-dab in the middle of a knitting session.

"You're a million miles away and I don't think

you've knitted a stitch," Belinda Murphey said, breaking through her reverie.

"Are you still brooding over losing out on the theater?" Marva asked.

"Umm..." Flynn shot a glance at Patsy, who was pushing her rocker faster than usual. They hadn't openly spoken about Jesse buying the theater out from under her, but everyone knew about it.

"She's not brooding. She's daydreaming about bridesmaid dresses and place settings and floral arrangements. How can she be brooding with that rock on her finger the size of Texas?" Terri teased.

Flynn looked down at the ring. It was ostentatious. And heavy. And it kept getting tangled up in the yarn.

"Yeah," she quipped. "I keep thinking that it'll come in handy living here on the river. Next time there's a flood and I see someone getting washed away by the current, I can just toss out the ring with a line on it and they can anchor themselves."

Raylene guffawed. "You could always use it as a doorstop."

"Or a paperweight." Marva snickered.

"It *was* nice of Beau to gift me with a dual-purpose engagement ring. I'll never fly away in a hurricane."

"So thoughtful of him," Patsy said. "Considering that we're four hundred miles inland."

"You know," Belinda added, raising her arm to block her eyes. "It's so sparkly it would make a great beacon in a power outage."

"In case I forgot to put batteries in the flashlight and all the candles in the house melted?" Flynn laughed.

"Exactly."

"Oh, oh." Flynn waved her left hand. "If some-one tries to grab me in Froggy's parking lot late at night, I can just crack them over the head with my ring."

"*Swwttt*," Marva said. "They'd be out cold."

"TKO."

"Comatose."

"And when the attacker came out of the coma, he'd probably sue you for assault with a deadly weapon."

Dotty Mae looked confused. "I don't get it. You can't do all those things with a diamond engage-ment ring. Even with a honker like that."

"It's a joke," Terri said gently. "You know Flynn. She's not the type to draw attention to herself, and a ring that size brings the spotlight. To ease the tension, she makes jokes."

"I don't," Flynn denied. "Do I?"

Everyone nodded, even Dotty.

"She also cracks wise when she's feeling over-whelmed. The more beleaguered she is, the snar-kier she gets," Carrie said, waltzing in from the kitchen. "It's her fatal flaw."

"Fatal flaw?" Patsy asked.

"Don't encourage her," Flynn said. "She's dating a guy who's getting a liberal farts degree. Appar-ently he's taking a literature class and she's absorb-ing it through osmosis."

"See," Carrie retorted. "Pure snark. She *has* to do it, even though she knows it will prove my point. Hence, her flaw is fatal. And FYI, Logan is taking creative writing."

"Always having to have the last word is Carrie's fatal flaw," Flynn muttered.

"Is not."

Flynn arched an eyebrow and took a purl stitch for dramatic effect.

"*Are* you feeling overwhelmed?" Marva asked. "You're adding extra stitches."

"What? Oh. No," Flynn lied. "It's the spotlight thing, like Terri said."

Carrie snorted and disappeared upstairs.

"Oh, will you look at the time," Patsy said. "I didn't realize it was after nine. We gotta hit the road, girls."

The Sweethearts gathered up their knitting, said their good-byes, and left Flynn waving at the front door. The minute they'd dispersed, Flynn slipped on a light sweater and headed down to the dock. She was feeling particularly lonely tonight.

And achy.

Those daydreams she'd been having were stirring up some powerful old emotions. Nothing like sitting on the dock and watching the water roll by to take the tension out of a woman's shoulders.

She padded over the decking, settled on the lawn chair, sank down, snuggled into her sweater, and breathed in the air. The wind tossed her hair into her face. She tucked it behind both ears.

The breezy summer night reminded her of Jesse. Of that night when everything changed.

Jesse. His name hung in her mind like a prayer. Why couldn't she stop thinking about him?

In the distance, she saw a boat headed upriver from the lake, its blue and yellow lights winking in the night. The motor was quiet, trolling slow. She watched it draw closer. She didn't recognize the boat as belonging to any of her neighbors on this side of the river, but it was pulling closer to the shore as if intent on docking at one of the slips. Her father owned a johnboat for fishing and there was the canoe, but they hadn't owned anything more ambitious since Floyd sold the ski boat to help pay for her mother's medical bills that insurance didn't cover.

The boat coming toward her was a ski boat. A very nice one. The driver killed the engine, let it drift toward her dock. Did she know who this was?

Flynn got to her feet, squinting into the darkness.

"Enjoying the evening, Dimples?"

"Jesse?"

He was standing up in the seat, guiding the boat in. "Ahoy there."

The boat bumped against her pier. She grabbed the rope he tossed. "This is Dr. Longoria's boat."

"That it is."

"What are you doing with it?"

"Making a little money on the side. It'll be awhile before the motorcycle shop is pulling in any cash. The good doctor said she was running funny, asked me if I'd take her out for a spin. Diagnosed it right off the bat. Clogged fuel filter. Cleaned her up and now here I am, making sure she's in top form."

"Oh."

"Thought you might like to go for a ride."

Flynn shook her head.

"Ah, come on. When was the last time you went out on a late night river cruise?"

Umm, never?

"Come on," he coaxed. "No one has to know."

"I've got to work in the morning."

"Don't give me that. Froggy's doesn't open until ten. That's twelve hours from now."

"Jesse . . ."

"I need to talk to you." He had one leg on the dock, one leg in the boat. She stood on the deck steps above him. He canted his head up at her, a sexy silhouette in the muted dock lighting. He wore blue jean shorts, a thin cotton T-shirt, and Nikes. The telepathy between them frightened her. She'd been thinking of him and *poof*, he'd appeared. A dark knight in a white speedboat.

"What about?"

"Let's take a little trip upriver. We won't be gone long. An hour, tops."

The way he said "long" made her pulse pound. Her gaze hung on his lips—full, angular, sardonic. She held her breath. Waiting for what, she did not know, but she felt it. This odd sense of impending change. And Jesse was the catalyst.

He ran his hand through the sheaf of whiskey blond hair that had fallen across his forehead, pushing it back with his fingers, showing off his masculine brow. Shadows cloaked his face, making him look for all the world like the outlaw who shared his name. He tilted his head, lowered his eyes, and cast her a come-hither look that had perspiration dampening her underarms.

She came down the steps toward him. Old feelings—both dangerous and exciting—shot up between them like Pop-Tarts from a toaster, hot, sweet, startling.

The moment stretched into a minute. They stared into each other, their breaths rasping in tandem.

Flynn's heart slumped back against her spine. Fear tap-danced in her belly. What did he want from her?

What did she want from him?

Nothing. There was absolutely nothing she wanted from him. When it came down to it, she barely knew this man.

But that was her brain talking. Her heart—oh, her treacherous heart—was feeling something else entirely. Could she trust the feeling? Could she trust him? Could she trust herself?

Her gaze hooked on his mouth. A mouth she yearned to kiss. A mouth that called to her in the middle of the night, in the midst of her darkest dreams. The forbidden fruit. Deadly, poisonous.

If she got into that boat . . . Heaven help her, she was *not* going to get into that boat.

Hypnotized, she found herself moving forward, getting closer. Not thinking, just wanting.

Jesse held out his hand.

Flynn never took her gaze off his face. They were both holding their breath, their fingers within touching distance. They were so close she could feel the heat of his skin.

So close. So easy.

But she should not, could not, would not.

Jesse touched his bottom lip with an index finger. The gesture wasn't calculated. Flynn could tell he wasn't trying to call attention to his mouth, he was just nervous because she hadn't taken his hand and he was trying not to show it. She recognized his tension in the tautness of his shoulders. Unnerved, just as she was by this chemistry that time and circumstances had not erased.

"I've got a proposition for you," he said, breaking the spell.

She drew in a deep breath, crossed her arms over her chest. Even in this breeze she could smell his warm, manly scent.

"Get in." He inclined his head toward the passenger seat beside him. "Let's take a ride and talk about Lynn's Yarn Barn."

CHAPTER EIGHT

Flynn, come what may,
we'll always have that night on the bridge.
—Jesse Calloway, yearbook entry, 1999

She got in.

Yeah, it was stupid. Yeah, it was courting trouble. Yeah, if Beau found out there would be hell to pay, but Jesse had uttered the magic words that made her step into Dr. Longoria's boat and plunk her butt in the seat beside him. Part of her couldn't help hoping he'd come to offer to sell her the theater.

He didn't say another word. Just started the engine and took off up the river, past the boat ramp, underneath the old Twilight Bridge.

Along the banks, bullfrogs hummed a deep-throated chorus. In the blue glow of the light on the stern, moths gathered. A fish jumped up, breaking the water with a smart slap. The air smelled rich, loamy. The breeze blew damp, coaxing a flutter from her curling hair, blowing it over her shoulders.

She knew where he was headed as surely as if he'd told her. She wasn't surprised when he took the fork in the river, following the tributary north to the underground caves and the swimming hole where they used to meet. When they reached the spot, he cut the engine, threw out the anchor. Gently, the boat rocked. He said nothing, just leaned back in the seat and cupped the back of his head in the palms of his interlaced hands.

She didn't ask why he'd stopped, what he was doing. She knew from the way he closed his eyes and inhaled deeply. He was savoring his freedom, breathing in the scent of Twilight, reliving old memories. This place got into your blood, slipped under your skin, twined around your heart. Flynn drew her knees to her chest and sat there watching him.

"Remember the time we went skinny-dipping right here in this same spot?" Jesse asked.

"We were in a canoe."

"That I borrowed from Clinton Trainer."

"Borrowed?" Flynn snorted. "You stole it."

"You say potato . . ." He grinned.

"No wonder Clinton had it in for you. You were a thorn in his side."

"It was fun seeing his face get red and watching the vein at his temple pop up."

"You were incorrigible."

"It's what you liked most about me."

She couldn't deny it. He was right. His boldness, his spontaneity, his fearlessness intrigued her, drew her. Probably because she was none of those things. The closest she came to any kind of rebellion was her smart-alecky take on life.

"I did the things you couldn't," he said, eyes still closed, his voice rumbling deep into the night air. "You lived vicariously through my antics."

"It was almost as if you had a death wish, Jesse."

"I was seventeen and stupid. So about the skinny-dipping?"

"What about it?"

"Wanna swim down memory lane?" He inclined his head toward the water. The look in his eyes was pure sex.

"Get naked? With you? In the lake?"

"That's kinda the idea of skinny-dipping."

"We have no towels."

That wasn't what she should have said. She should have said, *No way, Jose. No deal, Phil. Are you out of you mind, Clementine?* But instead she said, "We have no towels." As if she would do it if there were towels. Why had she said that? Why had she gotten into the boat with him?

Jesse leaned over, raised up the seat where the life vests were stowed, and pulled out two thick bath towels. "Ta da."

"You set me up."

Jesse laughed. "You don't have to do anything you don't want to do, Flynn." He stripped off his shirt. "But I'm going in."

"Jesse!" she exclaimed.

"I love it when you get all indignant," he said.

The sight of his bare chest shining in the moonlight drained all the starch from her indignation. She was female and human. He was male and muscled and in his prime. One look, and all she could do was stare.

Don't drool.

"I'm not going to puddle at your feet," she said, "just because you're hauling around a strapping six-pack."

"No?"

"Go ahead get naked. It won't faze me a bit." What was wrong with her? Why did she keep saying things she shouldn't? Nervously she twirled Beau's ring on her finger. Guilt played up and down her spine.

You're engaged to another man. You shouldn't be here with this one.

Jesse cocked a wide, wicked grin. "Your nipples disagree."

"What?" She glanced down; her nipples were poking hard against her bra and clearly visible through her T-shirt. She crossed her arms over her chest. "Frick."

Jesse laughed, toed off his sneakers, reached a hand to the snap of his jeans.

Flynn covered her eyes with her hands.

"Coward."

"Just because I don't want to get naked and have minnows nibble on my skin does not make me a coward."

Jesse hit the water with a soft smacking noise. She peeked through her fingers.

"Ah," he said, treading water. "This feels great. Refreshing."

"I'm happy for you."

"Come on in, Dimples. I promise I won't look."

It had been so long since she'd had a dip in the lake, skinny or otherwise. She never seemed to make time for the leisure activities she enjoyed.

"You don't know what you're missing," Jesse cajoled.

"You're just trying to stir up trouble."

"You could do with a little stirring up."

"Oh, believe me, you've stirred me up plenty."

"That's encouraging to hear."

"That's not what I meant."

"Right."

"It's not."

"Come on in. Keep your clothes on."

"Then I'd be all wet on the way back home."

"That sounds intriguing."

"You're completely incorrigible."

His chuckle rang out across the water. "God, this feels great. I didn't realize how much I'd missed it."

He made it sound so enticing. What would be wrong with taking a dip in the water? She didn't have to swim close to him. She could keep her underwear on. Urges pulled at her, the water called. Oh, what the hell. Flynn stripped off her T-shirt, wriggled out of her shorts, but kept her bra and panties on.

Jesse applauded.

"Knock it off if you want me to come in."

"Yes ma'am." He saluted her.

Flynn slipped off the side of the boat, but when she tried to swim free, something tugged on her panties. Dammit, she was caught. She reached around trying to figure out what had snared her.

"Something wrong?" Jesse swam up to her.

"My underwear hung on something on the boat."

"Here," he said, "let me help."

"Just stay away, you've caused enough trouble."

She treaded water in the darkness, her fingers fumbling at the material of her panties. "It's some kind of screw sticking out."

"If you'd just let me . . ."

"Get away." She kicked at him, and her foot made contact with his thigh. She felt the material of his jeans beneath her toes. "Hey! You kept your shorts on."

He laughed. "You're the one who closed your eyes and assumed the worst. Did you really think I'd get totally naked in front of you?"

"Hell, yes."

"Maybe it was just wishful thinking on your part."

"Oh, just shut up." She yanked at the panties, felt the material rip in her hands. Great! Now she was totally naked in the water with him.

"If Beau could see us now," Jesse said.

Flynn groaned. If Beau found out about this he'd be cut to the quick. And he wouldn't believe her that nothing happened. He would want to know why she'd gotten into the boat with Jesse in the first place, why she'd jumped into the water in her panties and bra. Why had she done those things? And what was she going to do now?

Get back in the boat, you idiot, and put your clothes back on. You are not wild. You are not sixteen. Wise up before you get into big trouble.

"Turn around," she said.

"What?'

"Turn around and close your eyes. I'm getting back in the boat."

"Okay." He closed his eyes, turned around in the water until he was facing the shoreline.

Hurriedly Flynn climbed the ladder. Just as she flung her leg over the boat, fully exposing her bare butt in the starlight, Jesse let out a long, low wolf whistle.

"Dammit, Jesse, I told you not to look!" Furious with him, she snatched up a towel, wrapped it around her bare body, and spun around.

He was still facing away from her. He hadn't looked. He'd just been teasing. His laughter rang out across the water. Hurriedly she got dressed.

"Can I open my eyes now?"

"Get back on this boat and take me home," she demanded.

"Yes, ma'am."

"This isn't funny."

"It's kinda funny," he said, scaling the ladder, his wet shorts clinging to his skin. He leaned over the side to pull up the anchor, the material molding snugly to the curve of his very sexy ass.

Flynn jerked her gaze away. She was *not* going to ogle him. "It's not the least bit funny."

"Your panties got caught on a screw, how is that not funny?" He grinned.

"Stop grinning."

"Not until you admit it was a little funny."

"Okay," she admitted. "Maybe it was a little funny."

He pulled on his T-shirt, sank down behind the wheel. "I'm sorry if I made you feel uncomfortable. That wasn't my intention."

"What was your intention?"

"Honestly?"

"No, lie to me." She snorted.

"I just wanted someone with me when I went

swimming for the first time in over a decade. And the first person I thought of sharing the moment with was you." His tone was poignant, wistful.

His words pulled the air right out of her lungs. "Ah, Jesse."

Were his eyes misting? Or was it a trick of the moonlight. He blinked, and his smile softened. "The thing about the theater was just a handy excuse."

"What about the theater?"

"We'll talk when we get back. I'm sorry about the skinny-dipping thing. I just, well . . . you look so damn gorgeous in moonlight, Dimples, the devil on my shoulder got the best of me."

She forgave him then. What else could she do?

He started the engine. The air was cool against her damp skin, but it felt good. Fifteen minutes later they were docked outside her house. Jesse leaned back in his seat, studying her with half-shuttered eyes.

"So what did you want to talk to me about in regard to the theater?"

"Would you be interested in renting out the top floor?"

The minute he said it, she knew it was the perfect solution. She wouldn't have to go into debt. She'd have the right kind of space in the right location. But how perfect could it be when she was having these very disturbing thoughts about Jesse? She was engaged to Beau, and even if she wasn't, Jesse threatened to turn her orderly world upside down. He'd done it before. He'd done it tonight and he would do it again. Of that she had not doubt. The man loved shaking up the status quo. Especially *her* status quo.

"I think that would be a really bad idea."

"How so?"

"Beau wouldn't like it."

"I didn't ask Beau, I asked you."

"Why do I get the feeling nothing pleases you more than getting under Beau's skin?"

"You misread me, Dimples. There's a lot of things that give me more pleasure than irritating Beau Trainer." The way he looked at her made it pretty clear what sort of things would give him pleasure.

"It wouldn't work."

"You'd be doing me a big favor. It'll be awhile before the motorcycle shop starts turning a profit and I could use the rent money."

No. Just firmly say no.

"I'd promise to keep my hands to myself. No more tricks like the fake skinny-dipping."

"*That* goes without saying. How much do you want for rent?"

He named a very reasonable price. Too reasonable.

Was he making the offer merely to cause trouble between her and Beau? Was that the reason he was really here? "You could rent it out to someone else for more than that."

"I could, but who better to rent to than a knitting store? All those motherly types coming and going. I'm sure to get a lot of casseroles as a side benefit."

"It wouldn't come without strings," she pointed

out. "Those kindly motherly types bearing bachelor casseroles would expect you to tinker with their cars."

"Small price to pay for homemade chicken à la king."

"You have been in prison too long if that's your biggest ambition." The minute she said it, she could have bitten off her snarky tongue. What in the hell was wrong with her?

Jesse laughed, and relief poured through her. She hadn't offended him. "So what do you say? Become my chicken à la king pipeline?"

"It's very tempting when you put it like that . . ." She wanted to say yes, to accept his offer, but there was the not-so-small matter of her fiancé. "But I'm certain Beau wouldn't approve."

Jesse got to his feet. "By all means, let's make sure that Matt Dillon signs off on this one."

She got to her feet as well. "Thanks for the offer. It was nice of you to think of me."

"Hey, it's the least I could do since I bought the place out from under you."

"I appreciate it, but I'm going to still keep looking for a place of my own," she said.

"I gotcha." He nodded. "I can leave the offer on the table for a month. But after that I really will need to get some rent money coming in."

"I understand."

They stood looking at each other, neither one of them moving. In an oak tree along the bank, an owl hooted eerily. Time and history stretched between them, a palpable thing. Tension rose up, curling through her, swirling around him, silently ensnaring them in the question of what might have been.

She dropped her gaze, but it landed on the length of his long bare legs. A trickle of sweat slid down the back of her neck in spite of the breeze rolling off the river. The pulse in her throat skittered, and she experienced a rush of sexual awareness so potent she had to bite down on her bottom lip.

His breathing sped up; she could hear him raggedly pulling air into his lungs, saw to her surprise that his hand was trembling oh so slightly. Bravely she lifted her head and met his gaze once more. He was staring at her so intently she wondered if he could see the bead of sweat that had traced from her neck, down her shoulder, and was now sliding slowly between her breasts. But he couldn't have seen it in the darkness. Somehow he just instinctively knew what was going on in her body.

She scurried out of the boat, relieved to have her feet planted firmly on the dock.

"Good night, Dimples," he murmured. "Sweet dreams."

Then he started the boat and disappeared into the darkness, leaving Flynn wondering what in the hell had just happened.

The next morning Beau dropped by as Flynn was getting ready to head out to Froggy's. Beau's appearance was a surprise. She hadn't expected him. She'd just stepped out on the front porch and was juggling her keys, ledger book, and glass of iced tea as she pulled the screen door closed behind her. She'd spent the night tossing and turning. Thinking about Jesse's proposition and how much she wanted to start the Yarn Barn and live up to the promise she'd made her mother.

"Morning," Beau greeted her, coming up on the porch steps and doffing his Stetson in one smooth movement. He leaned in for a kiss. It was nice, comfortable, perfunctory. She waited to feel some kind of tingle, but she didn't. Okay, that wasn't fair. It was a simple hello kiss. It wasn't designed to be knock-your-socks-off.

"What's up?"

"Nothing's up, just wanted to drop by and say hi."

"Hi." She smiled.

"I took the liberty of talking to some Realtors on your behalf," he said. "I hope you don't mind."

"No, I don't mind, that's fine. I appreciate the help." She pocketed the keys, tucked the ledger under her arm, and took a sip of tea. "So did you have any luck?"

Solemnly he shook his head. "There's nothing for sale anywhere even close to the town square, not even for rent."

Except for the space over Jesse's motorcycle shop.

"Furthermore, no one thinks anything will open up within the next year."

Flynn muttered a strong curse word. Beau frowned, but said nothing. She knew the look. He hated when she cussed. "Sorry," she mumbled an apology.

"With that in mind, I was thinking we should just go ahead with the wedding plans and then you can start the business after we're married."

Panic seized her. "But you promised me that I could get Lynn's Yarn Barn started before we made wedding plans. That was part of the deal. You can't renege on me now," she protested.

"I know it was, Flynn, but get realistic. It might be several years before the right property comes along." He touched her shoulder, gave her a soft smile. "I can't wait that long to have you as my bride."

Feeling cornered, she gulped, and then blurted, "Jesse offered to rent the upstairs floor of the theater to me."

Beau stiffened. "What?"

She repeated what she'd said even though she knew he'd heard her the first time.

"No." Beau gritted his teeth. "Absolutely not. I forbid you to rent from Jesse Calloway."

Anger and adrenaline pumped through her. "Excuse me? You *forbid* me?"

He put out a restraining hand.

She jerked away and ended up dropping her glass of tea to the porch, not even caring that it splashed on her legs. She shook the ledger underneath Beau's nose. "We are *not* married yet, mister, and you cannot tell me what to do. I have been taking care of my entire family since I was thirteen years old. I've worked and I've scrimped and I've sacrificed. And when my mother was on her deathbed, I made her a promise. I swore that I would open the yarn store that she never got the chance to open and give her knitting club an official home. And you have the audacity to stand there and forbid me to do this one last thing for my mother—"

"Whoa, whoa, whoa." Beau put up his hands in a defensive gesture. "That was a poor choice of words. I'm sorry, I didn't mean it, back up the chuck wagon."

Flynn clenched her fist; she was trembling all

over. She couldn't remember the last time she'd been this angry. Why was she so angry? "Do you want your ring back? Is that what you want?"

Beau paled visibly. "No, no, things have gotten out of hand, this isn't—"

"What do you think is going to happen if I rent the top floor of the theater? That I'll start getting tattoos and riding motorcycles?"

"No, of course no." He paused. "It's just that . . ."

"What?"

"Calloway's up to no good. He's trying to get even with me."

"Get even with you?" Flynn canted her head. "For what?"

"Umm, for my father arresting him and sending him to prison."

"That wasn't your fault."

"Try telling Calloway that. He's jealous of me. He's always been jealous of me, and he knows being friendly with you sets my blood boiling."

"Well, it shouldn't set your blood boiling, Beau. The man is simply trying to put his life back together." Was he? Or was Beau right? "He's been to prison. He's paid his debt to society. He's allowed to make a living. Find some Christian charity in your heart and forgive the man."

"I've seen the way he looks at you," Beau grumbled.

"A lot of men look at me that way, Beau. Haven't you been to Froggy's on Saturday night?"

"It's not the same," he mumbled.

"I'm engaged to you, Beau. You know I'm not the kind of woman who cheats. Even though we weren't officially together when you were in Iraq, I didn't date anyone else. Not to mention, the sheriff's office is right across the frickin' street from the theater. You could pop in and check up on me at any time. If you want this wedding to happen, then just let me rent the damn space and get on with it."

Beau swallowed, licked his lips. He looked at once both vulnerable and hopeful. Flynn suddenly felt extraordinarily sad and she had no idea why. "If I say yes will you set a date?"

Compromise.

Her heart felt leaden. "I'll set a date."

"Christmas?"

"That's only six months away!"

"Christmas?" he persisted, his eyes glistening darkly.

She could feel his controlled emotions simmering just below the surface. He was hurt and scared and looking for reassurance. But she was scared too. She didn't know what was happening to her. To them.

Compromise.

"It's cutting things close," she mumbled.

"There's plenty of time. My mother will pull strings. She can help you get everything organized."

"Christmas," she confirmed, and the tightness inside her chest loosened a little.

His shoulders relaxed, and a smile replaced the dark expression marring his features. "All right then."

"So I can tell Jesse that I'll take the space?"

The smile vanished at her mention of Jesse's name and the muscle at his temple pulsed. "Yeah."

"Okay, then."

"Fine, great," Beau said, "I'll call my mother and tell her the good news."

They were both breathing heavily, eyeing each other like adversaries, spilled tea pooling at their feet. Flynn felt like she'd just won a gigantic battle, but yet something niggled at her, something she couldn't quite put her finger on. It wasn't just the look in Beau's eyes or the defiant way he lifted his chin. She had the strangest feeling he was crossing his fingers behind his back, telling a lie but making it okay with the rationalization. But that was a ridiculous thought because his hands were on his hips. Whatever it was, she didn't trust the victory.

Because she had a feeling that this wasn't over. Not by a long shot.

Wrong. This was all wrong. Flynn building the Yarn Barn above Calloway's motorcycle shop.

Beau furrowed his brow, pressed his lips into a hard thin line, and paced the confines of his office. He could feel Flynn slipping away from him and he had no idea what to do about it. This wasn't fair. It wasn't right. He'd invested ten years into their relationship and he wasn't about to let her go without a fight.

Calm down. Be cool. Don't let your anger get the best of you. She agreed to set a date. That's progress. It's a step forward. You crowd her, you lose her.

He couldn't lose her. Not after all they'd been through. He'd just have to find some way to get rid of Calloway. Shouldn't be hard. He was a parolee. Wouldn't take much to send him back to Huntsville. It was up to him to protect Flynn. He'd failed with Jodi, but he wasn't going to make that mistake twice.

"Sheriff," Madge's voice came over the intercom. "Dr. Cheek is here. He'd like to speak with you."

Beau blew out his breath. "Send him in."

Madge buzzed the outer door, and a minute later Sam was standing in front of him, his dark brown eyes looking troubled. "We need to talk."

Beau motioned to the chair opposite his desk.

Sam shook his head.

"What's this about?' Beau asked, both annoyed and relieved for the interruption from his emotional turmoil. Sam wasn't a complainer. If he had something on his mind, he was serious about it.

"The old Twilight Bridge."

"What about it?" Beau crossed his arms over his chest, leaned against his desk.

"My boy got hurt on it taking a shortcut home from school. He fell through a hole in the runners, scraped up his leg pretty good. Termites are eating away the wood. It should come down or be rebuilt."

"You're right," Beau said. This was a cause he could get behind. He'd hated that damn bridge ever since the night he'd seen Flynn up there with Jesse. The memory—and the old anger—rushed through him, but he quickly squelched it.

"It's a hazard," Sam said. "You're lucky it was my kid and I'm not the kind of guy to bring a frivolous lawsuit against the town, but next time we might not be so lucky."

"Thanks for bringing this to my attention,"

Beau said, and clasped Sam on the shoulder. "I'll see what I can do."

For the rest of the weekend, Jesse worked on gutting the bottom level of the aged theater, pulling out all the old wooden seats, ripping down the screen, piling the debris into the back corner of the lot until he could haul it away later. Determined not to think about Flynn and what had happened—or not happened—on the river on Friday night. He was confused by his behavior, uncertain of why he'd taken her out in the boat. It had been stupid. He could have blown everything.

Hondo came by and pitched in for a while before starting a twenty-four-hour shift at the fire station. Jesse pushed himself hard, sleeping only four or five hours, going back at it again. Reveling in the punishing ache assailing his muscles.

Then at eight o'clock on Monday morning, after he'd already been working for two hours, he looked up from where he was pulling up the threadbare carpeting to see Flynn standing in the doorway. The sight of her caused his heart to skip a beat. She was here. In his shop.

Flynn was dressed in an oversized, loose-fitting pale blue T-shirt, faded blue jeans, and sneakers. Her hair was pulled back into a ponytail that made her look sixteen again. She held a sack in her hands from the Twilight Bakery.

"I come bearing breakfast croissants and hot coffee," she said, and her tentative smile swept over him like a gentle caress.

"To what do I owe this unexpected pleasure?" he asked, dusting his hands against his pants.

"I came to talk to you about the offer you made on Friday night," she said, digging around in her purse with her free hand. "Here you go." She tossed him a package of premoistened towelettes.

"What a little Girl Scout you are," he said, tearing open the package and cleaning his hands with the damp wipe.

"Hey, don't get smart. You want food or not?"

"Gimme." He reached for the sack. "How did you know I haven't had any breakfast?"

"You possess a lean and hungry look."

"Cassius from *Julius Caesar.*"

Flynn looked surprised. "You *did* pay attention in Mrs. Martin's English lit class."

"I'm far more than just a pretty face."

She smiled vaguely and from the sack pulled an egg and sausage croissant wrapped in wax paper. It smelled like heaven. She handed it to him along with a cup of black coffee. "Cream? Sugar?"

"Straight up works for me."

"Where can we sit?" She glanced around the empty, dusty room.

"The stairs?"

"Um . . . sure, that'll do."

They perched on the second step of the stairs, their thighs almost touching. Hot, horny images flashed in his head. He saw her sitting there completely naked, her knees primly pressed together. He took a bite of croissant and closed his eyes.

Stop torturing yourself.

"You okay?" Flynn asked. "Did you swallow wrong?"

"Yeah," Jesse lied, his voice coming out all hoarse and husky. She smelled so good. Like sunshine and orange juice and happiness. "I swallowed wrong."

"Ooh," she said, "you're about to . . . um . . . lose your sausage."

Flynn must have realized how that sounded at exactly the same moment Jesse realized the sausage patty was sliding out the pastry's buttery folds, because she audibly sucked in her breath.

Jesse jerked his hand back just as Flynn reached out and caught his meat before it could hit the step. Their eyes met over the sausage. She held it clasped delicately between the tips of her thumb and forefinger.

Blood pooled in his lower abdomen and he felt himself harden. Dammit.

"You want it back?" she whispered, her voice seductive as hell. Or was it his perverted imagination? Her hazel eyes were rounded wide and completely guileless.

He sucked a deep breath into his lungs and split apart the two sides of the croissant. "Load it on for me."

She nestled his sausage between the flaky buns. But he wasn't looking at his breakfast. Rather his gaze was glued on her. A few tendrils of dark hair had escaped her ponytail and were curling softly against her shoulders. Sunshine slanted in through the open window, bathing her creamy skin in a heated glow.

"There you go," she murmured. "Good as new."

Good as new, hell. What about the erection straining against his zipper? Good thing he had the wrapper in his lap for camouflage.

"How did you get out of prison early?" she asked.

It was the last question he expected, and it did the trick of deflating his arousal.

He shrugged. He didn't want to talk about it. Especially with her. "I was a good boy."

"Exactly how good?"

"Why are you asking?"

"I heard a rumor," she said, "that you did something heroic. The details were shaky. It's why I'm asking."

He snorted. "Where did you hear that?"

"I overheard customers talking at Froggy's. So there's no truth to it?"

"It's not a big deal."

"Big enough to get you released two years early."

"I really don't want to talk about it."

"Are you embarrassed about being a hero?" she prodded.

Just satisfy her curiosity, get it over with. "Look, there was an eighteen-year-old kid who came into lockup. He was terrified, made a bad deal with the wrong guys, found himself caught in between a turf war. He had no idea what he was getting himself into." Jesse gritted his teeth.

"I can tell this bothers you. You don't have to go into detail." She was acting all demure. Lowering her eyes, keeping those knees pressed tightly together. But he could tell the danger intrigued her. He saw the way her breath quickened, how the pulse at the hollow of her throat leaped with each pump of her heart.

"I was lucky in prison. I stayed of people's way, flew under the radar, and for the most part I got by unscathed; I'd already seen the worst the world has to offer. Prison was really no different than living on the streets or in some of the foster homes I'd been in. The worst part was the confinement. But this kid . . .." He paused. "He didn't know how to keep his nose clean. They were gonna kill him if someone didn't step in, and in all likelihood it would have erupted in a prison riot between two warring factions."

"You stepped in," she whispered.

"Lone Ranger to the rescue," he said, poking fun at himself.

"Did you get hurt?"

He fisted his right hand, held it out so she could see the flayed cut wounds across his knuckles. "Pretty minor, considering."

Flynn's face paled, and she made a low noise of sympathy and gently ran her fingertips over the jagged scars. "I'm so sorry for everything you had to go through."

"Hey, it wasn't your fault." He was reluctant to admit it, but her touch was unraveling his control, loosening the spigot on his emotions. "So tit for tat. What's happened with you while I was away? Other than getting engaged to Trainer?"

"My mom finally died last year," she said quietly.

"Yeah, Aunt Patsy wrote and told me when it happened. She was pretty torn up about it."

"Why didn't you write me, Jesse?" she asked in a rush. "Why did you send back the letters I wrote you?"

Old feelings roused in him—sorrow, sadness, disappointment. "I couldn't handle reading your letters." He shook his head. "And I knew if I wrote you back you'd keep hanging on to that childhood crap, and there was no reason for that. You had your life, and I was in a place you could never be."

"I would have come to see you."

"I didn't want you there," he said harshly. "Don't you get that? I didn't want you to see me on the ground, broken and damaged."

She drew in her breath. "I just wanted to help."

"You can't take care of everyone, Flynn."

Silence fell. They looked down at their half-eaten breakfast sandwiches, at their cooling coffee.

"I came to tell you I'd like to rent your upstairs room for the Yarn Barn," she said.

Jesse's pursed his lips. "Trainer know about this?"

"Yes."

"And he signed off on it?" Something smelled fishy in Denmark. He couldn't believe things were falling into place so easily. Jesse had learned a long time ago not to trust anything that came easily.

"Beau doesn't own me."

"I think he would disagree with that. Trainer's the possessive type." *Possessive enough to frame a man and send him to prison to eliminate him as a romantic rival.* But Jesse didn't tell her that. He knew she wouldn't believe him. No one but Patsy and Hondo believed him about Trainer.

"You're wrong about Beau. He's a really good guy," she said.

"Yeah, yeah. A real prince. What did you have to agree to in return?"

She bristled, got up, moved off the stairs. "That's none of your business."

"Let me guess. He pressed you to set a wedding date for sooner rather than later."

The look on her face told him he'd hit the bull's-eye.

"Are you going to rent me the space or not?"

He raised his palms, stood up. "Sure, sure. When do you want to start renovations?"

"Tomorrow?"

"Tomorrow it is," he said, and stuck out his hand to seal the deal. "Welcome aboard."

CHAPTER NINE

Jesse, I'll never forget our rendezvous.
You're destined for big things. I just know it.
—Flynn MacGregor, yearbook entry, 1999

Okay, so the sizzle between them still burned hot as ever, but it didn't have to mean anything. She would not act on it. She was no longer a teenager. She'd moved on, put the past behind her. She was engaged now.

Mentally girding herself for the onslaught of Jesse's devastating grin, Flynn parked on the square and wandered around to the back entrance. She was surprised to see the progress he'd made on the place since the previous day. The bottom level had been completely gutted right down to the cement floor.

The man was a worker, she'd give him that.

"Hey, Dimples," Jesse said, his voice echoing in the now cavernous room. He was ambling down the stairs, his arms loaded with junk he was apparently cleaning out from the upper level.

"Wow, I'm amazed." Flynn turned in a circle. "Did you stay up all night?"

"Not *all* night."

"But most of it."

"I've almost got the upper room cleaned out," he said. "Do you have any idea what you want to do up there? Paint? Wallpaper?"

"Actually, my mother picked out the wallpaper years ago. She had me buy it in preparation for the right place. Mom was a big believer in visualization. See it, believe it. I don't know why, it didn't seem to work for her."

"I think that's where you're wrong. Looks like her dreams are starting to come true."

His words brought a lump of emotion to her throat. Flynn splayed a hand to her neck.

"I did some visualization of my own," he went on. "Every night as I fell asleep in my cell, I'd imagine my own shop with a row of gleaming motorcycles that you could see through the display window."

"I'm happy for you."

"We could probably start the wallpapering, depending on how long you can stay," Jesse said.

"I can stay as long as I want."

"Sheriff got you on a long leash?"

Bite your tongue. Don't rise to the bait. "Uh-huh." She smiled sweetly.

By eleven, they'd finished clearing out the rubble, sweeping up the floor, and wiping down the walls of the large room that had once served as Pete Grissom's office. Flynn went home and dug out the wallpaper she'd purchased years earlier and stored in her mother's hope chest. It was adorable, knitting-themed paper decorated with colorful skeins, balls, and hanks. Amid the yarn, kittens frolicked—calicos, tabbies, Siamese.

"That looks like the cat that's been hanging around out back," Jesse said, nodding toward a gray tabby curled up in a pail of balled yarn. "I tried to chase it off two days running but she won't leave."

"Did you feed her?"

"*Phttt*." He pulled a macho face. "I'm starting up a business here, can't have a cat underfoot when you're running motorcycles in and out of the place."

Flynn noticed the tops of his ears turned red. "You fed her."

"Yeah, I'm an idiot."

"You're an old softie, that's what you are."

"Shh, don't let it get out."

"You ever have a pet?"

"No, and I don't have one now."

"That's what you think. You fed her, she's yours."

He shook his head. "I don't get attached. I know better. Getting attached . . ."

"What?"

"It's for suckers and fools."

Flynn could almost feel the pain in his voice. Jesse dropped his gaze, reached for the measuring tape. She let it go. What was there to say? Life had kicked him hard in the teeth. She couldn't teach him something he had to learn on his own. That you have to give love in order to get it.

They worked together in silence, measuring the

wall, cutting the paper to fit, wetting the back, smoothing it into place with sponges. Surprisingly, in their work, the hush felt uncomplicated and easy. Then Flynn spoiled it all by noticing they were moving in tandem—their arms sweeping out, mimicking each other's strokes, totally in sync. The tempo was spellbinding. Erotic. Almost like foreplay.

Unsettled, she stepped back and pretended to assess their work. She squeezed her sponge tightly, felt the gooey adhesive create a sticky web between her fingers. Jesse stopped working too and peered over at her, his bold stare caressing her intimately. The sharp crackling of sexual undercurrent rippling between them raised the hairs on Flynn's arms.

"It looks good," he murmured, but he was not studying the wall. He was looking straight at her and his voice was husky. "Real good."

Closing her eyes, she willed herself not to shiver, but then quickly opened them again. She felt too vulnerable here alone with him as it was. Shutting her eyes was just asking for trouble. "Real good," she echoed.

He reached out and took the sponge from her, his fingertips barely grazing her skin as he chunked both their sponges into the water pail.

"You thirsty?" Perspiration had plastered his cotton muscle shirt against his chest.

She was sweating too, but not just from the sultry summer day. She could smell the onion, garlic, and Italian sausage drifting up from Pasta Pappa's across the street. Heard the sounds of tourists walking along the cobblestone walkway outside the window, talking to one another above the more usual town square noises—the dinner bell ringing for the next seating at the Funny Farm restaurant on the corner, the rumble of a diesel pickup truck motoring by, the strumming guitar of a street musician entertaining for pocket change.

"Uh-huh," she whispered.

"Be right back." He hustled downstairs and returned a minute later with two bottles of water. He handed one to her.

It was cold and damp against her palm.

Without ever taking his eyes off her, Jesse tilted his head and took a long swallow from his bottle.

Her gaze tracked from his lips to throat. She watched his Adam's apple work, and she fought the shiver slipping down her spine. Fretfully she shifted her attention away from him, looking for something else to focus on. She surveyed the room.

It was fresh and homelike and inviting. Any knitter would feel at home here with the walls decorated with this pattern. But looking at it, Flynn felt . . .

Bogus.

Her big fat lie was splayed all over the wall right in front of her. *You're a fraud, a charlatan, an impostor.*

"What's wrong," Jesse asked, coming up behind her. He stood so close she could feel his body heat.

"I don't know if I can do this." She crossed her arms over her chest, held her body tight.

"Do what?"

"Open this knitting store. Run this business. Keep pretending I'm something I'm not."

"Flynn, you can do anything you set your mind to. I've seen you in action."

His words warmed, but more than that, the look in his eyes set her knees to rocking.

"Hang on," he said. "I've got something I want to give you. I was going to give it to you later, after we finished getting the room ready, but I think you need it now."

"You got me a gift?"

"Yeah," he said. "Ten years ago."

"Ten years ago and you still have it?"

"I'd stored it in the Harley's saddlebags and I'd forgotten all about it until I took the bike out of storage. Just stay here. I'll be right back."

Puzzled, Flynn watched him leave. She heard the back door creak open and then slam closed. Where had he gone? She sat down to wait, to finish her water, and that's when she met the cat.

The shy little girl peeked around the top of the stairs, eyeing Flynn with big gray eyes almost the same color as her fur.

"Well hello, Miss Tabitha." Flynn waited, letting the young feline come to her.

The tabby eased across the floor, sniffing delicately at the air.

"Wallpaper glue," Flynn explained. "Nothing tasty."

The cat inched closer. Flynn scratched her behind the ears. Miss Tabitha purred. Flynn was in love.

At the sound of Jesse's feet on the stairs, the cat jumped up and darted into the closet. "Hey," he said.

"You scared Miss Tabitha."

"Who?"

"The cat."

"You named her," he said. "We're toast."

"Can we keep her in the shop?"

"Looks like she's here to stay."

"Goody. I'll buy her a litter box and pick up some cat food."

Jesse stood there clutching a big pink box wrapped with a red ribbon. At the sight of it, her heart gave a funny little chug. His shoulders filled out the dimensions of his black muscle shirt with the Harley emblem emblazoned on it, and Flynn found her gaze sliding helplessly down the front of his shirt to the waistband of his jeans.

His belt was new, the silver buckle modest by Texas standards. His muscled masculinity made the pink box look incongruous, and the sight of it touched her more deeply than she'd expected. He'd bought her a present ten years ago, before he'd gone to prison, and he'd kept it all this time. Even when she hadn't believed in him, he'd still believed in her.

He handed her the box. "Open it."

Flynn untied the ribbon, lifted the lid. Inside, swaddled in red tissue paper, was a pink leather Harley jacket. She laughed. "Well, I'll be damned."

"Do you like it?"

"I can't believe you actually got this for me."

"I'd bought it for you a couple of days before graduation. I was going to give it to you . . ." He hesitated. "You know, after that night on the bridge. But I never got a chance."

"Jesse, I don't know what to say." She felt as if she'd been turned inside out.

"I'm giving it to you now so that you can see

you've got a way out. You don't have to be an impostor if you don't want to be. You've got the jacket, I've got the motorcycle. There's an open road stretching across America." When she looked in his eyes, she could almost believe that anything was possible.

"Besides, you're the most authentic person I know, Flynn MacGregor. Even if you can't knit."

Flynn met Jesse's gaze. He knew her so well. How could he know her this well? He knew her better than anyone ever had, even her own mother. It was eerie the way he could see straight into her. See her, understand her, accept her.

His eyes glistened with the same out-of-control impulses that were simmering through her blood. He moved toward her. She did not step back. "You're an amazing person, Flynn MacGregor."

His comment brought a flush of self-consciousness to her cheeks. She ducked her head, put the lid back on the box.

Jesse took another step toward her and then another.

Her pulse spiked.

He didn't stop until the tips of his boots touched the tips of her sneakers. He reached up his hand.

Flynn's lungs deflated.

His fingers landed in her hair. Unnerved, she flinched beneath his touch. "Wallpaper."

"Huh?"

"Wallpaper, stuck in your hair." He gently tugged it from her hair, showed her the scrap of wallpaper.

"Oh."

"You know," he said, "some guys might take advantage of a moment like this and try to kiss you."

"But you're not going to do that?" She meant to say it firmly, like a statement, but it came out hopeful, like a question.

His gaze nailed her to the wall, and he leaned in so close that their noses were almost touching. "No."

"That's good because I'm engaged to the sheriff."

"I know. I was at the party, remember. Me and Garth Brooks." He hummed a couple of bars from "Friends in Low Places."

"That was an awkward moment."

"Kind of like this one, huh?" His lips were almost on hers. "Flynn."

"Yeah?"

"I'm not going to kiss you."

"So you said."

Neither of them moved, but he was kissing her with his eyes. Thoroughly, completely. A blast of sexual heat rolled down her spine. His warm breath tickled her skin. He smelled so good. Flynn knotted her hands to keep from grabbing him around his neck and forcing him to kiss her for real.

"Please . . ." she whispered, meaning to add, *Let me go*, but her throat muscles constricted so tightly she couldn't say anything more, and his gray-blue eyes were so intense he'd snared her in a magical coil of sexual longing.

She felt it all at once. An earthquake rumbling through her. Desire and lust, hunger and longing. Guilt, sadness, loneliness. Craving and confusion. So much confusion. It fell in on her, heavy and stiff and too, too much.

His eyes were handcuffs; locking her to him. He tilted his head, inhaled audibly.

She tensed. Aching for him to kiss her, but terrified of where it might lead and what it might mean.

He took a step back.

Don't go, something whimpered inside her.

Bound by desire that knew no reason or restraint, Flynn put out her hand and touched his forearm. She had to kiss him or die on the spot. The recklessness bothered her, but it was something she'd been burying for a long time, and the urge would not be denied.

Heedlessly, Flynn wrapped her arms around his neck and held on tight.

Jesse shook his head.

She swallowed, moistened her lips, whispered, "Yes."

His eyes glimmered, and a grin tipped up his lips. It was like watching a red light turn green. She felt the rush of his emotions because they welled up inside her as well. Dark and dangerous and forbidden. She didn't think, just acted. "Kiss me."

"Dimples," he murmured. "I want to kiss you more than I want to breathe. But I can't, I won't. Not as long as you have Trainer's ring on your finger."

Jesse couldn't sleep.

He tossed and turned on the mattress in his Aunt Patsy's guest room. When she'd found out he'd been crashing on Hondo's couch, she'd insisted he move in with her. He'd been hesitant. Mainly because if Aunt Patsy figured out what he was up to, she would light into him with the rough side of her tongue. But she'd seemed so hurt that he'd stayed with Hondo and hadn't called her the minute he got out of prison, that when she came for him, he'd just gathered up his stuff and followed her.

His relationship with his aunt was complicated. He appreciated the fact she'd come to Arizona and rescued him from the foster home where he'd been living, but part of him—the part of him that had been eight years old and left completely alone when his mother died—resented her for not coming sooner. He knew it wasn't Patsy's fault. His mother had never told him about her, or her about him, but there it was. He felt what he felt.

But Patsy had been staunchly on his side after his arrest, telling him not to take the plea bargain even though her husband, Jimmy, the lawyer, had advised him to do so. Patsy was certain he would be exonerated. He hadn't been, and in the end, he should have taken Jimmy Cross's advice. His sentence would have been years shorter. Yet the fact that his aunt had believed in him wholeheartedly had meant a lot to Jesse. She'd known who he really was at heart.

Whereas Flynn . . .

Jesse sighed, flopped over on his side, punched his pillow. He couldn't blame Flynn for believing what everyone else in town believed. Trainer had filled her head with lies, poisoned her mind against him.

The old anger pushed up inside him. Trainer. The bastard.

He had to get out of here. Had to do something to put a headlock on these unwanted emotions.

Jesse threw back the covers, pulled on a pair of gym shorts and sneakers, and then slipped out the back door. He went for a run around the lake, pushing himself hard, flying over the jogging path until his legs ached. Normally running calmed him, but not tonight. The air was muggy and stagnant, but it smelled of freedom. Overhead the moon shone down and the stars twinkled while Twilight slept.

And all he could think about was Flynn. Even his revenge scheme against Beau couldn't compete. Everything was coming together just as he planned. He should have been excited, elated. Instead he was worried. He had one shot at this and he wouldn't blow it. He couldn't make his move too soon. That's why he hadn't kissed her when she'd practically begged him to, and nothing had ever required more of his self-control.

Ten years had only added to Flynn's sexual allure, making it almost impossible for him not to touch her in some small way. He adored her wicked sense of humor that she was just as likely to turn on herself as on anyone else. And he couldn't ignore the sharp-eyed intelligence that gleamed from behind her good-girl mien.

Jesse admired her grit and determination, and he even admired the way she stuck to her guns, even though she was clearly on the wrong track with this knitting store thing. The woman was as stubborn as he was. And she was going to be renting out the top floor of his motorcycle shop.

It was a serendipitous turn of events he could not have anticipated. For once fate had smiled on him, delivering him not only a legitimate reason for hanging around her, but giving him a meta-phorical sword with which to pierce Beau Trainer's arrogant armor.

Priceless.

He swiped the back of his arm across his sweaty brow and cornered the lake not far from the marina. Froggy's lay two miles north. Flynn's house was a half mile beyond that. He picked up the pace, kept thinking about how she'd looked in that loose-fitting T-shirt, how it draped softly over her breasts. She'd been trying so hard not to look sexy that she'd ended up looking even sexier in those faded jeans and those modest gold studs at her earlobes. The woman could make a tow sack look sexy. All she had to do was flash that double-dimpled grin and he was a goner.

But who was he kidding? He would forever be the kid from the wrong side of the tracks. He had no business believing he could have her for his very own.

No business at all.

He ran. Harder, faster, legs pumping, trying to outrun his demons, but it was useless. They hitched a ride wherever he went.

And then there he was. Where he hadn't realized he'd been headed all along.

The old Twilight Bridge.

He sprinted up onto the runners, lungs chugging. The wooden slats creaked and swayed beneath his sneakers. When he got to the middle, he stopped, panting hard, chest heaving, and bent over trying to catch his breath.

Then *bam!*

He was folded into the arms of the past. Jesse sank to his knees as the old bridge shimmered and memory eclipsed the present. He was back in time, on this bridge, right in this same spot, with Flynn in his arms.

He'd kissed her, cradling her head, and she wrapped her arms around his neck, pulling him down on top of her. The bridge swayed, adding to the heart-pounding thrill of the moment.

She wriggled against him with pleasure as his hand slipped up underneath her blouse, skimmed over her bare belly. He undid the hook of her bra, pushed her shirt up, then moved his mouth from hers, traveling down her neck, burning her tender skin as he went. He found her nipples, nibbled them lightly one after the other.

Flynn moaned softly, and the sweet sound drove him crazy.

He undid the snap on her shorts, eased his palm past the waistband, touched her through her panties, his mouth still softly suckling one nipple.

She threaded her fingers through his hair, whispered his name like a mantra. "Jesse, Jesse, Jesse."

He stroked her, steadily, firmly. She wriggled, breathed in a sigh. He increased the tempo, his fingers rubbing against the thin cotton, strumming her straining nub beneath the material.

And then she shuddered in his arms, let out a strangled cry, tightened her hands in his hair.

She came! He'd made her come.

A deep sense of pride swept over him, and he felt a tenderness for Flynn so strong and true it constricted his throat. He zipped her pants, hooked her bra, tugged down her shirt, pulled her into his arms, and rocked her slowly there on the swinging bridge.

Time passed.

It could have been hours. It might have been only minutes. They were caught in a blissful vortex stretching full of possibilities. They were young and falling in love and . . .

A pickup truck rumbled down from the highway. They paid no attention to the vehicle until it came to stop at the west end of the footbridge. A metal barricade erected at both ends of the bridge prevented cars from driving out on it, so even then, they didn't take much notice. The truck, which had been jacked up with a lift kit, turned on a row of bright off-road spotlights—the kind hunters used—that ran along the elevated cab, and blasted them with a blinding glare.

Flynn untangled herself from his arms. He could hear her breathing quicken. "That's Beau's truck."

The truck door opened. The sound of country-and-western music spilled out. Hank Williams. "Your Cheatin' Heart."

Jesse stood up, pulled Flynn to her feet. "Come on," he said. "Let's go tell him about you and me."

"No!"

He saw it then. The look on her face. Guilt, confusion, regret. She was *ashamed* of him. Ashamed of what they'd done. He couldn't have been more hurt if a wrecking ball had smacked into him, crushed his chest.

"No," she said, reaching out to touch his shoulder. "Let me handle Beau." She pointed to the east side of the bridge. "Go home now. We'll talk later."

She was trying to get rid of him. Hide him from her boyfriend. Sweep her little indiscretion away under the rug.

Despair stiffened his steps. He was pissed off at himself. Angry that he'd allowed his feelings to run away from him. He'd been so stupid to think a woman like Flynn could feel anything deeper than lust for a guy like him.

Idiot. Fool.

Contempt for his own foolish hopes ground him like a cigarette butt beneath a boot heel. His stomach sickened. His vision blurred. Blindly, he stumbled off the bridge.

Jesse gulped back the memory, stared down at the water. That moment had been one of the lowest in his life.

The next morning it had all turned around. Flynn called him to tell him that she was going to break up with Beau that night after high school graduation. His hopes had soared as swiftly as they'd been dashed the night before. He'd gone to the graduation ceremony, eager and happy, ready to declare his true feelings to Flynn and give her the motorcycle jacket he'd bought for her a few days earlier.

But he'd never gotten the chance.

Before he could enter the auditorium, Sheriff Clinton Trainer's men converged on his car in the parking lot. They'd pulled him out, forced him on the ground. Then the sheriff had yanked Jesse's keys from the ignition and made a beeline for his trunk as if he knew exactly what he was looking for.

Beau and Flynn had pulled up just in time to see

Jesse being stuffed into the back of Clinton Trainer's patrol car.

"Jesse!" Flynn had cried, and rushed over. Beau, he'd noticed, stood behind her smirking.

"Stay back." Clinton had come between Flynn and the patrol car. "This man is under arrest."

"For what?" Flynn had exclaimed.

"Possession of cocaine. Over a kilo, intent to distribute. And possession of an illegal firearm."

Flynn had looked into his eyes. "Jesse?" she'd asked, her voice small and tremulous.

He'd winked at her, all cocky bravado. "Don't worry, Dimples," he'd said. "It's not the worst thing since Vietnam."

CHAPTER TEN

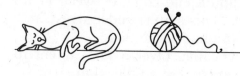

Beau, thank you for being my anchor.
—Flynn MacGregor, yearbook entry, 1999

After what had almost happened between her and Jesse, Flynn was determined to keep to the top floor of the theater and let Jesse have the bottom. He offered to help her finish the wallpaper, but she refused. She started entering the Yarn Barn by the side entrance, hustling up the outside steps rather than traipsing through the motorcycle shop.

Truth was, she was terrified of what she was feeling and what she might do if she found herself alone with him again.

And then there was Beau.

The fact that she'd been so tempted with Jesse, had almost crossed a line, rattled her to the core. Was Jesse just something she needed to get out of her system? Or did her attraction to him mean that her relationship with Beau was in serious jeopardy? She had a lot of thinking to do.

On Sunday evening Beau took her to see an action-adventure flick at the cineplex. She sat through the whole thing without seeing or hearing a word of the movie, her mind fidgeting with her dilemma. Were her feelings for Jesse real? Or were they leftover remnants from their childhood? What about Beau? What were her feelings for him?

On the drive home, he reached over, took her hand, squeezed it gently. "You've been very quiet tonight."

She rubbed her temple. "I have a bit of a headache."

"Have you given any more thought to going to the law enforcement convention with me next weekend?" he asked.

Great, she'd totally forgotten he'd asked.

"I've got to work at Froggy's next Saturday. Janeen is still out on her honeymoon."

"Can't you find someone to work for you? I'd like to have you there for moral support when I give my speech."

"You'll do fine. Besides, what would I do with myself all day while you're in workshops?"

"You could see the sights in Dallas."

"I've been to the grassy knoll and the School Book Depository. That's about the extent of tourism in Dallas."

"You're right," he said. "But it would just be nice to have you with me. You could stay in the room, order room service, get a massage and spa treatments. You never pamper yourself. My treat."

Okay, now she felt like a total shit. Wouldn't a good fiancée be jumping up and down to go with him? "Honestly, Beau, I'm a little nervous about leaving my father all alone for the weekend. Carrie is going on a weekend trip to San Antonio with her boyfriend, and if I go too, Floyd will be by himself and more vulnerable to temptation."

"Maybe next year then," he said.

"Next year," she echoed.

He walked her up onto the front porch, kissed her at the door. It was a good kiss, a sweet kiss, a kiss that once upon a time would have caused her to take him by the hand and lead him up to her bedroom. "See you tomorrow," he said.

"Good night, Beau."

Then she'd gone to bed and dreamed of Jesse. A hot, erotic, endless dream.

Whenever she was at the Yarn Barn, she threw herself into her work. Pushing herself until her muscles ached. She finished the wallpapering and started putting down the parquet flooring herself. She came early and stayed late. And Jesse gave her space, which sort of irritated her when she thought about it, even though she didn't know why. Was he avoiding her as much as she was avoiding him? She managed to go the whole week without ever seeing him.

But oh, she heard him. Each tread of his boot as he moved around below her, echoed in her ears. She brought her iPod, stuffed earbuds in her ears, but she still knew he was there.

On Friday, the day Beau departed for his conference in Dallas, she worked herself into a frenzy putting down the parquet, trying to douse her awareness of Jesse. She broke her fingernails and got splinters in her hands. Her knees throbbed from all the kneeling. At last she finished the floor-

ing. Great, now she could go home. Then she got
to her feet and looked down. For the first time she
noticed the mismatched design. Somehow she'd
gotten off track with the pattern. The floor was
going to have to be ripped up and the whole thing
done again.

"Son of a horse," she swore, and in frustration
kicked the stack of remaining parquet tiles, stubbing
her toe. "Ouch, ouch, dammit, dammit." She hopped
around on one foot, clenching her teeth against the
pain. The iPod in her ear blasted Gretchen Wilson's
"Work Hard, Play Harder." She ripped the buds
from her ears; the tinny sound spilled into the room
as she sank to the floor holding her toe.

Jesse came plowing up the stairs. "What is it?
Are you okay?"

"No, I'm not okay." She glowered.

Concern etched his face. He rushed over, sank
to his knees beside her. "What's wrong?"

"I stubbed my stupid toe having a temper tantrum."

He rocked back on his heels, a smile tugging at
his lips. "A temper tantrum? What about?"

"Look." She swept a hand at the mismatched
floor. "A week's worth of work down the crapper."

"Let me look at the toe." He reached for her
shoe.

The last thing she wanted was his hand on her
body. She swung her foot away from him. "That's
okay. It doesn't really hurt anymore."

"You've been working too hard," he said.
"Maybe you should take a page from Gretchen."

"Huh?" She blinked at him, too unnerved by his
nearness to snap to what he was talking about.

He picked up her iPod and handed it to her. "Work hard, play harder."

"I don't play."

"I've noticed," he said.

"I better get to work pulling up this floor."

"I've got a better idea." He touched her hand.

Flynn gulped, jerked back. "Um . . . what's that?"

"Let's go do something fun."

"Jesse," she said. "I'm engaged to Beau."

"Does that mean you can't have fun?"

"I don't want to have to deal with it if someone sees us out together."

"What if we went somewhere the locals never go?"

"Where's that?"

"Mini golf out on 377."

She laughed. He was right. The locals never played mini golf. It was always too packed with tourists.

"When was the last time you played mini golf?"

"When Noah and Joel were ten."

"Well, that's too long. Come on. Give yourself a break. It'll be fun."

"I don't know." She waved at the floor.

"I'll help you fix it." His eyes danced impishly.

She drew in a deep breath. "It's not such a good idea."

"I'll buy you a hot dog," he cajoled. "I promise, it's nothing more than two friends letting off some steam on a Friday night. We'll be out in public. Nothing to hide."

Honestly, the thought of getting out of the building was tempting.

"I'm going to look pretty dorky playing mini golf by myself, but hey, if making me look dorky is your goal . . ." he teased.

"Okay, fine," Flynn relented. "One round of mini golf.

Twenty minutes later, she had to admit to herself it wasn't a bad idea. They took her car because she refused to ride on the back of his motorcycle. They were outside in the evening breeze and she could feel the tension easing from her shoulders. It was amazing how much fun they were having doing something as simple as miniature golf. Flynn had played a few times, mostly bringing Joel and Noah up to the Puttery, getting them out of the house for some semblance of a normal childhood. But she'd never been here on a date. Not that this was a date. They were just hanging out.

"So seriously, Ol' Ramrod never brought you here?" Jesse asked, practically reading her mind.

"Ol' Ramrod?"

"Yeah, he walks like he's got a rod rammed up his back."

"Beau has good qualities."

"Not a many as you'd like to think."

"What's that supposed to mean?"

Jesse shook his head. "Never mind."

"He's been a good friend to me."

"I bet he has."

"You're jealous."

"Hell, yes. He's had ten years with you. Ten years I'll never get back no matter how many rounds of mini golf we play." Jesse brushed against her as he went to line up his putt, and she knew the touch was not accidental.

"He was in Iraq for four years."

"Okay, six years. It still sucks." He made the shot and looked up, and for one lightning-quick second she saw his heart in his eyes, but he quickly cut it off.

Her own heart moved, shifted in response.

"Your turn," he said.

"Oh yeah." She took her shot, ended up far away from the hole.

"Tiger Woods has nothing to worry about."

The wind changed directions, blew in off the lake, tossed Flynn's hair in her face. She could feel it starting to frizz. Irritated, she pushed it behind her ears. "Damn hair."

"What do you mean?" Jesse said. "You look gorgeous."

"I don't."

He chuckled. "I'm not going to argue. It'll just give you a big head."

"Too late, I'm already big-haired."

"You do have a lot of hair," he conceded.

He was looking at her like he loved big hair. He was standing so close she could smell his darkly sexy Jesse scent. A shiver swept through her, and she quickly turned away before he could see the desire in her eyes. She wasn't ready for these feelings. Not by a long shot.

"Oh, look what's up next." She pointed to the upcoming hole. "A castle. And it's got a moat and a drawbridge that raises and lowers. Hurry and put your ball in the hole so we can move on."

"My ball is already in the hole. You're the one gumming up the works."

"That's my ball?"

He inclined his head. "It is."

"I'm red?"

"Yeah."

"I can't be red."

"You're red."

Flynn narrowed her eyes. "Are you sure?"

"Why can't you be red?"

"Because Noah loves red. He's always red. And Joel is blue. Carrie likes yellow."

"What do you like?"

"Whatever is left over."

Jesse shook his head. "That's really sad."

"What?"

"The fact that you're so used to giving away your favorite color that you won't even claim it when it's yours." Jesse leaned over and fished his ball from the hole. "See, I'm green."

"I'm red?"

"You are."

"How did you know red was my favorite color?"

"You told me once. A long time ago. Before you brainwashed yourself into fulfilling everyone's needs but your own."

"And you remembered that?"

"Dimples, where I've been I've had nothing else to do but remember," he said. "There's another thing I remember."

"What's that?"

"You used to talk about becoming a teacher. Why didn't you do it?"

"I couldn't leave my mom."

"She's been gone a year."

"So? There's still Carrie and my dad and the twins."

"All adults who can take care of themselves. What have you done for Flynn? What steps have you taken to achieve *your* goals?"

"The Yarn Barn."

"That's not your dream."

"It is."

"Only by proxy."

They stood there looking at each other. All around them couples and families were laughing and talking and whacking golf balls through windmills and Eiffel Towers and into clowns' mouths. The moment stretched, awkward and unsettling.

"What was it like?" she asked softly.

"What?"

"You know." She wished that she hadn't asked it.

"Prison?"

"No Disneyland."

He laughed. "Not as much fun as those spinning teacups, but between that obnoxious Small World ride and prison . . ." He cupped his hands, palms up, moving them back and forth like a scale balancing. "Pretty much a tossup."

Flynn started humming the "Small World" song.

"Now that's just mean. That song should be outlawed."

She laughed. "The lyricist was clearly a sadist."

"They should play that in prisons," he mused. "To the folks on death row. They'd all commit suicide."

"Ooh, gallows humor. Dark and broody."

"I thought you'd appreciate it."

"I'm sorry," she said, softening her voice, "that you went to prison."

"Why? It wasn't your fault."

"You lost ten years out of your life. That's sad."

"The way I figure it, we're all in some kind of prison. Take you for instance." He pointed at her with the end of his putter.

"Me?"

"Just as a for instance."

She wasn't so sure about this; she putted the red ball, sank it into the hole. "Okay. As a for instance."

"You're trapped here, just like I was trapped in prison. Oh sure, you've got a bit more space, but in the end you go through the same routines every day. Your prison might not have four walls, but you're trapped just the same."

"But I could break my routine any time I wanted. I don't *have* to do it," Flynn argued.

"That's a good rationalization, but it's still a rationalization."

"What? Did you get a psychology degree while you were in the slammer?"

Jesse's smile was wry. "Something like that."

"It was bad, wasn't it?"

"I survived." He shrugged like it was nothing worse than a trip to the dentist.

She tried to imagine what he'd gone through and she couldn't fathom it.

"Here was my day," he said, reading her thoughts again. "Not so different from yours. Up at five-thirty. You get up what? Six?"

"Six-thirty," she mumbled. "But I don't like it."

" 'Course not. It's something you have to do, not something you want to do. Then there was cell count."

"I don't have that."

"Cooking breakfast for your family and getting them out the door for the day qualifies as cell count."

"Okay, I'll give you that."

"Shower." He ticked the items off with his fingers. "You do that. Lunch, ditto. Exercise yard, day room, for you the equivalent would be working at Froggy's. Followed by dinner, cell count, lights out."

She slid him a sideways glance, but she could read nothing on his face. "My routine varies."

"Oh yeah? When?"

"Christmas, holidays."

"Same thing as visitor days. See, prison, Flynn MacGregor's life, not so dissimilar."

When he put it like that, he had a point. Flynn moved onto the next hole. The one with the castle. "I'm going first," she said, hoping he'd drop the subject.

"The only real difference is that your trap is of your own making."

She hit the ball. It struck off the drawbridge just as it started to close and came bouncing back to her. "Oh yeah, like someone planted that kilo of cocaine and .357 Magnum in the trunk of your car."

His eyes glittered a warning, told her not to push, but he'd pissed her off. Because of his foolish youthful indiscretions, they'd lost precious time together. She was with Beau when she could have been with him. "You think I'm guilty," he said.

"I get it, you had a rough childhood. You lived on the streets, you needed money. Selling drugs was the only way you knew how." The truth was, she didn't understand. Plenty of people had bad childhoods without turning to crime.

Jesse tossed his putter onto the AstroTurf, narrowed his eyes, and stalked over to invade her personal space.

Flynn gulped, but held her ground.

"You've been hanging out with Trainer too long," he growled.

"What's that supposed to mean?"

Jesse looked like he might say something else, but he clenched his jaw shut and stepped back.

"What?" she demanded.

"Never mind. Forget about it. You're going to believe what you want to believe about me. You always have."

"It wasn't your cocaine?"

"No. Do you really believe that after how my mother died I'd ever take up drugs, much less sell them?"

"A lot of people do. What's the Hank Williams Jr. song to that effect? 'Family Tradition,' " she dared to challenge him.

"Do you drink like your old man?"

"No."

"I rest my case."

"Whose cocaine was it?"

"Why don't you ask your fiancé?"

"Beau has never done drugs. He would barely take an aspirin even when he came back wounded from Iraq."

"I know you feel some kind of connection with this guy, although for the life of me I can't figure out why." Jesse sank his putt with one stroke. "But he's not the saint you seem to think he is."

"Hole in one."

"What?"

"You got a hole in one."

"You're changing the subject."

"I am."

Jesse blew out his breath. "Okay. I'll let it go."

"Thank you."

He smiled at her to show no hard feelings, and her heart rate sped up. Flynn ducked her head and assiduously scribbled his hole in one on the scorecard with a fat, stubby pencil.

"Who's winning?" he asked, peering over her shoulder.

His breath was warm on her skin. He smelled like soap and motorcycles. Flynn struggled to ignore the heat flaring through her. "You just made a hole in one, who do you think?"

"That's why you're cranky. You hate to lose."

"I'm not cranky."

"You kicked a pile of parquet."

"What does kicking a pile of parquet have to do with mini golf?"

"You were mad because you messed up the floor."

"Yeah, all my hard work down the drain."

"Same thing as losing at mini golf. It didn't go your way, you get cranky."

"I'm not cranky," she snapped.

"Right." His eyes laughed.

"I'm not!"

His gaze honed in on her lips, then slowly eased over her chin to her throat, sliding on down to her breasts. "Cranky or no, Flynn MacGregor, you've got a body that makes a guy ache to do things he shouldn't do."

Instantly her nipples hardened. Traitors.

"Things that could land him back in prison." He lifted his gaze back to hers. "But you, Dimples, are worth it."

Her stomach tugged. Her heart swooped. Her palms went slick. Goose bumps spread over her forearms. "That's some pretty dangerous talk, Mr. Calloway."

"Going all formal on me, Miss MacGregor, isn't gonna change what's going on here," he said.

"There's nothing going on here but a game of mini golf."

"Sweetheart, denial ain't gonna make that river in Egypt disappear either."

"Hey," hollered a chunky man in a loud-print Hawaiian shirt. He was standing at the tee-off position at the front of the castle, surround by half a dozen kids. "Are you two going to play that hole or stand there flirting all night? Either put the balls in the ground or get a room already."

Jesse raised a hand at the guy. "We're getting out of your way." He picked up their balls, hooked his arm around Flynn's shoulder, and guided her off the green. "About that room," he murmured in her ear.

She pulled away from him. "You're just trying to start trouble."

"Am I?"

"You don't like Beau and you're using me as a tool to gig him."

"Ah, Dimples, is that what you really think?"

"You're going to deny it?"

He used the head of his putter to pull her back

toward him. "Gigging Trainer is not my primary goal, but if he gets pissed off in the process that's not my problem."

"What is your primary goal?" she asked, not knowing why she just didn't go to her car and drive away. Why was she staying here staring into his eyes when it was the absolute wrong thing to do? She thought about Beau at his conference in Dallas, and guilt sliced right through her.

"Dessert. I'm aching for something sweet. You up for a banana split at Rinky-Tink's?"

"There's no way I'm having a banana split with you at Rinky-Tink's."

"No way?" He arched an eyebrow.

"None."

"The fact that it's my birthday won't sway you?"

"It's not really your birthday."

"It is. June 11."

"I don't believe you."

"I can prove it." He took his wallet from his pocket, extracted his driver's license, passed it over to her.

Yep. There it was. June 11.

He gave her puppy dog eyes. "Don't make me spend my birthday all alone."

"You're manipulating me."

"Is it working?" he asked hopefully.

Five minutes later they were sitting in the back booth at Rinky-Tink's. She kept telling herself it was okay if people saw them together. She rented her shop from Jesse. It was his birthday. They were out for a little celebration. Just friends. Nothing wrong with that.

Would Beau think so? She pushed thoughts of

Beau from her head and tamped down the guilt. She'd tell him she went out with Jesse. No secrets. Nothing to hide.

Which was good, because there was no way to hide when you ordered the Birthday Banana Split Special. It came loaded down with the works, plus had the added attraction of sizzling sparklers, and it was accompanied by a trio of singing teens in short skirts.

"This is silly," she said once the song and been sung and the sparklers had burned out.

"But fun." He dipped his spoon in a hefty helping of cookie dough ice cream drizzled with caramel and topped with whipped cream and a cherry. "Open up."

"I'm not going to eat off your spoon."

"Scared of my germs."

"Frankly, yes."

"You're just chicken."

"I'm not."

"You're afraid of having fun."

"*Pul-leaze.*"

"Come on," Jesse coaxed. "Prove you're not afraid to have fun. Open up."

"Oh, okay, fine," she said, just to get him to shut up. She parted her lips, and he slipped his cold spoon into her warm mouth. Dang, it was delicious.

"Good, huh?"

"Sinfully so."

"You could use a sin or two, Flynn MacGregor."

The way he was looking at her made her feel as if she was sixteen for the very first time. Jesse made her realize how much of her childhood she'd really missed.

"Are you telling me you never shared a banana split with the sheriff?"

"Beau doesn't eat sweets."

"Of course he doesn't." Jesse said and took a big bite of ice cream.

"Let's not talk about him."

Jesse leaned in close, and her pulse kicked up. "I'm for that."

"People are looking at us," she said, suddenly aware that even in the back booth at Rinky-Tink's they were still open to public scrutiny.

"Let 'em. You worry too much about what people think."

"And you don't worry enough."

"You can't live your life to suit other people."

"Sure you can. I do it all the time."

Jesse looked at her with half-lidded eyes. "Yeah, but does it make you feel happy or just obligated to do things their way?"

Flynn raised her chin in the air, wriggled to a straighter sitting position. "I like helping people."

"I know you do," Jesse said. "What I can't figure out is why you don't like helping Flynn."

"Hey, I'm here with you, out in public, aren't I? Taking a risk, taking a chance."

"You are," he conceded.

"Happy birthday, Jesse," she whispered, realizing he hadn't had much of a childhood either.

"Thank you, Flynn." His eyes looked sad.

She dropped her gaze, put a hand to her stomach. "I'm so full," she moaned, and eyed the monstrous banana split bowl that was still more than half full.

"A little does go a long way."

"You can say that again."

"Wanna walk it off?" he asked. "There's something I'd like to show you."

She should have said no. Just as she should have said no to the mini golf and the banana split, but the truth was she was having fun, and in her world, fun wasn't easy to come by.

"Remember, I'm the birthday boy."

"That only works until midnight."

He glanced at his watch. "I have over two hours left."

What the hell? She'd come this far. "Let's go."

He left a tip for the banana split big enough to make the short-skirted trio squeal and giggle at him to hurry back. They stepped out of Rinky-Tink's to find the Friday evening tourist crowd had dwindled to a few groups and hand-holding couples.

"Where are we going?" she asked.

"Stroll through Sweetheart Park."

The air was languid. The white Christmas lights that perpetually decorated the park beckoned to them. They walked across the cobblestoned street to the soft grass of the park, traipsing over the long wooden footbridge.

Sweetheart Park was bordered on two sides by a narrow tributary of the Brazos. In the center of the park lay the Sweetheart Fountain. The fountain was a cement statue of two lovers in Old West garb embracing in a heartfelt kiss. Legend had it if you threw pennies into the park's fountain you would be reunited with your high school sweetheart. Belinda Murphey had a list of testimonials claiming it was true.

Jesse stopped beside the fountain. "Do you believe it?" he asked.

"What?"

"The sweetheart legend."

She shrugged. "As a self-fulfilling prophecy, maybe. Other than that, I'm not very superstitious."

"Guess that makes me the romantic." Jesse took a coin from his pocket, flipped it into the fountain's gurgling pool.

The gesture scrambled her up inside. What did he mean by it? She didn't want to analyze it. The idea of Jesse conjuring up his high school sweetheart was one she didn't want to entertain. Who had been his high school sweetheart? He'd gone out with many girls. She didn't recall there being just one.

"So this thing you wanted to show me . . ." she said.

He took her hand—she didn't resist—and led her over to the Sweetheart Tree.

The Sweetheart Tree was a two-hundred-year-old pecan thick with sheltering branches. In the past, hundreds of names and hearts had been carved into the trunk. The oldest name was that of the original sweethearts. *Jon loves Rebekka* had been carved in the center of the pecan, faded and weathered now, but the etched lines were still visible. Sometime in the 1960s a botanist had warned that if the name carving continued, it would kill the pecan, so a white picket fence had been constructed around the tree, along with a sign sternly admonishing: "Do Not Deface the Sweetheart Tree."

Jesse stepped over the white picket fence. Flynn held back. Crossing the fence felt like breaking the rules.

"Come on," he coaxed.

Gingerly, she followed him, her shoes sinking into the grass damp from where the water sprinklers had sprayed. He took her around the back of the tree. It was darker on this side, no Christmas lights over here.

"I'm going to have to boost you up." He pulled a penlight from his pocket, handed it to her.

She remembered another penlight, a dark cave, a wet kiss. "What?"

"So you can see it."

"See what?"

He knelt on the ground. "Just climb on my shoulders."

"This feels weird."

He patted his thigh. "Foot here."

She climbed him. First foot on his thigh, second on his shoulders, then both on his shoulders. He encircled her ankles with his hands. "Up and to the right, beside the lowest limb," he directed.

She flicked on the flashlight. "What am I looking for?"

"You'll see."

"Jesse . . ."

"Just look."

She shone the beam, feeling a little irritated and, oddly, a little scared. She didn't know what she was afraid of but she could hear the blood pumping in her ears. And then she saw it.

Jesse loves Flynn.

And underneath was the date Jesse had been arrested. The same day Beau had asked her to marry him for the first time and she'd said no. A battering ram of emotions punched her chest. Saliva dried up in her mouth.

I'm in trouble. Deep, deep trouble.

"You find it?"

She couldn't answer. She was that overcome. She sucked in a deep breath, shifted, and slipped off his shoulders, but he managed to grab her before she fell.

Grabbed her.

Held her.

Took possession of her.

His eyes were dark, knowing. Her heart was a drum, pounding, pounding. "You carved our names in the tree. It was outlawed and you carved our names in the tree."

"I am an outlaw," he said. "I don't play by the rules, and I was determined to prove to this damn town how much I loved you."

"Oh, Jesse," she whispered.

And that's when he kissed her.

CHAPTER ELEVEN

Flynn, don't sit under the Sweetheart Tree
with anyone else but me.
—Beau Trainer, yearbook entry, 1999

Ten years fell away.

Ten years of wanting, yearning, craving, dreaming, and hoping.

He was falling in love with her all over again and he was powerless to stop it from happening. His mouth drank her in. Sweet nectar. He could feel the crush of her soft breasts against his muscled chest. He loved the way her hair curled across his shoulder and tickled his nose when he held her close.

Growling, he pulled her closer, his hand slipping down to cup her butt cheeks. He nibbled her bottom lip, and then he tracked his mouth lower, going down to nuzzle the slender curve of her neck. He felt her go loose in his embrace, melt against his body. They could have been on the moon, he was that oblivious to their surroundings. He'd been hungering for this moment for so very long. Just to feel her in his arms was a miracle.

Jesse throbbed with need for her. His knees trembled with the power of it. God, how he wanted her. But he couldn't have her. Not now. Not yet. Not while she still wore Beau Trainer's ring on her finger. When he took her, he wanted her to be fully and completely his.

Still, his body refused to cooperate. He had to have another kiss and another and another. When he wrenched his mouth from hers, she made a soft mewling sound of protest. Moonlight fell on her, bathing her creamy skin in a soft glow. It was all he could do not to strip her bare and take her right there.

"You are so beautiful," he murmured.

Sexual tension pulsed between them, an erotic irresistible force.

She reached up to pull his head down again for another kiss, but he took her hands, stepped back, and shook his head. He gently kissed the knuckles of both her hands, felt her shiver.

"What are you doing to me?" she whispered.

He had to draw in a deep breath to control himself. He wanted to possess her. All of her. Now. The urge was primal and all-consuming. *Flynn, Flynn, Flynn.* Her name beat in his head with every pulse of his blood. He had to stop this now or he wasn't going to be able to stop at all.

Flynn, however, seemed to have ideas of her own.

There was nothing sweet or tender about the kiss she planted on his lips. Heat radiated from her hot little core, searing him all the way to his tonsils. She bunched the front of his shirt in her fingers. She tasted so good. Like chocolate-chip cookie dough ice cream, sensuous flesh, and delicious woman.

Mindlessly he threaded his fingers through her hair, cradled the back of her head in his palm, took the kiss away from her. Deepened it.

They were standing in moon glow, underneath the branches of the Sweetheart Tree, kissing as they'd never kissed before. In an open area for any and all to see. It felt wicked, and his dick got so hard he couldn't form a coherent thought. He knew he was playing with fire, pushing things too far, too fast. He could screw it all up. Ruin everything.

"This isn't smart," he murmured against her mouth.

"I know," she whispered back.

"We have to stop."

"Yes."

"It was stupid."

"Yes." Her arms were still laced around his neck.

He reached up and wrapped his hands around her wrists. "You're engaged to another man, and I know you're not the kind of woman who cheats."

That seemed to get through to her. She blinked, pulled back, looked ashamed. "I'm not." She blew out her breath, took another step back, shoved a hand through her hair. "Oh God, what am I doing?" Her face paled. "I gotta go. I gotta get out of here."

Looking dazed, she turned, spun away from him, stumbled over the white picket fence.

He reached for her.

She threw up her hands, fending him off. "No, no."

"Flynn."

"No, no, don't touch me, no," she pleaded. "I can't do this. I won't let you do this to me. I won't do this to myself. I won't do this to Beau. He deserves better. I deserve better. You deserve better."

He understood. She'd broken her own values, shattered her code of ethics by kissing him just as she had done ten years ago on that bridge. He was her Achilles' heel, and she resented him for being her weakness.

Jesse didn't try to stop her. He just stood there, watching her rush away across the grass, headed back to the town square. Guilt twisted his heart. His plan had worked too well. He'd upset her, and that wasn't what he'd meant to do.

Moments later, her Ford Ranger sped past him. Flynn's hands clutching the steering wheel, her gaze staring straight ahead.

He swallowed hard, closed his eyes, and crossed his hands in front of his swollen erection. Dammit, Flynn got under his skin in a way no woman ever had—and he feared that no other woman ever would. What was it about her that so beguiled him? It was more than her straight dark hair that went wild and curly with the humidity. More than those intelligent hazel eyes that tipped up when she smiled. More than those deadly gorgeous double dimples in her right cheek.

What was she doing to him with her sassy mouth and the sexy way she sashayed? His defenses were crumbling. His resolve was gone. The woman lit a fire in him that could not be quenched.

And he was so busy wanting her, he'd forgotten all about getting revenge.

Beau stood in the shadows watching the convict kiss his girl, fury spurting like hot lava through his veins. His hand went to the butt of his gun as he imagined himself pulling his duty weapon from his holster and shooting Calloway right through the heart.

The impulse terrified him, because he knew he was capable of it.

He'd killed before. In a war, yes, but he'd pulled triggers and men had died. Bad men, and the world was a better place without them, but anyone with a conscience felt regret when he ended the life of another. No matter how much he had it coming.

Revolt writhed through him. Devastation wrecked him. Loathing seethed in his gut. He felt betrayed and mortified. They were kissing underneath the Sweetheart Tree for everyone to see. Making a fool of him. Laughing at him. Deriding his office.

He didn't blame Flynn. He knew she was hypnotized by Calloway's evil charms. Seduced by the dark side. Lead astray by lust. Deceived by pleasures of the flesh.

And it was up to him to save her.

This was his mission. Rescuing Flynn by eradicating this delinquent force. In Beau's mind, Calloway embodied every criminal who'd ever broken the law. Every evildoer who had gotten away with his crime. He was the biker responsible for Jodi's death. In him, Beau even saw his father—lawless, arrogant, undisciplined. Calloway was a cancer growing on Beau's beautiful little town, and he had to be stopped. Even if that meant Beau had to compromise his principles to achieve his goal. Just as he'd been forced to do back in high school.

And yet even as rage whispered this into his ear, part of him reveled in self-flagellation for entertaining such thoughts. Bad impulses were bad impulses even when they came from good people, and this impulse to destroy Jesse Calloway hunkered like a black monster in his soul.

Beau fisted his hands, struggled with his hatred. He could not let himself become obsessed with destruction. If he did, he was no better than Calloway. He closed his eyes and swallowed back the vicious bile choking his throat. Swallowed it and fought off the sinister brute threatening to consume him.

"Sheriff?"

Opening his eyes, he saw Sam Cheek standing in front of him, his dogs on leashes sniffing at Beau's boots.

"You okay?"

"Fine." Beau bit off the word, then swung his gaze to the Sweetheart Tree, wondering if Sam had seen his shame. But the park was empty. Calloway and Flynn gone.

"You sure?" Sam looked concerned.

Beau nodded curtly.

"You haven't seemed yourself lately."

Yeah, well, you catch your girl kissing a con and

see how that makes you feel, he wanted to say, but of course he did not. Instead a twinge of fear ran down his spine as he whispered, "Maybe *this* is the real me."

The next morning, Jesse was right in the middle of installing shelving on the walls for the boxes of inventory he'd just received when Sheriff Trainer darkened his door.

"Hello, scumbag."

A chill shot up Jesse's spine the same way it had when he was a foster-care runaway living in the Arizona desert and he'd heard a very distinct kind of rattling noise. He looked up, screwdriver in hand, the smell of fresh paint in his nostrils. His instincts urged him to leap across the room and pummel the shit out of the man responsible for ruining his life, but retribution had been ten years in the making. He wasn't going to do anything to ruin that and send himself back to prison. Flynn's love was at stake. For her, he would do anything.

"Hello, Sheriff," he replied mildly, and slid him a narrow-eyed glance, part boredom, part threat, as if he was a fatted cougar, not hungry, but not opposed to toying with his prey for sport.

Trainer's hand rested on the butt of his duty weapon, a trigger-happy expression glinting in his eyes. The past decade had been kind to him. Being sheriff had puffed him up, slathering meat on his bones. But he hadn't gone to fat as many former athletes did. Rock-hard muscles bulged underneath the tin star on his chest. A white Stetson rode his head.

Jesse laid down the screwdriver and raised his palms. *Easy, easy, don't give him any excuse to play Wyatt Earp.*

"I know what you're trying to pull and it's not going to work," Trainer growled.

"Me?" He kept his game face firmly entrenched. He had street smarts going for him. All Trainer had were his badge and the gun. *That's all he needs to send you straight back to Huntsville.*

"Don't play me for a fool."

"I don't know what you're talking about." Jesse stiffened his shoulders. Hell, he'd known this wasn't going to be a cakewalk. You come messing around a beehive with a stick, you were bound to get stung.

Trainer trod toward him, the sound of his boots echoing loudly in the cavernous room.

Jesse didn't shirk, didn't blink.

Trainer invaded his personal space.

Jesse held his ground.

Trainer's gaze smashed into his.

Jesse sent it flying right back with a powerful visual lob. This was how he'd survived in prison. He never started anything, but he never ran from a fight either. On the outside he stayed calm, but assertive. Quiet, with a deadly undercurrent. *Don't tread on me.*

"She's precious," Trainer said.

"I know."

"Special."

"That she is."

"She deserves better than you."

"You too."

"Granted, but she's mine."

"She might have your ring on her finger, but you don't own her. Flynn has a mind of her own and she knows how to use it."

"You don't know her."

If Beau only knew the things Flynn had confided in him. Jesse could say he knew her better than Trainer could ever possibly know her, but if he did, he was sure his face would end up as a stopping place for the sheriff's fist. And more than likely he'd find handcuffs clamped around his wrists as well. *Don't give the bastard an excuse. He's itching for you to give him an excuse.*

"You need a bottle of water, Sheriff? You're sweating."

"You haven't changed a bit, Calloway, still full of shit," Trainer said, but he reached up to swipe his upper lip with the back of his hand.

They scowled at each other.

Jesse wasn't afraid of him, but he felt that same razor-blade edginess he got in the penitentiary just before serious trouble broke out. It was that sharp, thin awareness of impending disaster that led to him saving Josh Green's life and preventing a prison riot. But navigating that dark perimeter was precarious. Instinct wasn't a sure thing. Rather, it was a whispering nudge that, if followed, could lead a man to the brink of reason. Intuition was too often like toeing a tightrope, stretched taut and narrow, over a yawning abyss. One shaky move in the wrong direction and it was all over.

"Something else you want from me, Sheriff? Something more than the ten years you stole?"

For the first time, Trainer looked a little uneasy, a little uncertain. Jesse saw the flicker of fear run across the man's eyes, but he quickly shut it down. "You sent yourself to prison, Calloway. Don't try and blame it on me."

"Been denying what you did for so long that now you're believing your own bullshit?"

Trainer's jaw turned to granite. "I want to make one thing perfectly clear."

Jesse couldn't stop himself from reacting. Not when it came to Flynn. He took a hard step forward, flattened his chest against Trainer's, and stared the taller man squarely in the eye. Their noses were almost touching.

"Yeah?"

"You stay away from her."

"Gonna be kinda hard to do, Hoss, what with her working right upstairs from me."

"You know what I mean."

"You mean you want me to keep my hands off her?"

"Yes." He snapped off the word like breaking peanut brittle.

"Or what?"

Trainer looked taken aback. "Or what?"

"You said to keep my hands off her. That implies an 'or what.' What happens if I touch her?"

"Do I have to spell that out for you?"

"Come on, Hoss, be man enough to come right out and say it. Keep my hands off Flynn or you'll plant evidence on me again, just like you did the first time."

Trainer's eyes narrowed and his nostrils flared. "Just stay out of her way."

"And if I refuse?"

Anger pulsed the distended vein in Trainer's forehead. Jesse felt rather than saw him knot his hands into fists.

Duck! his mind yelled, but Jesse kept toeing the abyss. He was giving Trainer the rope, let the bastard hang himself.

"You touch her and you're a dead man."

"What if she touches me?" he asked. *Couldn't let well enough alone, could you?*

"You son of a bitch." Trainer cocked back his fist, threw a punch.

Jesse never raised a hand. He just let the beating happen.

"I saw Beau go into Jesse's shop and then he comes stormin' out five minutes later, fists all knotted up, face like a thundercloud. I go over to see Jesse, you know, to be neighborly, say hi."

"Who wouldn't?"

"I took him some cranberry walnut muffins."

"Well, of course you make the best cranberry walnut muffins in Twilight."

"Thank you. Anyway, I walked right in, and let me tell you, girl, you could have knocked me over with a feather. Jesse's right eye was swelling shut and his bottom lip was cut and bleeding."

"My heavens!"

"I'm telling you, I'm pretty sure Beau smacked him a good one. I asked Jesse what happened, but he claimed he ran into the door. Ran into the door, my left foot! Let me tell you, something's going on between those two."

"You suppose it has anything to do with Flynn

MacGregor? She finally accepted Beau's ring, but I've seen the way Jesse looks at her. That man's in love."

"Or serious lust."

"He *has* been ten years in prison. That's got to put the starch in a man's jeans."

"Penelope! You naughty thing."

"I'm just saying. Ten years without s-e-x . . ." She spelled it out.

Vida Lewis and Penelope Cantrell, two of the busiest busybodies in Twilight, stood gossiping at the fabric counter at Wal-Mart, while the checkout clerk flipped a bolt of forest green corduroy and measured off a yard. Flynn could only assume that the women didn't see her perusing the yarn and knitting selections a few feet over. Either that or they *wanted* her to overhear their pernicious gossip.

She had the urge to give the old biddies a piece of her mind, but she held her tongue and slipped out through the automotive center where she'd been having the oil changed in her pickup. No sense in giving them added fuel to the fires of their rumor-mongering.

However, their conversation dug right down into her brain. Had Beau gotten into a fistfight with Jesse?

Over her?

But how could he? Beau was at his law enforcement convention in Dallas.

Or was he? Had Beau somehow found out that she had kissed Jesse and come home early? Shame burrowed into her head, snuggled up tight next to Vida and Penelope's tittle-tattle. She'd cheated on Beau.

Her fingers fumbled the debit card as she paid

for the oil change. She was shaking so much she had to slide the card through twice before it was accepted. But it was only when she was in the Ford Ranger and flew past the cutoff that she took every single day of her life that Flynn realized just how upset she was.

After circling back, she took her exit and drove to the town square. She found a parking spot not far from the theater and didn't even take the time to feed the parking meter. Flynn sprinted around the back of the building—the front entrance was still boarded up with plywood—and dashed inside.

"Jesse!" she called.

Her voice echoed back to her in the empty, high-ceilinged room.

Jesse . . . Jesse . . . Jesse.

And then she saw it. Two drops of bright red blood spatter in the middle of the cement floor. Her body went at once icy cold and red-hot livid, and she knew what Vida and Penelope had said was true. Beau had beaten Jesse. She spun around, saw Jesse in the doorway, a cardboard box in his arms. The sun was behind him so she couldn't see his face.

"Fancy meeting you here, Dimples."

"Jesse." Flynn breathed and rushed across the room toward him. She stopped when she saw his face and raised a trembling hand to her lips. "Omigod."

"It's not as bad as it looks." He tried to grin, but only one side of his mouth crooked upward.

"Beau did this to you?"

"Who told you that?"

"Vida Lewis and Penelope Cantrell."

"Those two busybodies?" He shrugged and stepped across the threshold and then balanced the cardboard box between a pair of parallel saw-horses. "When did you start listening to anything they had to say?"

"You're telling me that Beau didn't have any-thing to do with this? Oh, your poor eye." His right eye was almost completely swollen shut. She raised a hand toward him. "And your lip!"

Jesse flinched, stepped back.

"I wasn't going to touch your face."

"Sorry, reflex."

"It looks horrible."

"No big deal. I've had much worse."

"It *was* Beau, wasn't it?"

"I ran into an immovable object."

"And would that immovable object be six-foot-four with a fist like a bowling ball?"

"Bowling ball?"

"Figure of speech. Why are you protecting him?"

"I'm not protecting him, I'm protecting me. I have no desire to go back to Huntsville. Your fiancé is the one with all the power."

"So he did hit you."

"Look, I've got work to do . . ."

"Were you fighting over me? Did he find out that—"

"Cute as you are, Dimples, it's not always about you."

That irritated her. She sank her hands on her hips. "Are you trying to piss me off?"

"Hey, you're responsible for your own emotions."

"You don't want me to care if you got your face bashed in? Fine, I don't care." She snorted out a breath of frustration, turned her head. Men. Stubborn as hell, all of them.

"Liar."

"What?" She whipped her head back around.

"You care."

"Okay, I care, but for the life of me, I don't know why."

He grinned at her as best he could through the swollen eye and busted lip. "Because I'm simply irresistible."

"Yeah, keep telling yourself that." She slung the strap of her purse up onto her shoulder and stalked toward the door.

"Hey, Dimples, where you going?"

"I've got an immovable object to budge."

Flynn marched from the theater across the street to the sheriff's office. "Where is he, Madge?" she asked of the dispatcher seated inside the protective cage at the front desk.

"He's in his office."

"Buzz me in."

"Sure." Madge hit the buzzer underneath her desk that unlocked the door from the lobby to the back offices. Flynn pushed her way through and barreled into his office.

"Flynn," Beau said. "This is a nice surprise. I've been calling around to caterers for the wedding and—"

"Stop!" she commanded.

He blinked at her. "What's wrong? Something's happened. What's happened?"

"You, you're what's happened. Why aren't you in Dallas?"

"They switched the time of my speech. I gave it last night, came back home early to be with you." He pushed back from his chair, came toward her, an expression of confused tolerance on his face. "You're upset."

"Don't patronize me." She raised both her palms, took a step back. "And don't touch me."

"I don't understand. What's going on?"

She slipped his ring off her finger, held it out to him. "I came by to give you this."

"What? Is something wrong with the ring? Isn't it big enough?" he asked.

"Don't play dumb. I know what you did and I'm breaking up with you, Beau."

He looked like she'd socked *him* in the jaw. "Wh—wha—" he stammered. "Haven't I been good to you? Haven't I been patient and understanding and—"

"You beat up Jesse Calloway."

The guilty look on his face said it all. "He's a convicted criminal, Flynn. Don't believe everything he tells you."

"Jesse never mentioned your name. He even denied you beat him up, but I know it was you. He's served his time, Beau. He's paid his dues. He has a right to live his life in peace. Why are you harassing him?"

"You've always had the hots for him, admit it," Beau said. "Secretly you're attracted to riffraff."

Flynn hardened her jaw. "Take this ring right now before I throw it in your face."

"I'm sorry, I shouldn't have said that, but I love you so much, Flynnie . . ."

"You've got a stupid way of showing it, Beau

Trainer." Rage and hurt burned her throat with unshed tears. She wasn't about to let him make her cry.

"You're my best friend."

"No, I'm not. You treat me like I'm your possession. Like you're a dog and I'm your bone."

"That's not true."

"Then why did you beat up Jesse? He can't fight you, Beau. He knows he'll go back to prison if he does. And you know it too. You were trying to get him to fight with you. Admit it. You're gunning for him."

"Why are you so hung up on Calloway?"

"Beau, you busted up his face!"

"I know what it is, you've got this need to fix everyone, and I'm not broken so you go looking to fill that need somewhere else. But you can't fix someone like Jesse Calloway."

"You're not broken? Excuse me, Beau Trainer, that gun at your hip doesn't make you superhuman. Nor does that Eagle Scout badge in your top dresser drawer. It's all just a cover because deep down inside you're nothing but a bully, just like your old man."

Beau's sharp intake of breath told her that she'd stepped over the line. Not only had she crossed the line, but it wasn't really true. Yes, Beau might have bullied Jesse, but that wasn't his basic nature. That was what made this all so unbelievable.

"I can't believe you're siding with this scumbag over your husband-to-be."

"You're no longer my fiancé." She tossed the ring on his desk. "I'm sorry, Beau, it's over. And this time I mean it."

His face shifted, he was trying to be rational, to get his emotions under control, but she could see the pain in his eyes. "We've been together for ten years, Flynn."

"We were together because it was easy for us both, not because we're right for each other. If we were truly meant to be, we wouldn't have allowed circumstances to stop us from getting married."

"You were the one dragging your feet, and now I figure out it's because you've been mooning over a convict for ten years."

"That's ridiculous. I wasn't mooning over Jesse. I was taking care of my dying mother and trying to keep my family from falling apart."

His graze drilled into hers. "Is it ridiculous?"

She made a derisive noise, but her stomach roiled. "Yes it is. I've never even dated Jesse."

Not officially.

"I saw you." He'd gotten his emotions under control. His face was marble now, impassive, cold. That immovable object.

"What are you talking about?"

"I saw you and Jesse last night. Underneath the Sweetheart Tree. Do you have any idea how that made me feel?" He went on in a voice so empty it chilled her to the bone. "You were mine, and when my back was turned you—"

"It was just a kiss."

"Don't give me that," he said harshly.

"It didn't go any further. I didn't cheat on you."

"Maybe you didn't screw him, but you cheated on me just the same. In your heart, and you know what? That's worse."

She could feel his distress. It hurt, knowing she

was hurting him. She hoped he didn't touch her. If he touched her, she feared she'd break into a million fragile pieces. "How is that worse?" she whispered.

"Pretending to love me when you wanted to be with him."

"Beau, I didn't pretend."

"Then if you love me, why are you breaking up with me?" He looked so sad.

It was her instinct to wrap her arms around him to comfort him. She hated to see people suffer. But she didn't want him to misinterpret the gesture. "Leave Jesse Calloway out of the equation. You and I, we're really too much alike to be a good fit."

"It took you ten years to realize this?"

"No, I just kept telling myself it was enough that you were a good person, that you cared about me and I cared about you. But Beau, it isn't enough. Not for me and not for you. The truth is you deserve someone who is wildly, madly, deeply in love with you. You deserve the woman who would have said yes the first time you asked her to marry you, circumstances and complications be damned."

"You're just upset."

"I'm upset with you, yes. But it's more than that. Why are you willing to settle for something less than you deserve?"

"I deserve you."

"You're attached to the idea of me."

"You're the one I want."

"I'm sorry, Beau, no. It's over." Then marshalling every bit of courage she possessed, Flynn turned and walked away.

* * *

For the next couple of days, all over town, Flynn imagined she heard the whispers.

"I heard she threw over the sheriff for that convict."

"You know how women act stupid over bad boys."

"Such a fool, Beau treated her like a queen."

"I thought Flynn had more sense than that."

"Her mother would be so ashamed."

That last one hurt the most, even if it was just conjured up by her own mind, because Flynn knew it was true. Her mother would be ashamed of the way she'd behaved. Why had she done it? What was this dark sway Jesse held over her?

She knew what her mother would say, because she'd heard her say it before. "Jesse Calloway is bad news, Flynn. I don't want to judge, because heaven knows I've made my own mistakes, but his mother died of a drug overdose. No one has any idea who his father was. He ran away from foster homes. No telling what all he's suffered. The boy's emotionally damaged. Even his Aunt Patsy admits he's troubled."

"But Mama," she'd murmured. "You don't know him like I do. Yes, he's got a tough outer shell, but that's just to protect himself. Doesn't Jesse deserve a chance?"

"Certainly, but you don't have to be the one to give it to him."

The truth was, Flynn didn't know if her feelings for Jesse were real or if he was just the catalyst she'd needed to break her engagement to Beau. Maybe her feelings for Jesse were nothing more than a desire to toy with the forbidden. She'd been good for so long, was he merely an excuse to indulge the bad-girl side she'd always struggled to deny? Was she making a big mistake? Was he just using her to humiliate his nemesis, Beau?

But no, you couldn't fake a kiss like the one he'd given her on his birthday underneath the Sweetheart Tree. The man wanted her. She had no doubts about that. And she wanted him.

He's been in prison for ten years. At this point he'd take a blow-up doll.

"It's Jesse," she murmured to herself. "He's not like that . . . he's . . . he's . . ."

What? The man who could ruin her reputation in the town that meant so much to her. Flynn was a people person. Being with Jesse could damage her standing in the community. Did she really want to risk everything that was important to her for the promise of great sex?

He's more to you than that and you know it.

Yes, but did Jesse know it? Was he toying with her, or did he want a real relationship? And if he wanted a real relationship, was she up to dealing with the fallout of loving an outlaw?

Love? Whoa there, Nellie. Aren't you putting the cart before the horse?

She agonized over these thoughts as she pushed her grocery cart through Branson's supermarket. It was after five and the store was crowded with working mothers in their office attire. She rounded the corner by a stacked display of Cheez Doodles, and there, standing beside the meat counter, inspecting a package of filet mignon with an upturned nose, was Kathryn Trainer.

Instantly Flynn braked, and then whipped her

cart around, intent on barreling away toward the dairy section as fast as possible.

"Flynn," Kathryn's voice rang out. "There you are."

Oh God, kill me now. Just strike me dead. Go ahead, slam me with lightning. Put me out of my misery.

"Flynn MacGregor."

She halted her sprint for the sour cream, forced a smile on her face, and turned back around. "Kathryn, I didn't see you there."

Flynn suppressed the sudden urge to reach up and feel to see if her nose had just grown an inch. Cringing, she braced herself for whatever onslaught Kathryn was about to heap upon her.

"Listen dear," her ex-future-mother-in-law said. She wore an expensive beige linen dress, June Cleaver pearls, and two-inch heels. "I've spoken to Father Geyette and he's very excited about performing the ceremony, but with all his duties on Christmas Day, he won't be able to officiate the wedding until late Christmas evening. Will that work for you?"

"Huh?"

Kathryn repeated herself and then added, "A young lady of substance doesn't say, 'Huh,' she says, 'Pardon.'"

"Pardon me."

Kathryn beamed. "Very good. Now about the time of the wedding—"

"You haven't spoken to Beau." Young ladies of substance probably didn't interrupt, but come on, let's be honest, she might be young, but she was no lady, and as far as substance went, well, after the expenses with the Yarn Barn, she had five hundred and sixty-seven dollars in her personal savings account. Not much substance there.

"He came to dinner last night, why?"

Oh, this was just great. Beau hadn't told his mother she'd broken up with him. The coward. Now what was she supposed to do? Tell Kathryn in the middle of the grocery store between the filet mignon and the Cheez Doodles that she'd kicked her son to the curb for acting like a jealous, possessive bully?

"I think you need to talk to Beau about the wedding."

"You're letting him make all the decisions?"

Flynn's throat tightened. She was his mother, let him tell her. "Just talk to Beau."

Kathryn reached out and touched Flynn's arm. "Is there something I need to know?"

The expression in her eyes was one of pure vulnerability, and it rattled Flynn. She'd never seen the formidable woman look anything but in total control. She opened her mouth to tell her, but she couldn't bring herself to say the words. When it came down to it, Flynn hated hurting people. She'd rather hurt herself than someone else.

Now who's the coward?

"Just talk to Beau," she murmured, then abandoned her shopping cart and scurried for the door.

CHAPTER TWELVE

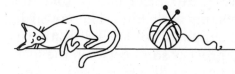

Flynn, get out and live a little.
—Missy Ivey, yearbook entry, 1999

Flustered by what had happened at the supermarket, Flynn returned to the Yarn Barn more mixed up than ever. Things were definitely over between her and Beau. The milk was spilled on that score and she was ready to move forward in her life.

But what of her and Jesse? Where did they stand? Was she ready to take their relationship to the next level? Was she ready to make it official? The gossiping she'd heard in her head would be minor compared to the real gossip that would come pouring out when their coupling was confirmed.

She went up to the Yarn Barn through the outside stairs, assiduously avoiding Jesse. She hadn't talked to him since she'd broken things off with Beau, and she wasn't ready for that encounter just yet.

A large rolled-up rug lay in the middle of the floor. Apparently the delivery had arrived in her absence and Jesse had brought it upstairs. She took from her purse the Swiss Army knife that Beau had given her for her birthday and cut away the plastic. She unfurled the oval braided rug and dragged it to the middle of the floor where she planned on positioning the rocking chairs she had on back order. Everything was coming together. She might not be able to keep her promise to her mother that she would marry Beau, but by gum, she was making Lynn's Yarn Barn happen.

She got to her feet, admiring her handiwork. She'd made a good choice. The room felt more homey and welcoming, and the neutral colors of the rug enhanced the appeal of the parquet floor she had redone after her mess-up. Her mother would love it.

"Here it is, Mom." She sat down tailor-style in the middle of the rug, closed her eyes, and let the moment sweep over her. She didn't often relax and let go, but she was trying. No one was expecting her at home. Carrie would be at her night class, her father was at Froggy's. She didn't have to be anywhere but here. It was an unusual sensation.

Relax. Just breathe.

The setting sun was slipping past the window when she felt the back of her neck prickle. She turned her head, and saw Jesse standing at the top of the stairs. His face was healing. The swelling was gone from his eye, but it was still a harsh color of purple, and the cut on his lip was almost closed.

She'd been so wrapped in savoring her accomplishment that she hadn't heard him come up. His eyes were on her, his gaze sultry.

"I've locked up for the evening. I was just about to leave," he said.

She got to her feet, caught his stare, inhaled it.

Those eyes.

They held the power of an electrical storm—sharp and hot. Ten years away had changed him. He'd always been intense, yes, but now there was a quiet wisdom in the back of those blistering eyes. And a sadness that tugged at something deep within her.

Jesse was her touchstone, she realized with a start. Why and how it came to be, she did not know, but when she looked into those eyes, she felt it.

He came across the room toward her, agile in his cowboy boots. The way he moved in his black Levi's—loose-hipped, fluid, self-assured—jiggled her insides, stole her breath. He smiled that rakish grin.

The sight of him set her heart to singing, stoked her longing. She felt hot and sticky and achy.

"Flynn," he said, "is it true?"

"Is what true?"

"I heard your broke your engagement to Trainer."

"I did."

He held his arms open then, just opened them wide. She ran to him unfettered, skipping across the parquet floor covered with the braided rug.

He swept her into his embrace and spun her around, and time seemed to slow to this one perfect moment when she had it all. The Yarn Barn was official, her father was off the sauce, Carrie was in school, and she was in Jesse's arms again.

She heard her heart pounding, felt his beat a

corresponding rhythm when she splayed her palm over his chest. She spied a smattering of dark blue paint on his neck. He'd spent the morning painting the front of the building. She planted a kiss on his neck, traveled up to find his earlobe. His familiar scent filled her nostrils, reached down and caressed her lungs.

Jesse.

He'd been at the back of her mind for years, even when she thought she'd forgotten about him or had mistaken how she really felt about him, and he about her.

Be careful, go slow.

She wasn't sure how much of this feeling she could stand. It was too strong, too wild, too un-Flynn-like. She was accustomed to being confident and in charge and considerate of other people's needs. Being with Jesse was like taking that five-thousand-piece jigsaw puzzle you'd spent every night working on for three months and heedlessly tossing it into the air.

But oh how she wanted him. And that was what scared her most of all. This desire—burning, raging, out of control. She knew for certain this feeling was what she'd been avoiding, why she'd stayed so long with Beau even when it wasn't fair to him. Beau made her feel stable. Jesse made her feel—*real*. And she simply didn't know what to do about it.

She wanted him, but there were walls between them. Prison walls, and not just the concrete kind. Intangible walls of loss and pain and nervous expectation. He could break her so easily. Split her heart clean in two.

At that thought, she pulled back, stepped from his embrace. She saw a shadow of something in his eyes. *Where do we go from here? Is it time? Is it right? Should we just take a leap of faith and jump? How do we start tearing down these walls? How do we keep from hurting each other?* The questions poured in on her, but she did not speak her doubts aloud.

Jesse was a man of action. Spur-of-the-moment, free as the wind. He didn't have the restriction of community. The fear of being cast out. Belonging meant more to Flynn than anything in the world. If she gave in to her sexual needs, would the town she loved ostracize her? Would she lose everything?

Before she had time to reconsider her emotions, he grabbed her arm, pulled her back against his chest, then brought his mouth down on hers in a kiss so firm and hungry she just went limp.

Whoa. Slow down. Her expectations were so high, she feared the plummet.

Jesse must have sensed her thoughts, because he cupped his palm under her chin and raised her face up so her eyes met his. "It's been a very long time for me, Flynn. I'm not sure if I remember how to do this, the niceties, the tenderness. I'm not sure if I can give you the experience you need."

"All I need is to be with you," she murmured.

"I'll try my best, but woman, you are so amazing." He ran his hands over her body, came to a stop at her waist, and let loose with a deep-throated masculine groan of appreciation.

"You didn't, after prison, find someone to be with?"

"I thought about it," he admitted.

"But you didn't."

"No."

"Why not?"

"I kept thinking no one could compare to you."

"Now you're putting me on a pedestal."

"What's wrong with that?"

"What if I can't live up to *your* expectations?"

"How about this? No expectations."

"You mean, don't have sex?"

"That's what I'm thinking. Let's just kiss and cuddle and feel each other up like we did when we in high school."

"You'd . . . be okay with that?"

"Would you?"

"Sure, sure."

"Okay, so just to get this straight, no expectations, no sex unless we change our minds midway."

Flynn licked her lips. "Right."

"Things get too overwhelming, you just say the word and I'll stop."

"You can do that?" She put a hand on his abdomen just above his belt buckle.

He swallowed visibly. "I'll try my damnedest."

The dark desire in his eyes rocketed her libido into orbit. "Me too," she whispered.

Slowly, Jesse pulled her up flush against his chest.

"Can you kiss," she asked, "with your sore lip?"

"To hell with my sore lip." He pushed her hair back off her shoulder and sank his mouth down on the side of her neck.

She felt the tingle all the way to her toes. He remembered her erogenous zone. His hair tickled her throat. His scent filled her nose, her soul. Musky clean and a little painty. He made her feel exposed, raw. He was dangerous. She was vulnerable. She was afraid of it, this vulnerability. She was accustomed to being strong, in control, in charge. With one well-placed kiss, he took it all away.

His teeth lightly nipped her skin, and he tightened his grip on her waist as her knees completely gave way.

Even after all these years, after all their time apart, he knew her body better than she did. Beau had never found her secret trigger spot, Jesse zeroed right in.

"Do you still like this?"

She couldn't answer, only whimper.

"Mmm, good to know. I love how you smell, like watermelon and little purple flowers. I love the way you taste, salty, yet sweet, like a PayDay candy bar. That's the way of you, Flynn, tart-tongued at times, but it's only to hide that tender, tender heart."

He skimmed his hands up underneath her blouse, his palms slipping over skin. His fingers skated around to unhook her bra, and the next thing she knew it was off her, flung somewhere across the room.

Magic. The man was Copperfield with a bra. Some things never changed.

Jesse took her breath, and her wandering thoughts, when he ensnared her lips with his hot, wet mouth and sucked her skin. Radiant heat mushroomed outward, across her shoulders, headed pell-mell for her breasts.

Her pulse leaped, bounded. Her nipples tightened. She reveled in the luxury of his embrace and took a deep breath. She inhaled, and his manly scent—motorcycle oil, fresh paint, pure essence of Jesse—filled her lungs.

They ripped at each other's lips, tearing away the veil of the past, revealing themselves to each other as they were today, in this moment, aching and hungry and open to each other, crashing the boundaries that had separated them for so long.

He lowered his lids, sultry, half-mast. Lust for her burned in his eyes, stiffened the length of him pressed hard against her.

"Do you want me to stop now?" he whispered. "Have we gone too far? Are you out of your comfort zone?"

She opened her mouth to tell him yes, it was too much, but no words came out. Instead she leaned over and nipped at his shoulder.

He felt so good. She felt so good. What he was doing to her felt too good. Everything about this man, his lips, his fingers, his tongue, his arms, his gray-blue eyes, the heady fragrance of his skin, made her want to beg for more, more, more.

Take me, take what you want, take everything, leave me stripped raw and bare and savagely sated.

The viciousness of her thoughts stunned her. She'd never felt so unbridled, so free.

More, more, take more. Let me give you everything I have to give. Lips and teeth and tongues and hard, wet kisses.

She was overpowered, overwhelmed, overcome, over-everythinged. Jesse was a fighter jet and she was in freefall. Nothing to grab on to, nothing to stop herself from plummeting.

His thumbs brushed lazily against her nipples,

tightened the already stiff peaks, driving her crazy. Her breath hung up somewhere between her lungs and her throat. No air, just the smell of Jesse.

Stop. Stop this before I lose my mind.

A throbbing ache pooled deep inside her womb. Reflexively she pressed her knees together, more to keep herself from falling down than anything else. If he wasn't holding on to her, she would probably already be on the ground.

His fingers fumbled. Copperfield having magic trouble? Fumbled with the buttons on her blouse, trying to undo them, finally he just grabbed her shirt and pulled it open. Buttons popped, hit the floor with a little *spit-spat* noise. Material ripped.

Her hands were on the hem of his T-shirt, dragging it up and over his head. *Bye-bye, T-shirt. Hello, hard-muscled man.* She whistled in a breath, traced shaky fingers over his striated chest.

Skin to skin. Chest to breasts. They were naked from the waist up and breathing like labored engines chugging up a steep grade. His pelvis was pressed tight against hers, and he was hard and long and thick. Was he as big as it felt like he was? A raw, nagging twinge bloomed between her thighs. His calloused fingertips scratched rough against her tender nipples. Her hands were cold against his heated belly.

Simultaneously they inhaled the same excited sigh.

"Wanna stop?" he murmured.

She grabbed for his belt. Panting, he pulled at the snap of her jeans.

Now, now, gotta have him. Can't wait, can't stop, can't think, can't breathe.

Jesse.

Reality. More intense, more nerve-wracking than her dreams. What if she didn't please him? What if he didn't please her? What if after all this time, all this waiting, they were bad in bed together?

"Shh," he said. "Stop thinking. You're thinking too much."

"How do you know?" she whispered.

"You've got the oddest little frown on your face like you're mentally arguing with yourself. I know you, Flynn MacGregor, you have a hard time just being in the moment. Be here with me now, Flynn. Don't think. Don't live in the past. Don't project into the future. Don't stand on the sidelines any longer. Stop ignoring your own needs. Shut down that noisy little voice and listen to your body."

"Okay, okay, I'll try."

"No trying. Do it."

"Yes, sir."

"Here, let me help you." He pulled off her shoes, tugged her jeans down over her hips. She kicked them aside.

Jesse knelt in front of her. He cupped her buttocks in his palms, looked up at her with complete and total awe. The light in his eyes shook her very soul.

"Beautiful," he cooed. "So, so beautiful."

The pleasure of his words, the expression of pure gratitude on his face toasted her skin, warmed her heart. He pressed his cheek against her belly, held her close to his head. She could hear her heartbeat pounding blood through her ears and felt hot tingles of delight race over her skin.

"Mmm," he murmured, lightly nipping the skin

just below her navel with his teeth. "You taste so good. Tender. Juicy."

"That's me, tender and juicy, just like chicken," she joked. She pulled in a shaky breath and lowered her lashes. *Keep kissing on down to the sweet spot*, she thought, but didn't have the courage to say it.

"Lucky for you, I love chicken."

His tongue was at the top of her panties, and for all practical purposes her mind had gone to mush. His hands were softly kneading her butt cheeks and his hair was tickling her belly and she was aware of absolutely everything. The smell of new rug, the ticking clock on the wall, the rich taste of lust on the back of her tongue, the sight of Jesse's teeth tugging on her white cotton panties, the feel of his warm breath against her achy flesh.

"Lucky me," she whispered as tiny little campfires ignited along her nerve endings. Everywhere his lips touched, she blazed.

A robust laugh rolled from him. He tilted his head and looked up at her, his eyes shiny with lust. His hands moved from her bottom to her waist. "Feel like you won the lottery, do you?"

"No," she said, "I feel like you won the lottery. I'm the prize here."

"Oh, you think so?"

"I know so."

"Such an ego," he said, and drew her down on the rug in front of him.

They were eye to eye, nose to nose, his hands still resting on her waist. For the longest moment he said nothing, did nothing except peer into her.

"Knock, knock, anybody home," she finally ventured.

"Gotta," he said.

"Gotta what?"

"Gotta have some of this," he said, and with a low groan, he tugged her against his chest for a soft, slow kiss. He drew her tongue from her mouth with gentle suction. He reached up and cupped the sides of her face with both palms.

Her hands got busy exploring him, moving them up his thick biceps to his shoulders. She dug her fingertips into his muscles, kneaded them. Heat rolled off him in waves, causing sweat to dew between her breasts.

Jesse made love to her with his mouth; in turn she combed her fingers through the sprig of hairs at his chest. "Woman," he mumbled against her neck, "you drive me crazy."

"Right back at you. You're not alone in the booby hatch."

He pulled her into his lap then, and she felt the throb of his erection through the fabric of his jeans. The man was enormous, and the pressure! Glorious pressure squeezed the floor of her pelvis.

She rocked against him.

He groaned really loudly this time—all masculine need and hungry arousal. She was hot, he was hot, the room was a frickin' sauna. They were kissing again, their tongues dancing, dueling, taunting. She dug her fingers into his skin and kissed him and breathed him and pushed her bottom against his stiff penis.

Sweetness vanished from his kiss. Tenderness?

Out the window. Everything was rough and primal and wild and carnal.

They were moving too fast, rocketed by passion and the past; she should tell him to stop, but her tongue didn't work. Who was she kidding? It worked too well. She was licking and tasting and teasing and having way too much fun to stop.

More. She had to have more.

His thumbs brushed her nipples, and she let out a hungry moan. Her hands were all over him. Touching, stroking, probing, exploring. Her head spun, her heart thumped, her skin burned. Her breasts tightened, her nipples beaded. Had she ever felt a pleasure this delicious? Yes. Once. On a bridge, long ago.

She was in his lap, riding his thighs, pressing her palms against the zipper of his jeans where his penis strained, dying to get out and come play. She groped him through the denim, feeling every hard edge of him.

He groaned.

The ache between her thighs was painful now. A wet, hot ache that swirled her brain. One of his hands stayed at her breasts, lightly pinching a nipple while the other hand crept down to give as good as he was getting. He slipped past the waistband of her panties, his thick finger searching for her most sensitive spot.

His hand was between her thighs, his thumb on her . . .

Oh, dear Lord, he'd found it.

She squirmed and wriggled, pushing against his hand. She was on fire, burning, burning. But she wasn't ready for this. "Jesse, wait . . ." She panted.

"You mean it?" His voice was ragged, disappointed. "You want me to stop?"

"Yes, no . . ."

Jesse pulled back, looked her squarely in the eyes. "Which is it? Yes or no?"

"I want you . . ."

"Well then, that's settled. I want you too." He slipped his hand back between her thighs; the air was sweet with the smell of her sex. Her scent caused his cock to twitch. She was so hot and wet down there. Wet and ready for him.

Jesse wanted her so badly. Had wanted her for ten long years. Lust pounded through him. This was it. She was finally going to be his. He shifted her in his arms, stretched her out on the braided rug, looked down into her face. "You are so beautiful," he whispered.

"You're not half bad yourself."

Gently, he parted her slick, warm flesh with his fingers. She was dripping for him, and when he slipped his finger inside her, she gasped and her eyes widened and she grasped his shoulders in her hands.

"Does that feel good?"

"Yes, yes."

He could feel her trembling against his hand. "You're so wet. You have no idea how much you turn me on. I want to kiss you here." He touched her clit. "Lap you up with my tongue."

Her muscles tensed and her breath grew shallow and quick.

"Do you want me to use my tongue on you here?" He lightly strummed the nub of her clit with his thumb.

"Uh-huh." She nodded. "Jesse," she rasped.

"Yes, sweetheart?"

"Please, please . . ."

He flicked his thumb against her clit, softer and faster.

"Please, please, I want you to . . ."

"I know."

"No, no—" Her words broke off on a strangled cry of pleasure. She moaned and clutched him and quivered.

His heart galloped. She was coming, big time. Her eyes widened and her face twisted up into a look of pure orgasmic ecstasy. Perspiration popped out on her face, and when she'd finished shuddering, he drew her to him, rocked her against his chest, feeling mighty damn proud of himself.

He nestled her in the crook of his arm, kissed her forehead, and ached to be buried inside her hot feminine body. She had no idea what this restraint was costing him.

"Oh my." She exhaled and looked up at him. "I've never . . . that was . . ."

"Flynn one, Jesse zero." He laughed.

"So that's how it is? We're keeping score?" Her eyes glimmered mischievously. Then she pushed him over onto his back and straddled him, her glorious breasts bobbing sexily in the light from the overhead fluorescent bulb. "You're in trouble now, bucko."

"Says who?"

"Says me. First thing, those jeans have got to

go." She undid the snaps of his jeans and grabbed hold of the waistband. "Hips off the floor," she said, but she didn't have to tell him, Jesse was already arching his back, his cock twitching to break free.

He heard her audibly suck in her breath when she got a good look at him, but when she touched the head of his shaft he was the one sucking in air.

She slid down his body until her butt was on his knees and her breasts were resting on his upper thighs and her tongue . . . hot damn her maddening tongue . . . was lightly flicking over his tip. She grasped his shaft with one hand, cupped his balls in the other.

"Jesse," she murmured. "I had no idea you were so big and juicy and beautiful."

He propped himself up on his elbows so he could watch her swirl her tongue around him. She glanced up, and her eyes locked on his. She winked, flashed her dimples, then ducked her head. The intensity of sensation quickly grew too much for him to fight against and he just sank back on the rug and let her have at him.

She toyed with him a moment more and then she drew him into her mouth, taking him as deeply as she could.

Jesse moaned as the heat escalated inside him. Her rhythm picked up. Her hands slid all over his body. Indescribable, this intimacy. His chest expanded, tightened. It was unlike anything he'd ever experienced. This took the meaning of sex to a whole new level for him.

"Yes," he hissed as she moved back and forth,

her hair a silky glide beneath his fingers. "Yes, yes, yes."

Flynn worked her magic, with her fingers, her tongue leading him into uncharted territory. He was on sensory overload as she gently guided him to a paradise he'd only dreamed of. But this wasn't a dream. The warm wetness of her mouth, the sweet taste of her lingering on his tongue, the heavenly smell of her feminine scent, the sound of her raspy breathing. This new awareness of him, of her, was breaking up his outer shell. All the old failures and disappointments fell away.

Her mouth moved over him without caution or fear. She pushed him past his knowledge of himself. He had never before been so physically possessed. His knees were quaking and he was as loaded and hot as he could ever be. Past thinking, with no coherent thought residing in his head, he was nothing but cock and ass and balls.

Relentlessly, Flynn pushed him forward. He was aching, gushing, throbbing, beating. He threw back his head and let loose with a primal cry, pleading for release from this magnificent torture, for the ecstasy he could almost touch.

Tingling. Pounding. Rushing.

He had no idea she was capable of wreaking such havoc. And then, just like that, it was upon him. Jesse tumbled. Jerking and trembling into the abyss, hurtling across time and space. Lost in the wonder of her awesome tongue.

He peered down, blinked. He could barely see. He lay there sweating, shuddering, panting for breath.

Flynn was sitting at his feet, smiling coyly, her lips glistening creamy and wet. She winked at him and swallowed his essence. She curled up on the rug beside him, spooned against his back. For a long while they just lay there together, not speaking, waiting for him to recover.

And then her cell phone rang.

She moved to get up. He grabbed her wrist. "Don't go, don't answer it."

"It might be important."

"I'm important. This is important. We're important."

"My family," she said.

When she gave him a look like that how could he deny her? He waved a hand. "Go ahead."

She scrambled off the rug, went for her purse, snagged up the phone. "What's up?"

Jesse rolled onto his side, watching her. In his eyes she was the most beautiful woman on earth.

"Okay, don't panic. I'll be right there." She hung up the phone, started putting on her clothes. "Oh crap, look at my blouse. You're hell on clothes, Calloway." Her blouse hung open, buttonless.

He grinned sheepishly. "Take my shirt."

She scooped his Harley T-shirt up off the floor, wrestled it over her head.

"What's up?" he asked.

"I'm sorry," she said, leaning over to kiss him. "For now it will have to stay Flynn one, Jesse one. They had a water main break down at Froggy's and my father is flipping out. Gotta go. See you later."

"Wait, wait." He got to his feet. "I'll go with you."

Flynn shook her head. "Nah, that's okay. Nothing I can't handle."

"But maybe you could just use the company."

"Relax," she said. "Bask in the glow."

Without another word, she plunged down the stairs, leaving Jesse feeling as if he was nothing more than her dirty little secret.

CHAPTER THIRTEEN

*"Which Bridge to Cross,
Which Bridge to Burn" by Vince Gill*
—Twilight High class song of 1999

Ten minutes later, Flynn pulled into Froggy's empty parking lot. Her father's car was there and so was Carrie's. The outdoor neon sign was switched off, but inside the lights blazed. Floyd must have closed up and sent everyone home after the water main break.

Feeling edgy and breathless, she pushed her fingers through her hair and let out a sigh, her mind webbed with thoughts of what had just happened in the Yarn Barn.

Jesse.

The taste of him lingered on her tongue, his smell loitered in her nose, her skin still sizzled from his touch, her ears hummed with the sound of his rich and sinful voice. When had he so completely captivated her?

Who was she kidding? She'd never gotten him out of her system. All this time she'd been using her mother's illness, her father's problems with alcohol, and raising her siblings as an excuse to avoid saying yes to Beau, because deep down inside she'd always been in love with Jesse Calloway.

The full realization of her feelings hit her. This was more than a schoolgirl crush. She'd been trying to deny it for ten years, but she couldn't deny it any longer. Flynn didn't know whether to throw her head back and howl at the moon, or giggle until her side ached. In the end, she did what she always did. She stuffed her own emotions to the side and did what needed to be done to help others. Inside Froggy's she found her father and Carrie ankle-deep in water with mops in their hands.

"What happened?" she asked.

"Ground must have shifted," her father said. "Central pipe in the kitchen burst. I knew the soil under the pier was eroding, but I didn't realize the foundation under Froggy's was so shaky."

Flynn suppressed a groan. This was going to cost a mint to fix, and insurance probably didn't cover it.

"Thanks for coming so quickly, sweetheart, but I managed to find the main cut-off valve," her father said, clearly proud of himself. "Imagine, I've owned this place for almost twenty years and I never knew where the water valve was located."

"Good work, Dad, now where's the wet vac?"

"We have a wet vac?"

"We do and it'll make the cleanup go much faster."

"Well, what do you know, I had no idea we had a wet vac."

Flynn bit her tongue to keep from saying, *That's probably because you were soused to the gills when I bought it*, but her father was doing his best. No need for sarcasm at this stage of the game.

"Keep mopping," she instructed. "I'll go in search of the wet vac."

After slogging on tiptoe through the drenched dining area, she headed out the back door toward the storage shed. She pulled the key ring from her pocket, unlocked the door, flipped on the switch, and stepped over a stack of plastic buckets that had seen better days.

Okay, so back to Jesse. How did he feel about her? That was the scary part. Not knowing if she was just a good-time fling for him. Or worse, was she just a tool with which to gouge Beau?

Ouch. That thought hurt. Especially since she'd just admitted to herself she was in love with him and that time and distance had done nothing to change her feelings. Was she being stupid? Was she just asking to get her heart broken?

Ah, there was the wet vac. She reached down, grabbed it by the handle, and lugged it toward the door. She'd just stepped out of the storage shed and was busy snapping the lock back into place when it happened.

The bang was so loud it rang her ears as if she were a punchy heavyweight who'd taken a hard fist to the temple. The windowpanes rattled. The ground vibrated. Were there earthquakes in Texas? Shocked, she spun around to see the river behind her light up in a crazy clap of over-the-top fireworks.

She wheezed in air. Blood slithered through her veins suddenly gone ice-cold. She was frozen, welded, watching. Seconds later she was in motion, abandoning the shop vacuum and sprinting at a dead run to the water's edge. Mouth agape, she watched burning debris rain from the sky.

It took a moment for it all to soak in.

The old Twilight Bridge—the place where she'd spent some of her happiest hours as a kid, the place where she'd had her first kiss (and her first orgasm at Jesse's wicked hands)—was gone.

Her mind sprinted. Her pulse skittered. She sucked in the acrid smell of burning timbers, watched the iron railings collapse, leaving only the brick and mortar support columns.

Someone had blown up the Twilight Bridge!

Instantly she was in motion, her hand reaching around to unclip her cell phone from her waistband, calmly punching in the numbers 9–1–1. Even as she functioned outwardly, inwardly her thoughts tumbled back to the past.

To that other night. To that other time. When Jesse had blown up the bridge. She recalled the exact moment he lit the match to the M80, grabbed her hand, and yelled, "Jump."

She'd never done anything so wild before or since. She'd taken his hand, taken a leap of faith, and jumped.

That explosion hadn't been nearly as loud or as forceful as this one, but in her sixteen-year-old mind, it had been just as spectacular. They'd hit the water at the same moment the powerful firecracker detonated. She gulped in air as they plunged deep into the Brazos, Jesse's hand still clinging tightly to hers. They surfaced in unison, bobbing up, falling back, floating with their eyes to the sky and their blood slipping quicksilver through their veins.

Together, they'd stared up at the gaping, smoking black hole. Something had nudged her elbow, and she realized it was a wooden plank knocked from the bridge's runners. The railings trembled like vibrating tuning forks.

She'd sat up treading water, realizing other planks surrounded them. The river was littered with planks. In the pale moonlight, they looked like long bones blanched ghostly white. Sadness rushed over her then as it was rushing over her now.

That blast had rendered the bridge undrivable. It had been closed to cars and unofficially designated as a footbridge. But this . . . this blast . . . was different.

The bridge that had held so many memories had been completely destroyed.

Along with the rest of the concerned crowd, Patsy stood on the Twilight side of the river's edge, immersed in the foggy midnight dampness, staring agog at remains of the town's beloved landmark, shivering in the knitted sweater she'd thrown over her pajamas.

Firemen bustled around them, dragging their big hoses back to the trucks. On both sides of the riverbank, red, white, and blue lights from the highway patrol cars strobed against the darkness. The air lay thick with the smell of charred timbers. Several people coughed against the smoke.

The old Twilight Bridge, built on the very spot where the original Twilight Sweethearts had met fifteen years after the Civil War had torn them asunder, was nothing but a pile of smoldering rubble. Looking at the ruins sent Patsy's stomach scraping along the bottom of her house slippers. She'd spent many childhood hours on that old suspension bridge—swan-diving off into the Brazos, picnicking with her friends and gabbing about boys, experiencing her first kiss with Hondo, escaping up there to sob her heart out when she lost their baby. Now it was gone, like so much else in her life.

She didn't expect it, this knife to the chest, but she knew her emotions were not just about the destroyed bridge. All around her people were shaking their heads, speaking in low, hushed voices about their memories of the bridge and the influence it had had on their lives.

A wake, we're having a wake.

Tears burned her eyes; blinking, she turned away. The acrid smoke was making her dizzy and nauseated.

A new batch of onlookers arrived and the tone of the conversation changed as the initial questions cropped up again.

"What happened?"

"Dunno."

"Pulled me out of a deep sleep. Set my dogs to barking."

"Who could have done something like this?"

"Had to be dynamite. Something much stronger than when Jesse Calloway set off that M80."

"Jesse *is* back in town."

Several heads swiveled to glare at Patsy. A ripple of apprehension raised the hairs on her forearm. This could turn ugly quick. Where was Jesse? She had to find him, let him know what was going on. Fishing her keys from her pocket, she headed toward her car parked haphazardly with dozens of others on the nearby boat ramp.

She sensed him before she saw him, his face in the crowd—hard-jawed, dark-eyed, all male.

Hondo.

He was in his paramedic uniform, crisp white shirt, blue slacks, stethoscope dangling from around his neck. She should have expected him to be here. There'd been an explosion. Of course he would have come with the fire crew to check it out, make sure no one had been harmed in the blast.

He sauntered toward her. Patsy gulped, reached for her door handle, and then froze when she realized she was completely blocked in by a minivan. She couldn't run away from him without drawing attention to herself. She was cornered.

Resolutely she squared her shoulders, took a fortifying breath, and met his steely gaze.

"Patsy," he said with a sharp nod as he rounded the bumper of her Crown Vic.

"Hondo." It took every ounce of courage she possessed not to flinch or glance away. Why had she come here? *Curiosity killed the cat.*

"Can we talk?"

"What about?"

"Jesse."

"Oh," she said, not really sure what she'd expected him to say. "What about him?"

"He didn't do this." Hondo waved at the downed bridge sticking up out of the water like some hellish bouquet of ebony bones.

"I know he didn't."

"You and I are the only ones." He was within two feet of her, closer than he'd been in years. "Everyone else thinks he did it."

"Based on what?"

"Past history."

"He was seventeen, he knocked a couple of holes in the aged runners with a powerful firecracker. He was a rebellious kid, having a lark. This is . . ." Patsy nodded toward the river. "Malicious destruction."

"Still, first time he comes to town he shoots off fireworks, causes the bridge to be closed to car traffic and turned into a footbridge. Now, the second time he comes back to town after spending time in the state prison. The explosives are bigger, the damage beyond salvage . . ."

"Whose side are you on?"

"Jesse's. I'm merely pointing out what the rest of Twilight will be thinking."

She wanted to ask him why he cared about Jesse so much, why he'd visited him in prison and loaned him the money to buy the motorcycle shop, but she was afraid of the answer so she avoided it, as she had for years.

"Especially Beau Trainer," Hondo said.

"Speak of the devil," Patsy muttered as Beau drove up.

"Are we the only people in town who think that pup is too big for his britches?" Hondo asked.

"Jesse," she said. "And Flynn."

"What's going on between those two?"

"Flynn and Beau or Flynn and Jesse?"

"Either, both."

Patsy sighed. She'd wondered the same thing herself. "The girl's conflicted. On the one hand she's got the lawman, on the other, the outlaw. One leads you to safety, the other straight to hell. Question is, which one is which?"

"Sounds awfully damn familiar."

Their gazes met, and for a flash Patsy saw pain in his eyes so stark it made her chest ache and her throat close off. "Yeah."

"Mrs. Cross, may I have a word with you?" Beau called to Patsy.

"Someone under thirty shouldn't have that kind of authority," Hondo muttered.

"Once upon a time you said trust no one over thirty."

"Yeah, well, once upon a time I was a dumbass."

They smiled at each other then; it was slight and fleeting, but it was a smile. A tentative truce after all these years? Patsy's heart fluttered.

"Patsy, a word," Beau repeated.

"I'll go find Jesse and warn him what's coming," Hondo murmured. "You keep an eye on little Big Britches."

"Thank you." She said it so softly she wasn't sure Hondo even heard her, but then he reached out, took her hand, and gave it a quick, reassuring squeeze.

One bridge had come down tonight, but was another unexpectedly being rebuilt?

She felt awkward and self-conscious, but she squeezed his hand in return. She thought of their past. Thought of her husband lying in a nursing home, crazy with Alzheimer's. Thought of her dead sister, Phoebe. Thought of Jesse and Flynn and Beau. Thought of the stupid things people did in the name of love.

Stupid, destructive, irrevocable things.

"Where's your nephew?" Trainer asked Patsy.

Jesse had been running along the river when he heard the explosion. He'd been jogging, trying to sublimate his physical needs and thinking about Flynn. But the noise and bright flash of light had jolted right through his bones. After that all he could think about was getting to Flynn and making sure she was okay.

He showed up just in time to see Trainer pestering his aunt.

From his place in the shadows, Jesse could see the stress on Patsy's face as she stood underneath the vapor flood lamp beside the sheriff. His pulse pounded. He knew who was going to be blamed for this. He also had a sneaking suspicion who'd blown it up. But no one would believe him. Reflexively, Jesse touched his black eye.

"I don't know," Patsy answered.

Jesse stepped from the darkness. "Quit badgering my aunt. I'm right here, Trainer. What do you want with me?"

Trainer whirled around and drew his service weapon. "On the ground, Calloway. You're under arrest for the bombing of the Twilight Bridge."

* * *

Moe called an emergency town council meeting to discuss the fate of the Twilight Bridge. Just before six P.M. on Monday evening, the movers and shakers of Twilight crowded into city hall. The air boiled with discussion of the downed bridge and speculation on whether Jesse Calloway was the culprit.

Flynn took a seat near the front beside her father and Carrie. She kept looking over her shoulder, watching the door, waiting to see if Jesse was going to put in an appearance. She'd learned through the grapevine that Beau had arrested Jesse the night before and that Patsy had hired a high-powered lawyer from Fort Worth who'd gotten him out on bail. Jesse hadn't come into the motorcycle shop that day, and when she tried calling him, his cell phone went to voice mail. Was he lying low on advice from his attorney?

At six sharp, Moe and Patsy took the podium.

Beau strode in, threading his way through the overstuffed aisles, marching right straight up to the front. He didn't sit, but stood with his back against the wall, arms folded over his chest, surveying the throng. His gaze lit on Flynn's. His eyes narrowed, his lips thinned, and he gave her a slight, curt nod. He looked as if he hadn't slept in a week.

Flynn saw the wounded pride in his eyes. Her stomach churned.

Patsy called the meeting to order. "First off, Sheriff Trainer has asked to speak to our collective." She moved aside. "Sheriff."

Beau stepped up to the microphone. "I'm issuing a formal announcement. The old Twilight Bridge has been condemned. It's a crime scene and it's been cordoned off. I don't want to see anyone hanging around."

"Exactly what happened, Sheriff?" Vida Lewis called out.

"We heard you'd arrested a suspect," said the hardware store owner, Mr. Ivey.

"I heard it was Jesse Calloway," someone else muttered. "That kid's been nothing but trouble ever since Patsy dragged him into Twilight."

"Is that true, Sheriff?"

Flynn's muscles tensed.

"I can't comment on an ongoing investigation," Beau said. "But I want to make it clear the bridge is off limits to everyone. We've already had people going down looking to take pieces of brick as souvenirs. My men have better things to do than chase off looky-loos."

"So that's it?" asked Dotty Mae. "The bridge that's been a mainstay of this community is gone. *Phhttt.* Just like that? Where will the young lovers go to neck? Where will the kids go diving in the summer? Where will the swallows nest?"

"Perhaps you should ask those questions of the person who decided to blow up the bridge." Beau's gaze fixed on the doorway.

All the heads swiveled in unison. Flynn was struck by how choreographed the moment felt. Like an exaggerated musical production. *Yes, we got trouble. Right here on the Brazos River.* And her head turned right along with everyone else.

Jesse slouched at the back of the room, shoulder braced nonchalantly against the doorjamb, that familiar laconic smile tugging at his lips.

A ripple of exclamations ran through the crowd.

Flynn's heart somersaulted.

"Anybody got something to say to me?" Jesse asked. "You best speak your mind now or forever hold your peace."

A dropping straight pin would have detonated the stillness of the room loud as a sonic boom.

"What?" Jesse sauntered forward, his gaze landing first on one person and then another. "No one wants to accuse me of anything?"

Several people studiously stared at their feet.

"What about you, Mrs. Qualls? I remember when you accused me of beheading your garden gnomes. You couldn't believe that it was your very own grandson, so you sent Clinton Trainer over to bust my chops. Remember that?"

The snooty Mrs. Qualls shook her head, her tight bun wobbled, and she splayed a hand to her throat. "I don't recall that at all."

" 'Course you don't. Selective memory loss. Nice to have." He moseyed down the aisle toward the front of the room. With each step forward that he took, Flynn's pulse quickened.

"What about you, Mr. Ivey? You accused me of shoplifting. Light bulbs, I think it was. And darn if you didn't have your poker buddy, Sheriff Clinton Trainer, shake me down. And wasn't it odd that when you later found those light bulbs in your storeroom, you didn't bother exonerating me."

Mr. Ivey's face paled. "How . . . how did you know I found those bulbs later?"

"I dated your daughter Missy for a while. She told me."

Mr. Ivey's complexion flamed from ashen to florid. "You? You dated my Missy?"

"More accurately, she dated me. She was the one throwing pebbles at my bedroom window, not the other way around. She's some kisser, that Missy. You tell her that the next time you see her."

Flynn felt simultaneously hot and cold. She knew Jesse was simply taking up for himself, the way he hadn't been able to do as a confused, troubled teen, but it made her uncomfortable. If she was being honest about it, she didn't want to hear that he'd enjoyed kissing Missy Ivey.

"Jesse," Patsy said from her place on stage beside Beau. "Did you blow up the bridge?"

"I did not."

"Then that's good enough for me. Let's move on."

"Whoa." Mr. Ivey shot to his feet. "You can't just sweep things under the rug like that, Councilwoman Cross. He's your nephew."

"Plus he's a convict," Mrs. Qualls said.

"Yeah," someone else threw in.

"I can prove I didn't do it," Jesse said. "I have an alibi."

That got everyone's attention.

"Yeah," Beau challenged. "Who?"

"I'm not revealing her name to you piranhas." Jesse did not look at her.

This is your chance, on your feet. Exonerate him. Flynn tried to move but her butt was welded to the seat. The truth was, she hadn't been with Jesse the minute the bridge had blown up.

It doesn't matter. You know he didn't have time to do it. Even ignoring the logistics, you know he didn't do it. Speak up.

She cleared her throat, tried to formulate a

speech. Jesse might not have been looking at her, but Beau sure was. His blister-hot gaze deep-fried her face. "An alibi witness isn't going to do you much good if she won't come forward," Beau said. "You sure she thinks enough of you to pull your bacon out of the fire?"

Was it her imagination, or was everyone in the room *except* Jesse staring at her?

"You should be ashamed of yourself, Jesse Calloway," said Mrs. Pickles, who ran the day care at the Ruby Street Baptist Church. "Lying about having an alibi."

"That bridge was a vital part of our history. It was one of the oldest viable suspension bridges left in the state until he blew it up the first time," declared Abel Hennessey, a local contractor. The man reminded Flynn of a bulldog with his jowly cheeks, smashed-in nose, and pugnacious set to his thick shoulders. "He done it once, ain't it likely he done it again?"

"It could be just as likely that someone blew up the bridge precisely because they knew you'd accuse Jesse," Patsy said. "Have you thought about that?"

"Have you thought about the fact that your drug addict sister gave birth to a criminal? And when you brought him to Twilight, you brought a viper into our midst?" Hennessey barked.

Things were turning ugly.

Quick, do something to calm everyone down. Flynn leaped to her feet. "Let's all take a deep breath. We don't know who dynamited the bridge. According to Fire Chief Rutledge, the investigation is still ongoing. Let's not jump to conclusions or point fingers. Instead, let's focus on what we can do about it."

She finally dared to look at Jesse. His gaze was inscrutable.

"Flynn's right," Patsy interjected.

"I want to put my bid in for the salvage job," Hennessey said.

"Before you start picking over the bones of the bridge," Flynn added, "I have an idea."

"Come on up here, Flynn, and tell us your plans." Beau stepped back from the microphone.

She eased down the row, climbing over knees, dodging feet, and ended up in the aisle not far from where Jesse stood. She didn't have the courage to look him in the eyes right in front of everyone, but she was close enough to feel his energy—thick, imposing, accusing. Head ducked, she scurried to the podium.

"As several people have pointed out," she said into the microphone, "the Twilight Bridge is an integral part of our history, but let's face it, even before someone blew it up, the bridge was in pretty sad shape. The railings were rusting out, termites eating up the boards, bricks coming loose from the pillars. We're lucky no tourists ever got hurt on it and sued the town."

Murmurs of agreement ran through the group.

"I propose we rebuild the bridge, salvaging and using as much of the original construction materials as we can."

"Good idea," Mr. Ivey said.

"Great suggestion." Mrs. Qualls's bun bobbled.

"How do you propose we pay for it?" Patsy asked.

"We could have a charity event."

Several people in the audience nodded.

Encouraged, Flynn continued. "Did anyone ever see the episode of the *Gilmore Girls* where the Stars Hollow Bridge suffered from Japanese beetles?"

"Oooh, I did. Wasn't that on the last season?"

"Don't you hate that the show went off the air?"

"It was my favorite. I miss Lorelai and Rory and Luke and—"

Flynn held up a hand. "We're digressing. Do you remember how they raised the money to fix the bridge?"

"Christopher, Lorelai's baby daddy and the man she was engaged to marry, paid for it," someone said. "He was rich."

Flynn waved an impatient hand. "Before Christopher stepped in."

"They held a knit-a-thon."

"Bingo." Flynn pointed. "If it was good enough for Stars Hollow, it's good enough for us. We could hold a knit-a-thon to raise money. Advertise it in the *Fort Worth Star-Telegram*. Make it an event not to be missed."

The room dissolved into excited chatter as the knit-a-thon idea caught fire. In a matter of minutes the town passed a measure to hold a knit-a-thon on the Fourth of July weekend to take advantage of the holiday traffic. That gave them two weeks to get ready, and they put Flynn in charge of organizing it.

Pride rode her shoulders as people shook her

hand. She'd taken lemons and turned them into lemonade. Citizens had come to the meeting disgruntled and looking for blood; they were leaving hopeful and enthusiastic. She'd proposed a plan and set it in motion. She was healing wounds and saving the Twilight Bridge.

She felt invincible.

That is, until she looked down the aisle and saw Jesse glaring at her as if she was the world's biggest hypocrite.

CHAPTER FOURTEEN

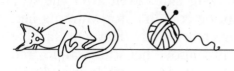

*Beau, too bad you were spoken for.
I hope Flynn appreciates you,
if not you know where to find me.*
—Missy Ivey, yearbook entry, 1999

Everyone filed out of the town hall meeting. Jesse stood by the door, staring down anyone who dared look him in the eye. He wasn't afraid of these people, this town. He was innocent. They were the guilty ones. Automatically assuming he'd done wrong based on the past. He didn't care about their small-mindedness. There was only one thing that bothered him.

Flynn. And the way she'd thrown him to the wolves.

Aunt Patsy passed by. "Will you be home for dinner tonight?"

He shook his head.

"Well, if you change your mind, if you want to talk about it . . ." She let her words trail off.

"I've got something else to handle first."

"All right. I'm there for you if you need me." Patsy left, and Jesse swung his gaze back to Flynn.

She was still on the stage, talking to a clot of ladies from her knitting club. Even after the way she'd wounded him, he couldn't stop wanting her. His gaze tracked over her body. She wore a blue jean skirt that hit just above her knees and a red cotton top that accentuated her dark hair and pale skin. It was the right outfit for this audience. Not too dressy, not too casual. Not flashy, but not stuffy either. She looked sweetly seductive, her clothing designed to sway people to her way of thinking. Jesse wondered if she realized she did that, dressed to persuade, convince, cajole, and win over. She was highly adept at getting people to like her.

A couple of the Sweethearts cast glances over their shoulders at him, closing ranks in a protective circle around Flynn. Growling under his breath, Jesse loped up on stage. He wasn't going to let her hide behind her posse. Marva Bullock shot him a dark look, but stood aside as Jesse approached.

"Could we speak in private?" he asked Flynn.

She looked uncertain, cast glances at her friends.

"Now," he said.

"Um . . . yeah, sure."

The Sweethearts didn't budge.

"It's okay," Flynn said, and wrapped her hands around her upper arms, her body language closing him out. "We can talk about the knit-a-thon tomorrow."

Reluctantly, the women gathered up their knitting accoutrements, purses, and bags and filed out through the side door.

"You want to sit down?" She motioned to the chairs the town council had vacated.

"Standing's good."

"Okay."

Silence stretched, long and uncomfortable.

She cleared her throat, swayed. He burned her face with his eyes. "Why didn't you tell them you were with me? You could have given me an alibi, but you didn't say a thing."

"I wasn't with you when the bridge went down."

Her words stabbed him right between his shoulder blades. "You hadn't been gone fifteen minutes when the explosion happened. There's no way I could have rounded up dynamite, driven over there, and blown up the bridge in that length of time. You know I'm innocent."

"I have no doubt about that."

"So why didn't you stand up for me?"

"What did you want me to do? Tell them we were making out in the Yarn Barn fifteen minutes before the blast?"

"Yeah, I did."

"Jesse . . ."

"You didn't want to look bad in front of the town. Breaking up with Trainer one day, going at it with me a couple of days later."

"You're being rude."

"I think I've earned the right."

She had the good grace to look chagrined.

"This is Trainer's doing," he said. "He's trying to turn the town against me, break us up."

"You're sounding paranoid."

"Yeah? Well, you try going to prison for a crime you didn't commit and see how mistrustful you become."

"Are you suggesting that—"

"Trainer blew up the bridge in an attempt to incriminate me? Yeah, I am."

"I can't believe that."

"Can't or won't?"

"Beau's not like that, he—"

"Beat me up."

She pulled her lower lip up between her bottom teeth and nibbled it, worry in her eyes. Was he finally getting through to her?

"Why didn't you share your certainty with the townsfolk who seemed mighty interested in carrying my head through the town square on a spike?"

"It's complicated."

"It's okay to spell it out for me. Remember, I didn't get to graduate from high school," he said sarcastically.

"I haven't told my family we're dating."

"Are we dating?"

"Aren't we?"

"Not from your behavior."

"Jesse . . ." She gave him a please-don't-back-me-into-a-corner look. But he wasn't feeling particularly accommodating. Not when she'd hung him out to dry. "I need to sit down. Do you mind if I sit down?"

He tried not to let it tug at his heart that her knees were trembling. He pulled out a chair for her. "Sit."

She sat, and then looked up at him. "You're going to keep standing?"

He narrowed his eyes, pulled out a chair, turned it around, and straddled it backward. "It's because of Trainer, isn't it? You don't want him knowing you were with me." He tried to keep the hurt from his voice. He didn't want *her* knowing she'd just shredded him to ribbons.

"No, yes . . . Jesse, I just don't want to hurt anybody."

"Too late for that, Dimples." Damn! Why had he said that? He was giving her all the power.

She raised a hand to her temple. "You're right. I'm a terrible person. I'm ashamed of myself. I'll go see the fire chief and tell him the truth. What's wrong with me? How could I have left you hanging out to dry?"

Jesse expelled a heavy breath of air. No matter how hard he tried he couldn't stay mad at her, especially when she was so good at punishing herself. "You're not a terrible person. There's nothing wrong with you."

"I am. I lie about being able to knit. Hell, I just organized an entire knit-a-thon and I have no idea what I'm doing. I cheated on Beau with you—"

"You didn't cheat. We just kissed, and that other stuff we did was *after* you broke up with him."

"Oh, believe me, I've cheated plenty in my mind. When I was with Beau I often pretended it was you."

"Really?" Okay, he shouldn't be feeling pleased over that last bit of information, but he did.

"What kind of person does that?"

"A normal human being."

"You want to know the truth of it?"

He reached over, touched her hand. "Yes, I do."

"I feel like I'm dancing as fast as I can, trying to please everyone I come into contact with. My father, my sister, my brothers, Beau, you, the Sweethearts, and even my mother. The Yarn Barn is for her, not me. I was trying to please the town tonight and that's why I didn't take up for you. If I'd taken up for you . . ."

"You were afraid they would cast you out along with me."

"Yes," she admitted, and he saw the fear in her eyes. "I sacrificed you because I was too big of a coward to go against the crowd. See, I really am a terrible person. I didn't stand by you when you needed me most."

"I wish I knew what it was like," he murmured.

"What's that?"

"To be so accepted by your peers that being outcast is your worst fear."

"I'm sorry." Her shoulders sagged. "How can I make it up to you?"

"By letting everyone know that we're seeing each other."

"Okay." She nodded. "I'm ready to do that."

"And one other thing."

She swallowed visibly. "Yes?"

He reached over to take her hand. "Stop beating yourself up, that's my girlfriend you're mistreating."

She looked at him from underneath her long dark eyelashes. His heart hammered at the vulnerability he saw in her eyes. She tried so hard to be everything for everyone. No wonder she felt pulled in a million directions. Her vulnerability touched him straight to his soul.

He wanted her so desperately. He'd never felt this way about another woman. He'd experienced it from the first moment he'd walked onto the football field at Twilight High and seen her on the sidelines with lively bumblebee-colored pom-poms, chanting, "Yellow and black, Twilight Tigers fight back. Goooo team, goooo."

Whether he liked it or not, he was connected to her in a way he'd never been connected to anyone. This was beyond lust, more than love. It was an unbreakable bond. He didn't understand it. He'd tried to deny it, but there it was. They were two parts of a single beating heart.

He bent his head and kissed her, inhaled her sweet, sweet flavor, felt it shoot through his blood, heady like a drug.

You're a sucker. She just let you take the fall and you're trying to tell yourself she's your soul mate? Bullshit. There's no such thing as love and you know it. Your own mother loved drugs more than she loved you.

He knew that ugly voice too well. It was the one that isolated him, kept him apart. Kept him distrustful and suspicious. Kept him on the outside looking in.

But you are on the outside. Except for your aunt and Hondo, the whole town believed Trainer.

And yet . . .

Some small part of him couldn't help hoping. Flynn made him want to hope, to believe that things could be different. She made him yearn for things he'd been without for so long. A tender hand to stroke his hair, a warm, soft body to wake up next to, someone who made him feel wanted, accepted, whole.

Wanting those things makes you weak and stupid.

He wished he could dismiss the need, the desire, but looking into those light brown eyes speckled with green, he was powerless against these feelings he had for her.

She'd betrayed him and he forgave her.

Damn him, but he was already lost.

Flynn was determined to make amends. Jesse was right. She'd chosen the town and her reputation over him, and she was ashamed of her cowardly behavior.

That was why she'd come to the fire station.

"Morning, Flynn." Hondo greeted her with a smile.

"Is the fire marshal here?"

"Yep. He just came in."

She found Chief Rutledge in the break room with a cup of coffee and a bear claw. He glanced up when she entered the room.

"May I speak with you, sir?"

Rutledge nodded and used his foot to push the chair across from him out for her. He held up a box from the Twilight Bakery. "Wanna doughnut?"

"No, thank you."

"Don't tell my wife I'm eating this. She'll have my ass in a sling." He pulled a napkin from the rectangular dispenser, set his bear claw down, and dusted sugar glaze from his fingertips. On the surface, he looked like anybody's dad. Paunchy, balding, reading glasses perched on the end of his nose. But his eyes were sharp, his posture alert. "What's on your mind?"

Flynn sat down and took a deep breath. "I know everyone's saying Jesse Calloway blew up the bridge, but he couldn't have done it."

"Oh?" Rutledge arched an eyebrow, but his inscrutable gaze never left her face. "How do you know?"

"Because he was with me. Or at least he was with me just a few minutes before the bridge blew. There was no way he had time to get to the bridge, rig it with dynamite, and set it off."

"Ah. You were with Jesse."

"Yes. We're renovating the theater together. He's turning the bottom half into a motorcycle shop, I'm making the top floor into Lynn's Yarn Barn."

"A tribute to your mother. I heard about that. She'd be proud."

"Thank you."

He stroked his jaw with a thumb and forefinger, leaving a bit of white bear claw glaze sticking to his chin. "So you were with Jesse."

"Yes."

"I thought you and Beau were engaged."

Flynn flattened her hand on the tabletop so he could see her bare ring finger. "We broke up."

"Does Beau know that?

"Jesse was with me," she said, dropping the whole conversational thread about Beau and their broken engagement. "He has an alibi."

"Why didn't you say something before?"

How did she explain it? "I . . . didn't want the

whole town knowing Jesse and I were seeing each other. The relationship is new and . . ."

"You didn't want to hurt Beau by flaunting it in his face."

Flynn nodded. "But I can't . . . won't . . . let Jesse take the fall for something he didn't do."

"It's nice of you to come clean and let me in on this," the chief said. "But I'm afraid your alibi does no good. Jesse's not off the hook."

Alarm spread through her. "What do you mean?"

The chief's eyebrows knit together.

"What is it?"

"You can't share what I'm about to tell you with anyone. Especially not Jesse."

Flynn gulped. "All right."

"Not even Beau. This is just between you and me."

Why was he telling her this and then swearing her to secrecy? Was he on some kind of fishing expedition? Was he trying to warn her? Whatever it was, Flynn had to know. "I promise not to tell anyone."

Chief Rutledge narrowed his eyes. "The dynamite was rigged to a timer. It could have been set up for days. All it took was one cell phone call and boom . . ." He slammed his fist against the table.

Both Flynn and the bear claw jumped.

"*Kablewy.*"

The following two weeks were a bit uneven between her and Jesse. They'd been friendly, often eating lunch together and helping each other set up their shops, but he hadn't asked her out on a date, and she hadn't issued any invitations either. They were feeling their way in the relationship, trying to find their footing with each other, and the ground still felt unsteady.

She'd spent a lot of time at Froggy's, helping her father make sure the repairs to the water main were done and getting estimates for the foundation repair. Luckily their insurance covered the bulk of damage. Thank heavens she'd had the foresight to insist on a flood policy.

Jesse's lawyer had told him that Chief Rutledge had found no evidence linking anyone to the bombing of the bridge, but they had discovered someone had stolen dynamite from the rock quarry upriver from Twilight. They had no further clues or leads. For now, Jesse was in the clear.

That put Flynn's mind at ease. She was left with only one niggling little concern. She was going to have to pretend to knit in front of a town filled with onlookers, while Carrie would be knitting the items in secret in the Yarn Barn and then smuggling the garments over to her. They'd rehearsed ways of maneuvering the handoff and the plan seemed fail proof, but still she couldn't help worrying that somehow she'd be found out.

And how would that look? The organizer of the knit-a-thon—the daughter of the woman who'd won three state fair blue ribbons—exposed as a fraud on the courthouse square.

Don't fret, it's going to be fine. You've managed to fool everyone for years. You even fooled your mother.

Honestly, everything was coming off without a hitch.

By the Fourth of July weekend, the Yarn Barn was almost finished. The supplies Flynn had ordered had arrived. She pried open boxes and filled up the cedar bins her father had built for her with hanks and skeins and balls of festive yarn, all the colors of the rainbow. Even though she couldn't knit, she had to admit there was something bright, comforting, and optimistic about yarn.

The airy aroma of silk, cotton, linen, wool bathed her in a quiet calm that came from methodically sorting and stacking the colors and types of fibers. The work came quickly, easily as she found her rhythm and took pleasure in her achievement. This was it. On Tuesday, she'd be ready to open.

By fulfilling her mother's dream, Flynn was hoping to find her center. The yarn store was simply the means to that end. If her store could bind the heart of the town square, if it could knit the Sweethearts together in a thread of community, hope, and love, then she knew that she would find her own center, even if knitting wasn't her personal strength.

She finished her task and stepped back to look at her handiwork. Floyd's diligent attention to detail had paid off. In his handcrafted cedar bins, the yarn captivated.

"I did it, Mama," she whispered into the silent confines of the room. "I made your dreams come true."

With jaunty spring to her step, she left the Yarn Barn and went out onto the sidewalk.

The knit-a-thon was scheduled to last the entire holiday weekend, running from Friday at noon to Monday at sundown. Entries had exceeded the cut-off limit, and Flynn didn't want to turn people away, so she and the Sweethearts had set up knitting stations all around the town square, not just on the courthouse lawn as previously planned—in Sweetheart Park, on the street corners, on the balconies of the storefronts. Along with big electric floor fans to keep the knitters cool in the Texas heat.

The money was raised in three ways: by entry fees, by selling the items they knitted, and by sponsors who donated money for however long the knitters knitted, like in a charity walk-a-thon. You knitted, the local businesses or private donors paid for your time and effort.

Sponsorship money rolled in. Ivey's hardware pledged a hundred dollars for every registered knitter who knitted for twelve consecutive hours. Not to be outdone, other businesses had made similar pledges, including the Ford dealership. They donated a new pickup truck to the grand prize winner of the knit-a-thon.

Moe had fashioned a tally board and raised it on the courthouse steps to keep track of the money raised. Terri and Marva had made two giant balls of yarn out of papier-mâché and a couple of matching knitting needles for the display. Outside her Sweetest Match office, Belinda set up a booth to sell the knitted items. Local restaurants got into the swing with portable food carts vending Italian meatball subs from Pasta Pappa's, tamales from Taco Hacienda, steak on a stick from the Funny Farm, fried chicken from Froggy's, and barbecued sausage from Texas Joe's.

The annual Fourth of July parade would kick

off the event in exactly two hours. At nine A.M. on Friday, everyone was in motion, setting up, preparing, organizing, and arranging. Flynn took a deep breath. It was going to work. She'd brought the town together for a common goal. Her chest swelled with pride. She'd done a good job.

On the walkway leading up to the courthouse, she found Carrie and Terri setting up the eye-catching artwork of yarn balls and needles. Carrie was on a rickety ladder, wearing purple short-shorts and a white midriff top. Flynn noticed several local boys had gathered around to watch, but none offered to help. Typical adolescent guy behavior.

"Shoo." She put on her best big-sister face, glowered, and waved her hands at the teens. "Go away or I'll put you to work."

Once the boys had scattered, Flynn turned to Carrie. "You're incorrigible."

"What I'd do?" She grinned.

"Dressing like that, climbing a ladder, toying with young boys' minds."

"Who me?"

"What would Logan think?"

"Who cares? We broke up."

"When did this happen?"

"Last week. You were right. He was pompous. Always correcting my grammar."

"Told you."

"You don't have to sound so smug."

"Stop wiggling around." Terri had both hands on the ladder. "And hurry up, I gotta pick Gerald up from day care in fifteen minutes. They're closing early for the parade."

"Go ahead and go, Terri," Flynn offered. "I'll hold the ladder."

"You sure? You've got a lot to do."

"Everything's running smoothly."

Terri winced. "Don't say that."

"Don't say what?"

"That everything is running smoothly, you'll jinx it." Terri was a bit on the superstitious side. She read her horoscope—Leo—religiously, wore an emerald four-leaf-clover necklace, and consulted Madame Drucilla out on Highway 377 whenever something went haywire in her life, even though the turban-wearing woman had twice been busted by the Fort Worth bunco squad.

"What could go wrong? All the yarn we ordered arrived, the rocking chairs are set up, Moe's here to collect the money, we have massage therapists at the ready to knead knotted necks—"

"Good alliteration, Flynn. Logan would love you."

"Everybody loves Flynn," Terri teased. "Beau, Jesse, now Logan, probably even those boys you chased off."

"They are in love with you, Flynn," Carrie said. "You think they were just ogling me? When you bent over that big basket of yarn . . ."

"They were not."

"They were too," Terri added.

"Stop it."

"Imagine, Flynn's a cougar, grrr," Terri growled. "Watch out. You're gonna have to change your name to Demi or Madonna."

"Don't you have a kid to pick up?"

"Luckily for you. Otherwise I'd spend the rest of the morning teasing you unmercifully."

Flynn took Terri's place at the base of the ladder and Terri went off to retrieve her offspring. It was already eighty-five degrees at nine in the morning and her blouse was sticking to her back.

Carrie leaned over, trying to artfully drape the rope, dyed to match the deep scarlet color of the papier-mâché ball of yarn, around the gigantic wooden needles so that it would look like a knit stitch.

Flynn's gaze wandered around the town square, supervising the bustling activity. Belinda was decorating her booth with helium-filled balloons and a cheery banner. On the corner, off-duty firemen were setting up a first aid station. And directly across the street, Jesse was parking his Harley on the sidewalk, setting up a motorcycle display. Polish rag in hand, he bent over the back of the bike, buffing up the chrome.

Flynn zeroed in on his tush, on compelling lines and honed angles as fine as his motorcycle. She licked her lips and felt something powerful stir inside her.

He bent over farther.

She tilted her head, studied the flex of his butt muscles underneath his tight jeans. Her mouth watered. Yummy.

Lust dug into her. She raised a hand, splayed it against her throat, swallowed hard, completely forgetting where she was and what she was supposed to be doing.

A group of women passing by on his side of the

street actually stopped, turned their heads, and caressed him with their eyes.

Jealousy blazed in her heart. Flynn's first instincts were primal, a feminine urge to claim her man, to cross the street, plant a kiss on his lips, and let the world know he belonged to her.

Beside her, the ladder wobbled.

"Flynn?" Carrie called down.

It didn't even register that her sister had called her name. Jesse had captivated her complete attention.

"Flynn!" Carrie's voice was urgent this time, snapping her from her trance. "Hold the ladder, please, I'm off balance and I'm about to—"

The last part of her sentence broke off as the ladder collapsed, falling into the giant ball of papier-mâché yarn. It spun off across the courthouse lawn as her baby sister tumbled yelping to the ground.

Chapter Fifteen

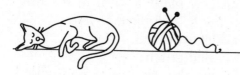

*Flynn, knit one, purl two, he-he,
your dirty little secret is safe with me.*
—Carrie MacGregor, yearbook entry, 1999

Flynn looked at Carrie's hand dangling from her arm at a very unnatural angle, her wrist ballooning like a puff adder. Nausea crowded her throat. Her head spun and she feared her knees might crumple right out from underneath her.

Don't panic. You can handle this. Carrie needs you.

"Let's get you to the hospital." She forced a smile, tried to look calm and cool, as she'd done many times in emergency situations. Flynn slipped an arm around Carrie's waist and tried to lever her up off the ground.

"Ow, ow, ow." Tears sprang to her sister's eyes. "It hurts, dammit. Bad."

"I'm sorry, how can I help? How can I make it better?"

"Just back off a minute and let me get my breath." Carrie sat on the ground, chuffing in air, wincing against the pain.

Several onlookers had seen the accident and came running over. From the corner of her eye, Flynn saw someone retrieve the oversized yarn ball before it rolled into the Main Street traffic.

"You better get some ice on that wrist," someone said.

"She needs a doctor."

Yes, yes she did. But how could Flynn leave when there was so much to do?

Patsy Cross put a hand on her shoulder. "Don't worry," she said, reading her mind. "I've got it under control. Get your sister to the doctor."

"But I'm supposed to be handing out the packets and showing everyone where they're supposed to set up and—"

"I'll figure it all out," Patsy said, "and recruit the rest of the Sweethearts to help, and if something gets left undone, well, then something gets left undone. You can't be everything to everybody, Flynn. Your sister is most important."

"Thank you," she whispered.

"Here's your ride, now go." Patsy nodded.

Flynn looked over and saw Jesse, helping Carrie up off the ground. "I can do that," she said.

"I've got it." Jesse guided Carrie toward Flynn's Ford Ranger, idling at the curb. The passenger side door hung open.

Flynn fell into step beside him. "How'd you get my truck started? I've got the key."

"Hot-wired it. I figured taking Carrie to the hospital on the Harley wasn't an option."

"Thanks, I think. You still remembered how to hot-wire a vehicle?"

"Hot-wiring a car's like making love. Once you know how, you never forget." His sexy tone made her heat up inside. "Remember when we—"

"Okay you two, I'm in pain here, save the trip down memory lane for later, huh?" Carrie grunted as Jesse helped her into the passenger seat.

"Thanks," Flynn said again. "We appreciate your help." She hustled around to the driver's side, Jesse close at her heels. She slid behind the wheel.

He placed his hand on the door. "Scoot over."

"What?"

"Scoot over, I'm driving."

"There's no need for that."

"Sure there is. You're shaking like a pound puppy."

"I'm perfectly capable of driving my sister to the hospital."

"Sure you are," he said. "But wouldn't it be nice if you just had a hand to hold on to?"

"I don't need you."

"I never said you did."

"Listen, Jesse—"

"For godsake, Flynn," Carrie snapped. "Just let the man drive us to the hospital. We get it, you're independent, you don't need anybody, you're the savior of us all, now get me to some drugs pronto or I'm gonna start screaming."

Flynn scooted over. Jesse got in and slammed the door. They took off, tooling past the throng of tourists that had already started lining the square.

Fifteen minutes later, Flynn paced the emergency department waiting room at Twilight General, arms crossed over her chest. "Why won't they let me in the exam room with her?"

Jesse lounged in one of the vinyl plastic chairs, looking far too comfortable for the atrocious seating. How did he manage that smooth, sexy, slouch? "Because they're examining her, that's why it's called an exam room."

"But she needs me. I'm her big sister. Hell, I'm her surrogate mother—"

"Calm down."

"I'm calm. I'm always calm in a crisis. I'm just frustrated. It's my fault she's there." Flynn knotted her hands. "I wasn't holding the ladder securely enough because I was—" She bit off the words before she said them.

"Was what?" Jesse prompted.

Staring at your butt. The man should be fined for having such a good-looking butt. "Umm, I was distracted."

"You have a lot on your plate."

"I do." *No more than usual. I was just too busy staring at your butt. Carrie was hurt because I was staring at your damn butt.*

"You must have walked ten miles in the last five minutes." He patted the seat next to him. "Come here, sit down."

"How can I sit down when my sister's in pain?" She gnawed a thumbnail. "It's all my fault."

"The nurses were coming at her with a Demerol needle just before they threw us out. I'm sure Carrie's floating pain-free right now."

"What if she needs me? What if she's calling for

me?" Flynn stepped to the wooden double doors and pressed one eye against the crack between them.

"She's not."

Flynn turned and sent him a flinty-eyed stare. Him and his sexy butt. "How do you know?"

"If she was asking for you they'd come get you."

"Clearly you have more confidence in medical professionals than I do."

"I just know getting yourself worked up isn't going to solve anything."

Flynn eased the door open a crack, stuck her foot in.

"What are you doing?"

"I need to check, make sure she doesn't need me for something. What if she's thirsty and they're too busy to get her a drink of water? She could be parched, and too dry to even call out water, water."

"This isn't Death Valley. See any sun-bleached cow skulls around? See any cactus? They'll give her water."

"You are such an optimist. How is it that you're such an optimist?"

"Flynn, get your foot back across the line. Read the sign. It says medical personnel only."

"Since when did you start paying attention to signs? Mr. Gone in Sixty Seconds lecturing me about following the rules? I've been in enough hospitals with my mother. I know the drill. The squeaky wheel gets the grease."

"Unless you're obnoxiously squeaky and then you get tossed out. Carrie's going to be fine. Now sit."

"You're sure? You promise?" She let out a huff of exasperation and reluctantly plunked down beside him.

"I promise." He reached out and laid a hand on hers.

Instantly she calmed. "I'm sorry, I'm getting testy with you and it's not your fault." *Your butt's fault, maybe.* "You hot-wired my truck for me and drove me over here and everything and I'm spouting off like you're my sounding board."

"Go ahead and spout. That's what I'm here for."

"I'm too hard on Carrie."

Jesse nodded. "She's not like you, Flynn."

"I know that. What's wrong with me? Why do I keep expecting her to live up to my standards instead of accepting her for who she is?"

"You have high ideals."

Flynn wrinkled her nose. "You make me sound like Beau. I don't want to be like Beau. He's too rigid. Am I too rigid, Jesse?"

"You're not like Beau." He slipped a hand to the back of her neck, and she melted against him. "And you're not the least bit rigid. You simply expect too much out of yourself."

A nurse appeared in the doorway. "The doctor has finished examining your sister. Would you like to come in now?"

Flynn shot to her feet. "Let's go."

Jesse took her hand, and her spirits lifted. Maybe everything would be all right after all.

They followed the nurse into the examination room. Carrie lay on the gurney, her face pale, her injured arm suspended from a sling on a rolling IV pole. Flynn plastered a cheerful smile on her face.

"Oh no," Carrie said. "I know that look."

"What look?' Flynn asked brightly.

"That everything's-gonna-be-A-OK smile you

always fished out for Mama's sake. It's bullshit, that smile. It doesn't convince anyone. Not Mama, not me. I must be dying."

"You're not dying."

"So why the perky smile?"

"I'm just trying to be positive. Rainbows, unicorns, kitties in a basket, all that upbeat stuff."

"Well stop it. My hand hurts like hell and it's my tray-carrying hand. You're going to have to find someone to fill my shifts at Froggy's. That should put a kink in your perk."

"Okay, this sucks. It's a nightmare. It's a disaster. The sky is falling. Does that make you feel better?"

"Actually," Carrie said, struggling with one arm to scoot herself up higher in the bed, "it does."

Flynn scurried over to help her sit up. Maybe fluff her pillow, offer her a sip of water.

Carrie's glower stopped her in her tracks. "I can make it on my own."

Flynn raised her palms. "Sor-*ry*. Just trying to help."

Carrie eyeballed Jesse. "He was holding your hand."

"What?"

"When you came in, he was holding your hand."

"Mmm, was he?"

Carrie snorted.

"What?"

"It's okay to admit you're with Jesse." She kept trying to wrestle her pillow with her good hand, but every time Flynn tried to help, she quelled her with a look.

"I'm not with Jesse."

"Because that would signal the end of the world," Jesse muttered.

Flynn spun to meet his gaze. "Well, I'm *not* with you."

He didn't say another word, just drilled her with his patented sexy stare, the one that made her itch and sweat and long to strip off her panties.

The doctor strode into the room, followed by a nurse pushing a big metal cart behind him.

"What's that?" Flynn eyed the cart.

"Cast cart," explained the nurse.

"Cast? Why does she need a cast?"

"Her wrist is broken. See here." The doctor stepped to a gray box mounted on the wall. He flicked a switch and the box was backlit, showing off the set of X-rays clipped to the front of it. It was an arm. Apparently Carrie's arm was broken, and anyone with half a brain cell could tell from the jagged line running across the base of the bone.

Flynn plastered the fingers of both hands over her mouth. "No, no, broken wrist. She can't have a broken wrist."

"She has a broken wrist," the doctor insisted.

"If she has a broken wrist, she can't knit."

"That's right. No knitting for our girl here for many weeks to come." The doctor held out his hand. The nurse opened up the cast cart, fished out supplies, and started slapping them one by one into his waiting palm.

"But there's knit-a-thon going on." Okay, she was officially sounding like an idiot, but the realization that she was totally screwed was finally sinking in. She met Carrie's gaze.

His sister shrugged. "It was bound to happen sooner or later."

"But this is the knit-a-thon. We have over a hundred entrants and dozens of sponsors and most of the town will be there and we have tons of tourists and—"

"And everyone will finally find out that perfect, infallible Flynn has a deep dark secret."

"I'm not perfect, I'm not infallible. I'm very fallible. That's why we're in this fix. I failed. I was staring at Jesse's butt and getting jealous over all the other women who were staring at his butt and I should have been holding the ladder when you needed me most, but I wasn't because I was staring at Jesse's butt. That's how fallible I am."

"You were staring at my butt?" Jesse straightened.

"Don't get cocky. You know your butt looks good in those jeans."

"You think my butt looks good?" He smirked.

"Actually, now that I think about it, this whole thing is your fault. For crying out loud, man, wear looser fitting jeans."

The nurse stepped back to check out Jesse's backside and made a she's-got-a-good-point face.

The doctor pulled Jesse aside. "Your friend sounds close to losing it. Maybe you could escort her back to the lobby."

"I heard that," Flynn said. "I'm not losing it. I don't lose it. I'm the thread that binds everything together. The twine, the string, the yarn. If I'm not there, it's all a tangled mess."

Kind of like your knitting.

Okay, so she was ranting, and Jesse had her

around the waist and he was dragging her off and she was just, well . . . What was she going to do about the knit-a-thon?

"Come on, Dimples, let's give the doctor some breathing room," he coaxed. "Let's go to the cafeteria for a Coke while they finish patching up Carrie."

Yeah, okay, he was right, no need to have a meltdown in the middle of the ER.

"What am I going to do?" she moaned when they were seated in the cafeteria. She sank her head in her hands. "Here I am the ringleader of this knit-a-thon. How am I going to compete? We had it all figured out. Carrie was going to be knitting the exact same garment I was supposed to be working on. When I took a break, the plan was for me to go across the street to the Yarn Barn, leave the piece I was working on and pick up the one she'd been knitting. Then she was going to come over, visit me with a knitting bag just like mine, and we'd swap out totes. Now everyone is going to know I'm a fraud and here I just opened up a yarn store. Seriously, who's going to buy yarn from a woman who can't knit?"

"Look at it in the grand scheme of things. Maybe it's a good thing this is happening."

"What are you talking about? This is a total disaster."

"People were bound to find out sooner or later."

"No they weren't. Carrie and I have had this going on for over ten years and nobody guessed a thing."

"So for the rest of your life you're going to pretend to be a perfect knitter while Carrie has to pretend she's got no talent for it? That's not fair to either you or Carrie."

"But I never did any of this for me. It was all for my mother."

Jesse shifted in his seat. "Isn't it about time you did something for yourself? You've been putting everyone's needs before your own and look, it's got you doing some goofy Lucy and Ethel scheming to pull it off. Do you really want to live your life like a 1950s sitcom?"

"No, of course I don't, I just—"

"Don't want to let people down."

"Yes, exactly."

"How about if I help you?"

Flynn laughed. "Please don't tell me you know how to knit baby booties."

"Not my specialty, Dimples, but causing a commotion, yeah I can do that. What if I make a distraction, or somehow destroy your projects. Big bottle of red wine dropped by your knitting basket?"

She laughed. "Okay, you made your point. I see how ridiculous I'm being."

He reached over and chucked her under the chin. "I got your back, MacGregor, all you've gotta do is say the word."

"Thanks," she whispered, her skin tingling from his touch. "I appreciate the offer, but you're right. I guess this is fate's way of telling me I need to stop lying about my knitting abilities and just take my lumps."

"How do you intend on handling it?"

"I'll set up and start knitting. When everyone

sees my work with the dropped stitches, backward stitches, and accidental increase, and asks what happened, I'll just fess up."

"Okay," he said, "but if you change your mind and need me to bail you out, just give me the word and I'll be there."

It felt good knowing he had her back, but there was something in his eyes she couldn't discern, something wistful and sad that made her want to crawl into his lap and wrap her arms around his neck. Then he blinked and the look was gone.

"Ms. MacGregor?" the ER nurse said from the doorway. "You can take your sister home now."

Two hours into the knit-a-thon, Flynn had managed fifty rows of knit stitches. They were sloppy, they were loose, but dammit they were perfect. No dropped stitches, no accidental increase, nothing looped backward. It was a glorious accomplishment and she couldn't share it with anyone.

The only two who could appreciate her victory were out of range. Carrie was snoozing at home, gorked on Demerol. Jesse manned his lemonade booth across the street. Flynn peeked over and saw him gabbing with middle-aged businessmen—doctors, lawyers, stockbrokers, playing at being badass bikers in their do-rags, chains, leather pants and vests, motorcycle boots, and wrist studs.

One gray-haired dude with a ponytail to the middle of his back wore a tattered black T-shirt that proclaimed: "Ride Hard, Die Young." Clearly he'd missed the boat on the dying young part.

"Uh-oh," Marva said. "Look who's headed our way."

Everyone glanced over to see Beau sauntering up the sidewalk toward them. Oh geez. Flynn ducked her head and concentrated hard on making a fresh row of stitches.

"Afternoon, ladies." He greeted them with a tip of his Stetson.

"Afternoon, Beau," the Sweethearts answered in unison.

Flynn felt his gaze on her, but she didn't glance up.

"You're looking fit, Sheriff," Terri said.

"Thank you, Mrs. Longoria. I'm feeling fit."

Go away! But of course he didn't. He just kept standing there right next to her rocking chair. She could see the tips of his boots.

"Flynnie?" His voice was soft.

"Yes?" Realizing she had no choice, Flynn raised her head and met his gaze.

"What's wrong?" he asked.

Quickly she dropped her hands into her lap to hide her knitting. "Um . . . nothing's wrong, Beau."

"I know you, Flynnie." He lowered his voice. "Something's bothering you."

"No. Nothing." *You, you're what's bothering me.* "I'm fine. Super, in fact."

"You know, just because you broke up with me doesn't mean we can't be friends. I still care about you."

"And I still care about you." It was true, she did. She cared about a lot of people. She tried her best not to glance over at the lemonade stand to see what Jesse was doing. She plastered a big fake smile on her face. "But honestly, nothing's wrong."

Beau cleared his throat, but didn't budge.

Seriously? Was he going to stand there all day?

"You can't lie to me," he said. "I see the signs."

"Nope, no signs." The smile was frozen on her teeth.

"It's in your knitting." He leaned over and tugged the scarf from her lap. "Look at this."

Yeah, isn't it cool? I did it all by myself.

He clicked his tongue. "Flabby stitches. That's not like you. Not like you at all. Normally your stitches are tight and controlled, just like you."

"I'm not tight and controlled," she snapped, feeling decidedly waspish.

"Sure you are, it's one of the things I admire most about you." Beau rested a hand on her shoulder, and it was all she could do to keep from swatting him away. "You're distracted. What's up?"

Irritation flared along her nerve endings like a bad case of shingles. "Yeah, okay, I'm distracted. Satisfied?"

"I knew it."

"What can I say? You're all-seeing, all-knowing. We oughta call you Beau the Omnipotent."

"I'm going to ignore that little bit of sarcasm, Flynnie, because obviously something's upset you."

"It's Carrie," supplied Dotty Mae, who was sitting to Flynn's right, purling a row of stitches on her afghan. "Poor girl broke her wrist putting up the papier-mâché yarn ball display. Flynn and Jes—" Dotty seemed to realize who she was talking to and finished with, "Um . . . Flynn took her to the hospital."

Beau's eyebrows dipped downward. "I'm sorry to hear about Carrie."

"Thanks for the sympathy, I'll let her know." Flynn ducked her head again, picked up her knitting, squinted hard at the stitches, hoping he'd get the hint and vamoose.

"Can I get you anything?" Beau asked. "Cold beverage?"

"I'm fine," Flynn said. *Go away.* So much for the tiny little pleasure she'd taken in knitting a flawless—if somewhat flabby—partial scarf.

"I'd love a glass of lemonade," Dotty Mae said. "Thank you so much for asking, Beau, you are a regular knight in shining armor, coming to the aid of thirsty damsels."

"Anybody else?" Beau asked the rest of the Sweethearts, who were gathered in a circle, knitting as a team.

"I'll have a lemonade as well," Marva said.

"I'm in, temperature's climbing and I'm already sweating." Terri fluffed the front of her white cotton blouse for effect. "Thanks, Beau."

"Raylene?"

Raylene held up a silver flask. "Got it covered."

"Ray!" Patsy said, "It's only three o'clock in the afternoon."

"Get your panties out of a bunch, Patsy. It's five o'clock somewhere in the world, and if I'm expected to sit here and knit for two and a half days I need some liquid incentive."

"Patsy?" Beau asked.

"What?"

"You want some lemonade?"

"Yes, thank you."

"I'd like one too," Belinda said, going for her purse. "How much is it?"

Beau put out a restraining hand. "Knitters drink free. I'll be right back, ladies. Flynn, you sure you won't have one?"

"I'm sure." She nodded curtly and didn't glance up.

"I still don't understand why you broke up with him, Flynn," Belinda said when Beau was out of earshot. "How many men would get lemonade for all of us?"

"Yeah, that's just what I want in a husband, a man who waits on other women hand and foot."

"Their breakup won't last," Terri predicted. "It never does. What's the longest time you two were broken up?"

"The four years he was in Iraq," Flynn supplied.

"But the minute he came back all wounded with that Bronze Star strapped to his chest, it was smoochie-smoochville again. Whatever is going on between you two, it will blow over. It always does."

"Not this time," Patsy muttered.

"Oh." Marva leaned in close. "What do you know?"

"Jesse took Flynn and Carrie to the hospital," Dotty Mae whispered.

"So is it Jesse?" Marva prodded Patsy. "Did he come between them?"

"People," Flynn exclaimed, "I'm sitting right here!"

"Yeah, but you won't tell us anything." Terri angled her torso toward Patsy "So, Pats, what's the scoop? Flynn and Jesse?"

As uncomfortable as the conversation was, it did take the focus off her knitting. Maybe she could

stuff the scarf in her purse while no one was looking and pretend she'd finished it. Slyly she slipped
the half scarf from her lap, and she was just about
to drop it in her tote bag when her father came
loping across the courthouse lawn.

Floyd wore a dark green apron emblazoned with
the Froggy's logo, and he smelled of fried chicken.
He looked good, really good. The best he'd looked
since her mother died. His skin had lost the sallow
cast and his face no longer looked bloated. His hair
was neatly trimmed, his chin freshly shaved.

"Hey, honey." He greeted her with a kiss on the
forehead.

"How's Carrie?"

"She's sound asleep."

"Selling a lot of chicken?"

"Swamped."

"That's great."

"Not so good, we're running out of chicken."

"You need me to go to the market?"

"I can't ask that, you're in the big middle of knitting. I thought maybe you could call Carlos—"

"That's fine, I don't mind." Flynn was already
up and out of the rocking chair, happy to have a
bona fide excuse to abandon the knitting. "Be right
back, ladies."

"If you feel your ears burning," Marva called
out, "you know we're gossiping about you."

"I wouldn't expect anything less," Flynn said,
and made her escape.

CHAPTER SIXTEEN

Trainer, sleep with one eye open.
—Jesse Calloway, yearbook entry, 1999

Sheriff Trainer trod across the courthouse lawn, littered with knitters in rocking chairs, and headed straight toward him. A bad feeling trickled down Jesse's spine. He squared his shoulders, looked Trainer in the eyes.

"How much did this bad boy set you back?" A ponytailed tourist caressed the Harley's fender with his fingertips.

"Found it wrecked, bought it cheap, rebuilt it myself," Jesse said, never taking his gaze off Trainer. He'd grown up in the desert. He knew you didn't turn your back on a rattlesnake.

Ponytail whistled, hunkered down to examine it more closely. "Helluva good job, man."

"My work is my best advertisement," Jesse said.

"Afternoon." Beau slid his Stetson back on his

forehead. His badge gleamed in the sunlight. Bastard probably polished it twice a day.

"What do you want?"

Beau rested his hands on his hips in that Wyatt Earp pose he affected. "Five lemonades for the knitters."

"Man," the ponytailed dude interrupted, "could you come over and take a look at my Ducati? She's been sputtering like a kid with the croup. She got worse on the drive over here."

"Could you hang on for just a minute?" Jesse asked Ponytail. "I have to find someone to take over the lemonade stand."

"You go on and help your customer, Calloway," Beau said. "I'll man the lemonade stand."

Something was up. He didn't trust Trainer. Not for a second. "Now why would you offer to do that?"

"I'm community-minded."

Jesse snorted.

"Besides, I know when I'm licked."

"What's that supposed to mean."

"Flynn. She wants you, not me."

Jesse's heart twisted, skidding like a bike in an ice storm. "She actually tell you that?"

"I got eyes in my head, Calloway."

"So she didn't tell you that."

"She didn't have to. I can see it on her face every time she looks at you."

"Does that mean you're steppin' aside?" Jesse tilted his head, tensing for an ambush.

"It means I'm calling a truce."

Jesse narrowed his eyes. He had no use for lawmen in general and this one in particular. "Why?"

"I only want Flynn to be happy," Trainer said, and he sounded sincere. "If she wants you . . ." Trainer swallowed, and his Adam's apple slid down his throat. "Who am I to stand in her way?"

"Man," said Ponytail, "can you help me or not?"

Jesse looked at Trainer.

Trainer shrugged. "I'm offering. Take it or leave it."

He felt like he was walking through a field of land mines, uncertain of where the explosives lay, but absolutely certain they were buried there.

"Let him run the lemonade stand," Ponytail said. "If you can't trust the sheriff, who can you trust?"

Jesse's thoughts exactly.

"Seriously, man, I'm scared to get back on the road on her. I'll pay whatever you think is fair." Ponytail slipped his wallet, which was attached to a chain linked to his belt, from his back pocket and started peeling off twenties.

"Yeah, okay. I'm coming." Jesse turned to Trainer, tossed him his apron. "Yellow lemonade is to sell, a dollar a glass. The pink lemonade is free for the knitters and festival volunteers. It's all yours."

When Flynn returned an hour later (she'd stopped by the house to check on Carrie and ended up heating her a bowl of cream of tomato soup with Cheez-Its floating in it, just like their mother used to make), she was surprised—but happy—to see the Sweethearts doing more gossiping and drinking lemonade than knitting.

A barbershop quartet had taken to the stage

outside the ice cream parlor, and they were belting out a surprisingly decent rendition of "Sweet Adeline." The crowd thickened. A beaming Moe pushed the tote board numbers up to two thousand dollars. It was going to take a lot more pledges and a lot more knitting to reach their target goal, but it was a great start.

"Hey," Marva called out. "Here's Flynnie, she's back."

"Come on," Flynn said, parking her butt in the rocker she'd vacated. "Don't call me Flynnie, I don't like it."

"You like it when Beau calls you Flynnie."

"No, I don't, but he does it anyway."

"So now that Flynn's back, who are we going to talk about?" Terri clacked her knitting needles together as swift as an iron chef sharpening cutlery.

"Oh, you know what I heard?" Belinda leaned in toward the group, her eyes bright.

"Don't tease, matchmaker," Raylene said. "If you know something juicy, spill it."

"It's about Emerson Parks," Belinda murmured.

"Who's Emerson Parks?" Flynn asked.

"You probably knew her as Trixie Lyn Sparks."

"I remember Trixie Lyn," Marva said. "Impulsive little thing. All red hair and freckles and spirit. She played the lead in *Annie* her freshman year."

"I really don't remember her," Flynn said.

"She was three or four grades ahead of you in school," Marva said. "And she was only in Twilight a few years while her daddy was working at the nuke plant in Glen Rose. It was the same time your mama got diagnosed with ALS. You had so much on your plate, you wouldn't have noticed if Santa Claus had moved in next door."

Flynn tried to picture who they were talking about, but couldn't.

"She was always telling everyone she was going to New York and make it big on Broadway. I'm guessing she changed her name to Emerson Parks."

"She went to New York and she made it all right, but not in the way you'd expect." Belinda nodded.

"Where you'd hear this?" Patsy said. "The *National Enquirer*?"

"What if I did?" Belinda was sensitive about her guilty pleasure. She loved reading the tabloids and took them at face value.

"Someone from Twilight is in the *National Enquirer*?" Raylene said. "Dish it up, woman."

"It's juicy gossip about hometown girl gone wrong in the big city." Belinda paused for effect and finished off her lemonade. "This is really good. I'm going to have to get another one. Anybody else want one?"

"I do!" Dotty Mae called out. "I don't know what Jesse puts in his lemonade, but it has some kick to it. What's he put in it, Patsy?"

"I don't know. That boy doesn't tell me anything."

"Get me one, too." Marva licked her lips. "It *is* tasty lemonade."

"Patsy?" Belinda asked.

"Oh, why not?" Patsy nodded. "Since it's free for knitters. Oops, looky there, I dropped a stitch."

"You can't leave us hanging," Flynn said to Belinda. "You haven't told us about Emerson Parks."

"Didn't I?" Belinda giggled, her eyes shining bright. "Well, remind me and I'll tell you when I get back." She waved a hand and toddled off toward the lemonade stand.

"Ladies, ladies." Moe strolled over. "Less talking, more knitting. We've almost sold out of all the items you've already made. We need more inventory." He clapped his hands. "Chop, chop, hop to it." Then he wandered off to roust another group of knitters with the same spiel.

"I can think of something I'd like to chop, chop," Raylene muttered, and stabbed her knitting needle through a loop. She was knitting with chenille, making a baby blanket.

"I can just see him as a sweatshop owner," Flynn said. "Cracking the whip over underage workers. Paying them in bananas instead of dollars."

"Sounds just like Moe. I worked for him as a teller when I got out of high school," Terri said. "He's docks your pay if you're one minute late coming back from break."

"Darn it, I dropped another stitch," Patsy said. "Anyone have this pattern?"

"You? Since when do you need a pattern for anything?" Raylene asked. "You've been knitting for fifty years."

"Since I started dropping stitches all over the place. I can't seem to remember what I'm doing. Where's my focus?" Patsy groused.

"Watch out, you might be getting Alz—" Marva bit off her words, looked chagrined.

Everyone's eyes widened at Marva's gaffe. Not cool to joke about Alzheimer's to a woman whose husband was afflicted with it. Patsy didn't looked up from her knitting, didn't react.

"My, my." Dotty Mae jumped in to pull back the awkward curtain of silence. "Since when did little Tommy Ledbetter get such a nice ass?"

"Dotty Mae!" Patsy said, sounding scandalized, but looking relieved at the change in subject. "He's barely twenty."

"I'm old, not dead. I can still appreciate God's work of art." Dotty Mae cocked her head and stared at the blue-jean-clad young man bending at the waist and dragging flour sacks from the bed of his pickup parked parallel to the courthouse lawn. Tommy worked as a delivery boy for Pasta Pappa's.

"Dotty's got a point," Raylene said, craning her neck for a better look. "Those biceps aren't so bad either."

Flynn took a gander at Tommy's rump. Meh. Not bad, but it wasn't in the same league with Jesse's. At that thought, she let her gaze wander back across the street toward the motorcycle shop/Yarn Barn. She couldn't see Jesse for the long line queuing up at the lemonade stand.

"Tommy joined the gym," Terri explained. "He's got a crush on Mr. Ivey's youngest daughter and he's buffing up to impress her. I've been training him."

"Well, it's working," Marva said. "You're a good trainer."

"You're a lucky duck." Dotty Mae sighed longingly.

"Who's lucky?" Belinda asked, coming back

over with a corrugated cardboard tray filled with cups of lemonade.

"Terri. She gets to train that." Raylene jerked a thumb in Tommy's direction.

"Ooh, seriously? You are lucky, Ter." Belinda handed out the drinks, and then returned to her rocker.

Dotty Mae sucked down half her lemonade in one long swallow. "Whew, this heat is really getting to me. My head's spinning."

"Flynn, you should try some of this lemonade. It's fabulous." Belinda extended her glass to her and then hiccupped loudly. "Excuse me."

Flynn waved the glass away. "I don't like lemons."

"Oh yeah, I forgot." Belinda giggled and hiccupped again. "That's good, leaves more for me."

"Hey," Raylene said, "how come I'm the only one knitting, except for Patsy, who's dropping stitches like a relief aid plane tossing care packages into a quarantine zone. Shake a leg, ladies."

"What's the deal, Ray? You applying for a job as Moe's manager?" Flynn asked. She hadn't even dug her half scarf out of her knitting bag since she'd returned from her errands.

"No, I'd like to see us raise enough funds to rebuild the Twilight Bridge, but at this rate, we won't make enough money to build a fence stile."

"What is wrong with this picture?" Flynn teased.

"That Ray is the one actually doing some work for once?" Terri hooted, her cheeks flushing a high pink.

Marva giggled.

Belinda hiccupped.

Dotty Mae snored.

Patsy dropped another stitch.

Raylene narrowed her eyes. "What is wrong with everyone? Excluding Flynn, you're all acting . . ." She trailed off, snapped her gaze from Patsy to Marva to Terri to Belinda and then over to Dotty Mae, who was sound asleep with her chin resting on her chest. "You're all stinking drunk!"

"Whoop, another first," Terri said. "Raylene's the sober one and the rest of us are tipsy. Hey, how come we're all tipsy?"

"I'm not tissy," Patsy slurred. "You tissy, Marva?"

"Not me." Marva shook her head.

"Me neither." Belinda hiccupped.

Dotty Mae sawed a few more logs.

Flynn stared. Raylene was right. They were all drunk.

Raylene grabbed Belinda's glass of lemonade and took a swallow. "Hey, you guys were holding out on me." She huffed. "Who's got the flask of vodka? Belinda?"

Belinda held up her hands. "I'm innocent."

"Don't look at me," Terri said.

"Me neither." Marva took another drink of lemonade.

"I didn't spike the drinks and I can't believe one of you did." Patsy sniffed.

Everyone turned to look at Dotty Mae, who was still snoozing.

Raylene elbowed Flynn. "Go through her purse."

"I will not." Flynn glowered.

"Then hand her purse to me and I'll do it."

"Dotty Mae couldn't have spiked anyone's drinks," Terri pointed out. "She hasn't left her chair all afternoon."

"If none of us spiked the drinks," Marva asked, "who did?"

Raucous laughter from the next knitting group over drew Flynn's attention. The group of ten women looked to be having as much fun as the Sweethearts. Uh-oh. Alarm spread through her.

She stood up, dropped her knitting into the seat of her rocking chair, and wandered around the knitting circles. Sure enough, everyone was giggling and joking and no one was knitting. They all had empty paper cups of lemonade littered around their rockers.

Moe apparently came to the same conclusion at the same time Flynn did. He came running up to her, a look of panic on his face. "They're drunk, they're drunk, they're all drunk. How can we have a knit-a-thon with inebriated knitters? This is a disaster. A nightmare. A travesty."

Flynn looked around. Across the entire courthouse lawn no one was knitting and everyone was slamming back pink lemonade.

"Someone must have spiked the lemonade with alcohol," Moe stated the obvious.

"Shit, Moe, we're selling that stuff to tourists!"

"Shh, lower you voice." He flapped his hands. "It's not *that* bad. There were two separate containers. The yellow lemonade is to sell to tourists. The pink lemonade was the free stuff for the knitters and the people working the festival."

Along the streets, tourists ambled past, many of them carrying glasses of yellow lemonade, but none carrying pink that she could see. Flynn blew out her breath.

"Someone is trying to sabotage the knit-a-thon," Moe said.

"Don't be so dramatic." Flynn tried to calm him

in spite of her own rapid pulse rate. "It's probably just some teenage pranksters."

"Or perhaps it could be the same person who blew up the bridge." Moe stroked his chin with a thumb and index finger. "Someone who doesn't want that bridge rebuilt."

"What are you suggesting?"

Moe looked over at the lemonade stand parked in front of the motorcycle shop. "I'm suggesting Jesse Calloway's behind it all."

Flynn didn't want to believe it, just as she hadn't wanted to believe it when Clinton Trainer had arrested Jesse for possession of cocaine and illegal firearms. "Don't go pointing fingers without proof, Moe," she said.

But inside, she had the same worry. Had Jesse decided to help her out of her knitting dilemma by spiking the lemonade? He had said he would cause a distraction for her if she needed it. Was that what he'd done?

"Flynn, my darling, why you looking so sad?" Her father's steps were sprightly and loose as he came toward her. His smile was bright, the light in his eyes even brighter. "Come here, give your old daddy a big hug and I'll make it all better."

Flynn's stomach roiled. "Dad, did you drink pink lemonade?"

"I did, darlin'. I did and it was luscious." Her father slung his arm around her shoulder and leaned in to kiss her cheek.

No, Dad, no!

"Your old man's lit." Moe wrinkled his nose.

As if she didn't recognize the signs. Her father had been trying so hard to give up the drink.

Twelve months sober and now this. Through no fault of his own, he was back to square one.

Despair wrenched her into knots. "Daddy." She gently took his arm. "Someone put vodka in the pink lemonade."

"*Nooo.*" He shook his head slowly.

"I'm afraid so."

"No." A strange look—a comingling of pleasure, shame, and defeat—crossed his face.

"Yes."

"No?" His tone turned pleading.

"I'm so, so sorry, Dad. Come on, we need to find your sponsor, get you to a meeting," she said gently.

"Can I have one more glass of lemonade first?"

"No," she said as kindly as she could, trying her best to control the fury trembling her knees. How could Jesse have done this? To Moe, she said. "Could you find Hondo and send him over here, please?"

"Handling it." Moe unclipped his cell phone from his waistband. "Hondo's manning the first aid station."

"How many glasses of lemonade did you have?" Flynn asked her father.

"Three . . . wait . . . maybe four or it even coulda been five."

She blew out her breath and guided her father through the yarn ball/knitting needle archway to sit on the courthouse steps.

He interlaced his fingers, stared at his hands. "I'm going to have to start all over again, aren't I?"

"Yes."

"I swear, I didn't know the lemonade was spiked,"

her father said. "At least not that first glass. I swear, baby, if I'd known I would never have drunk it."

"I know." She sat beside him, rubbed his back. In the past, she'd never cut him any slack where his drinking was concerned, but this was different. "You've been doing so well. This minor setback is nothing. You'll just begin again. It's okay."

Her father lifted his head, looked her in the eyes. "What did I do to deserve a daughter as good as you?"

"I'm not that good, Dad. I have faults and weaknesses just like everyone else."

"Not in my eyes, you don't."

"Flynn."

She glanced over to see Hondo coming up the steps. "Moe told you?"

Hondo nodded.

"Could you help Dad?" she asked. "I've got something I must take care of."

"Sure, sure." Hondo leaned down to take her father's arm. "Come on, Floyd. Let's go get a cup of coffee."

The minute Hondo and her father disappeared into the crowd, Flynn gathered her anger and her shaking knees and stalked across the courthouse lawn, blood pounding *boom, boom, boom* in her ears with each purposeful step. In her peripheral vision, she caught a glimpse of Moe—with a few recruits, Tommy Ledbetter of the fabulous young ass among them—prying cups of pink lemonade from the hands of inebriated knitters. But she was focused on only one thing.

She marched up to the lemonade stand, cutting in line ahead of the customers.

"Hey, Flynn." Jesse grinned.

"How could you!" she yelled. She hadn't intended on it coming out so loud, but she was so mad, she didn't really care.

"What's wrong?" His smile shattered.

"You know what's wrong."

"I don't."

"My father's drunk."

His gaze drilled into her. "Okay. How is that my fault?"

"The pink lemonade was spiked with vodka."

His eyes snapped liquid fire. "What are you accusing me of, Flynn?"

"You know."

People were gawking. Flynn could feel the heat of their stares.

"Let's go inside and discuss this."

Jesse took her arm but she jerked it away. "Don't touch me."

Instantly he dropped his hands. "All right, I can see you're upset."

"Damn right, I'm upset."

"Lemonade stand's closed folks," Jesse said, then stepped to the door of the motorcycle shop. He held the door open, waiting for her to enter before him.

A blast of cool air hit her, but it didn't soothe the heat burning inside her. Head held high, she marched past him. He followed her, and the door closed behind them. Several gawkers placed their faces against the outside of the glass. Jesse closed the shades.

"Now then, Flynn, just take a deep breath."

"Don't tell me what to do."

"Okay." He lowered his voice and raised his palms in a defensive gesture as if he was a hostage negotiator demonstrating that he was no threat to a crazed gunman. "Let me have it."

"What?" His tactic threw her off.

"The tongue-lashing, whatever it's about, let me have it."

"You spiked the pink lemonade."

"Why would you think that?" Jesse's gaze zeroed in and never left her face.

The room smelled of new rubber tires, fresh motor oil, and chrome polish. They were surrounded by an inventory of tricked-out bikes and motorcycle accessories. "Born to Be Wild" filtered softly through the music system. But Flynn was aware of nothing except the bitter taste of anger on her tongue and the solid ache in her heart.

"Um, let's see, you were running the lemonade stand."

"And you just automatically assumed that I spiked the lemonade." He grunted.

She wanted so badly to believe he hadn't done it. "I know your heart was in the right place. You were trying to help me out of my knitting problem, but getting everyone drunk was not the solution."

His eyes turned stony cold. "The lemonade container is sitting right out there on the street. Anyone could have spiked it when my back was turned, and yet you chose to believe it was me."

Guilt was rapidly replacing her anger. She *had* jumped to conclusions.

"Dammit, Flynn, I don't even drink."

"You drank champagne at my engagement party."

"Yeah, well." Jesse clenched his jaw, the muscles worked beneath his skin. "I was hurting a lot that night."

"You were?" Flynn swallowed, and felt the last bit of anger drain away.

"Hell, it tore me up inside to see you getting engaged to Trainer."

"It did?"

"Are you blind, woman? I wouldn't do anything to violate my parole. Not now, not after we've . . ." He trailed off.

"We've what?" she prodded.

"I was going to say after we made a new start, but I just realized we haven't. Not if you can believe I would do something like this."

"I'm sorry I jumped to conclusions. It's just that my dad got hold of some of that lemonade. He's been sober for a year, Jesse. He's been trying really hard and now . . ." Tears misted her eyes, but she blinked them back. She refused to cry in front of him. She tried not to cry in front of anyone. She was the strong one in the family, the big sister. She did her crying in private, alone and usually on the Twilight Bridge. But the bridge was gone now and she had nowhere to go to let it all out.

"That is a shame, Flynn, but I'm not responsible for what happened to your father and I'm damn frustrated that you don't stand by me. You didn't stand up for me at the town council meeting and now you just assumed I'd spike the lemonade."

"You have to admit, Jesse, that you've done wild things in the past," she said. "It's not outrageous for me to ask questions."

Jesse shifted his weight, folded his arms over his chest. "Yeah, okay, I admit I screwed up as a kid. I stole some cars. I shoplifted, but that was when I was in Arizona, living on the streets, trying to feed myself the only way I knew how. And then I came to this town, and from the word 'go,' I was labeled a bad boy. No one gave me a chance. Even when I played football so well they made me first-string quarterback, I still wasn't good enough to date girls like Missy Ivey. So yeah, I might have lived up to that reputation, acted out a little. I was seventeen with a huge chip on my shoulder. I did shoot off an M80 on that bridge. But out of everyone in this town, I thought you would believe in me. The whole time I was in prison, I tried hard not to think about you, but I couldn't get you off my mind. Some stupid part of me had this hope . . ." He pulled his palm down his face, let out a sigh.

"Jesse." She reached out to touch him, but he stepped away from her.

"When Aunt Patsy told me that after ten years of dating Trainer off and on you'd turned down four of his marriage proposals, I couldn't help thinking, maybe there was a chance for me, you know? Then I come back and find you're wearing Trainer's ring and I figured, Let it go, Calloway. The image you've been keeping of her in your head is nothing but a fantasy. And then you broke things off with Trainer, and damn if that sorry old hope didn't come charging back again." He shook his head.

"You're right. I've been treating you unfairly. I'm conflicted, confused."

"Well, let me unconflict you, Dimples. I'm taking

myself out of the running. I can't be with a woman who doubts my integrity."

"Are you breaking up with me? It's over?"

"Yes, ma'am," Jesse said. "Until you can prove to me that you're in my corner one hundred per-cent, the way I'm in yours, then yeah, it's over."

CHAPTER SEVENTEEN

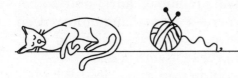

Jesse, the Jell-O has set, the sun has risen,
today is the day, we're out of prison.
Long live the rebels. My number is 555–9876.
Call me.
—Missy Ivey, yearbook entry, 1999

Jesse watched Flynn walk away, feeling as if someone had wadded him up, dropped him into a blender, and hit liquefy. It took everything he had inside him not to call after her, tell her to come back, swear that he was only kidding.

But he could not. Everything he'd worked for was at stake. He knotted his fists, bit down on his tongue. She'd accused him of spiking the lemonade. Did she truly believe he would do something like that?

He hadn't wanted to break things off with her. What he'd wanted to do, what he'd been having fantasies about doing all afternoon, was flip up the hem of her sexy little blue jean skirt, pull down her panties, bend her over the leather seat of a showroom Harley, and make her fully his, once and for all.

A watershed of dark emotions poured over him—anger, betrayal, remorse, hurt, and something deeper, sharper—a primal masculine need to claim her as his woman, mind, body, and soul, without any heed to the consequences.

Jesse couldn't, wouldn't do that. He still hadn't earned her trust, and until he did, he was not going to touch her again. No matter how hard it might be. If prison had taught him anything, it had taught him patience and the power of calm, assertive energy in overcoming any difficulty. He could wait for her to sort out her emotions and to fully believe that he had not been in possession of cocaine, had not bombed the bridge, had not spiked the lemonade.

Still, how was he going to keep up his resolve when Flynn came sashaying in here every morning, butt swaying as she climbed the stairs to the Yarn Barn. Stopping on the steps to bend over and scratch that gray tabby under the chin.

"Dammit," he cursed, and pressed a palm against his forehead. What had he gotten himself into? Why had he come back to Twilight? Being so close to her, having to keep his hands to himself was pure torture.

Frankly, he didn't know if he had the strength to handle it.

After the spiked lemonade fiasco, they called off the knit-a-thon for the reminder of the day. Even though they resumed knitting on Saturday, they'd lost momentum and ended up falling thousands short of the money they'd hoped to raise.

But Flynn had deeper worries. She took both Carrie and her father's shifts at Froggy's while Hondo dragged Floyd to Fort Worth for an intense round of AA meetings. During her breaks, she popped in to check on Carrie at the Yarn Barn. While her sister couldn't wait tables with her wrist in a cast, she could man the cash register and discuss knitting with customers. Flynn tried to keep her mind busy so she wouldn't dwell on the fact Jesse had broken up with her, but she couldn't seem to stem the churning in her gut.

Jesse was one hundred percent correct. She hadn't believed in him the way she should, and she didn't know how to go about fixing it. Thing was, it was easier to withdraw from him. Let Carrie run the Yarn Barn while she looked after Froggy's and her father.

And what of the desire that throbbed through her every time she had to pass by Jesse on her way into the yarn store? What of that?

Well, what could she do? He'd made it clear things were over between before they'd ever really begun.

"Okay, so the knit-a-thon didn't turn out as well as we'd planned," Flynn said at the next meeting of the Sweethearts' Knitting Club. "But we all had fun. Now we've got to figure out how to raise the rest of the money for the bridge. Are you guys in?"

"Count on me," Terri said.

"You betcha." Belinda nodded.

"I'm there." Marva plunked down in her rocker with a fresh cup of tea.

"Any ideas?" Patsy asked.

"We could have a wet T-shirt contest at the Horny Toad," Raylene offered.

"Um . . . you're not considering using us, are you?" Patsy asked. "Flynn and Terri are the only ones who could get away with it."

"Of course not. We'd get college girls, charge guys a hefty cover fee."

"I was thinking of something a little more wholesome," Flynn said. "Maybe an arts and crafts auction?"

"How about a picnic basket auction," Dotty Mae said. "You know, girl makes a nice little picnic lunch, boy bids on it. That's how Stuart and I became sweethearts. He bid on me at a church social."

"But Dotty, you can't cook," Terri pointed out.

"Stuart didn't buy it for my cooking. He said he was just looking to brush up against my Betty Grable legs."

"Actually," Patsy said, "it's not a bad idea. We could hold it during the sheriff's posse rodeo event at the end of the month. That'll give us time to advertise in the *Fort Worth Star-Telegram*."

"Ooh," Belinda said, "I can tie the event in with some of my matchmaking dates. Where should we hold it?"

"In the park, of course," Marva said, "underneath the Sweetheart Tree."

"Perfect," Flynn concurred. "Let's save that bridge for all the future sweethearts to come."

* * *

Just before noon on the day of the auction, locals and tourists alike gathered in Sweetheart Park right off the square. People spread out on the lush rolling lawn between the statue of the Twilight Sweethearts and the gazebo beneath the Sweetheart Tree.

Inside the gazebo, dozens of picnic baskets sat out on a long table. Moe took his place at the microphone, welcoming the participants and stressing that the proceeds from the auction would go to rebuild the Twilight Bridge. This year's Miss Twilight—seventeen-year-old Britney Wilks—stood at his elbow holding up the baskets as they came up for bidding.

"Britney's got potential as a letter turner," Carrie whispered to Flynn. "Doesn't she remind you of a young Vanna White?"

"That smile, those teeth, the vacant eyes."

"Look at this first basket, folks," said Moe.

Britney obligingly paraded the basket around the gazebo like a cue card girl in the boxing ring.

"Isn't that something? It's made out of sourdough, braided, baked, and shellacked so you can use it for a bread basket on your kitchen counter when you've eaten what's inside. Who could be that creative with a basket, you ask? Why, it belongs to Miss Christine Noble, owner of the Twilight Bakery, and if you've ever eaten her pastries you know you're in for a treat. But that's not all. Not only do you get the basket, you also get to share it with Christine. Isn't she a cutie?" Moe waved at Christine, who ducked her head and blushed prettily. "Let's get the ball rolling at fifteen dollars."

"Fifteen."

"Twenty."

And so it went.

"Look," Carrie said, ten baskets and several hundred dollars later. "Vanna put your basket up on the auction block. You're next. Whatcha got in it?"

Flynn snorted. "Fried chicken from Froggy's, what do you think? I'd cooked something special? Who has the time?"

"Hey, this auction business was your idea."

"No, saving the bridge was my idea. Blame for the auction belongs at Dotty Mae's door. So what's in *your* basket?"

"Froggy's fried chicken."

"Copycat."

"Like the idea is *sooo* original. Probably half the baskets up there have Froggy's fried chicken in them. You think Beau and Jesse are going to duke it out over your basket?"

Secretly, she had hoped Jesse was going to make a grand gesture and preempt the bidding, but since he'd barely spoken two words to her in the past three weeks, she wasn't holding her breath.

"Doubt it."

"What is the deal with you two?"

"Search me. If you find out, let me know."

"I have my thoughts on it. Wanna hear?"

"Not particularly, but I suppose you're going to tell me anyway." Flynn tucked two fingers of both hands into the back pocket of her jeans and forced herself not to scan the crowd for signs of Jesse. While not looking for him, she spied Beau standing head above everyone else over by the Sweetheart Fountain. He was checking out the gathering as well. Quickly she dropped her gaze and turned her shoulders toward her sister.

Carrie tucked an errant curl behind one ear. "You're the caretaking type."

"Now that's a shocker. Breaking news. Call the *Star-Telegram*."

"You're getting snarky. That means you're anxious. Are you worried that no one will bid on your basket?"

"Not at all. It's Froggy's chicken up for grabs. If nothing else I can count on the retirement community set."

"And Jesse," Carrie went on with her theory. "He's always had to take care of himself. He doesn't know what it's like to be nurtured and cared for. It's foreign to him. It makes him suspicious. If you're nice to him he's trying to figure out your angle. So when you give, it makes him question your motives. Giving is second nature to you. When he turns it down, you take it as a rejection."

"Wow, you learn all this in Psych 101? You're getting your money's worth out of that community college."

"I'm gonna let that go because I know you're jealous that I'm in college and you didn't get to go."

"Wise move." Flynn wasn't proud of it, but yeah, there was a grain of truth to her sister's accusation. From the corner of her eye she saw Beau moving closer to the gazebo, but there was still no sign of Jesse. Seriously, he wasn't even coming to the auction?

Could she blame him? Three-quarters of the town were convinced he'd sabotaged the knit-a-thon with vodka-laced pink lemonade. There'd been talk of banning him from joining the chamber of commerce, but the wind had been taken out of that argument when Jesse never applied for membership.

"And this lovely little basket here," Moe said, reading the tag on the handle, "is quite traditional. You got your red and white gingham check and the handle is tied up with a pretty red and white bow. Inside you've got your fried chicken with homemade biscuits, tater salad, and coleslaw." Moe pressed his nose to the closed wicker basket. "Smells like Froggy's." He looked out across the sloping lawn at Carrie and Flynn. "Which one of you MacGregor girls does this belong to?"

Carrie pointed at Flynn.

"Traitor," Flynn mumbled.

Moe looked at Beau. "You want to start the bidding, Sheriff?"

Flynn cringed, stared at her toes. "Do you see Jesse in the crowd?" she whispered to Carrie.

"What? You're asking me for a favor after accusing me of being a traitor?"

She tugged the hem of her sister's shirt. "Just do it."

"Okay, but you owe me." Carrie swiveled her head. "Uh-oh."

"What-oh?" Flynn's body tensed.

"Jesse's over by the paddleboat rental place talking to some girl I don't know. She's very pretty."

"A hundred dollars," Beau said.

The crowd gasped. Flynn felt a several dozen pairs of eyes on her. She raised her head, forced a smile.

"Do I hear a hundred and five?" Moe asked.

Not a peep, not a sound, not even a cricket chirped.

"Come on people, all proceeds go to save the Twilight Bridge," Moe cajoled.

Flynn darted a quick glance in the direction of the paddleboat rental office. Sure enough, there was Jesse leaning one sexy shoulder nonchalantly against the side of the shiplap building, talking to a young woman in her mid-twenties. Flynn recognized her. "That's Missy Ivey."

"Who?" Carrie asked.

"The woman Jesse is talking to."

"No. Really?" Carrie craned her neck. "She's lost a lot of weight and cut her hair."

"What's she doing back in town?" Flynn mused. "I thought she was engaged to some East Coast real estate big shot."

"Oh, you know how Mr. Ivey likes to exaggerate how good his kids are doing. But she does look really great. Jesse seems to think so too."

"Thanks for pointing that out." Flynn felt the stinging slap of jealousy. Jesse was moving on without her.

"Don't mention it," Carrie said.

"Anybody?" Moe asked. "You guys just gonna let Beau walk away with the girl?"

A lot of people were peering over at Jesse, but he never glanced over at the gazebo. Flynn's face heated.

"No? Okay." Moe smacked his gavel. "Flynn MacGregor's basket sold to the sheriff for a hundred bucks."

Beau stepped over to pay the fee at a nearby

card table set up with a bookkeeper to accept donations.

Vanna aka Britney picked up a motorcycle helmet. She held it over her head and pranced around the gazebo with it.

"Now this is our first basket from a man," Moe said. "Except you can all see it's not a basket, but a motorcycle helmet. Hang on a minute, while I see what's inside."

"What's this?" Flynn muttered, getting a very bad feeling about the helmet posing as a basket. "Who said men could enter?"

"Who said they couldn't?" Carrie cocked her head. "Don't be sexist."

Britney obediently trotted the helmet over to Moe. He reached in, pulled out an envelope, opened it, and read the contents out loud. "Ladies, are you ready to take a walk on the wild side? This basket contains a catered meal from Pasta Pappa's followed by a motorcycle ride on Jesse Calloway's Harley."

The women in the crowd went nuts, bidding so madly that Moe could barely keep up. "Twenty, twenty-five, thirty, thirty-five. Do I see forty, forty yes, forty-five, fifty."

Flynn stood up, raised a hand.

"Fifty-five . . . wait a minute Flynn, you can't bid on Jesse's basket. You're having lunch with Beau."

"I'm not bidding on Jesse's basket. It's not even a basket, for crying out loud." She gestured at the helmet in Britney's arms. "I just wanted to say something."

"In the middle of the auction?"

"It's important. His basket should be disqualified."

"What do you mean?"

"It's a catered dinner. The basket is supposed to contain the dinner. The idea is to make the dinner yourself."

"Just like you fried the chicken in your basket?" Moe asked.

"Sit down and shut up, MacGregor," a woman called out. "You're just jealous."

"She's a man hog is what she is," muttered someone else. "She wants her Beau and Jesse too."

Flynn's cheeks flushed. Carrie grabbed her hand and pulled her back down to the lawn.

Moe turned his attention back to the crowd. "Fifty-five, sixty. I see sixty-five, seventy, seventy-five . . ."

"One hundred and fifty dollars," Missy Ivey hollered.

That put a damper on the feeding frenzy.

"Anybody want to fight it out with Missy?" Moe asked. "No? Okay. Missy, you just scratched and clawed your way to lunch and a motorcycle ride. Next!"

Determined not to look in Jesse's direction again—if he wanted to have lunch with Missy Ivey, so be it—Flynn lifted her chin and smiled at Beau as he came up with her basket draped over his arm.

"Hey," he said, suddenly looking as bashful as a schoolboy on the playground.

"Hey."

He reached down to take her hand. What was she going to do? Not take it? He'd paid a hundred bucks for a chicken dinner that would have cost him ten-fifty if he'd gone straight to Froggy's for lunch.

Don't look over at Jesse to see if he's watching you take Beau's hand. Don't do it, don't do it.

She looked.

Jesse was staring at her.

Zap!

An electrical current that would have jolted the socks off a kite-flying, thunderstorm-loving Benjamin Franklin zipped through her. Holy shit. This attraction should be powering down, not up. It didn't appease her to see that, for a split second, Jesse looked as unnerved as she.

Missy Ivey was hanging all over Jesse. She had his helmet strapped to her head as a waiter from Pasta Pappa's fluffed out a red linen tablecloth over a picnic table with a flourish and a bow.

Jesse cocked an arrogant grin, raised a suggestive eyebrow.

Showoff.

Quickly, before Beau caught her ogling, Flynn jerked her gaze away. Oh, this was so fifth grade.

Beau's hand was at her elbow in that possessive way of his. Why was he always taking hold of her? Did he think she was too feeble to make her own way across the lawn to the picnic tables? She would have yanked it away except they were passing close by Jesse's table, now laden with a platter of chicken Marsala, a tray of lasagna, bruschetta, and a Greek salad.

Flynn's nose twitched at the delicious aromas.

"How's this?" Beau asked, picking the table

closest to the water so they could watch the ducks and the tourists in paddleboats.

"Great, fine." She could feel heat on the back of her neck. Was it the noonday sun pouring through the branches of the old pecan tree or was it Jesse staring at her?

She untied the ribbon from the basket, opened it up, took out the red and white gingham tablecloth. Behind her, Missy Ivey giggled. Flynn's stomach clenched.

Beau helped her set up the picnic spread and then sat down with his back to Jesse and Missy. He patted the seat beside him, but Flynn went around the table, pretending not to notice as she smoothed down the edge of the tablecloth and sat across from him. From this vantage point, she could see Jesse and Jesse could see her.

"You look pretty today." Beau doffed his Stetson and settled it on the table away from the food.

Stupidly, she'd worn a pink blouse, thinking, hoping . . . what the hell had she been hoping? That Jesse would bid on her basket? He'd made it clear things were over between them. "Thank you," she mumbled.

Beau reached across the table and took her hand in his. "I miss you, Flynnie."

"You see me in town almost every day, Beau."

"That's not what I'm talking about."

"I know what you're talking about." She eased her hand from his and started doling out the food on paper plates.

"I'd like you to give us another chance."

"Beau," she said softly.

"Are you still seeing him?" He said the last word harshly.

"If I was seeing him, I'd be sitting with him."

"You're sitting with me and you're not seeing me."

Touché. "We're not seeing each other."

Hope sparked in his eyes. "What can I do to earn your forgiveness?"

"Beau . . ." She poked at her potato salad with a red plastic fork. "I think maybe it's time for me to be without a man in my life. I've depended on you too long, and let's be honest, neither one of us has ever had a long-term relationship with anyone else."

"I don't want a relationship with anyone but you."

"How do you know? If you've never experienced it."

"I know," he said, hardening his chin.

She sighed. "We can't be together out of habit or fear of the unknown. That's not good."

"That's not why I want to be with you."

She raised her palms. "I need breathing room."

"I can give you that."

"Buying my picnic basket in a preemptive strike does not qualify as giving me breathing room."

"Flynnie, I'm just afraid if I give you too much breathing room you'll decide to fly away."

"You can't just force me to feel the way you want me to feel," she said.

"I'm handling this badly." Beau took a breath so deep his chest shuddered with the effort.

Empathy pumped through her until she peered over his shoulder and saw Jesse watching her.

Instantly goose bumps dotted her forearms, and

she stopped listening to a word Beau was saying. Her hands quivered and she clasped them in her lap to keep Beau from noticing. Jesse sat eight feet away, but she could feel the caress of his gaze as surely as if he was sitting beside her. Her breath came in short little gasps as if her lungs couldn't properly inflate.

Jesse brought a piece of bruschetta up and then slowly wrapped his mouth around it, all the while staring her down.

Thrown off balance, Flynn dropped her gaze and reached for a piece of chicken, nibbled on a thigh. But try as she might, she couldn't stop herself from peering over at Jesse again.

He looked like the baddest of bad boys. That insouciant slouch. That slow, mischievous grin. That insolent cock to his brow. The expression in his highwayman eyes that said, *Come on, I know you want me to do wicked things to you.* He was the sexy amalgamation of every rogue who'd ever graced the silver screen—James Dean, Marlon Brando, George Clooney, Russell Crowe, Colin Farrell.

His gaze slammed into hers, and she felt the impact hit the very center of her body. Click, snap, lock. He claimed her, chained her with his eyes.

"Flynn." Beau breathed.

"Hmm?" She wrenched her gaze from Jesse's.

"Are you listening to me?"

"Yes, yes, sure." She forced herself to focus on Beau.

"I'm not giving up on us. We've been through rough patches before. I know you have this fascination with Calloway. I get the whole bad-boy thing. I don't like it, but I get it. Except you're not a teenager anymore. You have responsibilities."

"Excuse me," Flynn snapped, "when have I not lived up to my responsibilities? I put my own life on hold because of my responsibilities. When *do* I get my own life, Beau?"

"I'm sorry." His voice rippled over the ridges of his mistake. "You're right. It's just that I don't want you to mistake falling in lust for the real thing. You can't let your libido rule your head. I'm willing to forgive you for dating him and . . ." Beau cleared his throat, hurt simmering in his eyes. "Um . . . and anything else you did with him. We were on a break after all, but—"

"This will probably come as a total shock to you, Beau, but I don't want or need your forgiveness."

Simultaneously he clenched his jaw, clenched his fist. "He's toying with you, Flynn. Listen to him over there laughing with Missy Ivey. You're nothing more than a game, a notch on his belt. I'll give you time, I'll give you space, but I won't lose you. Especially not to some low-life scumbag like Jesse Calloway."

"This isn't about me at all, is it, Beau? This is about the competition you've had with Jesse since high school when Coach Tinsley made him first-string quarterback and demoted you. You always have to be Twilight's top dog and Jesse threatens that. Because of your family's money and status, he's the only one who's ever threatened your place in the world, and you can't stand it because Jesse doesn't even care about being top dog. He usurped your position without even trying."

Beau's mouth flopped open, but then he slammed it closed. She'd pegged him and he knew it.

Flynn threw down the half-eaten chicken thigh, wadded a paper napkin in her palm, and got to her feet. "That's why you want me. So Jesse can't have me. I'm not a possession to be wrangled over."

He clamped a hand on her shoulder to stop her from walking away. "I'm trying to keep you from making a huge mistake."

"No, you're trying to cling on to a relationship that wasn't working. If you really love me as you say, Beau, you'll let me go."

Angst etched his familiar face. She'd kissed this man. Made love to him. He was the only one she'd ever gone all the way with, and yet all she felt was an empty sadness. She might never be with Jesse, but she could no longer pretend she could settle for Beau. They both deserved better.

"Flynnie, I . . ."

"Beau," she said, "please take your hand off me now."

"I'm not shutting the door on us." His stubborn chin hardened. "Not after everything we've been through."

They had been through a lot together. Supported and comforted each other during family sorrows and times of trouble. She felt compassion for Beau and she had respected him, but he was chipping away at all those good feelings. It was like finding hard, bitter slivers of pecan shell baked into your Thanksgiving pie.

"No?"

He wagged his head. "No."

"Not even if I am?"

"You don't mean that, you're just hung up on Calloway. But that's okay, because I'm going to prove to you what kind of man he really is."

Something about the way he said it, the look in his eyes, raised the hairs on her arms. "What are you talking about?"

"I'm not going to let anyone hurt you, no matter what I have to do to protect you." Then with that, Beau picked up his Stetson, settled it on his head, and walked away.

Leaving Flynn feeling as if she'd just been threatened.

CHAPTER EIGHTEEN

*Flynn, in the words of Neil Young,
you are like a hurricane.*
— Jesse Calloway,
handwritten note passed in government class, 1999

The remainder of the summer passed in a miserable swelter of dry August heat. The tabby took up permanent residence in the Yarn Barn. Flynn's life had always been too busy for a pet, and until Miss Tabitha she hadn't realized how much she'd been missing. She loved watching the little cat bat balls of yarn about the shop, and the customers spoiled her outrageously, slipping her treats or bringing her squeaky mouse toys. When the Sweethearts assembled in their knitting circle, Tabitha would curl up in Flynn's lap to have her ears scratched, giving Flynn the perfect excuse to drop her needlework. The cat was a lot of company. Who needed a man when she had Tabitha?

She managed to stay busy and, for the most

part, to avoid both Beau and Jesse. Because of the side entrance she could sometimes go a whole day or two without ever seeing Jesse, but if she listened closely enough, she could always hear him moving around or talking to customers in the shop below.

And as for Beau, he would tip his Stetson if he saw her in the street, but otherwise he kept his distance. For that, she was eternally grateful.

Unfortunately, Beau's mother wasn't so forgiving. She not only snubbed Flynn, but influenced her friends to snub Flynn as well. It bothered Flynn more than she wanted to admit. She was a people person, after all, but she couldn't live her life to please Kathryn Trainer. If the woman's friends wanted to be snippy, let 'em snip.

Her father attacked his renewed sobriety with dedicated vigor and insisted on taking over full management of Froggy's. Carrie got her cast off and she was back to knitting Flynn's projects. With extra time on her hands, Flynn spearheaded more projects to raise the rest of the money needed to rebuild the Twilight Bridge. The town council was in the process of taking bids from contractors. With any luck, they'd have a new bridge in time for the annual Twilight Christmas festival.

On the last Saturday in August, a group of home economics high school students threw a back-to-school knitting party at the Yarn Barn. They were having such fun gossiping about boys, knitting scarves, and playing with Tabitha, Flynn didn't have the heart to throw them out at nine when the shop normally closed. It was after ten when the last girl had gone home and Flynn finished straightening up for the night.

The air smelled of rain. Harsh wind whipped through the oak trees lining the square. She hunched her shoulders, locked up, and wished she had on long sleeves. Then she remembered the pink leather Harley jacket Jesse had given her, hanging in the supply closet waiting for cooler weather. She went back inside and slipped into it. The leather was soft against her skin. She hurried back outside, turned a nervous eye toward the sky, and headed down the side entrance ramp to her pickup.

She climbed into her Ford Ranger, started the engine, turned on the radio, and punched buttons looking for a local weather report. The announcer's voice spilled into the cab of her pickup, predicting heavy rains, high winds, and possible hail for all of North Central Texas.

Flynn sucked in her breath. She hated storms. Living on the river necessitated the worry of flooding. Plus Carrie and her father were gone for the weekend to pick up her twin brothers from basketball camp in Iowa. She'd be all alone in the house during a thunderstorm. Not an appealing prospect.

Just get home, go to bed, sleep through it.

The streets lay empty. Everyone else had already shut down, locked up tight. She drove past the park, headed for Highway 51, which would lead her home.

Lightning flashed. Thunder rumbled. Flynn squealed. She wasn't a wimp, but storms unnerved her. Fat raindrops spattered the windshield. She gripped the steering wheel with both hands, arms taut as guy wires. Seconds later, she was caught in a deluge.

Water pounded the hood with angry fists. Her

windshield wipers swiped uselessly at the onslaught. The wind shoved against the Ranger. Her
pulse quickened, her breathing grew shallow.

Without warning, the truck slowed, sputtered,
lurched.

Flynn pushed down harder on the accelerator.
But nothing happened. She stomped the foot pedal
all the way to the floorboard. The truck coasted
down a small incline.

Crap, crap, no!

Wrenching the steering wheel to the left, she
pulled over onto the side of the road just as the
pickup belched and stopped cold.

Okay, don't panic. She took a deep breath,
twisted the key in the ignition. The truck coughed
once, and then fell silent. No amount of additional
coaxing could bring the damn thing back to life.

The sky opened up like a chute, funneling an av-
alanche of water. Flynn could see nothing beyond
the windshield except rainy darkness. Dejected,
she pulled her cell phone from her purse, held it in
her hand, stared at it. Whom could she call?

Instinctively her fingers started to punch in Beau's
number, but she stopped herself before hitting send.
No, she didn't want to get into that. She pushed the
end button. Then she thought of Jesse, but realized
she couldn't remember his phone number, and she
felt odd about calling him anyway.

"You don't need a man to rescue you," she
grumbled. "Just call the wrecker service."

She moved her thumb across the keypad to call
directory assistance, when the low-battery warning flashed onto the display screen, mere seconds
before the phone snuffed itself out.

Supercrap! She'd forgotten to recharge the battery. Great. Now what?

She sat listening as the rain slowed from drenching to steady drumming. She was going to have to wait until someone drove by. Lovely. No telling how long that would take. This late at night in a thunderstorm, she might end up sleeping in the truck.

Several minutes passed—five, ten, fifteen. The rain slowed to a drizzle, but in the distance, she could see more lightning rolling in for a fresh round. Terrific.

In her rearview mirror, she thought she saw the bobble of headlights. She swiveled her head, peered out the back window. Not headlights plural. Headlight singular. Someone had a headlight out.

Or maybe it was a motorcycle.

Her heart gave a funny little squeeze. *Don't be ridiculous. Who would be out on a motorcycle on a night like this?*

"Jesse," she whispered.

In that moment, she knew it was he. Riding up like a dark knight in tarnished armor. The closer the headlight grew, the harder her pulse pounded in the hollow of her throat.

Compelled by an impulse she couldn't control, Flynn flung open the door and stepped out onto the wet asphalt. She stood arms akimbo, hair frizzing in the mist, facing in the direction of the swiftly approaching light.

Goose bumps of exhilaration carpeted her bare forearms. The air tasted as sharp as aged cheese. The breeze muffled the sound of the Harley engine but she could still hear it, rumbling ever closer. Her breath slipped rapidly from her lungs in hot little pants.

Closer, closer.

Suddenly the world flashed midnight blue in the stark heat of bolt-action lightning. In that split second of intense brightness, he looked like a fallen angel dressed all in black.

She heard a rushing in her ears, a thunderous swooping. Time evaporated, vanished into the ether. Nothing existed but this one moment in time, and she felt fully, completely alive. Her breath was wet; every beat of her heart was languid and loud—*boom . . . boom . . . boom.*

The Harley pulled to a stop inches from the toes of her sneakers. Jesse swung off the motorcycle, stripped off his helmet. He cocked a wicked grin as lightning bit the sky one more time.

Flynn gulped.

He held his arms wide, dropping the helmet to the asphalt.

And she ran straight into his embrace.

Their mouths locked hot and frantic.

Desperately, Jesse grabbed a fistful of hair at the nape of her neck and pulled her closer to him, spearing his tongue past her teeth.

Flynn softened her jaw and let him in with a quiet groan of pleasure.

An electrical surge, more powerful than the storm around them, ran through him. His cock hardened, scared the hell out of him it got so hard. He could chop wheat with a cock this hard.

She ran her hot little tongue around the inside of his mouth and Jesse felt himself unravel. He had to stop this before they ended up making love right there in the middle of the rain-slick road.

He broke the kiss. She smiled a soft, knowing smile, but didn't say a word. A silent understanding bound them together, tight as twine. He cupped her cheek, and she turned her face into his palm. That simple gesture of tenderness and trust made his legs quake.

Unnerved, Jesse bent, picked up his helmet, and then strapped it to Flynn's head.

Jesse stared at her in the darkness, frequently punctuated with bright flashes of blistering light, trying to put every emotion that was in his mind into his eyes for her to see. *I want you. Do you want me as much as I want you? Let's get the hell out of the rain and into a bed. Let's finish what's been ten years in the making.*

She looked back at him, never once blinked. Her gaze was steady and sure. Their eyes had been locked for only a second or two, but it felt like a lifetime. They drew in simultaneous breaths of air, exhaled on a sigh. The connection was solid, strong. A bridge angels could waltz across. In her eyes, he read the answers to his unspoken questions.

Yes, yes, yes.

He took her hand, led her to the Harley. He straddled it. She slipped on behind him, her arms hugging him around the waist. He started the engine, and they took off.

The rain rolled over them, falling from the sky, splashing up from the road, bathing them in nature, washing them clean. Flynn's arms tightened around him, and she laid her head against his back, her face turned away from the wind.

He'd never felt more alive. He wanted for nothing. He had his freedom, he had Flynn. Nothing else mattered. He yearned for her, burned for her, and now he was going to make her his, forever and always.

They zoomed through the darkness, a sexual bullet headed straight for its target—the river, her home, her bed. She was wearing the pink leather jacket he'd given her. A symbol of wildness and freedom. The wind rushed over their skin. The road sped away beneath his tires. Everything was slick and dark and dangerous.

When they reached Flynn's neighborhood, all the streetlamps were out. The community had lost power, drowned in blackness. Lightning flashes paved the way to her house. He pulled into the empty driveway. She nudged his back. He turned his head and saw her pointing to the covered carport. "Park underneath there."

He did as she suggested, parking the bike, killing the engine. Flynn was already off the seat, sprinting the short distance to the back door. Jesse ran after her.

Inside the mudroom he found her, heard her more than saw her, stripping off her clothes.

"Electricity's out," she said. "There's candles and matches in the drawer to your right."

He fumbled for the drawer, smelled fabric softener and laundry detergent. Blindly he got the drawer open, searched inside, found a votive candle in a small glass holder and a book of matches. He struck the match, lit the candle. Smelled sulfur, then vanilla. He set the candle on the laundry shelf, turned to look at Flynn.

At the sight of her bare skin, his libido lunged, strangling him like a choke collar.

Down, boy.

He told himself to look away, but he did not, could not. She reached her hands around to her back, unclasped her bra, and within seconds it joined her shirt in the dirty laundry basket.

His throat convulsed and his pupils widened, taking her in. Her fingers went to the snap of her jeans, and then she worked the zipper. The next thing he knew she was skimming the wet denim, along with her panties, over her hips.

Jesse couldn't move, couldn't think. All he could do was watch.

Flynn stood before him, totally nude. Her dark, damp curls hung to her shoulders, accentuating the creaminess of her pale skin and making her brown-green eyes look wide and innocent. Her beauty ripped the breath right out of his lungs. Hot lust licked him. The hairs on the back of his neck fanned. Inside his head an old Johnny Cash song strummed. "Ring of Fire."

"Jesse?" Flynn breathed, her gaze fixed on his.

Tender feelings rushed over him. He was there with her and she was stripped naked, exposing herself to him fully. He had fantasized about this moment for more than a decade.

Finally.

Finally.

And yet he couldn't make himself fully believe it was true. Jesse stared at her, unable to speak, terrified that if he said a word she'd disappear and he'd discover he was back in his cell in Huntsville and this was all an impossible dream.

"Is something wrong?" Flynn whispered. Her eyes filled with anxiety and she crossed her arms over her bare breasts. "I thought this was what you wanted."

With a start, he realized that his hesitation had made her self-conscious. God, he was such a dumbass. "Yes, yes, it is. Everything's perfect. *You're* perfect."

The anxiety vanished from her eyes. "You're soaked to the skin," she said, and reached for the hem of his T-shirt. He helped her wrench it over his head. "Mmm," she purred, and her eyes narrowed as she took in his chest. "Yummy."

"Flynn."

"Jesse."

His fingers itched to stroke her flesh, but he was afraid to make a move, afraid of ruining things.

"We've waited so long. I've dreamed about this so many times. I'm just scared that . . ." She paused, and he realized she was trembling.

Hell, he was trembling too. "We're setting ourselves up for disappointment?"

She nodded.

"You could never disappoint me, Dimples," he murmured, and closed the gap between them, folded her into his arms, and gently kissed her forehead.

God, she smelled so good. Like rain and summer heat. He pulled back, looked into her face, gauging her reaction. Her eyes were heavy-lidded, her expression sultry. He kissed her again, forcing himself to go slowly, to be tender with her. This moment was special, magical. He wanted to remember it for the rest of his life.

She ran her palm up his bare chest, splayed her fingers through the tufts of hair. With a low growl, he sucked her bottom lip up between his teeth, nibbling lightly. He felt so many things at once—desire, longing, love.

Yeah, love. He wasn't ready to say it yet, not until he knew if she felt the same way or not, but he thought it.

Love. He loved Flynn MacGregor. Without any doubt or reservation.

"Flynn," he whispered huskily, barely recognizing his own voice. He cupped her bare butt cheek with his palm and almost groaned out loud. Her muscles were taut but soft, a thrill to caress.

"Take me, Jesse, take me now," she begged.

That was all the enticement he needed. He bent to scoop her into his arms.

"You don't have to carry me," she said. "I'm fully capable of walking."

"I know that," he said, and started to stride from the mudroom into the kitchen.

"Wait, wait, candle."

"Right." He carried her over to the shelf so she could grab the votive candle. "Bedroom?"

"Upstairs, first door on the right."

He charged up the stairs, heart pounding. The first door on the right stood slightly ajar.

"Your family," he said suddenly when he reached the landing. For the first time since coming into the house, he thought about something other than getting his hands on Flynn.

"Gone for the weekend to pick up Joel and Noah from basketball camp."

"Both Carrie and your dad?"

"Yep."

"No chance they could walk in on us?"

"None at all."

"That's all I needed to hear," he said, and toed the door open.

Flynn lay stretched across her bed watching Jesse come out of his wet jeans. The candle flickered on the bedside table. Music whispered from the battery-powered boom box on her window ledge, spinning the soft sounds of Faith Hill's version of "Help Me Make It Through the Night."

Her heart lumped up in her throat. So many nights she'd lain in this very bed, imagining herself naked just like this, watching Jesse walk in through the door of her bedroom, just as naked. How many restless nights had she dreamed of him? Touched herself and pretended it was his hand, not hers? How many tears had she shed over him when he'd returned her letters unopened? Sobbing into her pillow, her tender sixteen-year-old soul shattered into a million little pieces.

As she lay there now, seeing Jesse stalking up to her bed, that lustful look in his eyes aroused all the old emotions, all the old dreams. He was beyond handsome. Strong, masculine, graceful.

Her stomach fluttered.

He had a sprinkling of light brown hair over his muscular pecs, knotted biceps, sinewy forearms with the strong veins of a natural athlete pumping blood through his magnificent body. He had a second swirl of light brown hair just under the scoop of his navel that narrowed down to darker, curlier hair, framing his . . .

His penis jutted forward, a divining rod, pointing straight at her.

Flynn sucked in her breath. Her inner feminine muscles twitched with awe and excitement. Absolutely nothing—*nothing*—could have prepared her for the heated jolt of sexual desire coursing through her veins.

"Condom?" she whispered.

"Wallet."

"You were prepared?"

"Have been since that night in the Yarn Barn."

"Good man."

He chuckled. "Come here."

Ten years her body had been aching for this. Ten years of buried yearning surged through her veins, and she forgot everything except her need for him. She was sixteen again—shiny and young and free of mistakes—and the boy she was crazy in love with was holding her, kissing her, fulfilling her every fantasy.

Jesse took her hand in his, pressed his lips to the back of it, then raised his head and looked into her eyes. "I missed you so much, Dimples."

The heartfelt note in his voice was her undoing. Here was this big tough guy laying his emotions on the line. "Jesse," she whispered, and planted kisses all over his face. "Jesse, Jesse. Are you really here? Is this really happening?"

"I'm here. It's happening. Finally, finally."

But even as he reassured her, it still felt like an impossible dream. How many times as a teenager had she lain in her bed imagining him touching her just like this?

Hundreds?

Thousands?

She stared deeply into his eyes, knew he wanted to be inside her as much as she wanted him there— swelling, filling her up, making her complete. *Let's build a bridge, span time, hurdle the hurts of the past*, she thought giddily. *Overwhelm my soul, seize my imagination. Take me places I've never been. Make my heart sing. Make my legs tremble. Lick my thighs. Kiss me happy.*

She felt him everywhere—on her skin, her mouth, her toes, her fingers, her heart. Juicy, sweet, hot.

His body.

What a body!

The sweet feel of his strong, hard chest against hers. She tasted, licked. Delicious. Her tongue lingered, in love with the saltiness of him. Water droplets dotted his shoulders, dripping from his wet hair. She put her lips to it, drank from his skin. Intoxicating passion.

He felt so good in her arms. So alive. Their legs intertwined. His arms were her blanket. Engulfed. They kissed with everything they had in them. Heart, soul, mind. Sweethearts lost and found again.

Biting need flowed like blood through her ventricles. Pulsating, quick, hot, strong. She writhed beneath him, breathing hard, her ears humming with pleasure. So much pleasure. His mouth was everywhere. Lips on lips. Lips on nipples. Lips on navel and ah, ah, lips on *those* secret lips.

Heat and steam and sweat. A noise sounded. Was that a tea kettle? She hadn't put on water for tea. That was no tea kettle, but rather her own keening sound slipping from her hungry, willing lips.

Their fingers were at each other. Plucking, rubbing, caressing, kneading. Their fingernails clawed at sheets, headboard, pillows, skin. Need. So much need. Lust and trust. They pulled in air with each other's scents. They were one, no more two.

Their breath came in harmony. She was on her back, looking up into his eyes. Gray-blue eyes that had seen so much hardness in the world. Then he closed them and gently buried his penis deep inside her.

In and out. He moved slow and sure. Their bodies undulating as he kissed her. Their souls tied, bound, connected. His nimble mechanic's fingers skating over her thighs in crazy, dreamy circles.

Every nerve in her body was alive, on edge.

His movements quickened. From slow to staccato, thrusting into her deeper, higher, faster. He was on fire. A wild man. But no wilder than she. Their rhythm was perfect, as if all the practicing they'd done in their midnight dreams had prepared them for this glorious joining.

He pushed her legs up over her head, opening her wide, entering her as deeply as possible, pounding her hard.

Too much pleasure!

Her mind went numb as waves of orgasm overpowered her. His noises were as rough and loud as her own. Their bodies jerked in unison. They clung together, glued with rain and sweat and love juices.

When it was over, they lay on their sides, looking into each other's eyes, smiling and smiling and smiling. Jesse reached for her right hand, took it, curled her fingers into her palm, and then gently placed it over her heart. "I love you, Flynn MacGregor," he whispered. "I loved you then, I love you now, and I'll love you forever."

They slept for a while and then awoke in the night to stroke each other.

"What made you come after me in the dark?" she whispered. "How did you know I was on the side of the road needing your help?"

"We're connected, you and I," he whispered.

"Honestly, how did you really know? I'm assuming you weren't just out for a midnight ride in a thunderstorm on a motorcycle."

"You're right," he said. "When I left the shop I passed by where you parked, saw what looked to be a gallon of cherry red syrup on the pavement."

"And that made you come after me? What? Did you think I had a cold?"

"It was transmission fluid," he explained. "You had a big leak. I knew you probably wouldn't make it home."

"You came after me."

"I did."

"My hero," she teased, curling against him.

He pulled her close, kissed the top of her head. "Nah," he said. "It was all part of my master plan to get you into bed."

"Well, it worked." She giggled, and then she quickly forgot about anything else as his mouth once again lit a furious fire inside her.

CHAPTER NINETEEN

Calloway, don't let me catch you in my town again.
—Beau Trainer, parting words on graduation day, 1999

Mockingbirds singing in the peach tree outside Flynn's bedroom window woke Jesse just after dawn on that Sunday morning.

He opened his eyes, felt Flynn's body on the mattress beside him. He tucked his hands behind his head and stared up at the ceiling, a happy grin on his face, a sweet aching soreness in his muscles. Idly he considered running his head underneath the cool cotton sheet in search of her warm, sweet thighs. But they'd already made love three times during the course of the night, and he thought perhaps she might be worn out. Besides, he was starving. They'd burned off a thousand calories, easy.

Quietly he edged out of bed and crept into her bathroom, washed his face, slipped on his jeans that were almost dry, and padded barefoot downstairs. He hummed to himself as he took eggs and bacon from the fridge, and slapped an iron skillet onto the stove.

The bacon was just starting to sizzle when he heard a vehicle pull up into her driveway. Shit, had her family come home? Jesse moved to the window for a peek outside.

He froze when he saw Trainer getting out of his cruiser, and he knew at once what must have happened. Trainer had seen Flynn's pickup broken down on the side of the road and he'd come to check up on her.

What Jesse did next was stupid as hell. Pure masculine ego, but he wasn't going to hide and cower. Boldly he marched out the back door, barefooted, bare-chested, flaunting, taunting.

The screen door slammed shut behind him. He spied Trainer standing beside his Harley, hands on his hips.

Trainer raised his head, took in Jesse's near nakedness. Bone-deep hatred flashed in his eyes. "Calloway." He spat out Jesse's name like it was a bad taste in his mouth.

"Trainer." Jesse arched an eyebrow, balled his hands into fists, sauntered down the porch steps.

"*You!*"

"Me."

"I'll kill you." Beau took a menacing step toward him.

"I'd love to fight you, man, I really would. We got a lot of old anger that needs expelling, but I'm not stupid enough to take the first swing at you. You're just itching for any excuse to send me back to prison. I'm not jeopardizing my freedom."

Beau rolled up his sleeves, stripped off his Stetson,

shed his holster and gun, yanked off his badge. "Forget my position as sheriff. This is between you and me." He put up his fists, circled like some half-assed boxer. "Let's settle this thing once and for all. I give you my word I won't arrest you."

Jesse used both hands to motion him forward. "Come on, big man, I'm ready."

And just like that, the bare-knuckled brawl was on.

Beau lowered his head, snorted like a bull, and barreled straight for Jesse's solar plexus.

"That the best you got?" Jesse scoffed, lightly stepping aside and grabbing Beau by the back of his shirt as he charged past. Jesse spun him around and punched him a hard, short jab to the jaw.

Trainer bellowed, came back at him, fists windmilling through the air. He clocked Jesse on the side of the temple.

Jesse's vision blurred, his ears rang. He jumped on Trainer's back, cinched him in a headlock.

Trainer spun around the yard, trying to buck him off.

A decade's worth of anger came pouring out of them both. The veins in Jesse's throat throbbed as hot blood rushed through his system. He drew air into his lungs in short, snorting gasps.

"Convict," Beau wheezed, trying desperately to grab hold of Jesse.

"Crooked cop."

"Bastard."

"Fuck head."

They slugged and pounded, lost their balance, fell in the flower bed, punching and kicking and rolling. First Jesse was on top, then Trainer, the scrap evenly matched. Trainer was bigger and heavier but Jesse was leaner and faster. Trainer knew precision military moves. Jesse had been schooled in down-and-dirty street fighting.

"Stop it! Stop it!"

At some point Jesse realized Flynn was screaming. The sound of her voice barely penetrated through his rage-soaked brain. He was mauling Trainer's hand with his teeth as the sheriff attempted to gouge his eyes out with beefy fingers. They were both covered in dirt and bits of butchered daisies.

"Dammit, I said stop it! The both of you are acting like idiots."

How could he stop? If he stopped, Trainer would get the upper hand, and he wasn't about to let that happen. They tussled, wrestled, grunted, and swore.

It took the sound of a handgun blast to shake them from their death lock on each other.

They broke apart panting, Trainer falling to one side of the yard, Jesse to the other.

Flynn stood glaring at them, Trainer's duty weapon pointed in the air. She wore a bathrobe and house slippers, her hair a wild, chaotic tumble of curls about her shoulders. Jesse grinned at her even as he felt his left eye swelling closed. She was the most beautiful thing he'd ever seen.

"Beau," she commanded. "Get up, get back to your job. Jesse, go put some clothes on. And both of you stop acting like children."

"I can't believe you fought him." Flynn gave Jesse a package of frozen peas to put on his swollen eyes.

Her heart was still galloping from the effects of their altercation. "He had every right to haul you off to jail for assaulting an officer of the law."

"He attacked me first."

"That's no excuse."

"He had it coming." Jesse slouched in the kitchen chair. The smell of burned bacon hung in the air.

"Beau is jealous of you. There's no need to rub his nose in the fact that you and I are—" She broke off without finishing the thought. What were she and Jesse? After last night she knew what she wanted from her side of the equation, but she didn't know what Jesse wanted. Maybe his goal all along was to take her away from Beau. That thought had her plunking down in the kitchen chair across from him.

"You and I *are* together," Jesse finished for her.

She met his gaze. "Are we?"

He reached across the table, took her hand. "After last night, do you really have to ask that question?"

Her heart fluttered with hope. So much hope. He was there right in front of her, wanting her, all she had to do was reach out and take his hand.

"I meant what I said to you last night, Flynn. I don't say these words lightly. In fact, I've never said them to anyone other than my mother, but I love you." He reached for her and pulled her into his lap.

She giggled and wrapped her arms around his neck. "So you've forgiven me for not standing up for you in front of the community and for accusing you of spiking the lemonade and—"

He slipped his palms up underneath her robe.

"Dimples, when it comes to you, I simply can't hold a grudge."

"Hello? Anybody home?" Carrie called out as the back screen door creaked open.

Instantly Flynn leaped from Jesse's lap. "You . . . you . . . you're home early."

"And while the cats were away the mice were gettin' it on." Carrie laughed, eyeing Jesse's naked chest. "Oh hell, what happened to your eye, Jesse?"

Flynn waved a hand. "Long story. Dad and the boys?"

"Right behind me."

Flynn didn't even have time to groan over being caught in her bathrobe in the kitchen with a semi-naked Jesse, because her father and brothers bumped into the kitchen with their duffel bags and basketball gear. The twins had changed so much in the three months they'd been gone, their faces settling into the masculine lines of adulthood, but they were still horsing around like kids. It struck her then that Jesse had been their age when he'd been sent to the penitentiary.

She ran to them, hugged them. Taking turns they picked her up, spun her around the room, laughing and telling her she'd gotten shorter.

"Oh," her father said. "We didn't realize you had company."

"Hello, Mr. MacGregor." Jesse got to his feet, extended his hand. Flynn could tell he was trying hard not to look self-conscious.

"Jesse." Floyd shook his hand.

"Hey," Joel said. "Who are you?"

Noah puffed up his chest. "And what are you

doing naked in the kitchen with our sister?" Noah looked at Flynn. "Does Beau know about this?"

"It's a long story," Flynn, Carrie, and Floyd all said at once.

Jesse was cool enough not to say anything. He motioned toward the stairway, indicating he was going to her room for his shoes and shirt.

"Who wants breakfast?" Flynn asked, rubbing her palms together.

"Me," said Joel.

"Starvin'," Noah chimed in.

"I'll cook it," Carrie offered. "You take care of your . . . *guest*."

"Thanks." Flynn flashed a smile.

Jesse came back downstairs. "I'm just gonna hit the road."

Flynn took his hand, led him outside. "Not without a good-bye kiss you're not."

They walked over to his motorcycle. Jesse leaned against it, drew her into his arms. "I know you've got some catching up to do with your family." He kissed the tip of her nose. "So I'll leave you to it, even though I had plans of spending the day in bed with you."

"Did you now?"

"I did, but that can wait. We've got all the time in the world."

The sentiment warmed her up inside. "Okay."

"See you tomorrow at work." He gave her one last kiss, then strapped on his helmet and straddled the Harley.

She raised a hand, her bare feet growing cold on the damp ground.

"Don't forget." He smiled. "I love you."

Flynn opened her mouth to tell him she loved him too, but she couldn't say it. Not because she didn't feel it, but because she felt it so strongly, she feared if she said the words he'd simply vanish and she'd never see him again.`

"Give me anutter whiskey, Earl," Beau slurred and pushed his shot glass across the bar.

Earl puckered up his face like he'd bit down on a lemon. "That's your sixth one tonight."

"Izza any you bidness?" Beau swayed on the bar stool.

"I know you're a big boy, but you don't drink like this, Beau."

"You sayin' I can't hold my likkor?"

"That's exactly what I'm saying. What's wrong?"

"Nothin'."

"What are you so angry about?"

"I'm not angry." He scowled. "I'm just tryin' to get things right."

"Okay."

"I work hard to get things right, don't I?"

"You do." Earl picked up a towel and started wiping down the bar, but he didn't pour Beau another shot of whiskey.

"What am I doin' wrong? I try and I try and I try to do the right thing. Whizzit all going to hell in a handbasket, Earl?"

Earl shrugged.

Beau pointed a finger at him. "Eggsactly. You don't know."

"Nope."

"Why does she like him better'n me? What's he got that I ain't got? Why do women like bad boys, Earl? Whazza appeal?"

"Dunno."

"I'm upstanding, principled." He puffed out his chest.

"You are."

"Damn straight."

"You push yourself too hard."

"No." Beau thumped the bar with his fist and pointed a finger at Earl. "No, sir, I do not. I don't push myself hard enough. I have to do better. Be better. I won't wanna be like him. I can't be like him. I'm good."

"Are you talking about Jesse Calloway?" Earl ventured. "Or your father?"

At the mention of his father, Beau's stomach roiled and whiskey burned back up his throat. "I gotta stop this."

Earl risked putting a hand on Beau's arm. "Let me get someone to drive you home." Beau flung his arm up, staggered off the bar stool. Earl stepped back. "Lemme alone."

He stumbled outside into the darkness. His pulse pounded erratically in his ears. His shoulders were tense, his spine straight in spite of all the whiskey he'd downed. *I'm good. I'm good. I'm good. It's up to me to stop the bad guys. I can't let this keep happening. I have to stop it. It's up to me. I can't trust anyone to get the job done.*

One way or the other, he had to get rid of Calloway before he destroyed Flynn. He had to fix this thing. Now. Tonight. And for the very last time.

* * *

Something woke Flynn in the middle of the night. An uneasiness settled deep inside her bones. She couldn't name it or explain it, but fingers of dread squeezed around her heart. And she had this one terrible thought.

Beau has done something to Jesse.

Gripped by a sudden desperate need to see Jesse, to touch his face, to kiss his lips, to hold him in her arms, Flynn swung out of bed at three-forty A.M. on Monday morning, tugged on her clothes, rushed downstairs.

I should have told him I love him. Why didn't I tell him I loved him?

On her way out the door, she almost tripped over the duffel bags Noah and Joel had left tossed on the floor. Mumbling under her breath about inconsiderate little brothers, she padded outside to her father's Ford sedan, started it up, and drove into Twilight. At this hour of the morning the roads lay empty. What was she doing out at this time of day? Why was she so anxious? Why was she letting her fears get the better of her?

Whatever it was, she couldn't shake the feeling something bad had happened to Jesse.

By the time she reached the town square, she'd convinced herself she was worrying for nothing, that she was imagining things, borrowing trouble, or suffering from the remnants of a dream she didn't remember.

She was about to turn the sedan around and head back home when an acrid smell filled her nose.

Smoke.

Her heart started a rapid thunder, rampaging in her chest like a caged bull. Bile rose in her throat.

Fire.

She saw it then, a column of gray-white moving up into the dark sky above the theater, confirming her worst fears. At once she knew where the dread had come from, what had pulled her from a deep sleep. She must have left one of the scented candles burning when she'd locked up on Saturday night. It had been burning for more than twenty-four hours.

The Yarn Barn and the motorcycle shop were ablaze!

Jesse was jogging around the lake. His mind had awakened him in the wee hours, worrying him with the thought that Flynn hadn't told him she loved him after he'd bared his heart to her. Did she love him or not? If so, why hadn't she said it? And if she didn't love him . . .

Doubt churned his head, so that he barely noticed when he caught a whiff of smoke. His nose twitched. Who was burning a fire in August? He followed his nose, swiveling his head around until he spied the plume rising in the sky. It was so close. Had to be a building on the town square.

The motorcycle shop! The Yarn Barn!

He took off at a dead sprint. Shit, shit, shit, why hadn't he brought his cell phone?

A minute later, he rounded Ruby Street just in time to see Flynn springing out of her father's sedan. What was she doing there?

They reached the front of the motorcycle shop

at exactly the same moment. Flynn had her cell phone to her ear. "Fire," he heard her croak. "On the square."

He could see the flames dancing in the window, leaping and jumping, spreading fast. Smoke wafted around them, billowing, building. Why was it spreading so fast? Was there an accelerant? Could this be arson?

"I caused it," Flynn moaned as sirens wailed in the background. "It's all my fault."

"What are you talking about?"

"I left a candle burning in the Yarn Barn." Her eyes rolled wildly, she wrung her hands. "It's all my fault, it's all my fault, I've ruined everything."

Jesse took her by the shoulders, forced her to look at him. "That's no candle. The fire started on the bottom floor. You didn't leave a candle going. This is not your fault. This is arson."

"Oh God," she exclaimed, and plastered her palm over her mouth.

"What is it?"

"Miss Tabitha is in there!"

Flynn stood watching in horror as the building she and Jesse had lovingly poured their hearts and souls into was chewed up by flames. Already the fire was so blistering hot, she had to raise her arms to shield her face from the heat.

Tabitha. The gray tabby was in there. Poor little cat.

"She's dead," Flynn whispered. "She's dying."

"No she's not." Jesse pointed.

She raised her head, saw Miss Tabitha's little face pressed against the upstairs window, her mouth opened in a yowl. Flynn let out a yowl of her own.

The next thing she knew, Jesse was kicking down the door.

She grabbed the sleeve of his shirt. "What are you doing? You can't go in there. Wait for the firemen. They're here." She waved at the fire truck careening around the corner of Ruby Street.

"It'll take too long. I can't watch that cat die," he said. "I've lost too many things in my life." Then he pulled loose from her grasp and plunged into the burning building.

"No! Jesse!" she screamed, but he was already gone.

Jesse didn't think. Just as he hadn't stopped to think when he'd rushed in to save Josh Green. He simply reacted, plunging ahead even as every sensible bone in his body urged him to flee.

Smoke filled his lungs. But he just kept going, driven by a personal need more intense than the primal urge of self-preservation. He was a good guy and he was desperate to prove it. To the town, to Flynn, to himself.

And besides, he sort of loved that damn little cat.

Blindly he charged up the staircase, heard the old timbers pop and hiss, felt the heat on his skin.

Get out, get out, his body urged.

He thought of Flynn on the sidewalk.

How stupid would it be if you died over a cat just when you and Flynn are finally getting together? Turn back, turn back now.

But he was already at the head of the stairs.

The floor trembled beneath his feet. Yarn was falling, bouncing from the shelves. He heard the cat mewling above the ominous crackling noises. He coughed against the choking smoke, pulled up the neckline of his T-shirt to cover his nose and mouth.

Smoke thickened, swirled. His lungs ached. His eyes burned. His blood pumped sluggishly. Jesse dropped to his knees, crawling as quickly as he could toward the window.

The terrified tabby hissed at him. But he understood. Fear could make you do strange and stupid things. He grabbed her up, ignoring the bite of sharp claws she sank into his skin. Clutching the wriggling cat to his chest, he staggered to his feet, but stayed bent over, keeping his head down, and rushed for the stairs.

And Jesse reached the landing just as the center support beam collapsed.

The firemen buzzed around Flynn, dragging hoses, spraying water, trying desperately to douse the flames.

"He's in there!" Flynn shouted above the noise of sirens and radios and burning wood. "Jesse's inside the building!"

"Jesse's inside?" It was Hondo, and the flash of fear on his face rattled her deeply.

"He went in after the cat. I tried to stop him—"

Hondo didn't wait for her to finish speaking. He grabbed a fireman, motioned toward the building, and they headed through the doorway.

The flame gave a low hiss and then something exploded, blowing Hondo and the fireman backward onto the sidewalk. They fell on their butts, dazedly shaking their heads.

"No!" Flynn screamed as terror struck her heart. She couldn't lose Jesse. Not now, not after all this time, not when she'd finally found the love she'd tried too long to deny. She rushed for the door herself, but Hondo struggled to his feet and managed to grab her before she could get there.

"It's too late," he said, his voice like a rasp. He held her tight, held her close. "We can't save Jesse."

"No!" She thrashed in his arms. "No, no!"

Inside the building a timber fell, shot sparks out into the streets. Flynn dropped to her knees. Around them, onlookers had gathered, and the EMTs were herding them back behind sawhorse barricades.

Hondo held her tightly around the waist. Flynn sobbed, a deep, heart-wrenching sound that she couldn't recognize as her own voice. "No, no, no."

The firemen raced about, while Hondo slowly helped her stand, drew her away from the fire. "No," she whimpered, and clutched Hondo's collar. "He can't be dead. I love him, Hondo. I love him so much and I never told him."

"I know," Hondo said, wet tears sliding down the big man's face. "I know."

He cradled her to him, holding her tight as her heart split into a million little pieces and her mind spun numbly in disbelief and denial.

"He knew you loved him," Hondo whispered. "He knew, he knew."

"Oh God," she groaned, the emotional pain hitting her right between the eyes. It hurt as badly as when her mother had died. Worse in some ways, because part of her had been relieved to know her mother's suffering was at an end. This was utter tragedy through and through.

"Hey!" a fireman shouted.

Simultaneously, Flynn and Hondo turned their heads. Suddenly there was movement from out of the shadows on the side of the old theater.

Magic. A miracle. It was Jesse lurching forward with something clutched against his chest.

Jesse looked straight at her, stared into her, and she stared into him, peered into his soul. *He was alive!*

And so was Miss Tabitha. The little cat peeked fearfully from the shelter of Jesse's arms.

Flynn ran to him, slipped her hand around his waist.

The firemen surrounded them, guiding them over to the ambulance. The paramedics took over. A firefighter pried Miss Tabitha from his hands. "We'll take good care of her. We'll get Steady Sam to check her out."

A soot-stained Jesse clasped Flynn to him. She squeezed, hugging him so tightly they both had a hard time breathing. Seconds before, sorrow and grief had held her in an iron fist, now the delicate wings of joy fluttered through her heart.

Alive. Jesse was alive.

She covered his face in kisses, not caring in the least that he tasted of soot and stank of smoke. He was there. He was alive.

"I love you," she murmured urgently. "I love you, I love you, I love you."

"I love you too, Dimples."

Hondo laid a hand on Flynn's shoulder. "I hate to interrupt, but we need to check Jesse out."

"Yes, okay, right," she said, stepping away, swiping at the tears of happiness sliding headlong down her cheeks.

"You stay right here," Jesse said, reaching out his hand to take hers while Hondo wrapped a blood pressure cuff around his other arm.

Jesse perched on the edge of the gurney, Flynn seated herself on the floor of the ambulance beside him, their fingers locked together. And that's how they sat, hearts and hands entwined, as they watched their dreams burn to the ground.

Hondo wheeled Jesse into the emergency room on the lightweight metal gurney. He knew Flynn was right behind him and he wouldn't have much time to tell the boy what he had to say. But after tonight, after watching him almost die, Hondo had to say it.

"You doin' okay?" Hondo asked, his voice coming out all rough.

Jesse gave him a wry grin. "I'll live."

"Listen," he said. "There's something I gotta tell. It's something I've been meaning to tell you for a long time."

"What's wrong, Hondo? You look like someone died."

"You may want to kill me when you find out."

Jesse frowned, winced. His face was covered in soot, and the parts that weren't were blistered red with first-degree burns. The kid needed pain medication, not to hear his confession.

"Never mind, I'll tell you later."

"It's okay, go ahead. Get it off your chest."

Hondo blew out his breath, plowed his fingers through his hair. "You want to know why I visited you in prison? Why I loaned you the money for the motorcycle shop?"

"Yeah."

Hondo splayed a palm to the back of his neck. He was having a hard time looking Jesse in the eye. "There's a good chance that I'm your father."

"Huh?" Jesse blinked, looked dazed, and then laughed. "For a minute there I thought you said you might be my father."

Hondo nodded miserably. "That watch you're wearing? It used to be mine."

"But . . . how?"

"You know your Aunt Patsy and I have a lot of old history."

"She's never talked about it to me, but yeah, I got that vibe."

"Well, it's a long story and we don't have time to get into it now, we'll talk when you're better, but the *Reader's Digest* version is that I ended up in Phoenix twenty-nine years ago. I was still doing drugs then, trying to stop, but not having much luck. I met your mother at a Narcotics Anonymous meeting and she looked so much like your Aunt Patsy that I . . ." He swallowed. "We'll talk later. Just know that I never knew about you until Patsy brought you to Twilight and I started doing the math and . . ." Shit. He couldn't do this. "I gotta go." He pointed at the door.

Jesse nodded. The kid looked overwhelmed and exhausted, but he didn't seem filled with hatred. That gave Hondo some encouragement. "Later."

Hondo pivoted, practically sprinted for the door, only to find Patsy and Flynn standing in the hallway.

Patsy stood staring at Hondo, her worst fears confirmed. Hondo *was* Jesse's father. She'd suspected. Had read Phoebe's diary where she wrote about having sex with Hondo. But in that same time period her sister had sex with several other men, and Phoebe wasn't above lying. Not even in a diary entry.

The news shouldn't have hurt as badly as it did. Twenty-nine years had passed. She'd been married to Jimmy all this time. Hondo had a right to sleep with anyone he wanted to sleep with, and yet she couldn't help feeling betrayed. He'd screwed her sister, made a baby with her.

"Patsy," Hondo said, and reached out to her.

She refused to look at him. Refused to acknowledge he even existed. The pain in her heart was almost as great as it had been when she thought he'd been killed in battle. Patsy simply linked her arm through Flynn's and said, "Let's go see my nephew."

CHAPTER TWENTY

Jesse loves Flynn
—Carved into the bark of the Sweetheart Tree, 1999

Jesse couldn't wrap his head around this newfound knowledge that Hondo Crouch could very well be his long-lost father. It startled him, but in all honesty, he found the idea appealing. Hondo was a good guy, even if he was flawed. But Jesse didn't have a lot of time to think about it, not with Flynn rushing to his side along with his Aunt Patsy.

"Hey," Flynn whispered, and gently kissed his forehead.

"Hey," he croaked, smiling at her. The motorcycle shop might have burned down but it was shaping up to be a pretty good day. Flynn had told him she loved him and Hondo had confessed that he might be his father.

"How are you feeling?" She perched on the edge of the bed beside him. It felt good having her there.

"I've had worse days. The doctor says I'll be fine. Some minor burns, smoke inhalation. They might let me go home later today."

"That's wonderful." Flynn patted his arm.

"Jesse Calloway."

At the sound of the masculine voice, Jesse, Flynn, and Patsy swung their eyes to the doorway.

Sheriff Trainer and Fire Chief Rutledge trod toward Jesse's bed. The gloating expression in Trainer's eyes told him this wasn't a social call.

"Jesse Calloway," Trainer said. "You're under arrest."

Jesse stomach flipped. Not again.

"What's this?" Flynn exclaimed, jumping to her feet.

"We found evidence of arson inside the motorcycle shop," Fire Chief Rutledge explained. "Jesse's fingerprints were all over a gas can we found in a Dumpster behind the property."

"What? No!" Flynn balled her hands into fists.

"Couple that with the fact that your boyfriend took out a three-quarter-of-a-million-dollar insurance policy, and you've got means, motive, and opportunity," Trainer said.

"This is bogus and you know it. Jesse did not start that fire," Flynn ranted.

"It was arson," Fire Chief Rutledge said. "There's no doubt about it."

Trainer's eyes locked with Jesse's.

Jesse knew what this was all about. Flynn. "You set me up again, Trainer. Bad habits die hard. You're trying to hold on to Flynn the only way you know how."

Trainer didn't answer him. He just clamped one end of the handcuff around Jesse's wrist, the other side to the bed rail. "You have the right to remain silent . . ."

"There's no way Jesse started that fire." Patsy paced the length of her living room floor. "I've hired the best lawyer I can afford, but that insurance policy makes him look guilty."

"Why did he take out such a big insurance policy?"

"Because he borrowed the money from Hondo, and if anything happened to the shop he wanted to make sure Hondo was paid back with interest."

It made sense. She believed it. She should have believed Jesse the first time.

"Clearly Beau isn't going to investigate any further. He's convinced Jesse burned down the shop to claim the insurance money," Patsy said. "I can't let Jesse go to prison a second time for a crime he didn't commit."

"Me either. We've got to take stronger measures," Flynn said. "We're going to have to conduct our own investigation. Somebody had to have seen something. This is Twilight, after all. Everybody knows what everyone else is up to."

"What do we do first?"

"Go door to door, asking lots of questions."

Patsy picked up her purse. "Let's hit it."

By the end of the afternoon Flynn and Patsy were completely discouraged. They'd canvassed an entire three-block radius around the motorcycle shop. While Twilight was a friendly town that took an interest in the business of its friends and neighbors, it was also a town that rolled up the carpet early. Few people had been out and about in the wee hours of Monday morning, and it seemed no one had seen a thing.

The last house on the block was a small frame bungalow that put Flynn in mind of a quaint English cottage. Rosebushes lined the walkway, and red geraniums peeked at them from white wooden window boxes.

"This is an exercise in futility." Patsy sighed. "Eloise Baron is deaf as a post. I'm sure she didn't hear a thing."

"Still," Flynn said resolutely, "we have to try. For Jesse's sake."

That pulled Patsy's shoulders upward. "You're right. We can't let Beau win."

Flynn knocked on the door. She had to pound on it several times before it swung inward, and a wizened little gray-haired lady peeked out.

"I'm sorry," Eloise Baron said, "I don't have any money to buy anything. I'm on a fixed income and—"

"We're not here to sell you anything, Mrs. Baron. I'm Flynn MacGregor and this is Councilwoman Patsy Cross. We'd like to ask you some questions about the fire on the square last night."

"Well, why didn't you say so? That was quite scary. Come right in." The woman swung open the door. "Would you like a cup of tea?"

"No thank you," Patsy said. "We don't want to trouble you."

"No trouble at all." Mrs. Baron toddled to the kitchen. They followed her. "Will Earl Grey do?"

"That would be fine," Flynn said.

Fifteen minutes later after much tea sipping and pleasantries exchanged with the elderly woman, they discovered what they'd gone there hoping to find. Around three A.M. Mrs. Baron had been awakened by the call of nature, and on her way to the restroom, she'd glanced out her bedroom window and saw a man running away from the motorcycle shop.

"Were you frightened?" Patsy asked.

"Oh no." Mrs. Baron shook her head. "Not at all."

"Why not?" Flynn asked.

"Because it was that nice Sheriff Trainer. I figured he was in pursuit of a bad guy. Funny thing though. I couldn't figure out why he was wearing gloves in this August heat."

"You go get Fire Chief Rutledge," Flynn said once they were back outside on Eloise Baron's front porch. "And bring him back here to hear what she has to say."

"Where are you going?" Patsy asked.

"It's time Beau and I had a long talk."

"Okay." Patsy nodded. "Good luck."

Rage fueled Flynn's every step as she marched across the street to the sheriff's office. "Buzz me in, Madge," she said to the dispatcher through gritted teeth.

Madge looked startled, but obeyed.

Flynn found Beau at his desk. She slammed the door behind her. "You rotten, low-down, lying, cheating son of a bitch."

"Whoa, whoa," Beau said. His face was scratched from his altercation with Jesse in her flower bed. "What's going on here?"

"Drop the act, Beau. I know what you've been up to. I've got to say I'm completely shocked. I would never have believed you were capable of such dirty dealings."

"What are you talking about?" Beau got to his feet.

"Mrs. Baron saw you running out of the motorcycle shop just seconds before the fire ignited," she accused.

Beau narrowed his eyes, planted his palms on his desk. "What are you saying, Flynn?"

"Did you start that fire?" She didn't expect the anguished expression on his face. He looked truly, deeply contrite.

"I didn't, I didn't . . . mean . . . it . . ." he stammered.

"It's a simple question. Did you start the fire or not?"

"I got drunk."

His admission took her by surprise. She'd never seen Beau drunk. "You got drunk?" she echoed.

"It killed me," he went on. "Seeing you with Jesse. Knowing he was touching you, kissing you." The face of the man she thought she knew contorted in a vicious expression that made him unrecognizable. "Doing *other* things to you."

She took a step backward, felt the first tickle of real fear at her throat. "I'm sorry if you got hurt, that was never my intention."

"So you didn't think it would hurt me to learn you were fucking him?" Beau broke off. She'd rarely heard him use language that strong, and it chilled her to the bone.

"I'm sorry."

"Yeah, well, I'm sorry too," he spat out.

"I'm not going to allow you to make me feel guilty for following my heart."

"You don't even know what that means. You've been sheltered by Twilight. You've never seen the world. You're so gullible. You have no idea what people are capable of doing to each other." He touched his shoulder where he'd been wounded in Iraq.

Clearly his scar went much deeper than the surface wound. Beau trod toward her, his boot heels smacking on the cement. His hands knotted into fists. Really big fists. Beau wouldn't hurt her. Would he? Flynn took a step backward, raised her palms. "Just settle down."

"I can't settle down. Too much is at stake."

"You were the one who blew up the Twilight Bridge."

Beau nodded, an expression of remorse on his face.

"You spiked the lemonade at the knit-a-thon."

Again, he nodded. "I'm sorry about your father. I had no idea he'd drink the lemonade."

Who was this man she once thought she knew so well? "But why?"

"I had to get rid of him."

Her blood ran cold. If he would blow up a bridge and spike lemonade, did that mean he'd done this before?

"Beau," she whispered. "Did you plant cocaine on Jesse? Were you the reason he went to prison?" It was all she could do not to fly at him in a rage and pound him with her fists. "Did you steal ten years of a man's life just because you were jealous?"

"No, no," he rasped. "He had a rap sheet, prior crimes. He was no angel. I had to save you. I didn't save Jodi and she's dead because I didn't step in. I couldn't let the same thing happen to you."

"You did it?" She dropped her head in her hands, overcome by the magnitude of what he'd done.

"Calloway is no good for you, Flynn, and you just can't see that. I had to save you from yourself. I had to show you what kind of man he was."

She raised her head, defiantly met his eyes. "That's what went wrong with this relationship, Beau. You, trying to save me. You're not my protector. You're not my savior. I'm responsible for my own actions and I have live with the consequences. Just like you're responsible for your own actions. You sent Jesse to prison, and when he came back to town, you went on a personal vendetta against him. Now you've got to live with what you've done."

"You're not listening to me," Beau said. "I tried my best to protect you from him, but like a moth to the flame you flew straight into the arms of danger. You were just like Jodi. What's wrong with women? They have a good man yet they gotta have the bad ones."

"You're mixing your metaphors," Flynn said, her snarky mouth trying to hop in to save the day, create some levity, snap him out of this weird trance he seemed to have fallen under.

"I did it all for you," Beau said, completely ignoring her attempt to shift the tone. "Everything was for you."

Flynn could hardly breathe, she was so shocked at how far Beau had deteriorated. How had he gotten so lost? "You found out about the big insurance policy Jesse took out on the shop. That gave you a motive to pin on him."

"People in this town do talk. Mostly all you have to do is buy them a meal and it's blab, blab, blab." He brought his thumb up in a repeated motion, using his two middle fingers to mimic chatter. His eyes were unnaturally bright. "I've always tried to do the right thing. You know that."

"You have," she said, ready to agree to anything if she could just see the old Beau again. This new guy was scaring the hell out of her.

"Then why am I losing you to a scumbag convict?"

"So you got drunk and you started the fire and tried to make it look like Jesse torched the place for the insurance money."

Her words seem to take the fight out of him. His shoulders slumped, his face went slack. "It wasn't like that."

"What was it like then?"

"I got drunk. I went to the motorcycle shop to see Calloway. He wasn't there and I just knew he was with you."

"Of course he wasn't there. It was three o'clock in the morning, but he wasn't with me."

"I was drunk. I hadn't thought it through, I just kept picturing him on top of you, inside of you." A startled sound ripped from Beau's throat and threw chills up her spine. "I got enraged."

"And then you burned the motorcycle shop down."

"No," he said hoarsely. "I admit it, I saw the gasoline can in the back room and a box of latex gloves on the shelf. It wasn't premeditated. It just happened."

Flynn nodded. Jesse had fueled up a motorcycle on Saturday so that a potential customer could take one of the Harleys out for a spin, and he kept latex gloves on hand for when he worked on greasy engines.

"I grabbed the can, spread gasoline all over the place, and then . . ."

"You lit a match and ran," she said flatly.

"No." He shook his head, ran a heavy palm down his face. "No. I . . . the smell of gasoline snapped me out of my drunken rage. I realized I was making a big mistake and I threw the gas can in the Dumpster and staggered out of there. That must have been when Mrs. Baron saw me."

"Are you saying the place just caught itself on fire?"

He shook his head, looked woeful. "There must have been a spark from the hot water heater pilot light that set off the blaze. I swear to you, Flynn. I did not light a match. I'm sorry I caused you to lose the shop. I know how hard you worked. I just want you back."

"It's too late for that."

Anguish pulled at his mouth. "I love you so much, Flynnie."

"It's the wrong kind of love. You're trying to use me to fill up an empty space in your life, in your heart. I can't do that. No one can fill it up except you, Beau. You have to look deep inside yourself and find what's missing. Only you can fix you."

"What are you going to do?"

"I'm not going to do anything. You're going to come clean to Fire Chief Rutledge and then you're going to contact the proper authorities and make sure Jesse is pardoned for the crimes he did not commit. Because if you don't, I will do it for you."

Flynn left the sheriff's office and raced back to the hospital, anxious to be with Jesse again and tell him how sorry she was for doubting him. She hurried down the corridor and burst into his room, only to find the bed empty and the deputy who'd been guarding Jesse standing in the hall chatting up one of the nurses.

"Where is Jesse?" she demanded of the deputy.

"Doctor just released him."

"What did you do with him?"

The deputy shrugged. "Beau said to cut him loose."

Some of the tension drained from her shoulders. "Where did he go?"

"I don't know, but he said he had some thinking to do."

Flynn left the hospital feeling numb with exhaustion. So much had happened over the last forty-eight hours, she could barely think. She drove around town looking for Jesse's Harley, but she didn't see it anywhere. Driving past the burned-out motorcycle shop, seeing it in ruins, made her stomach ache. She went by Patsy's house but no one was home. She headed over to the fire station. But neither Hondo nor Fire Chief Rutledge was there. Where was Jesse?

She didn't know what to do or where to go. She needed to do some serious thinking herself, but the house was full with Joel and Noah back home. She needed a space of her own.

Her cell phone rang. She dug it from her purse, palmed it. "Hello?"

"Rendezvous," Jesse said, and then hung up.

Flynn grinned and headed for home.

Once there, she dug the canoe from the garage, dragged it to the water, and paddled for their secret meeting spot.

The sun set on the horizon, descending into twilight. The air was alive with the sights and sounds of the river she loved so much. She paddled past the columns of the old bridge. The salvaged materials sat stacked on either side of the boat ramps, awaiting the start of the new construction. Her heart soared.

As she rowed upriver, it felt as if she was rowing into both her future and her past. In that moment she was sixteen again, sneaking off for a rendezvous with the boy she hadn't been able to admit she loved.

Jesse.

By the time she maneuvered the bend in the river and came upon the swimming hole, her heart was in her throat. There he was, on the bluff, waiting for her.

The dying sunlight cast him in an orange halo of light. Her bad boy, who at his core was very, very good. She docked the canoe against the bank. He was there, reaching down his hand to help her ashore. His left eye was black and blue, he had a long scratch on his forehead, and his skin was blistered bright pink, but he was the best-looking thing she'd ever seen.

"Flynn," he murmured.

"Jesse."

He stared at her for the longest moment. "You got Trainer to confess to everything."

"I did."

"You believed me."

"I should have believed you all along, Jesse. Forgive me for not believing you."

A smile quirked up the corners of his lips. "If you'll forgive me for sending your letters back to you unread."

"Done."

He looked a little uncertain, cleared his throat.

"Is there something you'd like to say?"

He nodded, took her hand. "Let's sit."

They sat on the bluff where they'd sat so many years ago and watched the sun disappear and the crickets start their chirping. "We've lost a lot of time."

"Yes."

"You've lost a lot of yourself."

"I wouldn't say lost."

"But you haven't had a chance to find out who you really are."

"That's probably true."

"You have that chance now. The Yarn Barn is gone. Your brothers are growing up. Carrie can take care of herself. Your father's gonna stay on the program."

She nodded.

"That means you're free. Free to be who you're destined to be, not what other people want you to be."

"What are you trying to say, Jesse?"

He looked deeply into her eyes. "I love you, Flynn. I love your smart little mouth and your sharp mind. I love how you take care of the people you love. How loyal and true you are. I love how you attract strays like Miss Tabitha. How you give so much of yourself without even thinking about it. I'm honored to know you, Flynn MacGregor, and I want to spend the rest of my days finding out more. I want you to be my woman. I want to ask you to marry me, but I can't."

"No?" Her chest got all achy.

"No. I can't hold you back. I won't. You need to explore. Find out who you are and what you want."

"I want you."

"You can't just rush into me."

"I'm not."

"I don't want you to ever have any regrets. I don't want to be the thing that ties you down."

"Oh, you goofy man. There's no escaping it. We're knitted up in each other. There's no denying it."

"Even if you can't knit?" He grinned.

"That's what I have the Sweethearts for. Besides, I don't need to look any further than my hometown for adventure. Everything I need is right in front of me." She looked at him, at the man she loved, and she knew it was true. "Being with you is all the exploration I need. You're just bad enough, Jesse Calloway, to keep me interested."

"Why didn't you say so sooner, woman?" he asked. "Now, how about we go skinny-dipping in those underground caves?"

Flynn laughed and stripped off her clothes. "Or," she said, "we could just stay right here and make love in the moonlight."

EPILOGUE

Flynn, embrace who you are.
—The Sweethearts' Knitting Club,
embroidered on a pillow, 2009

"I've got something to confess," Flynn said to the Sweethearts on the Friday evening following the fire. They'd met at her house again. All of them gathered around in their rockers, their hands busy with their knitting—Patsy, Terri, Marva, Raylene, Dotty Mae, and Belinda. Even Miss Tabitha was there, curled up in Flynn's lap. She cleared her throat. "I should have come clean a long time ago."

Everyone looked up at her, and she rested her knitting in her lap. The six women she admired most in town. The women who'd become surrogate mothers to her. The women who'd shared her laughter and tears. She was about to disappoint them, to shatter their faith in her. The lump in her throat swelled to a boulder.

"What is it, dear?" Dotty Mae asked.

"I . . ." She blew out her breath. "This is going to come as a shock."

Belinda reached over to pat her hand. "You don't have to tell us anything you don't want to tell us."

"But I do want to tell this. You guys deserve the truth. You've been there for me in bad times and good, but I feel like my secret is a huge barrier between us. Although, after I confess, you're probably not going to want me to hang out with you anymore."

"Good Lord," Raylene splayed a hand over her chest. "What on earth did you do?"

"Okay, here goes." She was having the toughest time pushing the words past her lips. She'd kept her secret for so long, it felt odd to just come out and say it. "I can't knit. Can't purl. I don't make scarves, I don't know a ripple stitch from a seed stitch. My mother was a world-class knitter and I'm a big fat fraud. And a liar. A big, fat, lying fraud. Carrie's been knitting all my projects for me."

Flynn expected to see stunned surprise on the faces of her friends. Instead, all six simultaneously broke into gales of laughter. "I'm serious." She frowned. "I can't knit to save my life."

"Honey," Marva said, "just how dumb do you think we are?"

Flynn blinked. "You knew?"

"A ten-year-old can knit better than you," Terri said.

"Ten-year-old, hell." Raylene hooted. "Miss Tabitha can knit better than Flynn."

"Excuse me?"

"No offense, honey," Dotty Mae added. "But your knitting stinks like year-old gym socks."

"You guys *knew*?"

All six nodded in unison.

Flynn was flabbergasted. "Why didn't you say something?"

"We were afraid that if you knew we knew, you wouldn't want to be in the knitting club anymore," Patsy explained.

"Wait a minute, let me get this straight. Even though I can't knit, you wanted me in the knitting club?"

"That's right."

"But why?"

"You're our heart and soul, Flynn," Marva said. "Don't you get that?"

"Me?"

"You're the thread that binds us all together." Tears misted Belinda's eyes.

"You complete us," Terri teased, mangling the *Jerry McGuire* quote to suit the situation.

"You're the one who remembers everyone's birthdays," Raylene pointed out.

"You send get well cards to our kids," Belinda said.

"You listen to our troubles," Dotty Mae contributed.

"You crack jokes that keep us in stitches," Patsy added.

"And you remind us so much of your mother," Marva went on. "Loving and giving and wise and sassy."

Something occurred to her then. "Did my mother know I couldn't knit?"

"She was your mother," Marva said. "Of course she knew."

"Well, why didn't *she* say something?"

"Because you were trying so hard to please her. She knew you gave it your all and that you just didn't have a knack for it."

"She praised the scarves Carrie made as if they were mine. That doesn't seem fair to Carrie."

"Honey." Marva touched her hand. "She was just so grateful to have you taking care of her. She wanted to boost your self-confidence. Besides, she and Carrie cooked up the scheme together."

"What!"

"They just wanted you to feel good about yourself."

"I don't get this." Flynn got up from her chair and paced the braided rug, distress knotting up her chest. "Why did my mother want me to start the Yarn Barn if she knew I couldn't knit? Why didn't she just ask Carrie?"

"Because she knew you needed us as much as we needed you," Patsy said. "You're so busy caring for others, you never realized how much you needed to take care of yourself. That's our job, Flynn, to take care of you."

Suddenly they were all crying and passing around tissues and hugging and dabbing at their eyes, and Flynn knew that no matter what happened, the Sweethearts would always be knitted up into one another's lives.

"Hey," Flynn said to Belinda. "You never did tell us the gossip about Trixie Lyn Sparks. What's that all about?"

"Oh, sit back and start knitting, girls, have I got a Texas-sized scandal for you . . ."

- Check Tribune pictures
- clip articles in Perspa tribune

$24 - 1 - 1 - 3 - 4 = 15$